BLACK BAGS

A RATIONAL MAN

BOOK TWO

ERIK HENRY VICK

RATATOSKR PUBLISHING

NEW YORK

RATATOSKR PUBLISHING
769 BROADWAY #1060
MANHATTAN, NY 10003

PUBLISHER'S NOTE: THIS IS A WORK OF FICTION. NAMES, CHARACTERS, PLACES, AND INCIDENTS ARE A PRODUCT OF THE AUTHOR'S IMAGINATION. LOCALES AND PUBLIC NAMES ARE SOMETIMES USED FOR ATMOSPHERIC PURPOSES. ANY RESEMBLANCE TO ACTUAL PEOPLE, LIVING OR DEAD, OR TO BUSINESSES, COMPANIES, EVENTS, INSTITUTIONS, OR LOCALES IS COMPLETELY COINCIDENTAL.

BLACK BAGS/ ERIK HENRY VICK. -- 1ST ED.
ISBN 978-1-951509-14-9

Table of Contents

For the *real* Gavin Gregory
who graciously allowed me to usurp
his identity for this series

There sat a seven-headed beast
Ten horns raised from his head
Symbolic woman sits on his throne
But hatred strips her and leaves her naked
The beast and the harlot
She's a dwelling place for demons
She's a cage for every unclean spirit,
Every filthy bird
And makes us drink the poisoned wine
To fornicating with our kings
Fallen now is Babylon the great

—Avenged Sevenfold

I hope you enjoy *Black Bags*. If so, please consider joining my Readers Group—details can be found at the end of the last chapter.

Chapter 1
Making a Killing

I

The air felt heavy and hot and wet, even at four in the morning, and it wrapped around him like a piss-hot blanket. But that was Miami. Black shadows danced in the sandy dirt beneath his feet, but darkness didn't impede his view of his date for the evening, the button of her tight shorts undone, the fingers of her left hand on her zipper halfway down, the arc sodium lights from the causeway above bathing her in soft, orange light. Her face bore an uneasy expression—one that bordered on fear. He stood stock-still, just looking at her, drinking her like a tall glass of clear, cold water. He knew the power of silence, knew how to use it to sing a coloratura of terror. Fear and pain and terror and panic—those were the fruits he lived on, and he knew how to cultivate each one, how to feed them, a master farmer.

He flicked the blade of the knife out from behind his thigh, reflecting creamsicle light—white from the pale moonlight, orange glaze from the arc sodiums up on the causeway—into her wide-eyed stare, and causing the light to dance along the razor-sharp edge of the blade. Her mouth gaped, and her breath stuck in her throat while his smile stretched, turning almost maniacal, and his eyes glinted orange. "Do what I say, and I won't have to kill you," he said. "Cooperation is key."

He liked that part the best. He'd spent hours and hours thinking about the moment he'd show the knife, rehearsing dialog in his mind, practicing the dance of light on the refined edge, practicing his expression, choreographing his movements, the turn and twist of his body, all of it designed to heighten his excitement, to increase her dread, in the moment of revelation, the moment he showed the knife.

She broadcast fright and anxiety and trepidation in waves he could feel crashing against his skin, and he knew what she thought—that he wanted to rape her. He felt a sense of satisfaction, of accomplishment that his little joke had succeeded. He moved the blade in a sinuous pattern, making the moonlight slide down the blade from hilt to clipped point, illuminating the dark—bright—dark—bright marbling of high-carbon and high-nickel layers forged into the steel. He slashed the air—two cuts almost too fast for the eye to follow— and stopped with the tip pointed at her face.

The woman squeezed her eyes shut, but to her credit, she didn't beg or wheedle. *Enough*, he thought and giggled. "Nah. I'm just playing around. Don't worry, sug."

Hot sweat prickled down the center of his back, ran down his flanks, and stood on his upper lip. *Next time, I'll wear shorts, like she did*, he thought, knowing it for a lie. The woman wore skin-tight denim short-shorts and a skin-tight pink cotton T-shirt that left nothing to the imagination. He wore baggy camouflage cargo pants that stretched from his scuffed combat boots to the black T-shirt he wore under the unbuttoned second-hand olive drab fatigue shirt. Her outfit, he felt sure, guaranteed she'd get laid if she wanted to, while his hid the knife—and several other goodies he might use before their evening together ended. Her outfit allowed her to dance and cavort without getting overheated. His soaked in the heat like water into a sponge.

He waited, not moving a muscle, not even blinking, waiting for her to open her eyes, stretching his patience, his self-control to the limit. When she finally peeked up at him, he smiled, and with a practiced, graceful flick of the wrist, reversed the knife so that he held it out toward her hilt first. "Take it," he said in a voice devoid of emotion, devoid of compassion, or anything human. "Go on, I want you to have it."

Her gaze flicked to the mottled blade, flicked to his waist, then back to his wrist and crawled up his arm, slithered up his neck, danced across his face—only meeting his hard eyes for the briefest of moments before dropping and darting away toward First Avenue half a block away. A hard smile surfaced on his face— that half a block of shadow and sugar sand might as well have been a mile. She shook her head without returning her gaze to him, a muscle beneath her right eye jumping, twitching, the only outlet for her anxiety.

He softened his expression with conscious effort and smoothed his tone. "Go on," he said softly. "Take it. You have nothing to fear—not from me." When she didn't move, he took half a step forward. "Really. I want you to have it." When she still didn't respond, didn't reach for the knife, his smooth voice cracked wide open, his patience cracked like thin ice underfoot, and his soft expression turned thunderous. "Take it! Take it, or I'll make you fucking scream!"

Again, her terrified gaze drifted to his face, and she bit her lower lip to stop its quivering. She lifted her hand, fingers shaking, but stopped only halfway to the knife. She peeked at him a third time—a rabbit looking up at a wolf.

"Don't make me say it again!" he snapped. "Because if you do, I'll say it with the fucking blade!" His harsh, staccato voice rolled around under the causeway arcing above their heads. He gave her a hard glare, and she reached for the hilt. He slapped it into her hand, and her fingers curled around it automatically. "There. Now you have the knife." He let go, and the fourteen-inch blade dipped toward the dirt. "Careful," he said. "That's a hand-forged Damascus blade!"

Slowly, as if she feared he'd snatch it away if she moved too fast, she drew the knife to her chest, clutching the Bowie in a white-knuckled grip. She wrapped her other hand around it and aimed the clip point at his belly, though she couldn't steady her hands enough to keep it from twitching and wandering.

A terrible grin spread across his face—a grin that would fit the face of any of the greatest villains on the planet. "There. You're armed and I'm not. Now, we can have some fun. Doesn't that sound good?" His spirit soared to strange heights, to locales both unfamiliar and unexpected. *Happiness? Is that what this strange emotion is?*

He had no idea. But the little game playing out in the hot, wet morning air made him feel…*complete.* None of the others had made him feel so good.

The woman darted a glance to the left and then to the right, but to the left lay a long, causeway-roofed black corridor of shadow all the way to Biscayne Bay, and to the right, a path through scrub brush and stunted trees and sugar sand and black, black shadows that led back to the First Avenue overpass—empty lanes, empty sidewalks. She stared up at him, slow anger creeping across her face, displacing her fear. "Help me!" she yelled.

He threw back his head and cackled at the moon. "Help!" he cried, mimicking her tone. "Help me! She's got a knife! She's going to stab me!" His shouts echoed around them like ravenous evil-eyed vultures, circling, circling, carrying on long past the point when the echoes should have faded.

She watched him through narrowed eyelids as he shouted and mocked her, slow fear leeching its way back into her expression, and her lips quivered as she asked, "What do you want?"

"Want?" He chuckled and did a little jig in the sand. "I just want to get to know you. Would that be so bad? I'll be the first to admit I have a strange sense of humor, and I didn't mean to scare you—well, I did, but like roller-coaster scared, not Jesus-fucking-Christ-he-is-a-psychopath scared." He bent forward a little, staring down at her in faux concern. "I thought we'd make a cute couple. That's why I picked you. That's why I wanted to give you that knife. I have another just like it. A matched set."

Her lip curled, and anger washed her face—quicker this time. "I thought you wanted…" She shook her head. "Not this sick fucking mind trip. I *was* ready to make love to you, to let you do whatever you wanted, but now?" She shook her head again and with more violence. "You're fucked in the head. Fucking sick. I'm out of here." She tried to sit up, but he planted a long-nailed hand on her forehead and pushed her back.

"That's a little rude, don't you think? A little insulting?" he asked in a whip-crack voice designed to cut deep. He stepped back, putting one worn-down combat boot next to the other, heels almost touching, then he squatted down, his groin an easy target if she were to kick. He rocked forward, slapping his hands down and gripping her legs tight. "My…father? It hardly matters. My mentor made the knives for me. Made them special. And for you, my dear—for this night—and when we're done, it will take pride of place above…above his…" His voice trailed away, and a confused expression sidled across his face for a moment. But then he cocked his head to the side and let a little of his true nature creep into his expression. "How else can I see what you look like on the inside?" he asked in a tone that evoked burning brimstone, mental institutions, snake-pits from the nineteenth century, and a torturer's workroom.

Her fingers squeezed the knife, trying to steady it as she raised it to point at his throat. The muscles of her right thigh bunched beneath her smooth, tanned skin, but neither her foot nor knee so much as twitched. She gasped and tried again, but not even her thigh muscle twitched on the second attempt.

He smirked at her, winked at her, leered down at her, then drummed grave-cold fingers on her foot. "Let's get started, eh? This morning won't last forever—more's the pity." A muscle in her cheek twitched, and he frowned at her until the movement stopped. His expression hardened, cold and dead, and his eyes bored into her own, glowing orange in the arc sodium light that slithered through the darkness from First Avenue. Concentration made merry in his eyes, and he peeled the fingers of her left hand slowly back, then flung the appendage away to slap at the dirt at her side. She grunted, but her hand stayed where it fell, and her expression became one of true terror, the expression of a woman who knows death has come to call. Her gaze begged, wheedled, pleaded with him, and slow anger stirred in his belly.

He took hold of her arm, and his face twisted with effort. Slowly, her right elbow began to bend. Her wrist twisted next, bringing the mottled belly of the Bowie around until that fine edge brushed against the pink cotton sheathing her belly. She screamed and tried to wriggle away from him, but it was as if her body had become part of the earth beneath her—as though she'd grown roots and they held her fast.

A lone car thump-thump-thumped across the concrete slabs over their heads. His fierce expression twisted into a madman's grin, becoming savage, vicious. His head turned a little to the side, and he squeezed his eyes into slits, cheeks quivering, but whether from anticipation or effort, not even he knew.

He only knew the time for holding himself back, the time for pretending at emotions that were foreign, unknowable to him, had ended. He felt as if he knew her every frantic thought, her every blistering sensation, her every dread. He felt as if he'd become part of her, that he could taste her dire foreboding, her redoubtable certainty that she was about to die. He drank her terror like fine wine, ate her despondency like an hors d'oeuvre—just a taste, a nugget of flavor, a hint of what was to come.

The Bowie's blade flicked across her pink-clad belly, parting the cotton as Moses did the waters, exposing delectable snow-white skin, so much at odds with the marvelous tan on her legs. The scalpel-sharp blade danced and weaved back and forth, back and forth, nipping her here, leaving a burning trail, biting her flesh there, another burning trail, another slice, another poke, constant motion, constantly increasing pain and terror, leaving red snakes in its meandering wake.

He shuddered as white-hot pain showed in her expression—a phantom pain dancing across his own belly. "Yessss," he hissed. "Isn't this glorious? Aren't you having *fun*?"

With great, muscle-shaking effort, her lips parted, and her jaw creaked like wood about to break as her teeth opened. As her tongue twitched, he narrowed his eyes, snapping his head from side to side, and he slammed those pearly whites, her perfectly straight teeth that had cost her parents thousands, together with the force of a hammer striking an anvil. "No, no," he whispered. "You've said *enough*."

He cocked his head to the side, watching hot blood paint a portrait of pain on her flanks, drip, drip, dripping to the gray dirt, making it black, like his soul. "Oh, I think you can do better than this," he said. "Don't you?"

Her eyes widened, and a muffled moan escaped from deep within her chest.

"Well, I think so, and that's really what matters. Don't you agree, sugar?"

Tears pooled in her eyes as the knife flicked upward, the clip point moving toward her throat, slitting the pretty pink T-shirt to the collar, leaving blood welling from the shallow red line the Bowie had left from her belly button to her sternum.

"Well, that won't do, will it?" he asked her. "It's always awkward the first time you get naked with someone, right? Let's get it out of the way, shall we? Like a band-aid." He ripped her T-shirt away, exposing her breasts. With one tapered finger that seemed more claw than human appendage, he jabbed her right breast. "I was never much of a student," he said. "Always too busy planning my next conquest, my next caper. And I just didn't see the sense of a formal education given my nature, my abilities...my *proclivities*. Oh, well." He shrugged, then leveled his gaze on her face and stared into her eyes, showing her his sharpened teeth. "Would you believe I don't even know how those magical mounds work? I mean, what are they? Bags? Milk factories? Dirty pillows? What?" Beneath him, her eyes rounded until he could see white all the way around her hazel irises. Again, he flicked her right breast with a long finger, his long sharp nail leaving a scratch through her areola. "And what's this part? Why is it a different color?"

Her lips quivered, and her eyes rolled like those of a horse trapped in its stall as the barn burned around it.

"Oh, I love this! You're so much more fun than the others!" He drew her zipper the rest of the way down with a dainty hand, pinky finger extended like at a formal tea. "I really have no idea how I'll get these off if you don't help. What do you say? Hmm? Cooperation is the first step of teamwork, right?" He gave the open waistband a desultory tug. "I guess we could cut them off with our knife if you'd like." The Bowie danced to the bottom of the zipper, more tears leaking down her cheeks, more red snakes cavorting on her belly.

He turned her hand, putting the flat of the wide Damascus blade on her lower belly, then slid it between her skin and the black lace peeking out from her fly. He grinned and winked at her, and her hand jerked, slicing through the thick denim, stabbing through it, ripping it to shreds as if the shorts were no more than tissue paper rather than thick denim. More blood welled from her butter-smooth skin, this time, a bright red arrow pointing at her sex.

"I'll take it from here," he said, already reaching down to tug the rest of her clothing away. He gazed down at her crotch for a full minute. "Maybe I should've just fucked you," he mused. "You're very pretty down there."

A single sob wrenched its way through her throat and out between her teeth.

"Oh, fine!" he snapped. "I try to be nice, to pay you a compliment, and this is how you act?" He lifted her right hand, and grinned as it shook like a leaf, then rotated it so the tip of the Bowie rested beneath her right nipple. The point of the blade snicked back and forth, leaving tiny cuts and scrapes as she struggled against his hold. "Oh, you'll ruin it." He glared at her, and the blade steadied, grew still. "I'm dying to see what's inside those beautiful bags of fun." He laughed. "Well, that was poor form, wasn't it, sugar? After all, we both know you're the one who is dying." He cocked his head as though a thought had just occurred to him. "I reckon that means it doesn't really matter what the fuck you think. Right? I mean, that's right, ain't it, sugar?"

She jerked, her head rocked back, and a scream tore from her throat as the knife blade slid through her nipple. It plunged another quarter inch into her flesh, then he relented, rocking back on his heels, one hand going to his own chest. He grinned down at her. "Oh, my dark lord, that feels so good."

He lifted the knife, drew it toward her face, skittering from side to side and flinging blood to and fro. The wide blade hovered over her lips for a moment before tweaking at the tip of her nose, leaving more blood. "This is really better than fucking, you know?"

He stood and smiled down at her. "Time for the real fun to start. You don't mind, do you, sug?" He flicked his claw-like fingers, and the knife floated over her left eye. With another gesture, he dipped the Bowie into the kitten-soft flesh beneath her eye socket.

Time, it seemed to him, stopped for a while. Instead of seconds tick-tick-ticking, it was her life's blood drip-drip-dripping as the knife lifted, cut, lifted again, stabbed down into soft, yielding flesh, and on and on and on—an eternity of torment for the woman, and eternity of ecstasy for him.

As the last of her life bled onto the sand, he frowned, the marvelous feeling already fading, already dissipating into the morass of his cold thoughts. *Too soon*, he thought. He grimaced and made her hand slash across her chest, chopping the wide-bladed knife into her breasts, but it wasn't the same now that death had claimed her, and her nerves were no more than angel hair pasta. He dropped his head, a disappointed eight-year-old, and cried a little.

He gazed at her, supposing she'd been more than just beautiful while warm blood still powered her flesh. She'd probably dangled dozens of men on strings of lust, all wanting to peel those shorts away and penetrate her the way humans did—and the dark lord knew she was willing, after all. She'd said so. He sniffed and shrugged. He'd never seen the attraction of fucking. Rape, sure, but not fucking.

Not a living girl, anyway. His eyes dropped to her crotch, and a ghost of a smile flickered across his face again.

Chapter 2
The Agent's
Return

I

FBI Behavioral Analysis Unit, Quantico, VA
Monday, 7:44 am

Yawning and ignoring the queasy, greasy feeling in his guts, Special Agent Gavin Gregory poured yet another cup of coffee—his fourth of the morning. The queasiness came from the other three cups, while the greasiness came from the jet lag earned by spending a month in the middle of the Pacific Ocean. His guts insisted it was the middle of the night, that all sane men should still be asleep. He glanced at the whiteboard the BAU used to track active cases as he stirred Splenda into his coffee, recognizing most of them, frowning at the death tolls that had risen while he lounged on the beach and made love to his wife. When his gaze slid to the case in green, his frown became a grimace—green represented a possible new series of murders.

He turned away, slurping bad coffee that no amount of sweetener could help. He'd seen the blank Agent In Charge box on the new case but denied the little voice in his head. *Surely Pete won't drop a new case in my lap the first day back.* He thought he could even believe it…at least until he finished another cup of joe.

"Well, look at you," said SAIC Pete Fielding. "As tan as a native Hawaiian and looking all kinds of rested." Gavin shook his head and sipped his coffee to hide his grin. Pete walked over and lay a hand on his shoulder.

"All kidding aside, Gav, I hope the time helped you two."

Nodding, Gavin pointed at the whiteboard with his coffee cup. "Same old song and dance while I was away."

"It never stops." Pete frowned, and his eyes danced over the names written in red on the board—the active cases. "But forget that for now. Let's have a 'welcome back' chat."

"That sounds ominous, boss."

Pete chuckled. "Ominous? Me? I'm a teddy bear. Come on, it won't take a minute." He peered at Gavin over his glasses. "Besides, you don't have anything pressing. Right?"

"Right you are, boss." Gavin followed the SAIC into his office and took a seat while Pete closed the door, grinning at the phrase he'd lifted from his new reading obsession—the one Maddie had introduced him to on their trip.

"So. How was Hawaii, really?"

"Good. Relaxing." For the most part, it was even true. He hadn't had any dreams—*nightmares*—since that last one in the exam room of Kingdom Cross Psychiatric Hospital. But still...he had felt unknown eyes watching him at odd times during the trip. Paranoia, Maddie had called it.

"And you and Maddie?"

Gavin sipped his coffee. "We had a lot of time to talk. It was good. We worked some things out." He chuckled and grinned. "Though, Maddie got me started on Joe Abercrombie's books, and…well, I got a little obsessed."

Pete nodded, a faint grin echoing Gavin's. "The motel give you any trouble about the extra days?"

Gavin shook his head. "They were very accommodating. Thanks for that."

"Glad to do it, Gav. It was the least I could do after that nightmare in Manhattan." Pete pinned him with a probing stare. "Speaking of which… Everything is good about the…about all that you two shared?"

"You mean being kidnapped by a sociopath?" Gavin forced a grin to his lips and hoped it was convincing, though it felt anything but. "We had a few virtual sessions with a Bureau counselor. Maddie had the worst of it—he had her longer and was more intent on terrorizing her. She's confused on some points, but she's dealing with it."

Pete nodded and dropped his gaze to his blotter. "And you?"

Gavin shrugged and took a sip of coffee to hide his unease. "Yeah. I'm fine."

"Right. Now that we have that out of the way, maybe you can give me the real answer."

Chuckling, Gavin nodded. *Should've known Pete would see right through that*, he thought. "I'm pissed, Pete. At myself, at The Smith, at those HRT guys"—he held up his free hand to forestall the objection Pete would feel obligated to raise—"I know there was nothing they could do, but dammit, I'm still mad at them."

"Everyone understands that feeling—especially those Hostage Rescue Team guys. They've been pestering me about making a formal apology to you and Maddie for the entire six weeks you've been out." He looked Gavin in the eye. "The real question is: How are you dealing with that anger?"

"The only way I can," said Gavin with another shrug.

"Then I guess that will have to do…as long as you *continue* to deal with it." Pete treated him to a stern gaze. "You *will* tell me if it gets out of hand, and I'll get you more help…arrange a leave, whatever you need. You know the drill."

"Of course."

"Good, then that's settled. Gloria wants you two to come for dinner. Sunday, or whatever day is better for you two."

"Tell her thanks. I'll have Maddie call her later."

"Good."

"Then…" Gavin stood up.

"There's something else," said Pete in a pensive voice.

"Uh oh. Am I grounded again, Dad?"

Pete gave him a half-smile and motioned him back to his seat. "I know you were pretty shaken up in the hospital, Gavin, but…" Looking uncomfortable, Fielding sighed and looked away.

"Spit it out, boss. I'm a big boy."

Pete returned his gaze to Gavin's. "It's probably nothing. Let's get that out in front of the rest of this."

After a sip of coffee, Gavin nodded. "Sure."

"I've had several calls from Kirk Haymond."

Gavin arched his eyebrows. "What did he want?"

"He's of the opinion that you and Detective Denders haven't been completely forthcoming."

His stomach dropped to somewhere near his ankles, but Gavin forced a smile to his lips and chuckled. "About what?"

"I can't say that the same thought hasn't crossed my mind, Gav. My gut tells me you held something back. The feeling started in your hospital room."

Another sip of coffee bought him a couple of seconds of thought. *What did Denders say when Haymond asked him this question? Damn it, I should have called Jim last night like I'd planned.* He turned his free hand palm up and looked Pete in the eye. "Come on, Pete. You've known me for a long time. I don't leave pertinent facts out of my reports."

Pete nodded. "I know that, Gav." He steepled his fingers in front of his face. "So… What *impertinent* facts did you leave out? Because that expression that danced across your mug just now confirmed to me that you did leave *something* out of your report."

Gavin killed the last of his coffee and set his mug on Pete's desk. "Okay, okay. Angel Kirk…"

"She's in Dr. Esteves' care in Kingdom Cross Psychiatric."

"Good. She's going to need all the help she can get, I think."

Pete narrowed his eyes a bit. "What about her?"

After a deep breath, Gavin leaned forward in his chair and gazed at Pete earnestly. "Debbie—Dr. Esteves—knew the DNA evidence probably belonged to Angel. She and Kirk were good friends, see, and when Angel disappeared, she'd been traveling—tracking The Saint Mary Psycho in a way, his back trail. Esteves thought she'd run afoul of him, and when the DNA came back as female, she suspected he had Angel and was using her to throw us off the scent." He relaxed back into the chair and put on his most convincing smile.

But Pete didn't return the smile. He stared at Gavin, instead. "There's more," Pete said, and Gavin grimaced.

"Yeah. Okay." He sighed, brushing a hand through his hair. "Okay. The Smith knew Debbie—or I should say it the other way around. Anyway, The Smith knew the patient known as Joe Doe—Debbie's star patient. His real name is Tom Madsen, and he was a psychiatric technician in Millvale, Pennsylvania."

"At that hospital you went to check out? Briar Patch?"

"Ridge. Briar Ridge State Mental Hospital. And, yes, that's where Tom worked. A bunch of people disappeared there, including Tom. The… The Smith bragged about it when he had Maddie and me in that room…" He shuddered, unable to help it. "That's how

I learned Tom's real name. He used Tom the same way he used Angel. Framed him up for The Smith's first set of murders—maybe more. If we ran Tom's DNA from the Virginia sequence, it would match. The Smith…he's not like other serial killers, boss. He breaks all the rules. Switches up his ritual as it suits him. Changes identities like I change my socks. I—"

"You don't think he's done yet, do you? You don't think he'll stop."

Gavin shook his head. "No. It's just a gut feeling, but I think if he's still able, he'll keep killing. He really is diabolical, Pete. Not like most of them. A true criminal mastermind. The trick will be figuring out how he's altered his routine, which crimes are him, and which are your garden variety serial killer." He searched Pete's emotionless face, trying to assess how well he was deflecting the question. "He…he told me that he killed others. He claimed he was The Saint Mary Psycho, that Madsen's DNA would match those crimes, too. Also, claimed responsibility for The Hangman's killings down in Texas."

"You believe him?"

Gavin rocked his hand back and forth like a seesaw. "That's what Angel was doing when he grabbed her—following his back trail, investigating those killers, checking to see if it was possible. Let's just say that as of yet, I haven't found a reason *not* to believe him. Not yet."

Pete leaned back in his executive chair. "The marks."

"Right."

"But there are no other cases where the victims were marked with the Gaelic letter gay."

Gavin shrugged. "He said differently. He went on to say we were looking in the wrong places, but maybe he was saying that to make us chase our tails. Those cases are old, and if the ME on the body didn't catch the marks, decomp will have erased them."

Pete shook his head. "Then what?"

"We need to screen new bodies for the mark—both on the small of the back and everywhere else. We need those MEs thinking outside the box we built for them by only saying the marks would be on the small of the back." Gavin frowned. "And he might switch up his method of making the marks—burns or lacerations, anything. He could brand them or make incisions or find a new way of tattooing his marks. We'll have to change the bulletin."

"We can do that." Pete leaned back in his chair, making it creak as he shifted his weight. He tilted his head to the side and gave Gavin a shrewd look. "Is that it, then? That's all of what you've held back?"

What does he know? Gavin returned his gaze but said nothing. *I really should've checked in with Jim.* He drew a deep breath and let it out slowly. "Like I said, I've never withheld any pertinent facts from my reports."

Again, Pete steepled his fingers, resting his elbows against his flanks and leaning back in the chair. "There are still many unanswered questions about how this case ended."

Gavin shifted in his seat and frowned. "Pete, let's stop playing this game. I'm not a perp. Just ask me what you want to know straight out."

Fielding sighed and dropped his hands to his lap. "Help me see the sense of it, Gavin. You said The Smith freaked out and ran, but he had a vehicle right there, and instead of taking it, he dropped the keys and fled on foot? And he sedated the four of you. He easily could have thrown you in the back of the van, right? Instead, he left you all sleeping. For goodness's sake, he didn't even kill anyone. It seems…out of character."

Forcing a smile and a chuckle, Gavin said, "Pete, if I could get inside The Smith's head, we would've caught him way back in 2007."

Pete rubbed his eyes with his middle finger and thumb, then pinched the bridge of his nose as if he were developing a world-class headache. "You know what I mean, Gavin. What spooked him? What made him panic?"

"I was sedated, remember? Memory's gone all fuzzy."

Pete nodded. "It just doesn't make sense, Gavin."

"Since when does anything make sense in this job? And The Smith cases are worse than most in that regard."

"Yeah, I guess. But we *try* to make sense of it, right?" Pete leaned forward, resting his forearms on the blotter of his desk. "You know you can tell me anything, right, Gavin? I don't care what it is. I know the kind of agent—the kind of *man*—you are. Whatever it is that you're holding back, I can help you with it."

"And if there was something pertinent, Pete, I would tell you. As it is…"

"Okay, then."

They sat in silence for a moment, then Gavin said, "Are you going to tell me about the green case in Miami, or do I have to read about it in the papers?"

Pete shrugged. "So far, it's only a blip on the radar. We haven't received an official request from Miami-Dade PD yet. They've found the bodies of three mutilated women, and that's where it gets strange. The ME says all the wounds were self-inflicted."

"What, some kind of cult activity? Masochism gone wrong?"

"From what they tell me, the wounds are extreme. Horrendous. The ME says he can't imagine anyone having the willpower to self-harm in the ways the bodies have been cut."

"ME's have been wrong before, and I'd think those cutters down at USP Lee might differ. But, if he can't see them harming themselves, then someone else had to do the cutting, right?" Gavin picked up his empty coffee mug and waved it at the door. "I'm still on Hawaii time. I need another cup."

"Right."

"Think Miami is going to ask?"

"I do. I spoke with the lieutenant—Bobby Truxillo—running the task force a few minutes ago, and if it were up to him, we'd already have an official request. It's politics. The mayor doesn't want to look weak." He gestured toward the door. "Go get your coffee but keep this little puzzle in the back of that huge brain of yours. Let your over-active imagination chew on it."

Gavin nodded and got to his feet. He walked back to the coffee machine, but instead of pouring himself another cup, he set the mug on top of it and headed for the stairs.

Outside, a warm early-summer breeze caressed his cheek and ruffled his hair. He already had his cell phone out, opened to his contacts list, and as he strode away from the building, he tapped his thumb on Jim Denders' picture.

It rang twice before Jim answered. "Well, if it isn't the surfing FBI man," he said in his squeaky tenor.

"Not much of a surfer, I'm afraid."

"How was the trip? How's Maddie?"

"Good, to both questions. How are things in the Big Apple?"

"Same shit, different day. The Smith case has stalled, as you might imagine, but at least there are no new bodies. Maybe that close call scared him away."

Deep inside, Gavin felt a knot untie. He hadn't realized until that moment how much stress he had been carrying, how much fear he'd harbored that Glacadairanam had gotten right back to his games while Gavin and Maddie relaxed in Maui. "Well, that's a relief."

"Things being what they are, I'll take it."

"Speaking of things being what they are, I just had a strange conversation with my boss."

"Figures. Haymond has been riding my ass for the entire six weeks."

"Yeah, Pete said something about Haymond thinking we'd held something back."

"What did you tell him?" Tension sang in Denders' voice.

Gavin sighed. "I had to tell him something. Pete's just known me too long… I told him that Debbie knew Angel and suspected The Smith had her. I said she believed he was planting Angel's DNA at the Manhattan crime scenes."

Jim grunted. "And that was enough to satisfy your boss?"

"Hell, no. I also told him about Millvale, about Tom Madsen, and said The Smith had admitted to doing the same thing with Tom's DNA between 2004 and 2014."

"Smart. That way if they run any comparisons…"

"Yeah, that's what I was thinking. Pete's not entirely satisfied, but he let it go for now."

"Haymond isn't satisfied either, but he ain't letting anything go. He's been giving me the stink-eye for weeks." In the background, someone yelled Jim's name. "Listen, Gavin. I got to go, but we should talk again later. Maybe after work? We can conference with Debbie so we all have the same story."

"Sounds like a plan. Be safe."

"I'm a cop, remember? The guys that run toward the shooting."

"Yeah, well…duck while you run."

Denders snorted and clicked off. Gavin slid his cell phone into his jacket pocket, then shoved his hands into the pockets of his pants, tilted his head back, and enjoyed the cool breeze.

2

1289 Welcrest Drive, Minnieville, VA
Monday, 6:13 pm

Gavin pressed the button on the garage door remote and killed the ignition. As the door rumbled down, he closed his eyes and relaxed into the seat. He was dog-tired and wanted a second or two to decompress. He'd seen the two cars parked on opposite ends of his block—unmarked FBI cars. Pete hadn't said anything, but it would be just like him to provide some HRT oversight for a week or so—just to be sure.

For a moment, he wondered if either of the teams parked outside had been on duty the day Glacadairanam had kidnapped Maddie, and the sour burn of fruitless anger twisted in his guts. He pushed those feelings aside—after all, they did no one any good.

All in all, Pete was more friend than boss, and Gavin felt more than a little guilty keeping the truth about the wrath child from him—whatever wrath child meant. But friend or not, Gavin did not want a psychiatric evaluation sidelining him. After six weeks away, he was ready to get back to it, to get his mind in gear on something other than Sand dan Glokta's twisted character.

The door to the kitchen opened, and Maddie stuck her head out. "Gavin? What are you doing, silly?"

"Making sure I got all of that hooker's lipstick off of my collar."

"You'd better. It's hard to get that greasy crap off. Can you sit out here for a while? I've got to get my lovers out the back."

Laughing, Gavin opened his door and got out. "Hell no. I want to see these guys. I've never seen a vampire before." Some of the mirth drained from Maddie's face. "At least not the ones who sparkle and glow in the dark."

"Yeah, well, my vampires aren't like that, anyway."

Internally, Gavin berated himself for a fool. "Sorry, hon. It's too soon, I know. I wasn't thinking."

"It's fine, Gavin," she said, half-turned back toward the kitchen, and then smiled. "That...*thing* was no vampire. And he barely sparkled at all."

"No, he wasn't." He stepped closer and gave her a kiss on the cheek. "I have no idea *what* he really was. What's a wrath child, anyway?"

"Let's not talk about it, okay?" Maddie turned to face him and put her arms around his waist. "I'm just glad we got away from him. I'm glad you didn't…"

"It's over, honey." He wrapped his arms around her and gave her a squeeze. "We got away, we took our vacation, and here we are. Glacadairanam is in the past."

Maddie nodded, then rested her cheek on his shoulder.

"In other news, Pete suspects something."

"That's not good. Should you just tell him everything?" Her warm breath tickled his neck.

"What would I say? 'Hey, Pete, let me tell you about this weird ghost-demon-monster thing I ran into on The Smith case.' He'd desk me for sure. Hell, he'd commit me, maybe. Even if he didn't, I'd spend at least six months talking to a head shrinker. It's the FBI, honey. They don't do supernatural."

Maddie chuckled. "Oh, come on, Gav. I've seen the X-Files."

"Exactly."

"You used to think Gillian Anderson was cute."

"Yeah, but then we watched The Crown, and now I can only see her as Margaret Thatcher."

Maddie sighed and stepped back. "As much as I'd like to stand here and let you hug me for an hour or two, our dinner's on the stove, and if I don't get back to it, we'll have to order out." As Gavin released his hold on her, she turned and walked into the kitchen proper. "Oh, a letter came for you. It's on the island."

"A letter?" Gavin walked into the kitchen and circled the island to look down at the letter-sized manila envelope resting there. "Who from?"

"No return address," said Maddie. "That postmark makes it look unofficially official, though. Someone in the Bureau?"

Gavin picked up the manila envelope and turned it over. The back was pristine—no return address there, either. He flipped back to the front. Whoever had sent it had printed the shipping label, but the postmark set an alarm bell ringing in his brain. "No, it was mailed from Langley," he muttered. Then, he glanced up at Maddie and shrugged. "Who do we know in Langley that might send us something?"

"No idea, Gav. Open it and find out."

"That's why you get paid the big bucks, honey. You know how to cut right to the middle of it."

"No, I get paid the big bucks because I write kick-ass paranormal romance with vampires that don't sparkle." She flashed a grin at him. "And for future reference, they don't need lipstick, either. All the blood."

"Good to know. Any idea where vampire hookers hang out?" He flipped the envelope over and slid a table knife under the flap, ripping it along its length. Butterflies danced in his belly, though he couldn't exactly say why. Glacadairanam never bothered with postage. His mind went back to his room at the Pod 51 Motel, and Angel Kirk's journal, which the little beast had slid underneath the door. That had also been in a big manila envelope. He shook his head and fished inside the envelope with his index and middle fingers, pulling a single sheet of vellum from the envelope. A flowing, fancy script covered both the front and the back of the sheet. His gaze rose and tracked to the refrigerator—Glacadairanam had taped his only other communication to its front. Gavin had finally seen the note after their release from Bellevue. It had been scrawled in a childlike hand—no fancy calligraphy involved.

Maddie glanced at him over her shoulder. "What's the matter?"

"Nothing." He looked down at the letter. It read:

> Dear Agent Gregory,
> Please let me start with an apology. This letter is bound to get you riled up, and I've gone back and forth in my mind on sending it until I've worn a path through my brains. You don't know me from Eve, I know that. You ain't got no reason not to toss this letter in the trash right now, but I hope you won't. And that's a bit of a lie because I know you ain't about to do that. "How can she know that?" you're thinking.
> I know you think of yourself as a rational man, and that's okay. But there are many, many things

in this world, Mr. Gregory, that don't fit in your rational view.

I am one of those things. The path I've walked tracks smack-dab through what you might call the irrational universe.

You ain't know me from Eve, like I said, and you ain't got no reason to believe me. So, I'ma give you a sample of my talents. I'm what the scientists call a telezitonic— which ain't nothing but a ten-dollar word for a remote seeker, as me and mine say, a bird dog. I find people, Agent Gregory, sometimes from far away geographically and sometimes from far away in time—though those kinds of viewings is rare.

You go right on thinking I'm a lunatic. It's fine by me, Agent Gregory. But, in a day or two, you gonna catch a flight south, a flight down to Miami, Florida of all places, and if you go messing around down there without knowing certain things, chances are you gonna die and leave that pretty girl of yours a widow.

So, let's get this dang show on the road, and let me get about the business of convincing you I'm not a crazy woman. More than a month back, Agent Gregory, I had a night terror starring you. In it, I was standing on a street in Manhattan, staring into a dark alley. I stand there, waiting for something, but I don't know what. That alley is full of creepy noises and the promise of pain everlasting, but you step forward anyway. I knew you the instant I saw you: Gavin Gregory, Special Agent for the

Federal Bureau of Investigation Behavioral Analysis Unit. Something was waiting for you in that black maw of an alley—something dark and hateful. Then there was this funny little chirp—not funny ha-ha, if you know what I mean—and I woke up, ready to scream my blame-fool head right off. A cold sweat covered me, leaving me shivering and hot at the same time.

Gavin took a shuddering breath, and Maddie glanced at him over her shoulder. "Everything okay?" she asked.

Gavin nodded and began reading again.

Anyway, I started the first writing of this here letter that very second, with the sound of that peculiar little chirp still ringing in my ears.

Does that dream mean anything to you? That chirp? I'm fare-certain it does.

Sometimes, I find people I need before I know I need 'em—and that's the case here—but I'll dance that waltz in a minute.

Whatever was in that alley, it had evil intentions toward you. I know that much without so much as a single doubt. I traipsed after you—not physically, mind, but in my mind's eye, in my visions. I watched over you, Agent Gregory, while you fought that little beast, while you fought for your lovely wife's life as much as your own. Later, I watched you board that fancy airplane and fly to Hawaii.

I watched you sleeping there, Mr. Gregory, in a fancy hotel, your beautiful bride slumbered next to you. Your sleep grew restless, as though one of your night terrors gripped you. You woke up, bolted out of bed, and checked that fancy room. You didn't like the shadows, so you turned on all the lights, though that ain't wake sleeping beauty behind you. When you satisfied yourself that the room was empty, you stepped out on the balcony and sat in one of them chairs out there. You put your feet up on the railing, just as calm as you please. You scrubbed your eyes with the heels of your hands. You chuckled to yourself and shook your head. You sat there for a time, content, but slowly all that unease returned. Your skin crawled as if something was a-watching you.

<u>And something was</u>, Agent Gregory—the little devil that rides people like horses, that wears 'em like a suit. You didn't see him because he didn't want you to see him, but he was right there, and I could see him just fine.

Gavin lifted his gaze from the page, and a shiver ran down his spine. He couldn't help looking around, peering into shadows, into corners. He hadn't remembered that night until he read the description of it. A black pit yawned in his stomach as he remembered the various moments when he'd felt someone watching him, the times he'd felt uneasy, the times the hair stood up on the back of his neck. Another shiver ran down his spine.

Maddie glanced at him over her shoulder once again. "What's wrong?"

"Nothing. It's…nothing." He turned his gaze back to the sheet of vellum and continued reading.

> That's going to put a fear into you, Agent Gregory, and I'm sorry as I can be about that. As I look now—the moment I'm writing this—*you are both safe*. That little devil went and growed bored with you. He's found other things to amuse him. Other people to please him.
>
> But, yes, he is still out there, Agent Gregory. Sooner or later, you will have to deal with him. But you ain't ready for him. If you seek him out now, he'll get what he wants, I reckon.
>
> But this here letter ain't about that little devil. Instead, it's about another devil down to Miami. A killer you're going to come to know. You see, I've had one of my little peeks at what's to come.
>
> Pack your bags, Mr. Gregory. You're going to Miami. You ain't prepared for what you'll face there, but I will do my best by you. Mayhap we'll meet face-to-face down there in Florida, or mayhap we will only speak on the telephone, but *we will speak*.
>
> Unless you find all this too irrational, child. And I apologize, but I can't resist that one little jab. I hope you can see it as I mean it, a joke, nothing more.

I hope to become your friend—if you can stand an old Black woman for a friend. I have things to teach you.

Think about it, if it pleases you. You don't have to believe every bit of what I've said, as long as you believe I've got your best interests at heart. When you are ready to talk about it, call me at 604-555-6344—you can always reach me through that exchange, no matter where I am.

I'm praying for you and your missus,
Adeline d'Clara

Gavin reread the letter, then folded it into thirds and slipped it into the pocket of his coat.

"Well?" asked Maddie, turning her gaze toward him. "Have we won three wonderful days at some beach resort?"

"Yes. All we have to do is sit through a short presentation on the ease of owning a time-share vacation property in Daytona Beach."

"My, we're so lucky."

"They'll even throw in a shark-skinner that doubles as a yogurt strainer."

"Will wonders never cease?" She shot a smile at him over her shoulder. Her smile faltered a little as she took in his expression, and she turned to face him. "What?"

"It's nothing," he said, folding the manilla envelope and adding it to the same pocket as the letter.

"Gavin." She crossed her arms. "You promised. Remember?"

"Nothing's certain," he said. "Miami-Dade Police Department has found three...cases. They haven't requested our help yet, but Pete spoke with the lieutenant in charge of the investigations, and it seems likely that a request will come as soon as politics permit it."

"So soon?" Maddie turned back to the stove and stirred something in one of the pots. "Can't he give you a week or so to..." She shook her head. "I promised, too," she said quietly. "Sorry."

"I feel the same way you do, hon," said Gavin. "But it's my job."

"Yes," she said, stirring the life out of the green beans.

"Oh," Gavin said, going for a light tone, "Gloria wants us to come to dinner. Pete mentioned Sunday but says whatever day you like will work."

Maddie scoffed. "I guess it depends on whether you're in Miami or not."

"Yeah," said Gavin with a sigh.

"Are you going to let me read the letter?" she asked in a neutral voice.

"It's—"

"Gavin."

He fished the letter out of his coat pocket, unfolded it, and lay it on the island. "I'm going to change clothes. Let's go for a walk after we eat. Like we did in Maui."

"It's a date," said Maddie, eyeing the letter.

3

1289 Welcrest Drive, Minnieville, VA
Monday, 6:47 pm

Gavin stacked the dishes into the dishwasher while Maddie read the letter. He kept stealing little peeks at her. When she reached the end of the letter, she flipped it back to the front and began from the beginning again. He was wiping down the counter when she blew out her cheeks.

"Do you believe her?" she asked.

Gavin finished the counters, then rinsed the sponge and set it in the drying rack. He pursed his lips and turned to Maddie. She stood on the other side of the island, the letter face-up on its quartz surface. "I don't know. Do you?"

"This stuff about the hotel. It's true?"

Gavin pressed his lips into a tight line and nodded.

She looked down at the letter, her lips a grim slash. "You thought it was over, that Glacadairanam was gone. I can see that." She raised her gaze to meet his. "And you did mention feeling like someone was following us, watching us." She shrugged. "I told you to stop being paranoid."

"It sounded pretty paranoid." He scrubbed one hand through his buzz-cut hair. "It still does. That letter doesn't change that."

"She knows about the guy in Miami."

"Anyone who watches the right news channels could know that."

Maddie blew out her cheeks. "But not about the events in the warehouse, not about that dream, not about that night in Hawaii—I didn't even know about that."

"No, and I'm sorry. I should've told you, but I thought it was just the dregs of all that mess getting out of my system," he said, shaking his head. "But I didn't tell anyone else, either. There's no way she could have known about it."

"Then…"

Gavin glanced at the letter and shrugged. "Come on. Let's go for our walk."

They left the letter on the island and exited through the garage. It was a fine night, and for a while, they walked in companionable silence.

"How could she know those things?" he asked.

"She says she's a telepath."

"No, not a telepath. A telezitonic, whatever that is. A bird dog."

"Didn't the FBI investigate stuff like that?"

"Not since I've been there," said Gavin.

"If what she said is true, she could be watching us right now. Listening in."

"I guess so."

Maddie stopped and grabbed his arm and pulled him to a stop. "Test her, Gavin. Call her up and test her."

He shook his head. "How?"

"Ask her to find us, to see us or whatever. Have her describe what we're wearing."

"Or," he said, wrapping his arms around her and pulling her close, "I could run her through the databases at work. See if she's a known con-artist or something."

"Yeah, but that wouldn't prove she's not a lunatic. That wouldn't prove she can do what she claims, and that's sort of the point of all this, right?"

"Yeah, I guess you're right."

"Finally, the man sees sense." She grinned and patted him on the chest. "No time like the present. Let's go back and call her right now. Come on, I'll race you." She took off running.

"Cheater," Gavin called, smiling and watching her run in those tight yoga pants.

Back in their kitchen, Gavin flipped the letter open and tapped in the phone number on the back. He put the phone down on the island and put it on speakerphone.

"Agent Gregory? Is that you?" asked a woman's voice, creaky with age.

"Ms. d'Clara?"

"Yes, that's my name. Heavens, child, I didn't expect you to call so soon." She trotted out her old-woman cackle, hesitated, then said, "Hello, Maddie."

Gavin raised his eyebrows, but Maddie nodded. "Hello."

"What, no questions about how I knew you was there?"

"No," said Maddie. "You can hear the phone's on speaker, and since he called your number, you know Gavin's read the letter. Ergo, he's at home with me."

Adeline chuckled. "Keep that one safe, Agent Gregory, and hold her tight. She's a good 'un."

"She is," he said. "But that's not why we called, Ms. d'Clara. Or is it missus?"

"Oh, I know that's not why you called," said Adeline. "I hope you'll both call me Adeline—all my friends do—or Miss Addy will do if you got to have some formality."

"Before we get to that, we hope you'll answer a few questions for us," said Maddie.

"Sure, child. If I know the answers, I'll give 'em over."

"First, how come you didn't think I'd call so soon?"

Adeline's rough chuckle came again. "It ain't like people think, divination. Fact is, not none of us who have the gift even understand how it works. It ain't something the Program studied, and it ain't something that young-uns seem to have."

"Wait. Can you or can you not see the future?" asked Maddie.

"Well, that's the question, ain't it? Maybe I see things that *might* happen, then I act, and because I did something, it happens. I don't know. I get these flashes or maybe a dream that's not a dream. Insight. Mayhap that's a better way to call it. But it ain't like I foresee every second of every day. And unlike my other gift, I can't *make* it happen. I think it's natural for bird dogs to develop the gift if they live long enough, but as I said, ain't a one who knows for sure."

"Bird dogs," murmured Gavin.

"Telezitonics," said Adeline. "Or TZs—whatever you want to name what I got."

"About that," said Maddie. "We'd like—"

"To test me." Adeline chuckled. "Didn't need no second-sight to know that was coming."

"Can you blame us?" asked Gavin.

Her laughter wound down, and Adeline hesitated a moment, as though she were considering her answer carefully. "No, child. I don't blame you none. There's plenty of things in this world that are outside the ken of normal folk. Your little friend in Manhattan being one example that stands up and salutes the flag."

"Right. I believe Glacadairanam exists—"

"That what he calls himself? That mess?"

"Yes."

"Sounds Gaelic. But that ain't nothing—it ain't even his true name, I don't think. Go on, Agent Gregory."

"I believe in him because I saw him. Spoke with him. *Fought* him. You see?"

"Sure, but he's trapped right between two worlds—ours and the one beyond. He can't do a thing without a horsey to ride. But that ain't what you want to jabber about. Go on and ask, son."

"Okay. If you can do what you claim, you can look in on us right now."

"Yes," said the old woman.

"Then…" Gavin shrugged.

"Then I should take a peek and tell you what you already know? That you were out walking, talking about me most like, then decided to come home and stand around your pretty kitchen and test me?"

Maddie's eyes widened.

"And that your pretty wife is wearing them tight-ass pants all the women wear these days. Yogurt-pants. And you got on that raggedy old concert T-shirt. That metal-licker one."

"Yoga pants and Metallica," said Maddie, though she'd paled more than a little.

"Well, sure," said Adeline. "Yoga and Metallica. That do 'er? That enough?"

Gavin looked at Maddie, and she looked back, then Gavin gave a little shrug. "That's impressive," he said. "Can you tell us what Maddie said right before we came back to test you?"

"No, child," said Adeline. "That ain't my gift, snooping. I can *find* people, but I can't listen in."

"Tell me this, can you look in on anyone anywhere you want?"

"Sometimes it don't work," she said. "Sometimes, I don't know, I'm too riled up or too wore out. Most of the prophesizing comes when I'm sleeping. Dreams, you know?"

"Your letter led us to believe you know a little about my last case."

"Well, some, anyway."

"That dream you talked about."

"That dream we *shared*?"

"Uh," said Gavin. "Sure."

Adeline chuckled again. "Child, don't fret so. How boring would this old world be if there was never nothing new to surprise you? What about the dream?"

"I must've had it… Well, I don't even know how many times."

"And?"

"And…it…"

"And it led up to one of them déjà vu things. The night you went back to that alley, then got in that van with that almost dead cop woman."

"Right," Gavin whispered.

"You want to know how come *you* could see the future?"

"Well, I don't know—" Maddie silenced him with a hand on his arm.

"You a rational man," said Adeline with humor in her voice. "I know it. You can't accept it—even when it happens to you."

"What's the answer?" asked Maddie. "How come he had that dream over and over again?"

"Child, I'm old as God, but I ain't Him. Mayhap your man has a little bit of psi. Maybe God just wanted to prepare him."

"A little bit of psi? Like the Greek letter?"

"Short for psionic. I know diddly about them Greeks, but you know scientists, always got to invent a new word for an old thing so people think they's important."

"You mean, Gavin could really be psychic?"

"I doubt that," said Adeline. "The Program's pretty good about identifying kids with potential early on. Then again, ain't no one in the Program God neither, no matter what some might think."

"The Program… Then there are more like you?" asked Maddie. She pulled out one of the barstools and sat on it.

Adeline cackled her old woman's laugh again. "There are many people like me and many with other gifts."

"What's this Program you keep talking about?" asked Maddie.

"Uh-oh," said Gavin. "I sense a book idea coming."

"Let's leave all that for a later conversation. I've got something on the stove, here, and I need to tend to it. Did I pass your tests?"

Maddie glanced at Gavin and shrugged. "For now, I guess so," he said.

"Fine, that's just fine," said Adeline. "Call me when you get down to Florida, Agent Gregory."

"If I catch the case."

"Oh, sure. *If*." Adeline cackled again. "You're a laugh-riot, child. That rational mind of yours just can't help itself, can it?"

"No," said Gavin, grinning, "I guess it can't."

4

Gavin sipped from his third cup of coffee, willing the caffeine into his bloodstream. He'd always heard traveling west to east was the worst kind of jet lag, and the five-hour difference between Hawaii and Virginia made him a firm believer.

"It's official," said Pete Fielding as he strode toward Gavin's desk. "Miami wants you."

"Doesn't everyone?" Gavin turned his office chair to face him.

"I hope Maddie won't hate me for sending you out so soon."

"She understands," said Gavin softly. "She doesn't love it, but she understands." He looked down at the coffee cup in his hands for a moment. "I'll go, Pete, but I'm going to need something."

Pete nodded. "I've already got around-the-clock coverage for her, Gavin. HRT overwatch—two teams, this time—"

"Yeah, I saw them last night. Thanks for that."

"—and I increased police patrols in your neighborhood. Would she allow someone inside the house?"

"I'll ask, but I doubt she'll want to go that far."

"Well, tell her I offered, anyway."

"I will," said Gavin. "What happened to break the log jam in Miami? Another body?"

Pete made a finger gun and shot him with it. "You should work for the FBI."

Gavin grinned. "Turns out I do."

"Then all that money spent on career fairs hasn't gone to waste. I'll have your tickets waiting for you at Reagan."

"What time's the flight?"

Pete looked down at his watch. "Two-fifteen. Plenty of time."

"Says the guy who doesn't have to tell Maddie I'm leaving."

"If you want—"

"No, no," said Gavin with a smile. "I prefer not to be strangled before I fly."

Pete grinned. "I always knew you were a smart one."

5

Gavin's carry-on rolled behind him, a yip-yip dog following its master, while his garment bag competed with his laptop in beating him to death with each step. The stained-glass wall-windows, and the Florida sun burning down through them, drew Gavin's gaze like a magnet. It even *looked* hot outside.

He served his time in the purgatory called baggage claim, then crossed through the terminal and stepped out onto the sidewalk. The air felt heavy and oppressive and thick, even at five in the afternoon, and it wrapped around him like a hot, wet blanket. The sun seemed to pound down on him, pounding the sidewalk, scorching it, in fact, and the strength of the glare seemed to stab him directly in the brain, like a lightning bolt to the *cabeza*. Cabs flooded the street, their exhausts adding to the queasy heat, horns wailing, pounding his brain to mush. His gaze found the dark blue Ford Explorer idling at the curb down the way, and he lifted his chin—a silent query—at the driver. A sun-bronzed man with dark hair in a tan suit got out and came toward him.

"Agent Gregory?" He held out his hand.

"That's me," said Gavin, shaking the cop's hand. "But it's Gavin."

"Karl Santana." He stood there a moment as a slow smile stole over Gavin's face, then he shook his head. "No, I'm not kidding. No, I don't play the guitar. And it's Karl with a K, not Carlos, though my mother argued for it."

"Okay," said Gavin with a shrug. He followed Detective Santana to the Explorer and threw his garment bag, his laptop case, and his carry-on in the back seat. He slid in on the passenger side, leather seats scalding-hot even through his pants. "Cripes, is it always this hot? Feels like an invisible wet blanket wrapped around my head."

Santana cranked up the air conditioner and fanned his face. "They say tan suits are supposed to be cooler. Bunch of bullshit, let me tell you. *Nothing* is cooler in the Florida sun." He loosened his tie.

"I can imagine."

"Imagine? You'll know it for a fact before you get out of here." He glanced over his shoulder, then squirted the SUV into the traffic. "But this isn't hot-hot, and it's really the humidity you feel. You've got to visit in August if you want to experience real heat."

"What's the humidity like?"

"About ninety or a hundred percent once summer gets a head of steam. Now, I'd guess seventy or eighty. It's what gave you the feeling of being wrapped in a steaming wet blanket." Karl pushed the SUV through the snarl of honking cabs and cars, all vying for the same spots on the exit road. "Where'd they stick you?"

"Stick me?"

"Hotel."

"Ah. They usually book me in the hotel closest to the department." He dug out his itinerary and squinted down at it. "Let me see… Here it is. Hotel Miami on First Street."

"Nah, First Avenue," said Karl. "And you really don't want to stay there."

"Oh?"

"You bet. What's your per diem?"

"Usually, they try to keep it under a hundred, but I can get a little more if there's a more convenient place."

Karl nodded. "Good. You want the Langfield Sun. Four stars instead of two, and you won't get the college parties like you would at the Hotel Miami. Plus, it's right on the bay."

"That sounds perfect."

Karl nodded once. "Let's get you checked in and drop your bags. Your boss said you'd want to go to the most recent scene right away. We can head over there as soon as you're ready. We'll get you briefed in tomorrow's meeting."

"Sounds good. Is Lieutenant Truxillo still running the show?"

"Do you want the press release answer or the reality of it?"

Gavin chuckled. "Let me guess. Your division captain is in charge for the press, but your lieutenant is running the actual investigation? Or are you?"

"Got it with the first one. And I'm the unofficial second." Karl flashed a lopsided grin at him. "Done this before, I guess."

"Too many times," said Gavin with a sigh. "But, hell, at least we have job security."

"You've got that right."

6

Virginia Key, Miami, FL
Tuesday, 6:23 pm

The Explorer creaked and bounced down the rough two-rut track that snaked away from Virginia Beach and disappeared into the scrub. "When was the body found?" asked Gavin, raising his gaze from the case file Karl had given him and glancing south at the Atlantic Ocean.

"Early this morning. Fresh kill. I got the call around seven, but the unies had already secured the scene and all that."

"How sure are you that she is part of the series?"

"If not one hundred percent, the next closest thing." Karl glanced at him, a strange expression in his eyes. "You'll understand when you see a body in person. This guy's signature is…" He shrugged.

"Unique?"

"Well, I was thinking 'a horror show,' but, yeah, unique works too. I've worked other serial cases… This guy is strange.

"You and Truxillo cracked The Bay Harbor Butcher, right?"

Karl nodded. "And The Skinner."

"Bloody cases."

"Yeah." Karl grimaced. "And so is this one. The perp either convinces his vics to cut themselves up or he does it without leaving a forensic trace. They're sliced up bad enough that they bleed out." Karl jounced them around a tight bend and slowed to a stop behind a row of police vehicles. "Here we are. I recommend ditching the coat."

"Good idea," said Gavin.

They got out, leaving their suit coats in the car, then Karl led him along a rough trail through the palmettos. They came to a clearing marked by crime scene tape. Deadfalls had created the clearing, creating a sort of natural wall ringing the light-golden sand. Karl pointed at a tall man standing near the edge, hands on his waist, glaring at the CSI team like an irate daddy. "That's Lieutenant Truxillo."

Gavin nodded, ducked under the tape, and approached Truxillo. The lieutenant turned and watched him in silence. "Lieutenant?" asked Gavin. "I'm Gavin Gregory, from the BAU."

"Profiler?"

Gavin nodded.

"Good. We need all the help we can get."

"I'm happy to hear you say that," said Gavin. "People tend to think I only come around to steal their cases, but I don't care about credit for busts. My goal is to help you find and catch your unsub."

"Good." He grimaced and held one hand toward the crime scene. "The local press is already calling him 'The Bogeyman.' It's only a matter of time until the cable channels start using it, and then…" Truxillo glanced at Karl. "This isn't like…"

"We may never understand him," said Gavin, "but we'll do our best to *catch* him anyway."

The lieutenant sighed and nodded. "Whatever you need, just tell Santana. He'll partner up with you while you're here."

"Will do. One thing I could use right now—and this is going to sound like it's right out of a movie—is a few minutes in the crime scene. Alone."

Truxillo gazed at him for a moment. "You're right. That does sound like it's out of a cheap slasher movie. But who am I to stand in the way of the FBI?"

"I appreciate it, Lieutenant. It helps my process if I can visualize the scene."

"Yeah, about that… No chalk outlines in this sugar sand, and the ME's already carted off the body. I can get you a complete diagram, though, and we have things staked out. And the blood's still there, of course."

"That'll work," said Gavin.

Truxillo gave him a terse nod, then turned and called the CSI team out of the scene. He got a diagram from the lead investigator and handed it to Gavin.

Gavin examined the drawing, noting where the body had lain and the trail of footprints—two sets entering the clearing from the north, one set leaving on a slightly different path. He looked at the lead CSI technician and nodded, then turned and walked into the crime scene proper. The kill site was almost in the exact center of the clearing—a roughly rectangular shape marked out by stakes. A huge quantity of dried blood turned the sugar sand into black muck. He squatted next to the staked-out rectangle, gazing down at the blood, assessing it, fixing the splatter in his mind, then he duckwalked to the larger set of footprints. The sand didn't hold tracks very well—more featureless depressions than tracks. Ten feet from the victim's final resting place, the tracks in the sand went back and forth, back and forth. "Did you pace back and forth while she died?" he murmured. The unsub had only come close to the victim once their paths diverged, spending most of his time in that churned-up section. "You watched, staying far away—far enough to avoid most of the blood splatter. But why? Didn't you do the killing? Was someone else here? Someone who carried her in, cut her up, while you supervised?" Gavin turned his head, scanning the scene, looking for something the CSI team might have missed, but it appeared they'd done their jobs well.

Gavin straightened, then walked to the churned-up sand. He stepped over it into pristine sand, then paced back and forth, keeping his gaze on the blood-stained sand. "Why stay back here? It's no fun back here, where you can't touch her, can't see her up close, can't *play* with her," he murmured. "Didn't you want to get your hands dirty? Didn't you want to watch death steal her away? Or are you just the observer, and your small-footed partner has all the real fun?" He counted the times he paced back and forth, comparing the mess he was making in the sand with the unsub's tracks. "How long did it take? Did you cut her before bringing her here? If not, why'd she come out here with you at all?"

A faint chirp sounded from across the clearing, and Gavin's heartbeat lurched into overdrive. With wide eyes, he stared at the scrub forest around them. But then one of the uniformed officers lifted his cell phone to his ear.

Christ, Gav. Get ahold of yourself.

It took him thirty-nine passes back and forth to churn up the sugar sand the way the unsub had. When he finished, he stopped and stared at the blackened sand inside the stakes. "You watched her suffer," he murmured, "but you didn't want to have your hand on the knife?" He glanced down at the diagram, scanning for the location of the knife, but it didn't appear on the diagram. "No knife?" He muttered, shaking his head. "Lieutenant?" he called. "Was the murder weapon recovered?"

Truxillo shook his head.

Gavin turned his gaze back to the bloody sand. "That's why you came close? Not to watch her die, not to be the last thing she saw, but to get your freakin' knife out of her dead hand?" He shook his head once more, then returned to the group of Miami police officers. "Was the quantity of blood right for the wounds inflicted?" he asked the lead crime scene investigator.

"Are you asking if the wounds were inflicted on-scene, I'd have to say yes. Also yes, if you meant to ask if it was enough blood to cause an adult to bleed out."

Gavin nodded. "And no one heard or saw anything? This witness who reported finding the body—"

"Anonymous call," grunted Truxillo. "Came in on our Crime Stoppers tip line."

"That's too bad," said Gavin. "It was probably the killer."

"Yeah, that's what we figured," said Truxillo with a sour expression on his face. "You done out there?"

"Yeah, I guess. I'm not used to this sand."

"Anything?"

"Maybe. I need to let it cook a bit."

"Don't let it cook too long. I don't want another one of these."

"Me, neither. I'd like to see the other scenes."

"Santana will give you the tour. We meet at seven each morning. I'll see you then?"

"I'll be there," said Gavin.

7

Santana bumped the car up on the sidewalk under the overpass and killed the engine. "This one was last Thursday. The one prior was eleven days before."

"And the first one?"

"Twenty-seven days before that."

"He's accelerating. Maybe overloading on it, going into a frenzy where he'll start making mistakes, get sloppy."

"Let's hope." Karl frowned and shook his head. "That's not what—"

"I know what you meant," said Gavin.

With a brisk nod, Karl opened his door. "Come on. It's away from the street a bit."

They climbed the ivy-encrusted fence, then walked into the claustrophobic cave beneath the causeway proper. Some enterprising fool had ripped down the crime scene tape and erected a shrine dedicated to someone named "Bottle Bob."

"What's this?" Gavin asked.

"Homeless guy croaked in the street the same night. Aneurysm. He's the reason we found the third victim tucked back in here. A motorist saw Bottle Bob lying crumpled on the sidewalk and thought maybe someone mugged him. She called 911, and when the responding officer arrived, poor Bob was long gone, but that cop did his job and looked around. He spotted victim number three from the sidewalk back there." Karl walked toward a water-stained row of support columns. "She was about here."

"Same as the Virginia Key victim?"

Santana nodded and heaved a sigh. "All cut up, blood everywhere. The ME says she did it to herself."

"The willpower it would take…" Gavin shook his head.

"I can't see how anyone could be convinced to do this."

"Maybe he holds someone in the victim's family hostage. 'Do it, or I'll do it to them.' That kind of thing." Gavin puffed his cheeks out. "It's surprising what you'll consider doing to save someone you love."

Karl's cheeks reddened. "Sorry. I forgot about your…"

"Abduction. Don't worry about it." He turned and looked back toward First Avenue. "But I'll tell you this for nothing, Karl. I'd have *chewed* myself to death to keep The Smith from hurting my wife." Gavin took a few steps toward the street, then turned and looked back. "This isn't very private. Any car driving past might see him, might see her cutting herself."

Karl nodded. "Or anyone walking by on the sidewalk."

"Old Bob?"

"We think so. We think maybe he came up on them while the girl was cutting herself and that the shock caused the aneurysm."

"And the ME fixed the time of death?"

"Between two and six in the morning—for both the vic and Bob."

"Is there much traffic at that time?"

"Foot traffic? Could be near the beginning of the window. There's a couple of clubs around the corner. Could be couples might walk over to the park for a little loving, though there's not much cover over there."

"How about vehicle traffic?"

"Sure. People leaving the clubs, folks driving in for work—there's always a construction project or forty in Miami."

"So why risk it?" Gavin turned back to stare at the cars going by on First Avenue. "I mean, he drove out to Virginia Key—presumably for some privacy—why make a kill right downtown?"

"There's a bar out there," mused Karl.

"On Virginia Key?"

"Yeah. Only two, though."

"And there are bars here…"

Karl met Gavin's gaze and grinned. "It's a long shot, here. But there's—"

"Only two on Virginia Key," Gavin finished for him.

Karl looked at his watch. "Hungry?"

"I could eat."

"Both of those places serve dinner."

"Let's go," said Gavin with a grin.

8

Tequila Jack's Bar & Grill, Miami, FL
Tuesday, 7:37 pm

The hostess walked them through the restaurant and out onto the deck overlooking the marina. The sun was making its slow dive for the horizon and painting the sky with brilliant oranges, ruby reds, and blinding yellows. The reflection of the sky danced on the marina's still water.

"Beautiful," said Gavin.

The hostess glanced at the sunset and nodded. "Can I get you two started with drinks from the bar?"

"I'd like a big glass of water," said Gavin. "I'm parched."

"Same," said the detective.

"Coming right up." The hostess turned to go.

"Before you run off, can you tell me if you know this woman?" asked Karl. He held a photograph out to her—showing the most recent victim lying on a stainless-steel autopsy table.

The hostess blanched and touched her lips with the tip of her tongue. After a moment, she nodded. "I think so. I think that's Sheila Masters. It's hard to tell, though, because…" She paled even further.

Karl flipped the photograph over. "Because she's deceased."

"Is that who…" The hostess closed her eyes for a moment. "Is she why so many cops are on the key?"

"I can't answer that," said Karl. "How did you know Ms. Masters?"

"She came in here a lot. She lived on a boat." She lifted a shaking hand and pointed at the marina. "Right over there."

"Do you know which boat?" asked Gavin.

"I didn't know her that well. Maybe…"

"Yes?"

"Maybe Marty—one of our cooks—knows. He was sweet on her."

Gavin and Karl exchanged a glance. "Is Marty working tonight?" Gavin asked.

"Sure. He's back in the kitchen."

Gavin nodded and looked at her name tag. "Caro, is your manager around?"

She nodded. "Andrea."

"I'm going to ask you to fetch Andrea," said Gavin, "but it's very important that you don't talk about this."

"At all," added Karl. "To anyone. Get your manager and then keep quiet until we've spoken with Marty."

"You don't think…" She shook her head. "Marty's one of the good guys. He'd never hurt anyone."

"You're probably right," said Gavin. "Still, it's best to let us speak to him and get him cleared. You understand, don't you?"

"Shuh-sure. Let me grab Andrea for you." When Gavin nodded, she turned and left.

"What odds are you giving that she won't warn old Marty?" asked Karl.

"Not good ones."

"You stay and talk to the manager. I'll go find the kitchen."

"Deal."

Karl got up and sauntered inside, whistling tunelessly under his breath. A minute or so later, a heavy-set woman dressed in all black came to the table, a puzzled frown on her face. "Caro said you needed the manager? I'm Andrea."

"That I do," said Gavin. "I'm Special Agent Gregory of the Federal Bureau of Investigation. I'm in Miami on a case, and it seems the victim, in that case, frequented your restaurant. Sheila Masters?"

"It doesn't sound familiar," said Andrea, her frown growing larger.

"Caro recognized her photo—or thought she did. She told us Marty might know more."

"Marty... Our cook?"

Gavin nodded. "I'd like to speak to him, but I don't want it to turn into a big deal. I'd like to ask you to get him for me, on some pretense. Would you do that?"

Andrea half-turned back toward the restaurant. "Of course."

"Before you do, could you look at this picture and tell me if she seems familiar?"

"Is there blood?"

"No," said Gavin, shaking his head. "But she is deceased."

Andrea pulled out a chair and sank into it. "Okay," she breathed.

Gavin flipped the photograph over, keeping his gaze on Andrea's face. She dropped her gaze away from his and looked at the picture.

"I've seen her," she said after a moment. "She's a regular at the bar. Party girl."

"Thank you," said Gavin. "Do you know if she was here last night?"

Andrea looked him in the eye. "She probably was. I can check my receipts."

"That would be extremely helpful. As soon as you can, please."

Andrea nodded. "Do you want Marty now, or after I check?"

"Now would be good."

She nodded again, took a deep breath, and stood. "I'll get him."

A few minutes later, Karl and a tall young man came out onto the deck, Karl walking slightly behind the man. "Agent Gregory," he said, "meet Martin Wilder."

"Hello, Marty," said Gavin, offering his hand.

"Um, hi." He gave Gavin's hand a quick, limp shake.

"Have a seat, Marty," said Karl, putting his hand on the cook's shoulder.

Marty sank into the chair Andrea had left pulled out. He played with the hem of his Tequila Jack's Bar & Grill T-shirt.

"Do you know a woman named Sheila Masters?"

Marty's gaze darted back and forth between Gavin and Karl. "What this about?"

"Did you know her?" asked Karl. "It's a simple question."

"Yeah, I know Sheila."

"When was the last time you saw her?" asked Gavin.

"Last night. She came in—like usual—for Happy Hour. She stayed until closing." Again, his gaze darted back and forth between them. "Listen, I don't know what you've been told, but Sheila and me, we're just friends."

"Caro said you might be sweet on her?" asked Karl.

Marty swallowed. "That's true, but it isn't reciprocal, okay? We're friends and that's all Sheila wants. What's this about?"

Gavin rested his hand on the face-down photo. "I'm going to show you this picture, Marty, and it might upset you. Okay?"

"Well, I don't know..." His gaze locked on Gavin's hand, though, so Gavin flipped the picture face up. Marty gasped. "Is that... That's an autopsy table."

"Yes, Marty, it is," said Karl. "This woman was murdered last night."

Marty closed his eyes, breathing heavily. "God damn it," he muttered. "*God damn it!*" He slammed his elbows on the table and buried his face in his hands. After a moment, he shifted his grip and snarled his fingers into his hair.

After exchanging a look with Karl, Gavin said, "I know it's a shock. You cared for her, that much is obvious."

Marty puffed out his cheeks. "I tried to get her to slow down, to get out of her lifestyle a little. But she always said she was too young to take life seriously. That she had years to…" He shook his head sadly.

"Did you see her last night?" asked Karl.

"I did," said Marty, heaving another sigh. "At the bar—as usual—slamming tequila with some weird dude."

"Weird how?" asked Karl.

"Like… I don't know. He was dressed weird, and his skin looked…" He pumped his shoulders up and down. "His skin looked bleached. Like everyone said Michael Jackson did, but this dude was Latino. At least I think so."

"Can you describe him in detail?" asked Gavin. "If we got a sketch artist down here, could you help produce a sketch?"

"I don't know…"

"All you'd have to do is tell the artist what you saw. The artist will draw it, then you tell him what needs to change." Karl leaned forward. "It would be a huge help."

"I know it's probably the last thing you want to do today, but it could help us get justice for Ms. Masters," said Gavin.

"It might be our best chance of catching the man who did this." Karl tapped one long finger on the ME photo.

"Put that away," said Marty in a shaky voice.

Karl flipped it over.

"Yes, I'll help with the sketch. Someone needs to tell Andrea."

"We'll take care of that," said Gavin. "In the meantime, can you tell us how the man dressed weird?"

Marty's gaze flicked toward Santana, then back to Gavin. "Yeah. He was, I don't know, six foot. Maybe. He had an army jacket on, even in this heat—you know, the olive drab long-sleeve shirt they wear. He didn't look like a pick-up artist—not like Sheila's normal fare. You know, he wasn't all flash and whatever. But he had a wad of cash and he wasn't shy about it. I could smell his gross cologne from the other end of the bar, and—"

"Gross, how?" asked Gavin.

"Musky, maybe a little rank. Like an animal smell."

Gavin nodded. "Go on."

"He had on baggy camo cargo pants and that fatigue shirt worn like a jacket over a black T-shirt. I think he had on lace-up boots. Expensive-looking boots but like worn out. His skin was so white he seemed to glow a little in the darkened bar." He paused for another shrug, then locked eyes with Gavin. "And his eyes were strange. Like a weird color. Gray. Pale blue maybe."

"That's pretty detailed," said Karl.

Marty shrugged. "I was a little jealous. Sheila and I were supposed to hang out after closing, but once I saw that asshole negging her, I knew that plan was shot."

"Negging?" asked Gavin.

"Yeah. You know, hitting her with a mild insult, being a little judgmental. Sheila was a sucker for that."

"Okay," said Gavin. "What else? Facial hair? Skinny?"

"Yeah, he was pretty skinny. I don't think…I don't think he had a beard or anything."

"Did you see what he was driving?" asked Karl.

Marty shook his head, then dropped his gaze down. "I… Look, it pissed me off, okay? That she was going to stand me up right in front of me, without even an apologetic look."

"She knew you were there?"

"Oh, for sure. But that's so Sheila, though, you know? She'd get hooked by a flashy dude or some skeezer pick-up guy, and it was like she got tunnel vision." He heaved another sigh. "Especially if the guy negged her. Then it was like she had something to prove. That she could conquer the guy." He looked at Gavin. "I told her about negging. That it was a thing, a tactic to get a girl interested right away. That pick-up artists brag about it…" He shrugged his shoulders wearily. "Unfortunately, Sheila had blinders on when it came to me."

"How so?" asked Karl.

"She thought everything I said was a line and everything I did was a calculated move to get in her pants."

"Getting back to what the guy was driving, you didn't see his car?"

Marty shook his head. "He bought her a couple of shots at last call—I mean, how obvious can you get? Then he acted all polite, pulling out her barstool, giving her his hand, helping her down. They walked toward the door, and I went back in the kitchen to close down the line."

"Okay, that's super helpful," said Gavin. He turned his gaze to Karl. "We'll get that sketch artist out here as soon as he's available." Karl nodded. "In the meantime, maybe we should speak to the bartender."

"Nah," said Marty. "There were three of them last night, and we were pretty busy."

"On a Monday?" asked Karl.

"Yeah. It used to be dead, but then we started running nickel beer and fifty-cent shots. Mondays are crazy around here now."

"Did one particular bartender serve them most of the time?"

Marty shook his head. "The bar's a big rectangle, and they tend to get run ragged."

"Still," said Gavin. "Can you give us their names? I'm sure Andrea can give us the addresses."

"Legand Druss, Joanna Shannow, and Diego Dunn."

"Great." Gavin jotted the names in his notepad, then got out a card. "If you remember anything else, you give us a call. It doesn't matter how insignificant you might think it is, tell us right away."

Marty took his card and looked at it for a moment, then took Karl's. "No problem."

Gavin stood and held out his hand. "Thanks, Marty. You've helped a great deal. We'll get that sketch artist rolling out here."

"Yeah, okay," said Marty. He shook Gavin's hand, then Karl's. "Just promise me that you'll catch the guy."

"We'll do our best," said Gavin. "And that's considerable."

Marty met and held his gaze for a moment, then nodded. "People will think Sheila had it coming."

"*We* know better," said Karl.

"No one has it coming," said Gavin.

Marty nodded and sniffed, then turned and went back inside the restaurant. Gavin and Karl exchanged a glance. "Jealousy?" Karl asked. "Spurned lover?"

"Maybe," said Gavin. "But that doesn't explain the other three."

"Yeah." Karl pursed his lips. "I'll call the station, tell Truxillo what's up, and get that sketch artist out here. Then, maybe we can finally grab a bite."

"Right," said Gavin, "but, I think I've lost my appetite."

By the time the sketch artist finished with his work, he and Karl had interviewed the three bartenders—none of which remembered serving Masters or her mysterious date—and Gavin was exhausted. He slumped in his chair at the table they'd commandeered for their stay at Tequila Jack's.

Karl gazed at him with a critical eye. "I was going to suggest we catch a late dinner, but by the look of you, I'd better get you to your hotel."

"Yeah," said Gavin with a sigh. "I'm still fighting jet lag." When Karl cocked an eyebrow, he went on, "The wife and I had a month in Hawaii."

"Must be nice," said Karl.

"It was. It really was."

9

Langfield Sun, Miami, FL
Tuesday, 8:36 pm

Gavin stepped through the door, then let it snick shut behind him. He gazed at yet another typical motel room, short entry hall with the closet and the bathroom hanging off opposite sides, main room cramped by the two queen beds. He walked to the end of the closest bed and sat with a sigh. He flicked on the television—not really interested in it but wanting to dispel the hotel silence for a few minutes—then flopped back on the bed.

He fished his phone out of his pocket and dialed Maddie's number.

"I told you, Frank," Maddie said after the first ring. "He's gone all the way to Miami. I'm waiting, and my pool needs cleaning if you know what I mean."

"Miami's not that far," said Gavin. "Besides Frank is the plumber. The pool boy is Michael, and he's decidedly batting for the other team."

"And plumbers can't clean a pool?"

"Not like FBI agents can."

"Wish you were here to make good on that," said Maddie in a sultry voice.

"Yeah," Gavin said. He drew a deep breath in and let it whistle out between his teeth.

"That bad?" Maddie asked.

"No, not really. I'm just exhausted. The heat is… Let's say I have a better understanding of what Hell must be like. But we have a description and a sketch already."

"Oh, that's great!"

"Yeah."

"Then why don't you sound happy?" Maddie asked.

"For one thing, exhaustion. For another, the unsub is pretty brazen—he picked up the last vic in a busy bar. Didn't seem to mind that tons of people saw them leave together. It strikes me as odd—like he's not concerned about getting caught."

"Oh."

"Tomorrow, Karl and I are going to check the bars near where other victims were dumped, but I think we'll find more of the same."

"Karl?"

"Yep. Get this: his name is Karl Santana. Karl with a K."

"You're making that up."

"Nope. He even has a little routine all worked up. 'No, I'm not kidding. No, I don't play guitar. And it's Karl with a K, not Carlos, though my mother argued for that.'"

"Wow. His parents must have hated him."

"Or wanted to give him an interesting name to keep him humble."

Maddie laughed. "Oh, a real 'Boy named Sue,' type of life."

"Yeah." He yawned in a breath, then blew out his cheeks. "God, I'm parched."

"You sound exhausted. I'll let you get some rest."

"No, not yet," said Gavin. "I think we'd better call d'Clara."

"Get some water, right now, Mr. Gregory. You sure you want to call her?"

"Not at all," he said with a chuckle. "I'm still not sure what to think of her act." He got up and crossed to the minibar, frowned at the seven-dollar bottle of water, then grabbed one anyway.

"Then you've decided not to believe her?"

"Well, I didn't say that, but… Psychics?"

"I don't know. I think it's easier to accept there are psychics in the world than it is to believe in little monsters that wear people like clown-suits."

"True."

"Why don't you conference me in?"

"You don't mind?"

"Of course I do. That's why I offered, you giant dork."

"I'm too tired for sarcasm, dear."

"Too bad, love, because I'm *never* too tired for sarcasm." She made the sound of a cracking whip. "Chop-chop, boyfriend. Frank's on his way over."

"Wouldn't want to keep the plumber waiting," said Gavin in a dry tone. He pulled the phone away from his ear, hit the add call button and found the contact he'd made for Adeline d'Clara to conference her in.

"Hello?" croaked Adeline in a rusty-saw voice.

"It's Gavin Gregory. Maddie's tied in as well."

"Are you in Florida, then?"

"Yeah," said Gavin. "Been here all afternoon."

"See there? I told you so," she said. "And you're calling because you've decided to trust me? To believe me?"

"I'm…" Gavin shrugged, even though no one could see him do it.

"Let's just say that Gavin is trying to keep an open mind."

"I see," said Adeline.

"What's your interest in this case?" Gavin asked. "I mean, why bother with all this?"

"I'm looking for somebody," said Adeline. "A man. I believe he's in Miami. In fact, I'm almost sure of it."

"I thought your power let you find people."

"Most of the time, it does. This person can hide from me. But I need to find him, so I'm helping you, in the hopes that you can lead me to him."

"Why? Do you think he's involved in my case? You don't even know he's in Miami, right?"

"There are other ways of finding people than using my gift. And he is capable of the kind of crimes you are investigating."

Gavin shook his head. "Ms. d'Clara—"

"Are we back to all that, child?"

"—do you know how often I hear something like that? Do you know how many times reports like that have been correct in my career? Zero."

Adeline chuckled. "First time for everything, *Agent Gregory.*"

Gavin sighed. "Why do you think the person you are looking for is capable of being a serial killer."

"He had a very bad time growing up."

"So did millions of other people. There's got to be more to it."

"I ain't going to argue."

"Good. Tell me who you are looking for and why you are really helping me."

"I don't know what he names hisself now. And my reasons are the same as I just said."

"In my experience, help is rarely free."

"Again, I ain't going to argue with you."

"Then tell me the price of your help."

"By helping you, I'm helping myself. Your killer will either be the man I'm looking for, or he'll know where to find him. And if it turns out my thinking's dead wrong, I can scratch Miami off my list."

"And if he is? He'll be imprisoned," said Maddie.

"We'll deal with that when the time comes."

Gavin snorted. "That sounds ominous. I'll tell you right now, no matter how much you've helped me, when I catch him, I won't turn him over. He's going to jail."

"Yes," said Adeline. "I wouldn't ask you to let him go. He belongs in captivity."

"As long as we're clear on that."

Adeline chuckled. "Yes, child. Clear as a summer's day."

"How did you meet this man you're looking for?" asked Maddie.

"You remember me saying there were a lot of people with God-given gifts like mine?"

"That's kind of hard to forget," said Gavin.

Adeline chuckled. "I guess it could be, at that. Well, back when ole' Harry Truman was president of these here United States, he formed a committee to look into reports of the communists developing psychic spies and killers for their army. Because of my gifts, and because of my association with a man—a doctor, but not the medical kind—who was researching what made people like me tick, I was one of the members of that committee." She paused a moment. "Well, that's a tiny fib. The man I talked about, *he* was the committee member, but he brought me around to them meetings and sent me in his place, now and again."

"Okay," said Gavin in a carefully neutral voice, and Adeline chuckled.

"You might've heard about the committee. President Truman called it by the code name 'Majestic.'"

"The Majestic 12? Seriously?" asked Gavin.

"What?" asked Maddie. "I've heard of that."

"What's got your man up in a tizzy is that the FBI investigated the so-called secret documents about the committee leaked to some of them UFO nuts and decided it was all a big lie. A whaddaya call it."

"A hoax. That's right," said Gavin.

"But what your man doesn't know is that *we* leaked those fake memos."

"Why would you want the FBI to investigate?" asked Maddie.

"So what happened would happen. We wanted the FBI to conclude them documents were fakes. We made it obvious."

"No, I mean, why would you do it at all? Why not keep hidden?"

"Ah. It was one of them campaigns you do to make your enemies forget about you. There's a fancy word for it, but I forget it."

"Disinformation," said Gavin.

"Yessir! That's it. Disinformation." Adeline's voice had left its rusty saw quality behind as she'd spoken.

"Why did you need to discredit—"

"Because, child. There were some other people—*capable* people—looking in the wrong places. Looking in the wrong closets."

"I don't understand," said Maddie.

"That committee of twelve grew into a project, then a program. A black program—you ken what I mean? A *secret* program. We call it the Program—with a capital P, mind—these days. Back then, folks called it Project Majestic, and that caused us all sorts of problems. A drunk Congressman let that name slip, and boy, did that cause trouble for us over the years."

"I have a tough time believing in a secret program that has existed for…what, seventy-four years?"

"You might be surprised, child," said Adeline, "to know the number of black projects your tax dollars pay for."

"No, I wouldn't. But black projects are short-term, used to develop a specific thing, then made public. Like the F-117, the Black Hawk, and the Manhattan Project."

"Yes, some of the black projects work that way. But others do not. Like the one those CIA boys ran from 1953 to 1974. MKUltra they called that one."

"That ended in the sixties," said Maddie. "I read about that in college."

"Yes," said Adeline. "They said it ended in 1967, but it didn't. If you care for the truth, it didn't end in 74, either. It changed names and went right along. It only did that because of that Rockefeller Commission."

"And how has your Program managed to stay unnoticed?" asked Gavin.

Adeline chuckled. "Child, you remember I said there are other people with other gifts?"

"Yes."

"Some of them have something the scientists call teletechnitic abilities. We call 'em fixers."

"What does that have to do with keeping your group secret?" asked Maddie.

"Fixers fix people's minds. Rewire 'em like. They can reach inside your head and make you forget you know something."

For a moment, no one said anything. Then, Gavin said, "You're talking about mind control."

"Yes. And no. It's not like in them movies. Not like someone climbs inside you and takes over—well, not fixers anyway. Not like your beastie. When a fixer reprograms you, you never know it. One day, you know about the Program, the next, you just don't."

An icy lump of irrational fear formed in Gavin's guts. "That's despicable."

"Mayhap it is, but it can also be good. Imagine, Agent Gregory, a world where all your serial killers are identified as children and *fixed* so they never turn to killing? Rapists, cured. Psychotics, corrected."

"If your program has these fixers, why do we still have serial killers, rapists, and psychotics, then?"

"Because it ain't magic. There are limits—the fixer's psi rating, for one. The fact that they need to be physically close to the one they're fixing, for another. And it's the rarest of the gifts."

"I don't know," murmured Gavin.

"Let me tell you a story about a project I helped develop. It was one of the blackest of the black projects, a secret project within a secret program." She paused as if a thought had just struck her. "Oh, I'd forgotten that…"

"I'm almost scared to ask," said Gavin.

"Pay attention to the one called Fry. He might help you understand your little devil."

"Glacadairanam?"

"The very one." She slurped a drink. "Now, this all happened in April of 1963. April 10th, it was. I was crammed into the back of a plain-Jane Ford van, with my team…"

Chapter 3
Seeker, Bigot, Soldier, Fry

I

Dallas, TX
April 10, 1963, 6:33 pm CST

Adeline sat in the back of a Ford panel van, crammed in with the members of her team. They'd been sweating for hours, and they all stank, but she was especially self-conscious because the team's pusher, Gerald T. Cooper, was a dyed-in-the-wool racist and not too shy to share the fact with her. He'd already complained that she was "dirty," and "smelled funny" in her hearing—probably purposely so. She shifted to get blood flowing to her left leg, which was all pins and needles from her hip to her toes, and Gerald grunted and gave her the eye.

"Cut it out, Gerry," said the other member of their team, Sally Eldridge. She was their snoop, and she knew better than anyone what a pig Cooper was, no matter how much he treated *her* like a queen—she was White, of course. She turned her gaze on Adeline and said, "You move all you want, Addy. Hell, if Gerry wasn't so fat, he'd never know you was a-movin' at all." She smiled at Adeline, even as Cooper shifted his bulk so he could turn his back on both of them.

"Thank you, Missus Sally," said Adeline.

"Hush, now. None of that missus business, Adeline. This isn't the forties, no matter how much Fat Gerry wishes it was."

"Just hush your dang mouths, the both of you, and hurry up," said Cooper. He glared over his shoulder at Adeline. "You're the bird dog, find your little friend so we can get on with this and get the hell out of this van."

Adeline nodded, then closed her eyes and separated her consciousness from her body. She scanned the street, looking for the candidate—he'd blown the meeting, but that meant squat since his connection to reality was tenuous, to begin with.

She sent her consciousness out through the side of the van and stopped dead in the center of the road until the van cleared out. The street was quiet, being around supper time on a Wednesday, but she wouldn't find the man she was looking for sitting at any dining room table with his missus and little ones. No, sir, not him. His missus was a fifth of bourbon, and his little ones were beer chasers.

She floated up, up, up, taking a moment of pure joy at gravity's diminished hold on her, then turned her attention to the alley running behind the buildings on Belmont Avenue, seeking the kind of places where hobos and men down on their luck might congregate. When she had no success there, she drifted skyward again and crossed over Belmont to check the alley on the other side. She glided down the alley, wondering if the angels took the same joy at flight as she did.

She passed a row of over-stuffed garbage cans, and there he was, in the middle of the row, back propped against the wall, smelly garbage cans to either side, his ratty Army duffel bag between his long legs. He wore the same clothing he had every time she'd seen him—knee-high combat boots, baggy fatigues with FRY stenciled above the right pocket and the shadows of patches on the shoulders, including the upside-down chevrons of a first sergeant. She drew her disembodied form to a halt, hovering six or seven feet above him.

"Say hey, sugar"—he turned his bleary-eyed gaze upward—"what are you doing down this way?"

She frowned down at him as he couldn't possibly know she was there—her astral body was pure imagination on her part, and even if it wasn't, he couldn't see her.

Fry grinned up at her. "Smile, it's prettier."

In the van, she opened her eyes. "Next block over," she said, exhaustion singing its sad song in her voice. "On the left-hand side. Combat boots, fatigues, Army duffel at his feet."

Gerald grunted and thumped on the back of the bucket seats where the two "physicals" sat up front. "Hear that, Al? Go get him."

The big guy in the passenger seat didn't move, didn't even twitch to indicate he'd heard him, but the driver put the van into first gear and let the clutch out slowly. Two blocks rolled beneath the van's tires, and he pulled over to the right, then glanced at the passenger and nodded.

Al grunted, then opened the door and stepped down into the street. He thumped on the double doors that opened in the rear of the Ford van as he passed around the back of the van and into the alley. Gerald got up and walked stooped over to the rear, where he pushed both doors wide open and waited.

When Al came back, he had Fry by the bicep, the man's duffel bag in his other hand. "In," he said. He glanced at Adeline. "He's drunk." He shoved the duffel bag under Sally's bench.

"Yes," she said.

Fry grinned, leering at Sally, then he put one booted foot up on the van's bumper and grabbed the doors to pull himself up. He stood there a moment, seemingly on the verge of laughter. His almost-white, pale blue eyes gleamed in the feeble light thrown by the van's dome light, and his lips parted, turning his already wide grin into something that screamed about insanity and murder on dark nights. One look at the man's face dropped Gerald to the bench next to Adeline like a butcher's maul to the forehead.

To her, the man seemed almost handsome, but in an unwholesome way, and on the heels of that thought, he turned toward her and winked, then waggled his eyebrows. "Once you go Black..." he said in a stage whisper. "Mmm-hmm, sweet, *sweet* brown sugar."

She dropped her gaze to his worn and mistreated combat boots, considering the miles he must've walked in them to wear the heels down so low, their leather uppers scuffed and scarred and stained by many a barroom brawl turned bloody. He reeked of alcohol and worse.

"Well, slide the fuck over, old hoss. Let me sit next to your nigger squaw."

"Christ on a crutch," muttered Sally.

The man's fevered gaze slid over to her, and her face blanched. "If there's time, you can have that ride you're dreaming about. If not, there's always room for three in my bed." His face twitched, cheeks bunching as though chewing a great big wad of chaw, but his smile never wavered. When his gaze slid to Gerald, the fat man raised a hand between them as though to ward off a physical attack rather than a harmless look-see. "Sorry, chummy," said the man. "I think you'll have to visit Rosy. I'm the jealous type." He turned back to Adeline and sat on the narrow metal bench between her and the door, a wave of bitter cold washing across her, then he leaned forward to look at Gerald once more. "Get a move on, fatass."

Cooper launched himself across the van to sit next to Sally, who was staring at the newcomer in that intense way she got when digging through someone's memories.

The man's eyes widened to show the sclera all the way around as he tipped his head back and opened his mouth a little to let a decidedly black tongue out to rasp across his lips. "My, oh my," he mused. "Ain't this gonna be fun? Ain't we gonna have us some fun tonight? Shit, yeah, sugar." As he spoke, his teeth snicked together like shears, and the sound made Adeline think of her nipples between those teeth. The man broke his gaze with Sally and grinned sideways at Adeline. "I like the way you think, darlin'." Heat and stink and hateful happiness wafted off the man, making Adeline feel a little lightheaded.

"Gerald, Sally, meet Mr. Fry. Mr. Fry, meet Gerald and Sally."

His bright-eyed gaze tracked back to Sally's face, color rising to bright spots on his high cheekbones. "That name'll do as well as another, but you can drop the mister. I don't stand on formality." He cocked his head to the side, first gazing at Gerald, then Sally, then turning to Adeline once more. "Well, now. Let's say we get on with whatever it is we're going to do." He hooked a strap of his duffel with one well-worn boot and dragged it over. "This bottle won't get itself drunk, now, will it?"

Gerald cleared his throat, reduced to the level of a nervous thirteen-year-old at his first boy-girl dance by Fry's cold presence. The fat man picked up the rifle case and hugged it to his chest. Fry glanced at him, then cocked his head. "Yes," he breathed. "That'll do fine. Just fine. Made in America, unless I missed my guess. .30-06?"

Gerald nodded, looking pale and worn out.

"M1903. Springfield"—Fry turned his gaze on Adeline once more—"and I was right. It's American."

He's a latent snoop, Sally sent to Adeline. *I don't think he even knows he's doing it.*

Fry threw back his head and laughed, then winked at her.

2

Turtle Creek, Dallas, TX
April 10, 1963, 9:33 pm CST

Fry unzipped the rifle case and slid the Springfield out, peering down at the optics for a moment, then grunting. "It'll do, hoss," he said, flashing a savage grin at Gerald as the driver of the van pulled over.

"Good," said Gerald. "Don't worry about a thing. I'll work the bolt for you, Adeline will find the target in the house, and Sally will guide your aim and tell you when to fire."

"Well, ain't y'all thought of everything?" He lanced each of them with a hot grin that made Adeline's blood run cold. "Y'all sure you don't want me to do this on my own? I don't mind. Hell, I like y'all. I'll do it on the cheap."

"No," said Gerald with a brisk shake of his head. "It's got to be done like I said."

Fry sniffed and tilted his head a little. "Not sure I cotton to being told what to do, old hoss." His voice was as smooth as cream, but there was iron behind it—iron ground to a razor-sharp edge.

Gerald darted a glance at Sally and swallowed hard. "It's a test, see? A…whachamacallit?"

"A proof of concept," said Adeline, then she dropped her gaze in the face of Gerald's glare.

"It'll cost more," said Fry. "I don't like the idea of having *her*"—he tapped his temple—"in my head. So many secrets, y'all see?"

"Fine," said Gerald. "I'll go with you. It's easier for me to do my part if I can see the rifle, anyway. Sally can relay Adeline's findings to me, and I'll whisper in your ear."

Fry gave a slow nod, then said, "I s'pose it'll do." He loaded two rounds into the rifle's internal magazine with a precision of movement that made Adeline think of a surgeon. He opened the side doors and stepped out, sparing a moment to wink at Adeline. "Be right back. Don't you run off nowhere."

When he stepped away from the van, Adeline blew out a shaky breath.

"You sure picked a good 'un," said Gerald. "Was the devil too busy?"

"Hush up, Gerry. Let her do her work, and you get on with your own." Sally nodded at Adeline and gave her a small smile.

He sneered and rolled his eyes at them where they could both see, then followed Fry out into the alley, swinging the doors shut, but not enough for the latch to engage.

Once again, Adeline sent her consciousness out of the van and flew down the alley toward the target's house. She overtook Fry as he sauntered down the alley, the Springfield tucked under his arm. His rolling stride was punctuated by the clop-clop of his sprung boots. As she slid past him, he turned his face toward her, his eyes locking on her and following her progress, and she saw that they were orange, not blue as she'd thought. His madman's grin stretched, and his eyes seemed to glow for a moment before he pointed down the alley.

Adeline tore her awareness away from him and found she'd drifted to a stop. *Come on, girl*, she thought. *Pull yourself together*. Behind her, she heard Fry's dry chuckle.

Ignoring him, she flew down the alley, streaking through a well-tended lawn, then around the house to the front yard. Turtle Creek Boulevard got its name from the wide creek that it ran parallel to, and Adeline hovered in the front yard a moment, enjoying the moon dancing on the creek. But a faint tug pulled her around to face the house once more.

She slid through the front door of 4011 Turtle Creek Boulevard and followed the irresistible pull into the dining room, where she found the target sitting at his desk with his back to the window that opened onto the backyard and the alley beyond. She opened one eye, letting her attention split between the van and the target's dining room. "I have him," she said aloud in the van. "He's in the dining room working at his desk. It's cattywampus in the corner."

"Relaying," murmured Sally.

Adeline closed her eyes, returning her attention to the target. She slipped out the window and found Fry's position without effort. His maniacal grin and orange eyes seemed to glow in the dark for a moment as he gazed up at her, then he raised the rifle and put his eye to the scope. "Where?" he asked Gerald.

"She said he's in the—"

"Dining room, yeah. Better do your thing, dummy," he murmured to Gerald. The bolt of the rifle worked by itself, slamming open and closed faster than any man could have moved it, and Fry exhaled, held his breath, and squeezed the trigger. The report slammed through the evening's stillness, echoing down the alley. Before the report faded from her senses, he was already half a block away, walking easy, worn-down boot heels pounding on the concrete, the Springfield tucked under his arm once more. Gerald struggled to keep up, his gaze darting around like a scared rabbit.

Adeline turned and slipped back inside of the house. The target wasn't dead, though blood dripped from his forearm. He stood in front of his desk, staring at the hole in the wall, then turned and ran for the stairs. When he came back downstairs, he charged out the back of the house, holding a pistol.

She snapped back to her body in the already-moving van and opened her eyes wide. Sally and Gerald sat across from her. Fry was peering out the windows in the rear doors. "Failure," she said. "Walker's injured, but not badly."

"You *missed*, you miserable rat-fuck?" demanded Gerald.

Fry whipped around, his ever-present grin blazing as bright as the noon sun, his baleful blue eyes pinning

Gerald to his seat. "*Rat fuck*?" he snarled, though his smile remained constant, spittle flying. His eyes widened, seeming to burn, leaving orange embers in his eye sockets. In two giant steps, he was in front of Gerald, looming over him, rifle tucked under his arm, forgotten.

Gerald began to choke, his hands flying to his throat, though Fry hadn't touched him.

"Al!" Sally shouted.

The tires shrieked as the van fishtailed around a corner, throwing Fry into the side doors, which flew open. For a moment, Fry teetered on the edge, then his feet slipped off the edge. He latched onto the doorframe with his free hand, skiing across the asphalt on those sprung combat boots of his. He roared like an enraged lion, fiery eyes nailing Gerald to the opposite wall of the van. "*RAT FUCK*?" he screamed.

Gerald convulsed, foam spattering from his mouth and coating the front of his shirt, bright red flecks speckling the white. His eyes bulged, and his lips darkened toward blue. He jerked his chin from side to side as though strangling.

Fry began to laugh, an angry, crazy sound, chattering into the night like a machine gun, maniacal whoops interspersed like orchestral hits.

"Al!" shouted Adeline.

Al spun around, then came into the cargo space at full speed. He kicked out, catching Fry in the chest with his own military-issued combat boot, though he cared for his, shined them a deep, glossy black. Fry seemed not to notice, his full attention burning into Gerald's eyes. Al shuffled back to try again, but his feet caught in Fry's duffel bag, and he stumbled into Gerald. He kicked the bag away, sending it at Fry, and the canvas bag bounced off his chest, then flew out of the van and away.

Fry snapped his mouth shut, snapped his head around, and peered into the van's wake. Then he let go of the van and was gone with the staccato snap of leathery wings deployed in a hurricane.

Gerald kicked his feet and tore at his throat, peeling back flesh with his dirty fingernails.

"The doors!" yelled Sally as she turned to try to help Gerald.

Al lunged to the open side doors and peered behind them, then grunted and slammed the doors closed. When he turned back, he'd gone as pale as a ghost.

"Is he following us?" Adeline asked in a tea-kettle shriek.

Al shook his head. "He's gone."

"Gone? You mean, he's given up?"

"No. He's *gone*. Him, his duffel, and the rifle. Poof."

Adeline turned to the rear of the van and went to the doors, peering out the dirty windows.

The street was empty—Fry had disappeared into thin air.

3

The van's tires crunched down the rough gravel road, bouncing through potholes with abandon. The road twisted through the overgrowth, mirroring the creek beside the road.

Gerald lay on the floor of the cargo box. He'd died within minutes of leaving Fry behind—or Fry leaving *them* behind—and the van smelled of his last meal, of the blood gouged from his own throat, of the mucus and blood he'd choked up.

Sally hadn't said a word since Gerald had drawn his last breath. She sat, arms folded, head down, on the metal bench, bouncing and swaying with the movement of the vehicle.

Adeline felt her exhaustion to the marrow of her bones, her mind blank, head aching, stomach churning. *Who was that?* she asked herself for the forty or fiftieth time. *Fry sewn on his chest, and yet, he'd said 'That name'll do as well as another' as if Sally was wrong, as if he didn't care what we called him.* Her gaze drifted to Gerald's face, then to the dried mucus, foam, and blood covering his chest. *Not only latent snoop. Latent pusher, as well? Or something else? Something* more?

The van rumbled to a stop, the driver glancing back in the rearview mirror. "The safehouse. Stay inside and keep the drapes shut up, until someone comes for you."

Adeline nodded once, then glanced at Gerald.

"We'll take care of it," said Al in a curiously high-pitched voice. He jumped out and opened the side doors.

"Come on, sugar," Adeline said to Sally, then remembered the word on Fry's lips and shuddered. "Let's get inside and get some rest."

Sally lifted her horrified gaze from Gerald's cooling form and met Adeline's. Slowly, she raised a hand to her mouth, covering her lips with shaking fingers.

Adeline held out her hand. "Come on, now, Missus Sally."

Sally shook her head but accepted Adeline's dry grasp, allowing the older woman to pull her to her feet. Once Sally was on her feet, Adeline wrapped her other arm around the snoop's shoulders. "Come inside," crooned Adeline. "I'll make tea."

"With gin in it," Sally croaked.

"Any-which-a-ways you want it, child."

Sally lifted her chin and let it drop. She kept her gaze away from Gerald as they stepped over him, then descended the folding step to the grass of the old farmhouse's dooryard.

The house had seen better days—peeling paint, cracked windows here and there, untended planting beds. Behind the house loomed an old red barn, but by the old hay and dirt smell, it hadn't seen use for a long time. Adeline led Sally to the farmhouse door and up the steps into the entry hall. A staircase ascended on the right-hand wall, just after a pair of closed pocket doors. Opposite the pocket doors was an archway that led into the parlor. A thick layer of dust coated every horizontal surface, and Adeline grimaced at the disused odor of the place.

"Well, it could be worse," said Sally in a sour tone.

"Sure," said Adeline with a wry smile. "It might have burned down."

Sally ventured a wavering smile, then took a deep breath. "No, that would make this mess better. Let's get that tea. We can dust tomorrow."

Adeline nodded, and together, they found the kitchen.

"You said Fry was a latent snoop."

"Yeah," said Sally with a shaky sigh. "It seemed effortless. Maybe an unconscious adaptation."

Adeline nodded, pursing her lips. "Still, he must have more than just telepathy."

Sally's gaze dropped to the floor. "Gerald."

"Ayup."

"Latent telekinesis, maybe," said Sally in a low voice, "but I didn't sense that from him."

"It's possible he ain't know it, hisself. Mayhap you couldn't sense it because he don't *know* he possesses the ability."

"It could be," said Sally. "The only thing is…"

"Go on, Missus Sally."

"Just Sally, please, Adeline." She made herself busy getting down two teacups and washing them in the farmhouse sink under the window overlooking the dooryard. "The only thing is…his telepathy felt… There was something…*strange* about it. Wrong."

"With that man, how could anything seem otherwise?"

"Yeah, I guess so."

"He could see me," said Adeline without meaning to speak. She lit a burner and set a tea kettle on.

"When you were scouting?"

"That's right."

Sally shook her head. "That's impossible, right?"

Adeline could only shrug. "A lot of things about that man seem impossible. His smile, first off."

"And his eyes…" Sally shuddered, then rubbed her upper arms briskly as if she'd taken a chill. "They"—she shot a furtive glance at Adeline—"changed, right? They were blue, but they changed to red?"

"More orange, unless I imagined it."

"If you did, I did."

For a few minutes, neither woman spoke, both staring at the tea kettle as if they could hurry it along. Finally, the kettle shrieked at them, and Adeline took it off the fire while Sally found the tea bags in the cabinet and set out their cups.

"What do you suppose was in that Army duffel bag?" murmured Sally.

"Whatever it was, *he* thought it was more important than watching Gerald die."

"Yes… And the way he talked"—again, a shudder ripped down Sally's spine—"about being willing to do it. Killing Walker without help, I mean." Her face burned crimson, and she averted her gaze.

"Did you…" Adeline found an old bottle of honey and put a dollop into both cups of tea. She took a deep breath. "When you was in there…in his mind, did you…"

Sally's eyes snapped shut. "His thoughts were chaotic, malevolent. What he had in mind for us…" She shook her head hard enough to dislodge the brunette bun atop her head. "More torture than sex. It was like he wanted to debase us, to turn even that simple pleasure into pain. More rape than loving."

Adeline nodded slowly. "An awful man." Yet her voice contained a wisp of regret.

"He *hated* us. I think… I think he planned on killing us all."

"Then why go along with the test? Why do what we asked?"

Sally took a long, shuddering breath. "I sensed amusement. A kind of…*pleasure* at the thought of murdering someone. And curiosity. As though he wanted to see what we were planning." She gazed into Adeline's eyes and took a deliberate sip of her honeyed tea. "Do you think you could…" She dropped her gaze.

"Find him? I'm sure I could. I think he'd be like one of them lighthouses on rocky points by the beach." Adeline shivered. "But I don't think I'd want to. Not *ever*."

Sally nodded. "Yes, but what if he…" She took another sip of tea, her hand shaking and slopping the tea over the cup's edge.

"You get that feeling off him? That he would want to come hunting after us?"

"No. That is, not like it was a plan. He seems to live in the moment, to do no planning. He *reacts*."

Adeline nodded. "Yes. His connection to reality is tenuous." For a moment, Sally's gaze zeroed in on her face, a frown of confusion there, and Adeline looked down at her teacup.

"He does the first thing that pops into his mind with no thought for the consequences. He moves from one second to the next with dancing, graceful steps, without any idea of the melody, the rhythm, or even the steps he just took."

Adeline swallowed some of her tea, her gaze resting lightly on Sally's.

"I didn't get a sense of identity, either. What did he say? 'That name'll do as well as another.' He wasn't deflecting, that was his true feeling—names don't matter to him. At least not *his* name. He doesn't care what anyone wants to call him."

"Except 'rat fuck,'" said Adeline. "He seems to mind that."

Sally gazed into her teacup. "Except that. Gerald was a pig, a racist, a misogynist, everything that's bad in the world…but he didn't deserve…*that.*"

"No, he didn't," said Adeline, though she thought a bigot like Gerald T. Cooper just might have deserved what Fry dished out.

"You know what Fry was thinking when he did it?"

Adeline shook her head.

"He was thinking about how he'd find some whisky tonight. Whether he could pawn or trade the rifle, and if so, how much he could get." Sally blew out a breath. "Can you imagine? He was killing Gerald and thinking about getting drunk—as if once he'd decided to kill him, he no longer mattered."

"Child, I don't think anyone matters to that man. Not ever."

4

Program Safe House, Dallas, TX
April 11, 1963, 8:45 am CST

That'll be him, Adeline thought. *He's already in Dallas. He'll want to hear it firsthand.* She stood at the big window in the living room, watching a dust cloud grow nearer with each passing breath. Sally fidgeted on the couch behind her, taking deep breaths, turning them into sighs, making little sounds of boredom.

As the dust cloud resolved into a black Caddie coming down the gravel road much too fast, Adeline lifted her hand to pat at her hair. She nodded to herself and turned a shaky smile on Sally. "Pull yourself together, Sally. Car's almost here."

"This ain't my first rodeo, Addy."

"Mayhap not, but he's in that car."

"Who is?"

"The Man."

Sally's complexion paled a little. "What makes you say that?"

"This project is important to him. He's already in Dallas planning the next steps. He'll want to know what went on, why we failed."

"But Fry—"

"Listen to me now, Sally," said Adeline in her most authoritative voice. "Are you listening?"

Sally swallowed what she wanted to say and nodded.

"Good. The Man doesn't want to hear about a bogeyman running loose. He doesn't want to hear that a wild talent is living in Dallas—especially not one who isn't quite right. Especially one we can't point to, can't prove even exists."

"But Al and—"

"They don't matter, Sally. They're *physicals*. To the Man, they might as well be bugs."

Sally took the news and thought about it a moment while Adeline peeked over her shoulder to check on the black Cadillac's progress. "What do we say about Gerald?"

"We tell him what happened. That he started to choke, he grabbed at his neck, then he started foaming at the mouth, eventually coughing up blood."

"An aneurysm."

Adeline shrugged. "It doesn't matter. We're not doctors, and neither is the Man—at least not a medical one. Don't make guesses, just tell him what happened." She turned toward the window, watching the car sliding into the dooryard. "And whatever you do, Sally, do not lie to him."

"Then it's true? About him, I mean?"

"You bet your ass, Sally. You bet your ass." Adeline moved toward the door, standing behind it, waiting for the Man to come bounding up the steps. She heard his pounding steps on the walk, heard him jump to the porch, and she flung open the door just as he raised his hand to knock.

A smile played at the Man's lips as he blinked at her, his magnetic, magical eyes seeming to beckon her. "You cheated," he said in a mild voice. He wore a pitch-black suit, white shirt, and narrow black tie over a pair of plaid tartan P.F. Flyers tennis shoes.

"Did not! A herd of buffalo couldn't have made more noise." The Southern patois with which she usually spoke was gone, replaced by something cultured, polished.

He glanced down at his shoes. "The salesman said these things would let me walk in absolute silence."

"I'd say that man lied to you, Sir."

The Man chuckled and stepped into the entry hall. "And how are you, Adeline d'Clara?"

"I'm well, Sir. I'm tired from my exertions, but I'm still breathing."

"And the world is a better place because of it." He stepped past her and into the living room, his fingers trailing down her forearm, and Adeline glanced outside, then closed the door.

"Just you?"

He turned back and smiled at her. "Disappointed?"

"Not at all," she said and meant it.

"Good. I'd hate to think my act is getting tired."

"Never in life," she said.

The Man glanced at Sally and sighed. "Alas, we can't spend all day in idle banter. You know why I've come."

Adeline nodded. "Shall we sit around the dining room table?"

"Let's," said the Man, turning on his heel and leading them into the stuffy room. He sat at the head of the table and motioned them to seats along the sides, opposite one another. "I understand your team took a casualty."

"Yes," whispered Sally. "Gerald Cooper."

The Man nodded. "Cause?"

"I don't know," said Sally. "He collapsed, choking and tearing at his throat."

"Foamed at the mouth," added Adeline. "Then spit up blood."

"Shame," said the Man, his brisk tone belying the sentiment. "Was his demise the reason the operation failed?"

"No," said Adeline. "Gerald worked the bolt in a blur. The…*candidate* fired, but the bullet struck the brick window surround, shattered, and deflected off trajectory. Walker took some shrapnel to the arm from the fragments, but that's all."

The Man turned a hard-eyed stare on Sally. "You were in contact?"

"Yes, with Gerald," said Sally, paling a bit more. "He…" She grimaced at Adeline. "That is, the candidate, was—"

"He was a lunatic, Sir," said Adeline. "He prattled on the ride over, all kinds of sex-talk focused on Sally and me."

"He even offered to perform the proof of concept for money—alone. He was very focused on buying whisky."

"Ah," said the Man. "A tramp."

Adeline nodded. "Yes. Disposable. No family ties."

"And was he disposed of?"

Sally and Adeline exchanged a glance. "Al—one of our physicals—tried to hurl him from the moving van, but Fry jumped before he could."

Sally swallowed hard. "When we last saw him, he disappeared out the side doors of the van, moving fast, chasing after his duffel bag."

The Man sat back, crossed his arms over his chest, and bounced a penetrating gaze back and forth between them. "Hmm." He peered into Sally's eyes, then nodded. "Then why did you fail?"

"Bad luck?" asked Sally, and the Man scoffed.

"All we could do, Sir, was find the target, communicate his location inside the home, and work the rifle's bolt," said Adeline. "We couldn't control Fry directly—or even communicate mind to mind, as he wouldn't have it—and, to ensure success, we need to control the shooter in the Big Show. This candidate is unsuitable for that task, at any rate."

"Ah. So." The Man looked down at the tabletop and hummed a single note. "This project is important. Highest priority."

"Yes, Sir."

"We can't afford to risk the future of Majestic on a poorly conceived operation. He must not be allowed to drag us into the light."

"No, Sir." Adeline nodded, thinking about John Kennedy and his plan to publicize Majestic.

"And from what you've just told me, this idea of mine *is* poorly conceived."

Adeline shook her head. "No, Sir. The operation would work if we had a team of five."

"More pushers? Control the trigger, aim the rifle, work the bolt?" he asked.

"I was thinking one bird dog, one snoop, one pusher, one fixer, and a puppeteer."

His eyes widened a little. "Puppeteering is a new discipline. Fixing, even more so."

"I know," she said softly. "But the bird dog finds the patsy and later, the target—in this case, rides right there in the car with him. The snoop is on comms duty as you might expect. The pusher works the bolt— Gerald proved last night that no mere man can move the bolt faster than a pusher. The puppeteer drives the patsy from the moment he wakes up until the moment after the motorcade passes by, giving him the steadiness the shooter will need."

"And the fixer?"

"Mindwipes the patsy and any witnesses."

"Ah, counterintelligence, then."

"Just so," she said.

The Man returned his gaze to the table and hummed a bit more. "Well, it is something that requires careful consideration," he said at last, "but I think you might be onto something." He flashed a sunny smile at her.

Adeline returned one of equal wattage, feeling warm inside for the briefest of moments before Fry's leering, lecherous grin filled her mind's eye, and his voice sounded in her mind, repeating the same two phrases over and over: *Say-hey, sugar. Smile, it's prettier.* A chill raced up and down her spine, but try as she might, she couldn't banish the voice or the smile.

"Of course, we'll need another proof of concept run," said the Man, his intelligent gaze boring into her own.

"Yes," said Adeline, "but perhaps I can take a more…supervisory role?"

"Whatever you think is best, my dear"—he held up one finger—"as long as the next test succeeds."

"It will, sir. The Big Show as well."

"Very well," he said in his deceptively mild voice. "I'll leave it to you."

Chapter 4
The 800lb.
Monster in the
Room

I

"Hold up. I like a good story as much as the next guy," said Gavin, "but what you just told me is complete fiction. Let's leave the Walkin' Dude out of it for a second, and—"

"I don't know who that is, child," said Adeline gently.

"Never mind. It doesn't matter," said Gavin.

"He means your hocus-pocus man. The guy who fired the rifle," said Maddie.

"I don't see how we can leave Fry out of it. Plus, we should talk about how—"

"The FBI determined Lee Harvey Oswald took those shots at Edwin Walker from that alley."

Adeline chuckled. "Ayup, that they did, but ain't it the same FBI that said Project Majestic was bogus? What do you reckon could have led them to believe Lee Harvey Oswald was a man of such unique talents and skills? As I recall, he weren't nothing but a ne'er-do-well. What made 'em discount the eye-witness account that there was *two* men in that alley—two *White* men, mind—while at the same time ignoring the testimony that Oswald didn't resemble either of the men he saw? And how, pray-tell, did Oswald, who couldn't drive at all, drive that getaway car?"

Gavin let the silence drag for a moment. "Oswald was the most likely suspect. He shot the President seven months later with the same rifle."

"*Did* he?" Adeline chuckled again. "Agent Gregory, your own lab determined them bullets fired at Walker were of a different alloy than the ones recovered from the assassination. And, that Mannlicher-Carcano rifle was a 6.5mm—not powerful enough to penetrate the brick window casement. The Dallas Police Department determined the bullets fired at General Walker were .30-06 caliber. Even General Walker said no 6.5mm bullet could've gone through his bricks and then on into the wall."

"People have been arguing about this for a long time, and I doubt either one of you can change the mind of the other." Maddie took a breath. "If I get the drift of your story, Ms. d'Clara—"

"No, no, child. Call me Adeline. Addy."

"I think your story is leading up to a claim that you were involved with the assassination of President Kennedy, and that all the points of contention about the shooting can be explained away by the inclusions of psychics," said Gavin.

"I didn't bird dog for the Big Show team, but I know who did, though he's long dead, and I helped with the planning. The Man did go along with my suggestion as to the team makeup. A puppeteer ran Oswald right up until that last shot was fired."

Gavin took another deep breath and let it out slowly. "Adeline, I can't—"

"You don't have to take me at my word, child," she said in her gentle voice. "You can find out for yourself. All them records from the Program are digitized—though the Big Show's records would have been sterilized. I'm sure I can get you a look at 'em. You can believe what you can see with your own eyes, right, Gavin?"

"Maybe," said Gavin in a thoughtful voice. "*If* they exist."

Adeline cackled. "Ayup. If they do. Read up on that snake, Fry. There's more to him than what I could see, and the Man had some doings with him after Dallas—against my say-so. The results will interest you, I should think."

Gavin suppressed a yawn, rubbing his watering eyes with the heel of his free hand. "I don't know what to think about this. Any of this."

"Wait on them documents. See if I'm lying," said Adeline with a smile in her voice. "Satisfy that rational mind of yours."

"It can't hurt, can it?" asked Maddie.

"I don't know about that," said Gavin, "but I'll take a look."

"That's fine, child," said Adeline. "Right fine. You get them files and read 'em."

"Right now, what I need is sleep," said Gavin. "I'm so tired I don't know what makes sense anymore."

"Mayhap a good sleep will settle your mind some," said Adeline. "Call me anytime, Gavin."

After Adeline disconnected, Maddie asked, "Well? What do you think?"

"I felt better about her before this phone call."

"You're going check her story? Through work, I mean?"

"Uh-oh," he said, smiling. "Sounds like my author wife is hooked."

Maddie laughed. "Well, it would be a great story."

"Even without sparkly vampires?"

"My vampires *do not sparkle*," she said, then laughed again.

"Yeah, but should they? That's the question."

"They decidedly *should not*."

"You're the expert."

"Say that again? I didn't quite hear you."

"I said, I better call Pete before it gets too late."

"No, I think you said something else."

"Me? No, I'm sure that's all I said."

"Uh-huh. Come home soonest, hey?"

"That's the plan. I don't want to find Frank's stuff in my closet."

"Ha ha," said Maddie. "Love you, asshole."

"Right back at you. I'll call in the morning."

"Good night, Gav. Sleep good."

"You, too." He disconnected, then dialed Pete's cell.

Pete picked up after only one ring as if he were waiting for Gavin's call. "How's it going down there, Gav?"

"Progress already," said Gavin. "We have a sketch."

"An eyewitness already?"

"Maybe," said Gavin. "And that bothers me."

"I can see why. He's not scared of the investigation at all—not scared of getting caught. But that doesn't mean he's confident he can elude you. Maybe he's batshit crazy."

"That would make catching him easier, that's for sure. But that's not why I called."

"No?"

"I've come across a bit of a strange story that may bear on the case. I don't know what to think of it, so I'm hoping you can dig up some information for me."

"Sure. What do you want to look in to?"

Gavin sighed. "I need to know if there is, or ever was, a black project called Majestic, or maybe the Program. I need everything we can get on a woman named Adeline d'Clara."

Pete whistled. "Even if we get a peek into those black files, they will be so redacted as to be worthless."

"I figured as much, but redacted records prove the thing exists, at least."

"How does this tie into the case?"

"A woman going by the name of Adeline d'Clara says the killer is from Majestic."

"And who is this woman?"

Gavin took a deep breath and blew it out. "She claims she's a psychic and that Majestic is a program for developing covert operatives. You know, psychic covert operators."

The line went quiet, and Gavin thought he could hear the faint voice of a woman screaming at her husband beneath the static. "Gavin, I—"

"Please, Pete. I'm not saying she's not crazy, okay? But I need to know whether listening to her is an utter waste of time, or if she might—as crazy as her story sounds—know something actionable. She says she knows who the killer might be. I need to know if she's credible."

"She sounds more like a lunatic," said Pete.

Gavin grimaced as he thought about her bizarre story. "Sure. Absolutely. That's where I'd lay my bet, but if even she is, maybe she knows something that can short-cut this investigation…and if we ignore it because she sounds crazy…"

"Yeah, I get it. I'll type it up and put in the request tonight. Don't expect an answer anytime soon, though. You know it doesn't work that way."

"Yeah, I know. Thanks, Pete."

"Don't thank me yet. They may ignore us."

"But you're at least willing to try."

"God knows why," said Pete with a sigh. "If it was anyone else… Get some rest if you can. It seems like your unsub is accelerating."

"He is," said Gavin. "Thanks again, Pete. I'll talk to you tomorrow."

"Right."

Gavin disconnected, and five minutes later, he was in bed.

2

A hotel room
Tuesday, 11:44 pm

Gavin snapped awake, thinking he'd heard something. A scream? He flung the bedclothes off and leaped from the bed, landing in a ready crouch, naked as the day he was born. He blinked the sleep from his eyes and opened them wide, willing them to adjust to the gloaming, but he could see nothing, could sense nothing in that impenetrable darkness. He crept around the room, checking dark corners, jerking the closet doors open, looking anywhere an intruder might hide. Once he finished, he stood there shaking his head, fighting the urge to begin all over again.

He snapped on the lights, then glanced back at the bed and sighed. Maddie slept on, oblivious to his insanity. No scream, then, *he thought.*

He shook his head and pulled in a lungful of the crisp, cold air-conditioned air. The hair on the back of his neck still stood at attention, so he went through the room again, looking for a little ghost, for the wrath child he'd met in Manhattan, listening hard for anything like a chirp.

Again, he found nothing, and again, he shook his head and took a deep breath of cool air. Nothing.

There's nothing here. We left Glacadairanam back in New York. We're safe.

He walked to the sliding doors and peeled back the thick drapes, moving with as much stealth as he could manage, honestly amazed he hadn't already woken Maddie. He unlocked the slider, grimacing at the loud click the lock made, and opened it.

Salt from the offshore breeze tickled his nose, and he breathed deep. He loved the smell of the ocean. His eyes slid shut, and he reveled in the breeze, the salt, the cool night air. His breathing, ragged with tension during his search of the room, returned to normal, and he shoved his hands into the pockets of his warm-up pants, his feet sweating in his running shoes.

He stretched, eyes still closed, and drew in a deep breath that stank of garbage and human waste and blood and imminent death. He froze, arms stretched above his head, mouth hanging open, eyes squeezed shut in denial. He stood there, waiting for something to happen.

What am I waiting for? *he asked himself. He had no answer, could think of nothing he wanted to see or smell or feel or…*

Or hear.

He opened his eyes. Better to see it coming, *he thought.*

The balcony and the beach beyond it were bereft of sound—the moonlight rendering the scene as a silent black and white film from a bygone era, artsy and cold.

Something thudded, down there on the beach. And again, something thudded, the beat of a telltale heart, the sound of the headsman's ax striking true, the sound of a body dropped onto beach sand just above the waterline.

MADDIE! *a voice inside him cried, and he snapped his head around.*

Leaden darkness greeted him, a living, breathing thing of terror, of murder, of deeds done in the deep dark of a cavernous subterranean crypt. He shivered, the cold offshore breeze penetrating his camo cargo pants and T-shirt, penetrating his skin, his mind, his soul.

He couldn't see more than a few paces past the balcony's metal railing, couldn't see the beach, couldn't see the sand or what had just thudded down onto it. Maddie! *his soul cried.*

The thud sounded again, horrid, the step of an enormous monster, the beat of a heart winding down to meet the end, the sound of a child's body bouncing off a car bumper, of a man's fist on a woman's face, the sound of a corpse falling into the bottom of its secret grave far back in the nightmare trees.

He peered into the Stygian darkness, the irrational, impenetrable black. He closed his eyes, then opened them wide, once, twice, and again, willing his vision to slice through that darkness, a sharp knife into flesh. He spun around, wanting to check the bedroom, to check if Maddie slept on, safe in their hotel room, but there was no hotel room behind him, only an alley, the alley, THE ALLEY, its mouth leering at him, looming over him, barbaric fangs stabbing down toward him.

He stepped back, one arm up to ward off whatever awaited him in that alley, and his butt bumped into the railing. He cried out, spun around again, and again smelled the salt on the air, heard the breakers rolling in, saw the golden sand. Relief danced through him, and his anxiety drained away.

A dream, *he thought, willing his pounding heart to slow, to return to a more dignified rhythm.* A dream, that's all. *He sat in one of the lounge chairs and put his feet up on the balcony's rail.* But if it was a dream, how did I get out here on the balcony? *The voice that spoke those words sounded young; a pre-teen boy scared of the dark.*

Shut up! *another voice cried.* It was a dream! *Only* a dream!

He scrubbed at his eyes with the heels of his hands, and before he dropped them, a cold soundless offshore gust struck him in the face, bringing with it the smell of dead animals and skunk and rotten food and human flesh burned to a crisp over an open flame. Something on the beach clanked, steel against steel, then something thudded, once, twice, again, and Gavin froze, hands covering his eyes like a small child.

He didn't want to see the thing thudding toward him from the beach. He didn't want to see the ghostly little creature at its side, the shadow-winged goblin with a bifurcated tail drawing substance from the night air, from the darkness, from the offal-stench on the frigid wind. He didn't want to see it, but a pair of blazing red eyes stabbed through his eyelids, twin spotlights of hatred, of evil, of wanton murderous lust.

When Glacadairanam chirped, Gavin jerked his eyes open and away, jerked away from the railing, stumbling away against the cold glass sliding door, his heart stumbling away against his ribs, all in perfect, utter silence. He stared at Glacadairanam, and the little bastard winked.

"Say hey, sugar," a monstrous basso voice said, echoes descending below human hearing, rattling the balcony like the promise of a massive earthquake to come. "Took me a bit, but I found my way. Let's you and me visit a spell."

"Leave me the fuck alone!" he shouted. Everything became still, the world screeching to a silent halt— everything that was, except his shout echoing and echoing and echoing.

"Not sure I cotton to being told what to do, old hoss." The smooth basso voice rolled around Gavin like thunder, vibrating beneath his feet. "No, sir. Don't cotton to it at all." The last two words burned ragged on the breeze.

Gavin stared into the abyss, twitching his gaze from place to place in the darkness, spinning from side to side, looking for the owner of the voice. Then, that horrible voice laughed—a maniac's laugh as he sharpened his ax, frenzied whoops interspersed with the screams of dying children, an orchestra of gibbering, crazy sounds jumbled together, the evil chattering of a thousand psychopaths plotting and planning in the secret darkness—and Gavin had the sense of something huge looming in front of him. He faced forward, dread circling around him like a shark. Something drew his gaze upward.

An immense face hovered above him, orange-red eyes shining down on him—the direful face of a man given wholly to evil and murder and mayhem and wanton destruction...to death—both hidden by the darkness and born from it, part of it. The awful man grinned a death's head grin, then his eyes flicked toward the open slider to the motel room. "Who's the babe?" A massive obsidian tongue flicked out of enormous cadaverous lips, tasting the scents on the air, and then the mouth yawned wide, exposing gigantic fangs.

Gavin screamed and...

3

Gavin lunged out of bed, a scream echoing in his ears, flinging the bedclothes off, eyes wide, peering into the dull red-orange light cast by the alarm clock's LED screen. His heart thundered in his ears, and his breath came in ragged gasps. Tears wet his cheeks, snot dripped to his lips, cold sweat dripped from his body. *Crying? Was I crying in my sleep?*

Nothing moved. Nothing loomed down at him from the darkness above, nothing chirped, nothing thudded, nothing creaked. He was in his hotel room in Miami. *Safe. I'm safe. Maddie's safe.*

"What the fuck was that?" he asked the empty room. "Where did that come from?" His traitorous gaze slid to the slider that opened onto his balcony—the balcony that overlooked Biscayne Bay rather than a golden beach caressing the Pacific. He dragged his gaze away from the dark rectangle and almost ran to the light switch. He swept them all upward, and bright white light splashed across his hotel room, obliterating the shadows.

"A dream," he murmured. "A dream, that's all." He sank to the edge of the bed, his back to the balcony. "Just a dream," he said firmly.

But he couldn't get that madcap voice out of his head. *Who's the babe?* The phrase went round and round in his mind, whispered, shouted, screamed, muttered. Gavin closed his eyes. "A dream," he muttered.

He lay back on the bed, tugging the bedclothes into a semblance of order, then pulling them to his chin. Only then did he permit himself a glance at the sliding glass door and the darkness beyond. For a heartbeat, he thought he saw a face—a laughing, leering face full of baleful fangs—in the darkness.

"That's it!" he snapped. He flung aside the covers and walked around the bed to the sliding glass door. He'd meant to jerk the curtains closed immediately, but the scene outside captivated him—the soft swell of the bay, a moonlit kiss atop every swell. He stood for a moment and drank it in, feeling more of the nightmare's stress seeping away. When he could grin and mean it, he pulled the curtains closed and went back to bed.

4

Langfield Sun, Miami, FL
Wednesday, 6:53 am

As Karl pulled into the portico, Gavin stood in the lobby, looking out into the early morning sunlight, but in his head, he was back on that blackened, soulless beach from his dream. When Karl blipped the Explorer's horn, Gavin jumped a little, then grinned ruefully. He pushed through the doors, the Langfield Sun's gilt logo glinting in the sun, and got into the SUV.

"Morning," grunted Karl.

"Glad you didn't insist it's a good one," said Gavin with a grin.

"How's the Langfield?" Karl pulled out of the portico and looped around on Chopin Plaza, then found a spot in the light, early-morning Biscayne Boulevard traffic to squeeze into.

"It's nice. Thanks for the rec."

"No problemo. The Hotel Miami is great if you're twenty and have a fake ID to buy beer. Not so much for anyone else." Karl glanced at his watch and grimaced, then goosed the accelerator and began cutting through the traffic.

Gavin's phone chirped and he dug it out of his coat. "This is my boss," he said. "Sorry." He thumbed the accept button and said, "Hey, Pete."

"Gavin," said Fielding. "I sure stirred up a hornet's nest with the request for information on Majestic. I've already had two emails from the A.D."

"Uh—"

"In the first one, A.D. Johnston wanted to know, and I quote, 'why in the hell does the BAU need USAP files for *anything*?' The next email was less polite and a little repetitive. I got the distinct impression that the big people are pissed we even know the name Majestic. It goes on to officially order me personally, and any member of the BAU to, and I'm quoting here, 'cease and desist any avenues of investigation relating to the debunked Majestic Project.'"

"I'm sorry, Pete. I didn't—"

"Nah, you didn't know. Neither did I. I did run the d'Clara name from home last night. Want to guess what I found out?"

"She doesn't exist."

"Bingo. She's *never* existed, Gav. No records at all. Ever." Pete grunted, then a car door slammed. "Which fits if she's part of some crazy black project."

"It fits just as well if she's a lunatic."

"Right."

"Did Johnston deny that Majestic existed?"

"You know how it goes. 'We can neither confirm nor deny,' blah, blah. But he didn't mind making it clear I'd better not ask again."

Karl cut through the intersection at Fifth, hitting the light very yellow, then accelerated hard.

"Yeah." Gavin sighed and ran a hand through his close-cropped hair.

"Reading between the lines of those emails, I think it's safe to assume Majestic exists, don't you?"

"Yeah, but what is it?"

"That's a little harder to extract from the subtext," said Pete.

"I guess I'll—"

"Listen, Gav. I've got to hang up. Johnston is in my office, with a who-pissed-in-my-Wheaties look on his bulldog mug."

"Oh, shit, Pete. Tell him it was me."

"Nah, don't sweat it. Talk later."

Gavin hung up and slipped the phone into his coat pocket.

"That sounded like a fun phone call," said Karl as he swung into the gated parking lot at the Second Avenue MDPD Station. "But tell me later—we've got about two minutes."

5

MDPD, 400 NW 2nd Avenue, Miami, FL
Wednesday, 7:03 am

Lieutenant Truxillo nodded at them as they snuck in the back door of the briefing room. A map of Virginia Key was on the projector, Tequila Jack's circled in green, the location of the last crime scene in red. "Thanks to Santana and Special Agent Gregory, we now also have a sketch." He twirled his finger, and the screen changed to the composite drawing. "We've got copies for you, and it's on the intranet as well. We're going live with it on the noon news." He glanced at Gavin. "Before I introduce Special Agent Gregory, I want to emphasize that he is here at *my* request. He's one of the good ones, and I expect you to make his job easy. Okay?" His steady gaze traversed the room. "Agent Gregory?" He held up an inviting hand, and Gavin walked to the front of the room.

"Hello," he said to the gathered officers. "I'm Gavin, and I work in the Behavioral Analysis Unit at Quantico. I've been in law enforcement for seventeen years—or twenty-three if you count my stint as an Army MP. I recently had a friend that summed all that up as 'keeping assholes in line.' I guess I can't disagree." He flashed a smile and earned a few chuckles. "My point is—"

"Agent Gregory is being a little humble," said Truxillo. "His pedigree includes The Smith—including both the Virginia series and the recent Manhattan series—Richie Arbarth, Wild Bill, The Mauler, and a bunch of others I can't remember."

Gavin nodded. "I've worked on quite a few cases—hunted quite a few serial killers—some I've caught, some I've missed." He gave a fast shrug. "It goes with the territory. But I've learned from every unsub I chased. I've learned that each case has its own rules, but there are similarities, consistencies."

A detective in the third row raised his hand. "Like what? Are you talking about signatures? Posing the bodies?"

"It's true that each serial killer has his own signature, but it may not be something as obvious as posing. And though it does happen, most signatures are not what the word implies—they most often are not personal flourishes meant to link the killer and the victim—not a mark like The Smith left us. Think of it more as an imprint of the killer, something that reveals the unsub is an organized killer where everything is planned to last detail or an unorganized one who kills in a bloody frenzy with no regard for leaving evidence behind. Those broad classifications allow us to assume certain things as we build a profile. Usually, the crime scene is the most revealing thing we have on any individual killer, but we can't get pigeonholed by that. We have to look at all aspects of the crime, not just the scene."

"What do our scenes tell you?" asked Truxillo.

"The first thing isn't good. The unsub has no fear he'll be caught. None. He—"

"How can you know that?" asked the detective in the third row.

"He murders at the scenes, right? And the scenes aren't in secluded, isolated spots. Take the First Avenue scene: anyone walking or driving on First Avenue might have seen him, might have dialed 911. He didn't care—"

"Or he wants to get caught," said the detective in the third row.

Gavin shook his head. "In my experience—and the experience of my colleagues in the BAU—no serial killer wants to get caught. They simply love what they do too much. However"—he held up one finger—"they might get bored, sloppy, or even reckless, but generally speaking those that do are prolific—have killed and killed until it no longer turns their crank. The other possibility is that the unsub has been able to kill other victims that maybe haven't been identified as murder victims or even found. In such cases, the perp will sometimes get a sense of invulnerability, a sense of power, and he may take bigger and bigger risks to heighten his pleasure. And yes, I do mean 'he' as almost all serial killers are males." Gavin met Truxillo's gaze. "That's why these crimes worry me. The risk to the public grows in such cases. Not only might the unsub kill his preferred type, but he will most likely kill anyone who stumbles across him at the scene. Because they are willing to take more and more risks, the chance of that happening increases with each kill." Gavin nodded at the detective in the third row. "Another thing you might have heard is that once established, the signature always presents in the same way. That is often true, but many serial killers admit to tinkering with it—a victim might inspire them, or the scene might offer something new, and the killer plays around with the signature. They are always seeking a better buzz, a longer-lasting high."

"What is *our* killer's signature?" asked Karl.

"Though I don't fully understand it, I'd have to say the antemortem mutilations made to look like the victim performed them. From the Virginia Key scene, it's clear that our unsub stands well back. He paced a lot at that scene but only approached the victim one time once they entered the glade. In fact, if there were any evidence to suggest it, I'd suspect a second murderer—one who stayed by the victim and forced her to make the cuts or did it all himself while the partner stood back and directed the action."

"Yeah, that part doesn't make sense to me," said the detective in the third row.

"That he hangs back?"

"Yeah. I thought these assholes wanted a front-row seat at the time of death."

"Think of the power he must feel in commanding the victims to injure themselves, then watching them do what he tells them to do. And that's a potential insight into his personality. Now, this is preliminary, just my initial thoughts. He may have been in a situation as a child where he felt he had no control over anything. Maybe severe abuse or degradation but also maybe being shuttled around to different foster homes or facilities. Perhaps these situations occurred at the hand of his mother or older sister. Then, he might latch onto a revenge fantasy, where he is compelled to make *them* do as *he* says, rather than the reverse."

Truxillo nodded. "Sounds reasonable. But the ME tells me that some of these injuries are beyond what any sane person would do to themselves."

Gavin nodded, his expression grim. "I haven't had the chance to meet with the ME, so the only thing I can add here is that there are ways to motivate people to do things that sound impossible when you're not in their shoes." He glanced at the other detectives in the room. "Some of you may be aware that The Smith abducted my wife and held her captive in an effort to draw me in. And it worked. I voluntarily stepped into his vehicle without a weapon and without backup. What we kept out of the media was his intention to force me into murdering his victims for him." He shook his head as a heavy silence fell over the room. "Obviously, we escaped before I had to make that choice, but let me tell you—as I told Karl yesterday—I'd have chewed off my own arm to keep that bastard away from my wife. If you think you'd react differently, I'll just say that I did too, prior to six weeks ago." He let them stew on that for a few moments, then said, "The unsub is most likely Caucasian or perhaps Hispanic since we have two Caucasian women and one Cuban as victims. The witness said he's light-skinned, light-eyed, whatever his ethnicity. He's probably between thirty and forty-five—that comes from his discipline at the scenes, especially Virginia Key—all that hard-to-believe pacing so far away from the victim as she cut herself and died. I believe he's using the same knife for each victim, but that's based on psychology rather than forensic evidence. He has the urge to dominate his victims, to humiliate them, to show the world how much power he has over these women. He's brazen— and for that reason alone, it's likely he will try to insinuate himself into the investigation, so be careful who you discuss the case with. Check credentials of men claiming to be press. Know your surroundings;

keep track of the faces nearby. A profile generally includes more detail, but I'm just not sure of those details yet. It's a work in progress, and I'll have more information as we amass more evidence." He glanced around the room, meeting each gaze. "I'm here to help you collar this guy—I don't care about credit for the bust. I care about nailing this bastard. Feel free to ask me anything, and I'll do my best to explain if I can."

The guy in the third row raised his hand, then said, "How many do you think this guy will kill?"

Gavin shrugged. "Most serial killers murder until they get caught or grow too old to handle the physical requirements. Sometimes, older perps will find other ways of committing their crimes or other ways of scratching that itch. But what I'm trying to say here is this: If we can't catch him, he will go on killing until he simply can't do it anymore."

"Okay," said Bobby Truxillo. "If there are no other questions, let's hit it, ladies and gents. We are on a timer, and that timer seems to be accelerating. I want to know more before the next body drops. Examine the composite. Check your sources. Ask around at the crime scenes. Get me something. Results, ladies and gentlemen. We need results."

As the detectives filed out, Truxillo strolled over to stand next to Gavin. "You don't paint a pretty picture."

Gavin gave him a single nod. "It's not a pretty picture. We stop him, or he goes on killing. I failed to stop The Smith, and he came back strong. Christ, the bastard almost killed me and my wife. That's not pretty. That's *scary*."

"Yes," said the lieutenant with a grave nod. "But you *do* think we can get this guy?"

"I have to think that, or what's the point of my life. And, statistically, there's every chance we *will* catch him. The question is: How much damage will he do before we get him?"

Truxillo's lips pressed into a thin line.

"But," Gavin went on in a gentler tone, "I think you and your detectives are on top of things, Lieutenant Truxillo. And we already have the composite. That's a big deal."

Truxillo nodded. "Thanks to you."

"No, thanks to Karl over there. He had the idea to check out Tequila Jack's. He'd have gone out there with or without me."

Truxillo nodded. "What are your plans for today?"

"We're going to hit up those clubs near the causeway crime scene once they open. We'll cruise by the others, looking for a pattern to the scenes, to the locations. But the first thing I'd like to do is talk to the ME."

"You didn't mention that both of the scenes you've looked at were close to bars."

"I don't want to pigeonhole your detectives. I don't want them thinking that the FBI said he only kills girls from bars or that he will always kill near one."

Truxillo nodded. "Ah, that makes a lot of sense."

"Like I said, I've learned from every case—even the ones I botched."

6

Karl cruised by the Jackson Memorial Hospital complex, then turned into the parking lot for the Medical Examiner Department across the street. He found a space not too far from the door and rolled into it.

They got out, went inside, and Karl led him to the elevator, then up to the second floor. He stopped next to an office with Dr. Timothy Powlesland on the nameplate and knocked on the doorjamb.

"Come," said Powlesland from behind a massive mahogany desk.

As they walked inside, Karl made introductions, then flopped into one of the chairs across from the ME. Gavin took the chair next to him and smiled.

"A visit from the FBI," murmured Powlesland.

"I'm here working on this series," said Gavin. "I'd like to talk to you about the mutilations."

Dr. Powlesland leaned back in his chair, put his elbows on the armrests, and folded his hands across his torso. "Ugly things, the wounds."

Gavin nodded. "They almost always are in cases like this."

"Yes, but usually, the wounds are inflicted by the murderer. These victims…" The pathologist shook his head.

"Any signs of hesitation?"

"None. Each cut is sharp-edged and deep."

"I was told you don't believe the victims *could* carry out some of the cuts."

"That's true. The pain would be excruciating, yet the cuts are smooth, continuous. Even if you were to make the same wounds on yourself, the excruciating pain would cause you to react—to hesitate, to lighten your pressure on the blade, to jerk your hand away. Like I said, none of that would be under conscious control. Our bodies have a built-in aversion to pain. Survival, Agent, is a powerful motivation."

"What if the perp had someone you love?" asked Karl. "Threatening them, you see?"

"Yes, I understand," said the pathologist. "But as I said, these drives are often unconscious ones, involuntary."

"Our problem is that at the last crime scene, the unsub only came close to the victim once. He spent the rest of the time pacing back and forth—at least thirty-nine passes back and forth is my estimate."

"I'm scheduled to do her postmortem this morning, so I can't say for sure that her wounds are the same as the others. Maybe he tried something new."

Gavin shrugged. "It's possible."

"Well, I'll know when I get her on the table," said Powlesland. "I'd offer to do it now, while you watched, but we have a staff meeting in a few minutes."

"We trust your conclusions, Dr. Powlesland," said Gavin. "We're just trying to make sense of this."

"I know, Agent Gregory. My fear is that there is no sense in this."

7

South Pointe Beach, Miami, FL
Wednesday, 8:32 am

Standing atop the pile of rocks that formed the jetty on the edge of South Pointe Beach, Gavin turned in a circle. "This is more like it," he said. He pointed at the high rises to the northeast. "Did you guys canvass up there?"

Karl nodded. "And it was worth a whole lot of nothing. It was a dark night. Overcast. No one admitted to sitting on the balcony; no one saw anything."

"Yeah," said Gavin with a shrug. "Is there a bar around here?"

"Throw a rock, you'll hit one. This is Miami Beach."

"Will Truxillo spring for some unies to canvass?"

"I think so," said Karl. He got out his phone and called the lieutenant, strolling back toward the parking lot.

Meanwhile, Gavin turned and studied the jetty, which, by the look of it, marked the limit of a dredged channel to the intracoastal. A pier ran along the south edge of the jetty with seating every ten yards and a covered section down at the end. "Risky," he muttered. "All those potential eyeballs on you. Then again, at night..." He shook his head.

He tried to find a thread into the murder, but the scene was forty-two days old. Plus, it was a tourist spot, and too many feet had gone up and down that pier, soaking up a bit of sun on South Pointe Beach or frolicking in the Atlantic. It no longer had the feel of a crime scene.

Gavin didn't expect much from the canvass, either. Forty-two days was a long time to remember some guy you might have seen in a bar while you got your drink on. He shook his head and sucked his teeth, wondering for the thirteenth time since they'd arrived what time the clubs over by the First Avenue scene opened.

Grimacing, Karl picked his way through the sand and stood at the base of the jetty. "Seen enough?"

Gavin nodded and started picking his way back to the beach. "How'd you do?"

Karl grunted. "He's sending over a couple of knotheads who pissed him off. They're barely functioning adults, so don't expect much."

"It's a long shot in any case."

Karl sniffed and looked down at his shoes, lifting one foot and trying to shake the sand off.

"I've seen enough," said Gavin. "Forty-two days…" He shook his head.

8

Milam Dairy Road, Miami, FL
Wednesday, 9:58 am

Karl pulled a U-turn on Milam Dairy Road at the intersection with Corporate Way, then bumped the Explorer up and over the sidewalk and parked in the grass on the other side. He jerked his chin toward the sculpted shrubs. "He put her behind them."

"Is there a clearing?" asked Gavin, looking at the wild underbrush at the end of the maintained landscape.

"Yeah, behind that crook at the end. That's where he put her, fifteen days ago."

Gavin nodded and got out of the SUV. He left his coat in the car and, as he walked away, loosened his tie and unbuttoned his top button, already hot. He skirted the shrubs, stepping through the red-dyed cypress mulch, wrinkling his nose at the odor of husky decay. "At least he didn't drop you in there," he muttered, looking at the wild growth of underbrush beyond the manicured grassy area.

There was a small flat space behind the curve of shrubs, maybe the size and shape of the Ford SUV Karl drove. He walked through it, his gaze on the ground, hopelessly looking for something other eyes might have missed. When he reached the chest-high wall of shrubs, he looked over it. "Anyone driving by should have seen you back here," he muttered. "Did you stand upright? Pace the way you did at the Virginia Key scene? And why not take her deep into that jungle?" As he asked himself that last question, he turned to look at the wall of green foliage—palms, oaks, pine trees, all strangled by palmettos and wild bushes. He wiped the sweat from his brow and tried not to feel like he was wasting his time. "But this is a little less sheltered than the jetty, isn't it? Did it excite you? The prospect of someone seeing you? Catching you in the act?"

He stared at the ground, trying to imagine where the woman had breathed her last. He knew the general area from the crime scene map, but he couldn't *see* it.

His phone jangled, and he jumped, then rolled his eyes and answered. "Gregory."

"Agent Gregory? A mutual friend said I should call you."

Gavin glanced at the caller ID on his phone. "Unknown Caller," it said. "Who's this?"

"Okay, this is how it's going to go. You don't ask me questions that could land me in jail or worse, and I won't tell you lies."

"You know my name."

"True, and you don't know mine. That's how I want it."

Gavin sighed, looked up at the bright blue sky, then shrugged. "Okay. Who is our mutual friend?"

"No names. But she's sweet and old and trying to help you out."

"I'm looking for records—"

"Yes, yes. Our friend said your official channels are drawing blanks. Are you—"

"How would she know that?"

"Our friend has…certain gifts."

"Not ones that would allow her to know that."

"Okay, our friend also has friends with certain other gifts. Okay? Does that satisfy you?"

"Okay."

"Good Christ. She said you were a pain in the ass, but…" He blew out a breath. "Are you somewhere we can talk without someone overhearing your side of the conversation?"

"I am. Standing in the bushes if you want to know the truth."

"What is it you need me to do?"

"Didn't our friend tell you that?"

"I need *you* to say it."

So that I'm incriminated. Gavin grinned a sour grin. "Right. I need information relating to our friend and a black program called either Majestic or the Program. Good enough for your recording?"

"Good enough. What our friend wants me to get you is dangerous. Dangerous to me, but also to you, if the wrong people find out you've got it. Say people who work in Langley, Virginia. Tell me you understand the risks."

"I understand the risks."

"Go on."

"I need as much as you can get on a guy called Fry. Also, all you can get on the Program. And someone called the Man."

The caller coughed, sounding almost as if he were choking. "*Fuck that*, dude. Are you suicidal?" he grunted. "And that's coffee all over my keyboard. That gets added to the bill."

"The bill?"

"You didn't think I'd risk my ass for free, did you?"

"I guess not."

"Something like this, the price isn't the standard rate. There will be extra expenses—blinds, relays in other countries."

"Will all that take long to set up?"

"I've *already* got all that set up, but if I'm going to blow it all on a crazy run like this, I expect to be made whole so I can set it up again."

"I see. How much?"

"Watch for an email from legion at anonymous. That's L-E-G-I-O-N at A-N-O-N-Y-M-O dot U-S."

"Legion at anonymo dot us. Got it."

"In the email will be a long ass number— a bank code wrapped in nonsense. Chop off the first five digits and the last nine, then copy them down backward. Then wire a payment of two thousand dollars into that account."

"Did you say two thousand?"

"Too rich for you? Too bad. That's what it costs for me to get started."

"No, it's fine." Gavin shook his head. He'd thought the hacker was talking about real money, and that he'd have to go to Pete for a special account. As it was, he'd cover the cost and simply expense it.

"That gets you up to ten megabytes of text data. If I can't get anything, you're still out the two grand."

"That's fine. What happens next?"

"Once I see the money in my account, I'll make the run. If I get anything, I'll email you an executable, a worm. The worm is going to make a few changes to your Bureau laptop, including writing the data you want into a hidden directory on your hard drive. Before—"

"If it's hidden, how will I find it?"

"That's a *very* good question, Agent Gregory," the hacker sneered. "And if you'd let me finish, you'd already know the answers. So, can the newb shit and let me tell you what to do."

Gavin pursed his lips. "Got it."

"I hope so, dude, because Majestic is ultra-black—know what I mean by that? Super-secret. Taking a run at a government server is bad enough—if you get caught, that's your ass in federal prison for a long time. This is beyond that. This is…this is blowing up the Death Star, okay?"

"But you can do it?"

"*Of course I can*! But I want you to know right from the start: if I get busted, I'm totally giving you up and testifying so I get a shorter term." He blew out a harsh breath. "Anyway, once I see the money in that account, I'll get started. If you don't hear from me, it means I'm working. I'm not going to go in there like the Marine Corps hitting a beach. I'm going to tiptoe around. I'm only going to take what I think is safe to get."

"That's good. Careful is good."

"Glad you agree, because it's my way or the highway."

"I get that," said Gavin, suppressing a sigh. "Anything else?"

"Bet your ass. Download the worm on your laptop. It will start itself, and you might see weird shit on the screen. Let it run on the laptop; when it finishes, you need to hit four keys at once to unhide a folder named Black. Okay? You need to hold down control, alt, and the shift key while you press the tilde—that's uppermost on the left—"

"I know," said Gavin.

"Well, fucking bully for you, man. Once you can see the Black folder, log in to your mailbox from the phone and open the same email. It's going to munch on the record of this call and zap any record of my emails."

"And that'll do it?"

"Yeah. The folder will delete itself if anyone else logs into that laptop—whether you've seen the data or not—so keep it safe. If you lose it because some IT wank at Hoover remotes in, you're fucked."

"Okay."

"Right, you know what to do?"

"I do."

"Then go check your email."

The call went dead before Gavin could say anything else. "Well, goodbye," he muttered. He cast one more look around the little hidden space and frowned. "I'm getting a feel for you, pal, and I'm going to get you. Hear me?"

He stood for a moment longer, perfectly still, as though waiting for an answer, then he turned and walked back to the car. He jumped in, hating the way the sweat prickled across his neck and stuck his shirt to his shoulder blades.

"Gonna be a hot one," said Karl in a mild voice.

"Already is, Karl." He held his arms out, letting the chilly air from the vents shoot past his cuffs and up his forearms. "I don't know how you do it every day."

"For one thing, I never have to shovel snow. I try to remember that in August. For another, you get used to it." He dropped the Ford into drive. "Well, that's a damn lie, but it sounds good, right?"

Gavin chuckled.

"Where to?"

"Any bars nearby?"

"Truxillo would know. He lives pretty close."

"Let's ask him for likely places our Don Juan might have hit up." After glancing at his watch, Gavin shook his head. "Still too early for the clubs near the causeway, right?"

"Yeah. I'll call Truxillo."

"I need to find some Wi-Fi."

"On it," said Karl, pulling the SUV off the curb.

9

Mall of the Americas, Miami, FL
Wednesday, 10:48 pm

Gavin pushed out of the crisp, cool air of the Mall of the Americas into the hot, wet air of Miami and grimaced. His laptop bag hung from his shoulder. He logged into his email on his phone and frowned at the screen as it blinked black, then rebooted. He walked to the Explorer and slid in on the passenger side.

"Did you get it all taken care of?" Karl asked as he slid into the passenger seat.

"Yeah, I'm all set. Thanks."

"Sure," Karl said with a shrug. He dropped the Explorer into gear and pulled out. "I spoke to Truxillo again and relayed your question. He says most of the places out here are restaurants—sports bars and like that. But he said we should try this martini bar that's maybe ten minutes from the second scene. It's 'trendy.'"

"Oh, good," said Gavin with a smile.

"Better yet, I called. They're having a store meeting in a half-hour. We're invited."

"Better and better. I wore my trendy tie."

Karl glanced at his plain blue tie and smiled with one side of his face. "Oh, that's trendy, all right."

10

The Olive, Miami, FL
Wednesday, 11:28 am

Gavin and Karl stood at the edge of the dance floor while The Olive's staff cast covert glances at them from the black leather booths where they sat. He watched them watching Karl and him, noting the ones that *didn't* look. Suits, short haircuts, and sensible shoes—everyone knew they were cops. The question he saw in almost every eye was, "What kind of cops?"

"Before we get into the specials and the acts booked for the next few weeks, I've invited Detective Santana"—he held up a hand to cut the few nervous titters from the staff—"and Special Agent Gregory to be with us today. They have questions relating to a case, and both Marsha and I expect you to give your full cooperation." He turned and held out his hand.

As they had discussed, Karl stepped forward, then walked a few steps away. "I'm Detective Karl Santana, and no, I'm not joking about the name. Also, no, I don't play guitar." More titters followed that, and Karl cracked a grin. "Now that we've got that out of the way…" He paused, then took two more steps away from Gavin—again, as planned. "Agent Gregory and I are here today on a serious matter."

Gavin watched as the waitresses and bartenders turned their heads toward him and gave a little smile and wave combo. When Karl spoke again, he watched those heads turn back. Most of them would give Karl their attention, but some would want to watch the FBI agent, and they could no longer do that while pretending to look at Karl.

"That serious matter is the murder of a young woman who may have frequented this bar. We've brought pictures, but I have to warn you: they were taken at the morgue." He handed a stack of copies made on a color copier at the office supply store down the street to the manager, who passed them out.

While that happened, Gavin watched, an easy smile on his face.

"This woman was killed a little over two weeks ago. Does anyone remember her?"

No one spoke, though a few turned the copies over.

"She may have spent time with this man"—he handed copies of the composite to the manager—"and they may have left together."

When no one spoke, Gavin said, "He dumped her mutilated body in the brush near Milam Dairy Road." That got them talking—to one another and in harsh whispers. "Don't you think she deserved better?" Every face turned his way. Every gaze locked on him.

"Don't you think her *family* deserves better?" asked Karl, his chummy tone replaced by that voice all cops learn over time—the voice of command.

"Don't you think they deserve *justice*?" demanded Gavin. That time, some of the staff members cut their gazes to the floor instead of looking at him. "Because I *do*. I'm here to help get justice for this young woman, for her family."

"Speak up if you recognize either of these people. Even if you don't know for sure," said Karl in a softer voice.

"We're not here to hassle you," said Gavin. "We don't give a shit about the pot in your car."

"Or your unpaid speeding tickets," said Karl. "All we care about is this young woman."

"Now," said Gavin, "who recognizes one of them?"

A too-skinny blonde woman raised a tentative hand. "Maybe," she said, but then considered another moment and nodded definitively. "I remember the guy in the picture. I got a creepy vibe from him despite the awesome tip."

Gavin nodded. "Thank you. Did he pay with a card?"

She squinted at the ceiling for a moment. "No, I think cash. A big bill." She turned to a man sitting in the booth behind her. "You remember, Mark? He had a hundred or something. He gave you crap about—"

"Yeah," said Mark, looking at the blonde. "He wanted his change in ones. I told him I didn't have seventy-nine ones." He turned to Gavin and dipped his chin. "He glared at me and said something about calling the manager." Mark shrugged. "It was busy, and we were three-deep, so I gave him three twenties, a ten, a five, and four ones and walked away."

"I thought he was going to jump over the bar and hit you," said the blonde.

"Was he with the woman?" asked Karl.

"I don't think so," said the blonde waitress. "He was busy ogling all of *us*."

"Did anyone else see him? Or the woman?" asked Karl. "Anything you might remember could help."

"For instance, did anyone see the car he drove?" asked Gavin.

"Or what time he left?" asked Karl.

"Or any scars or tattoos?"

A burly guy in a tight black T-shirt raised his hand. "I was on the door that night," he said. "I think he drove a Chevy two-door but an older one."

"How old?" asked Karl. "Eighties? Nineties?"

"No, not ancient like that. Like a 2010 or something."

"What color?" asked Karl.

"White, but the gloss coat was gone."

"I don't suppose you noted the license plate?"

The big man shrugged. "Sorry."

"No, that's alright," said Gavin. "Normal people don't." He gave the man a grin.

Karl walked to the first booth and passed out his business card. "If you remember anything, please give me a call at this number and leave me a message. You don't have to say your name if you don't want to, but please call and share what you know."

"In the meantime," said Gavin, "keep that composite sketch handy. If you see someone who looks like they match, do *not* confront him. But please try to get a license plate or driver's license number."

"Or a name," said Karl. "Then dial 911."

II

Eleventh Street, Miami, FL
Wednesday, 5:08 pm

After spending the afternoon traipsing up and down Eleventh Street, going from club to club near the

First Avenue crime scene in a fruitless canvass, Gavin felt hot and wrung out. His throat was scratchy—sore and dry. He was looking forward to a long shower and clothes that didn't smell like he'd run a marathon in them—that and about a gallon of water. The SUV felt like an oven as he climbed in, and he grimaced.

"No shoveling snow," Karl said with half a grin. He cranked the engine over and then turned the air conditioning to Max.

"Right. I'm almost ready to welcome that chore." He fastened his seatbelt, then loosened his tie and unbuttoned his top button.

"Hey, at least we got absolutely nothing for our efforts."

"There's that," said Gavin. "I suppose it was too much to ask for every club owner to be as cooperative as The Olive's."

"We were lucky there."

Gavin nodded. "So, what do we know? The unsub picked two of the victims up at nearby bars. We don't know one way or the other about the First Avenue victim or the South Pointe Beach vic."

"Right. Two out of four. Want to give me odds on the other two?"

"That's a chump bet," said Gavin. "We just didn't talk to the right people back there." He glanced at the wing mirror.

"True. We can always come back." Karl put the SUV in gear, then pulled out. The street was one-way headed west, so he drove up to Miami Avenue and turned south. "Should we get some dinner?"

Squinting at the wing mirror, Gavin said nothing.

"What's up?" asked Karl.

"Eh?" asked Gavin without lifting his gaze from the mirror. "Oh. No on the dinner, I think. I need ten or twelve hours in the shower."

Karl rolled his gaze to the rearview. "What's got your attention?"

"Probably paranoia. Maddie—my wife—says I'm full of paranoia." He chuckled but didn't turn his gaze away from the wing mirror. "See that black Dodge back there?"

Karl nodded. "Yeah."

"Have you seen it before?"

After taking another look in the rearview mirror, Karl shrugged. "A lot of Chargers in Miami."

"Matte black ones?"

Again, Karl shrugged, then checked his blind spot and changed lanes. "What's special about it, other than the color?"

Gavin shook his head. "Not sure, but I feel like I've seen it around a lot today."

Karl turned his gaze to the rearview as he slowed for the stoplight. "See if he follows us." He flicked on the turn signal as they approached Tenth Street. Behind them, the black Dodge slid into the left lane. "May be nothing," Karl murmured. "Maybe he just wants to get to Biscayne. Traffic might be as bad, but the scenery is better."

"Sure," said Gavin. He could make out two figures in the car but nothing else.

Karl swung the Explorer onto Tenth Street, and a moment later, the Dodge followed. At the next light, Karl turned north onto First Avenue—also one-way—without signaling. "Let's see what he does with that."

The Charger drove straight through the intersection and continued east. Gavin nodded. "Maddie's almost always right."

Karl chuckled as he turned west on Eleventh and headed back to Miami Avenue.

12

Langfield Sun, Miami, FL
Wednesday, 5:48 pm

Wrapped in the crisp air of the lobby, Gavin watched Karl pull out of the portico. He'd almost turned away from the glass doors when he saw the matte black Charger idle west on Chopin Plaza toward Biscayne Boulevard. As the car passed the hotel, the passenger leaned forward and squinted at the lobby doors.

Gavin pushed the door open and walked out, switching on his phone's camera and starting a video.

He jogged out to the median, then stepped out into the west-bound lane. He zoomed in, but before he could get the license plate, the Charger roared around the corner onto Biscayne, leaving a little of its tires behind. Gavin sprinted across the southwest corner of Bayfront Park, but by the time he hit Biscayne Boulevard, the Charger had disappeared.

Breathing the hot, humid air made him feel a little nauseous as he dialed Karl's number and wiped sweat from his face. The detective picked up on the first ring. "Change your mind about dinner?"

"That Charger was just here. At the Langfield Sun. I think they are following you."

"I don't see them. You sure it was the same car?"

"It seems a little too coincidental, doesn't it? *Two* matte black Chargers in twenty minutes? And they raced away when I tried to get the plate."

"Hmm. That's suspicious."

"You think?"

"Still nothing in my mirrors. You want me to swing back? Move you to another hotel?"

"No. I think they're after you, Karl. After all, they followed you onto Biscayne, and the passenger saw me in the lobby. I'm sure of it."

"Well, I still don't see them if they are."

"Keep your eyes open. Maybe they're rotating tails."

"Will do. And you call me if you change your mind. It's no hassle to get you moved."

"Sure thing."

"I'll talk to you in the morning, otherwise."

"Yep." Gavin hung up, then retraced his steps to the hotel and went up to his room, his mind churning. *Two people in the car, so it's unlikely it was the unsub,* he thought. *And they sped away, so it's not MDPD, and unlikely to be any other agency. Then who?* He shook his head and peeled off his coat and tie, sniffing his coat and wrinkling his nose. He finished disrobing and put the suit out for dry cleaning.

Stepping into the shower, he ran the water as cold as he could stand it, letting the shivery-goodness sluice over his tired flesh. By the time he stepped out, some of his fatigue had gone down the drain with his spent sweat. He pulled on a pair of shorts and went over to the sliding glass door, thinking he might sit on the balcony awhile, but then remembered the heat and sat at the small round table in the corner and opened his laptop instead. He grabbed another seven-dollar bottle of water and opened the Black folder.

13

From Program records
Marked March 11, 1963, 10:52 pm

Digitized from written memo #12X83475

TO: The Man

FR: Miss Adeline

SUBJECT: Recruitment report

Dear Sir,

With regard to our last conversation, I've been diligently looking for someone we can recruit for use in the proof of concept test you ordered. I believe I've found the perfect candidate.

Full disclosure: there's something strange about him. He isn't Program material, but he is sufficiently loose in the morals department.

Also, he claims he's anti-government, but it is my (and Sally's) feeling that he couldn't care less who is in power. He's a devotee of chaos and works to provoke it via whatever methods are at hand.

But I don't like him. There's something strange about him, like I said, but at the same time, something compels one to pay attention to him when in his presence—something magnetic about him. And potentially dangerous, I should think, but controllable. Let's leave it at that.

With your permission, I'll proceed with the Walker test.

Adeline d'Clara

14

From Program records
Marked March 13, 1963, 09:52 am

Digitized from written memo #12X83491

TO: Miss Adeline

FR: The Man

SUBJECT: RE: Memo #12X83475

Proceed.

We need to know if this will work or not. The Big Show isn't far away, and in that, we can't fail. This is your highest priority, Miss Adeline. Do not fail me.

As to the strangeness, we're all a bit out there, right? Would he be suitable for the Big Show?

The Man.

15

From Program records
Marked March 15, 1963, 12:52 pm

Digitized from written memo #12X83512

TO: The Man

FR: Miss Adeline

SUBJECT: RE: Memo #12X83491

My intuition says this new recruit is wholly unsuitable for the Big Show. Too much of a wild card, though I've misjudged people before.

Adeline d'Clara

16

From Program records
Marked March 20, 1963, 09:17 am

Digitized from written memo #12X83535

TO: Miss Adeline

FR: The Man

SUBJECT: RE: Memo #12X83512

Miss Adeline, don't worry about your wild card. If we proceed, he'll be managed—even if we need one of the new fixers to do it. In the meantime, please focus on the Walker test and ensure we fully explore the viability of the team makeup. Please do your best to emulate the time constraints of the Big Show—I know, I know. This is our first attempt, and there are bound to be problems. Just do your best. It's always been good enough for me.

The Man.

17

From Program records
Marked March 23, 1963, 12:52 pm

Digitized from written memo #12X83566

TO: The Man

FR: Miss Adeline

SUBJECT: RE: Memo #12X83535

I'm not worried, Sir. I believe he is unsuitable, but you see more of the picture than I do. I bow to your greater insight—as always.

As for doing my best, you know I will. I'll ride herd on this test, and we will know how to proceed after the operation succeeds.

Adeline d'Clara

18

Gavin stared at the last digitized memo. *I'll be damned*, he thought. *She was telling the truth*. He sat back, shaking his head. He leaned forward and reread the five memos. "Maddie's going to love this," he muttered as he reached for his phone and dialed her number. She picked it up on the second ring and said, "Frank, I told you no more phone sex. I'm waiting for a call from Gavin."

"I've never understood phone sex," he said.

"That much is very clear to me." Maddie chuckled. "Want to practice?"

"More than anything, but…"

"Oh, serious time?"

"Yeah, sorry. I'd be too distracted to do you justice."

"That's okay. I'd rather have the real thing. What's up?"

Now that he had her on the phone, he wondered if he should share the memos with her. If he did, it made her complicit in the hacking, plus, if Majestic was real and they took umbrage at the theft, it could put her in danger. "Uh… Nothing much. I…"

"Gavin," she said in a soft voice. "We talked about this."

"This is different."

"How so?"

"If I tell you, it could put you in…get you in trouble."

"It would put me in danger?"

Gavin blew out his cheeks. "Yes."

"Are you in danger?"

"I could be. I could be in trouble, too."

"Aren't those the same thing?"

"Not in this case. The trouble could incur Federal prison time. The danger will come from another direction. A deadlier one."

"Oh. Then Adeline was telling the truth, and you don't want to tell me how you got the confirmation."

"Sometimes, my love, you are too smart for your own good."

"Did Pete help?"

"Pete tried to get us a peek into some files. It didn't work."

"Oh. Then you—"

"This is where you stop trying to figure this out."

"Oh. Okay." She hummed tunelessly for half a breath. "Tell me what you found out." After Gavin relayed the contents of the memos to her, Maddie said, "Let's call her."

"Yeah?"

"Yeah. If what she told us last night is true, I want to hear more. Not about JFK. I want to hear about the crazy guy."

"Fry. Her unsuitable wild card."

"Yeah. Don't you want to hear more?"

"I do, and I don't at the same time." He got up and went to lie on the bed. "I had a nightmare last night."

"The alley again?"

"Sort of. No. Not just that, anyway."

"Yes, no, maybe?" She giggled.

"It's complicated," Gavin said without a hint of good humor.

"Want to tell me about it?" she asked.

"I was in Hawaii. It was the night Adeline talked about in her letter. I got up and checked the room, then went out on the balcony. There was something out there…"

"Glacadairanam?"

"Him, too. And the smell of the alley."

"Something new?"

"Yeah. It was huge. It…spoke to me."

"What did it say?"

Gavin covered his eyes with his forearm. "Remember in Adeline's story? Fry said hello to her?"

"Say hey, sugar," said Maddie, and Gavin winced at hearing those words in her voice.

"Yeah, and something about not wanting anyone to tell him what to do?"

"He said, 'I'm not sure I cotton to being told what to do, old hoss.'"

"Yeah," Gavin said as a shiver raced up and down his spine at hearing those words in her voice. "That's it."

"And that's all?"

"No." He drew in a shaky breath. "He…"

"He threatened you?"

"No. Not me."

"Oh." She hesitated for a few breaths. "I was in your dream?"

"Yes. It was like that night in Hawaii. I was on the balcony; you were inside sleeping."

"Okay. Then what?"

"I woke up."

Maddie was quiet for a few moments, then she said, "Gavin, you'd just heard Adeline describe Fry and how he talked. It was on your mind, and so was your recurrent nightmare. We talked to Adeline about that night before last, remember?"

"Yeah."

"So, there you go. It was just a nightmare, Gav."

"That's what I thought about the alley dream."

"That was different."

"Why?" he asked. "How?"

"Because you had it again and again. It was part of the case. None of this is part of your case, right?"

Gavin shook his head. "I can't see how."

"So, there you go. Your beautiful wife has figured it out again."

Relief and trepidation raced round and round in his head. "What if you're wrong?"

"Then we'll deal with it when we know for sure. Okay?"

"I guess. But do me a favor? Stick close to the HRT guys."

"Don't worry about me, Gavin. I'm fine, and the HRT guys are around."

"Okay."

"Let's call her."

"Okay." Gavin dialed Adeline's number and conferenced the calls together.

"Hello, Gavin," said Adeline.

"Maddie's here, too."

"Hello, Maddie. How are you, child?"

"I'm fine," she said. "How are you, Adeline?"

"I'm right as rain. I don't need no precognitive powers to know you're calling because you found out I told you the truth last night."

"No?"

"No, child," she said. "Tell me what you've found."

"Memos," said Gavin. "I've only read a few. Five, actually, from the spring of 1963."

"Ah. Them memos between the Man and me. From before the Walker attempt."

"Yes, from March."

"Then you don't know all of it."

"No, I guess we don't." Gavin grunted. "If I had to guess, I'd say we don't know any of it for sure."

Adeline laughed, and when her mirth had exhausted itself, she said, "Let's shift directions a little, leave all that Dallas stuff behind for a bit. Let me spin you another story, Gavin. A story about my…my friend, Jamilla. With her little baby in tow, she took an airplane to Western New York—coming to visit me and spend a week playing in the big lake. When she got off the plane, she lost her little one. And not just for a minute or two, Gregorys. No, she lost him for good that afternoon in June."

Chapter 5
Life in the Fast Lane

I

Rochester International Airport, Rochester, NY
June 12, 1998, 3:33 pm EST

Jamilla had only looked away for a moment. One lapse, one moment of giving in to her fatigue, one single distraction—a good-looking twenty-something diesel yelling at an old woman—one little flick of her gaze that strayed for a heartbeat too long, and her son disappeared.

"Kai!" she cried, twisting her head this way and that. "Kai, come to Mommy!"

A cool, dry hand slipped into the crook of her elbow. Jamilla turned her head to stare into the piercing gray eyes of the statuesque blonde who'd come up beside her and taken her arm. The woman looked familiar… *Maybe one of the flight attendants?* Jamilla thought. "Thank God! Have you seen my son? He's—"

"Be quiet," the woman said in a dead voice as cold as her glare. Her tone, more than anything, chilled Jamilla into compliance. "We have your son, Jamilla. He's safe. And so are you"—She cocked her head and narrowed her eyes—"for the moment."

Jamilla jerked her arm, trying to pull away, but the woman's grip on her arm tightened like the jaws of a pit bull.

"Stop," said the blonde in a bored-sounding, cold voice. "We have Kai, and—attend me well, Jamilla. We have him and there's not a thing in the world you can do about it." Again, her frigid tone gave Jamilla pause. "But…" She let it linger there, let the promise hang in the air between them—the perfect carrot. She lifted her chin, and her assessing gaze probed Jamilla's features. "But I might make a place for you where he's going. That's within my discretion. Oh, things have already gone beyond 'Mommy,' and you will no longer fill that role in Kai's life."

Hot panic sluiced into Jamilla's bloodstream like magma flowing down the shoulders of a volcano. She gave her arm a savage jerk, and this time, the blonde let her. "If you think I'm going to—"

"Don't be ridiculous, Jamilla. I'm offering a chance—a place in proximity to your son. A *safe* place. You will see Kai every day, though I doubt we'll allow him to ever see you. Don't cause a scene. Don't make me change my mind."

Jamilla twisted her head from side to side—looking for help. Looking for a cop.

The blonde's hand rose, and she flicked one perfectly sculpted nail to one side. "There," she said in her infuriatingly calm voice. "The 'men in blue,' if you will." Then, she said it again, but this time, it was the stick. "But…"

Jamilla snapped her head around to meet the blonde's cold, gray-eyed gaze. Her panic had left her, replaced by a cold, murderous rage. "But what, you bitch?"

The blonde smiled, her perfectly painted lips parting to reveal perfect white teeth. "At least you're an astute judge of character." Again, she cocked her head and hit Jamilla with a probing look. "Or maybe you have some of what Kai has." Her delicate shoulders rose and fell. "Either way, it really doesn't matter. But…" She turned her hand over and moved it from person to person in lazy sweeps of her forearm. She twitched past the obnoxious hunk that had distracted Jamilla, then paused and came back. The blonde's face drew down into a grimace of concentration, but her body remained loose, relaxed.

The twenty-something doubled over and puked on the tile beneath his feet. He clutched his belly and gasped as the blonde snapped her hand into a fist. She twisted her fist as though wringing out a washcloth, and the man grunted and went down to one knee.

"What are you doing?" Jamilla asked in a small voice.

"An…object…lesson," grunted the blonde. Again, she cranked her hand over, and this time, the man let out a little yell of pain. His hand drifted up to his chest, fingers digging into his pectoral muscles, then he pitched forward onto his face.

The blonde turned a satisfied smile on Jamilla and quirked her eyebrow. "Lesson learned?"

Jamilla couldn't take her eyes off the man who'd fallen into his own emesis. He didn't move, didn't try to roll out of the foul mess. She didn't even think he was breathing. "How… What…did you do to him?" Jamilla murmured as gate attendants ran toward the man.

"What I can easily do to you." The blonde's smile twitched into a smirk. "You should also know"—again, she pointed to the two cops lounging near the coffee counter, utterly disinterested in the dying man—"we own *them*."

Jamilla glanced over, and both cops met her gaze with dead doll eyes. The bitch beside her nodded, and one of the cops hit them with a jaunty two-fingered salute, then hitched his Sam Browne and nudged his partner.

"So," said the blonde, "are you coming with me, or are you going with them?" The bitch didn't even say it.

She didn't have to.

Jamilla had known the second her gaze met the dead glare of the cops…she either went with the blonde bitch, or her trip would end in a landfill.

2

Airborne somewhere over the Midwest, USA
June 12, 1998, 4:15 pm EST

Jamilla glared at the living Barbie Doll who sat opposite her. Inside, fury thrummed through her like vibrations through a high-tension wire, but she tried to keep her face from showing it. For her part, the Barbie-bitch hardly glanced in Jamilla's direction.

The jet they rode in was one of those cush-job corporate jets—all leather and expensive wood—and besides the pilot, co-pilot, and a bored-looking flight attendant who looked like a high school student, the plane was empty. When Jamilla returned her gaze to the blonde, the woman was staring at her, a lopsided grin on her perfect face.

"Took you long enough… Most mothers notice right away," said the woman.

"Fuck you, Barbie."

The blonde woman laughed and nodded. "I get that a lot. If your intention was to wound me, you'll have to be more creative." She tilted her head to the side, allowing her long blonde hair to cascade over her shoulder, and gave Jamilla a heavy-lidded look. "You can call me, Bethany."

"Fuck you, Bethany. Where's my son?"

"Tut-tut, Jamilla. I've already told you that part of your relationship with Kai is over and done. We never transport new admissions via air. It's too dangerous."

"Dangerous? He's eleven."

"Yes. He's young, impulsive, upset. We can't rely on him to maintain his control—if he even has control of his gifts yet." Bethany shrugged. "Sometimes the children don't understand their new reality. They lash out, and on an airplane, that always ends in disaster. Fatal for everyone, not just their minders." She hooked her thumb over her shoulder. "Imagine if I snuffed the pilot and co-pilot. What would happen?"

"We'd die," said Jamilla.

"Yes." She picked a piece of lint from her linen pants. "We can't risk children like Kai. You and the plane's staff are expendable, but Kai is not."

"And I suppose you aren't either."

"Very astute," said Bethany. "As a graduate of the Program, I represent a significant investment—not to mention the loss of my abilities."

"What the fuck are you talking about? New admissions. Graduate. You act like you've kidnapped us in order to put Kai in some school."

Bethany nodded. "And that's exactly what we've done—enrolled Kai in a special school. A school for kids like him, taught by people who understand his unique gifts." She leaned forward and lay her hand on Jamilla's knee. "You *should* think of where we're going as a boarding school. A prep school. And thank your lucky stars that we deemed Kai a desirable new admission. Otherwise…" She let it loom there, unsaid.

With her skin crawling at the other woman's touch, Jamilla shifted in her seat, moving her knee out of reach. "You like doing that. Leaving something to linger in the air like a bad fart."

Bethany shrugged and sat back. "Not every thought needs a voice to be heard." She leaned her head back on the luxurious headrest and closed her eyes. "We'll be there in a few hours. I'd catch a nap if I were you."

Jamilla scoffed. "And if I were you, you detestable bitch, I wouldn't close my eyes around me."

A subtle half-grin appeared on Bethany's lips. "Yeah? I have nothing to worry about, Jamilla, and we both know it."

She wanted to snap back, wanted to lean across the aisle and slap the white off Barbie-bitch's perfect face, but she couldn't. Not so long as there was a chance to get Kai back.

However slim that chance might be.

3

The van stank of sweat and unwashed bodies, and it turned Kai's stomach. He lay on his side in the windowless cargo compartment. The fat White man who'd grabbed him at the airport—the one who smelled unwashed—drove the van, his gaze never straying from the ribbon of tarmac that stretched toward whatever depravity was in Kai's future. He got no sense of the man's intentions—the man was a curious blank to Kai. Where most people's thoughts seemed to scream and holler, the driver's mind was silent. "Sir?"

The man's gaze swiveled up to the rearview mirror—the kind the school bus back home had. One that let the driver see every part of the van at once. "This will go better if you keep your trap shut, kid."

"But—"

"What did I just say?" The man's right eye widened, making him look a little crazy.

"Can I at least sit up front? I get car sick."

"You gotta puke? Puke. Shit? Piss? Same answer." The driver returned his gaze to the road. "But you ain't coming up front, and we ain't stopping anytime soon. I'll hose this bastard out after I drop you off. Now. Shut. The. Fuck. Up."

Kai heard the steel in the man's voice and bit back the questions he wanted to ask. *Who are you? Where are you taking me? Where's my mother?* He shook his head, and a desperate sadness swooped down on him like a hunting kite striking its prey. He swallowed past the painful lump in his throat and fought back the hot tears. He didn't want to give the asshole the satisfaction.

He sat up, crossing his legs beneath him, and stared at the back of the man's head. Kai had never tried to get inside someone's head before—he'd never needed to try. But this pig of a man's mind was different. Closed off.

Kai made getting inside the pig's head his top priority.

4

In the desert, Southwestern AZ
June 12, 1998, 8:43 pm MST

The jet bounced hard, and dust plumed into the air each time the wheels touched the dirt landing strip. Jamilla gripped the wide upholstered arms of her seat, anxiety eating away at her belly, her eyes riveted on the window, watching the cacti and ugly terrain whip by.

Across the aisle from her, Bethany chuckled. "Nothing to worry about, Jamilla. Our pilot is quite accomplished at these backwoods landings. He flew for the military before coming to work for us." The aircraft slammed into a pothole, and even Bethany grimaced. "Still, it seems this runway could stand some attention. I'll mention it."

"What kind of school exists out here in the desert?"

With another lopsided smile, Bethany winked at Jamilla. "The kind that doesn't want a lot of attention. The kind that wants to be hidden."

"Wonderful," said Jamilla.

"Actually, it is."

"You shouldn't have picked Kai and me. We have people who will miss us. People who will ask questions."

Bethany shrugged and looked out the window.

"No, I mean it. My people will ask questions, and they have the juice to get answers."

Bethany smiled a little. "We know all about 'your people,' Jamilla. We have the answers that will satisfy them." She turned away from the window to look Jamilla in the eye. "This isn't our first rodeo."

The plane taxied up to a squat building—the only structure Jamilla had seen from her vantage—and the flight attendant who should've been in high school opened the door and lowered the built-in steps.

"This is us," said Bethany, popping her seatbelt and standing to stretch. "Come on." She turned and walked up the short aisle toward the door.

With a silent snarl, Jamilla followed her out of the plane, then turned in a full circle. "What the fuck kind of airport is this?" The squat bunker she'd seen from the plane really was the only building. There was no fence, no parking lot—the whole field was nothing more than a single runway hacked out of the buckhorn cholla and ocotillo.

"The kind that is invisible," said Bethany. "Let's get inside." As they walked toward the building, the plane idled up, then taxied to the end of the runway, and, engines shrieking, took off into the night sky.

"I hope this place has HBO," muttered Jamilla.

Bethany chuckled. "That's good. And good for you, keeping your spirits up." She approached the building and worked a combination padlock hanging from a rusty chain that secured the only door Jamilla could see. The weather-beaten concrete block building wasn't much to look at—four unpainted walls with a rusty metal roof. "After you," said Bethany, holding the door open.

Jamilla walked inside and curled her lip. The interior of the twenty-by-twenty building had an old concrete slab for a floor but no furniture, no counters, nothing except a wide pillar in the center of the room. "What kind of school—"

"Give it a rest, Jamilla," said Bethany with a sigh. She closed the door behind them, then said, "Okay. We're in."

Jamilla turned to face her, anger in her eyes. Outside, the chain rattled, and then the padlock snapped shut.

"Cute," said Jamilla. "How's your friend outside going to get in?"

Bethany flashed that lopsided smile again.

"I'd like to beat that fucking smile off your face."

Bethany rolled her eyes and shook her head. "Go on"—she lifted her hand to point behind Jamilla—"let's get going."

Jamilla whirled around, and instead of the solid concrete wall that had been there a moment before, there was a gleaming, stainless steel elevator. "But…"

With a condescending laugh of the my-how-cute variety, Bethany stepped past her and into the elevator car. "You can stay up here if you want, but you'll be trapped. No one's scheduled to come in for a while."

Dropping her gaze to the ground, Jamilla stepped in beside Bethany, and the elevator doors slid shut without a sound. There were no buttons or controls, but the elevator began to sink, nonetheless.

"The school is underground?"

Bethany nodded. "And before you ask, the kind of school that wants to be hidden."

They rode in silence for a minute or two, then the elevator slowed to a stop. The doors whisked open, and Bethany sighed. "Home sweet home," she said, then stepped out of the elevator. "This is one of the staff levels. Come on, let's get you a billet." She turned back and extended a hand to Jamilla. "Come, or sleep in the elevator—either way, I'll be comfortable in my quarters."

Jamilla stuck her head out of the car and looked both ways down the concrete block corridor. The walls were a pale shade of seafoam green, except for five colored stripes, and the floor was polished concrete. Brushed steel doors appeared at regular intervals. She stepped out into the hall, and the elevator doors closed behind her.

Bethany pointed at inch-wide colored stripes. "In case you get lost. Green is for staff living areas, White is administration, black is for ops, yellow is for instructor living areas, and blue is for recreation areas."

Jamilla cocked her head and put her index finger in the middle of the red stripe. "And red?"

"Red is off-limits. Never set foot in a red area, unless directed to do so. The penalty is very severe, and this is your single warning. No excuses, no reasoning. Punishment comes immediately on discovery. No trials, no arguments."

That's where they keep the kids, Jamilla thought. *I've got to get in there.*

As though she could read Jamilla's thoughts, Bethany sighed. "I warned you." She turned and walked off down the hall.

Jamilla had no choice but to follow her.

5

Kai rocked in the rear of the van, his shoulder blades rubbing against the dirty metal walls. He hadn't blinked in a long time, and his dry eyes stung and burned. His breathing was slow and even.

The van's driver—a disgusting pig of a man if Kai had ever seen one—hummed tunelessly or made such a mess of the melody that Kai didn't recognize it. The tires hummed on the road's surface. Kai didn't know how far they'd come, but the driver did. They were southeast of Columbus, Ohio, but Ohio wasn't their destination. Kai had pulled that much out of the blank the man projected.

He almost knew the man's name. Almost.

The man planned to skirt around the northern parts of Cincinnati and then Louisville. After that, the route grew hazy in Kai's mind, but it was enough to know where he wasn't going, and that was any place he knew anyone.

"I'm looking for a place to pull over and catch an hour's sleep. If you haven't shit and pissed and barfed up back there, I'll take you into the woods and let you do your business."

A self-satisfied smile lit on Kai's lips. He'd exerted a lot of mental energy trying to convince the fat man he was tired. He couldn't calculate his chances of getting away—the man's curious blankness hid a lot—but there *was* a chance.

Maybe the only chance he'd get.

The driver's seat creaked as he swiveled his fat-jowled face around to peer into the back. "But if you pull any funny business, I'll make you regret it. That much I guarantee."

"I'll—" Kai's voice squeaked and cut out. He coughed to clear his throat and then tried again. "I'll be good. I promise."

"I've never met an eleven-year-old that could make that promise stick, so I'll make *you* a promise. You make me run after you, I'll beat you unconscious, then hog-tie you and leave you face down back there. This ain't my first rodeo. I've delivered better than you on time. Never had one get away. You hear me, boy?"

"Yes, but I'll be good."

The man scoffed and turned back to watch the empty road. "Soon as I find a cut-off, then." After that, he opened his mouth in a tendon-popping yawn.

Kai grinned at the sound of it.

6

Adeline d'Clara sat bolt upright from out of a deep, satisfying sleep. She blinked in the dark for several heartbeats, then got up and shuffled to the door of her small room to flick on the light switch. The pale light from the single, unshaded overhead light settled over her bedroom like early morning mist.

She knew it wasn't morning without peeking through the curtains—her internal clock told her that much. With that uncomfortable, almost sick feeling that plagued her when she was awakened too soon, she crossed the room in three steps and pulled out the straight-backed cane chair, then settled into its stiff embrace. Her back ached, as usual, and not to miss out on the party, so did her hands, wrists, ankles, and toes. She loosed a soft sigh, ignoring her discomfort and trying for that serene state of mind that would allow her to recall her dream. She shook her head at that and scoffed.

"That was no dream, Adeline d'Clara, and you know it. That was a triple-A foretelling, and a real doozy of one," she muttered. Soothsaying often came at the price of lost sleep but didn't leave her feeling so wrung out, so used up. An omen, perhaps—a hint of what might come if she didn't act.

She leaned forward and clawed the small glass of water from the center of her desk and sipped it, smiling a little at the sensation of the cold liquid trickling down to the parched parts of her. "That *was* a harbinger, and it was a *powerful* one. So what are you going to do about it?" She'd picked up the habit of whisper-talking to herself ages before, and try as she might, she couldn't seem to kick the habit.

She caught sight of her spindly legs and sighed at the itchy, ashy skin covering her shins. She glanced at the lotion on her desk, then sneered. "Focus your mind, girl!" she snapped. "Don't let it go to waste!"

The "it" was her dream of prognostication, of course, and if it had brought her out of a deep sleep, it was important. She leaned back in the chair and closed her eyes. She drew in a deep breath and held it while she dropped her hands from her lap to dangle at her sides, then drew them back. She let her breath trickle out of her, bringing her hands forward and up as she did so, only stopping when she had no more air to push and with her arms extended out straight, her hands open, accepting at eye level. She opened her inner eye, the part of her mind that sometimes throbbed with the need to *see* and cast it about, trying to catch the tail of her dream and ride it back to that special place where all things were possible.

7

Adeline marveled at the feel of the air caressing the underside of her wings. Each time they stroked the air, she caught the barest sight of them in the tails of her eyes, and had she a mouth instead of a beak, would have smiled with joy at the glimpse of her black plumage glistening in the moonlight. Since she couldn't smile, she croaked her call to the night, challenging the wind, the moon, the very stars themselves.

No bird answered her majestic cry—none dared— but something below seemed *to call out to her, to pull her attention downward.*

Or, perhaps, someone.

Someone who radiated familiarity and anger and fear. She tucked her wings and streaked downward—a bullet fired in anger at the cold, hard earth below. Her eyes swept the puny surface-bound creatures scuttling across the ground below. Her gaze found a boxy thing (a van, *said an unbirdlike voice within) that belched foul poisons into the pristine air, and once her gaze touched it, she knew the person who called out to her was within. She ruffled the feathers of her tail, altering her streaking dive to intercept the thing.*

When the box (the van, a part of her insisted) slowed and turned off the stinking black ribbon (a road!) she screeched her defiance and altered course again. She blazed over the treetops, flying by instinct alone, her eyes rage-filled orbs, her talons itching for flesh to rend and tear.

She tucked her wings for half a heartbeat, dropped under the summer canopy of the oak and hickory trees, then snapped her wings open, cupping them to catch the air, shoving her taloned feet out in front of her, widening her tail feathers. She picked her spot—a fat limb that extended out over the top of the stink box (van) and snatched it, digging in her claws. Wings outstretched, she stood stock-still for a moment, testing her balance, testing the limb. Then, she settled and cocked her head to the side so she could look down at the reeking thing (the van) beneath her.

A massive human made the box's strange flat-folding wing (the van! door!) and climbed out. He looked around, twisting his head back and forth but never bothering to look up, trapped and mentally stunted by gravity. He plodded around the front of the box (van! van van VAN!) into the twin beams of magic sunshine (headlights) and peered into the forest on the other side. After a moment, he grunted to himself and turned back to the van.

Mentally stunted as he was, he missed the red fox skulking through the trees in search of a juicy rabbit. He missed the white-tailed deer standing frozen a mere fifty steps into the trees. He missed the larks, the great horned owl that stalked them. He missed everything.

The soft human opened the van's side with a metallic shriek, then stood staring inside. "Remember what I said, kid. I meant every goddamn word."

"I meant what I said, too," said the piping voice of a boy-child.

Something inside her flared and spilled bitter panic into her veins. Her talons dug into the flesh of the poor hickory tree that had done nothing to deserve it. The boy-child (Kai!) was the someone that had called to her. He was in danger and seeing the big human threaten the boy-child (Kai! Kai!) awoke her kin-sense. The desire to drop onto the human's head and scratch out his eyes was very real and extremely hard to resist.

Somewhere off in the woods, a bobcat squalled, and for a moment, everything and everyone froze, everything and everyone stopped breathing and stared into the shadows with widened eyes. Below her, the large human gave an uneasy laugh.

"Just some dumb bird, kid. You need to pee or not?"

"Yessir," said the boy-child Kai.

"Then get on with it. Or pee back there, but you're the one who will have to sit in it."

"I'm coming out." The boy slid to the edge and put his feet down on the ground.

Her eyes wanted to dilate with the power of her urge to protect him, to sweep him into the sky and out of reach from the fat man—but that was an insane thought. She was too small to meddle in the world of the humans.

But then she saw the expression the boy-child Kai wore, and she knew he didn't need the help of a mere raven. The fat man didn't notice the boy-child Kai's look—he was too busy staring into the woods and jumping at shadows.

The boy-child Kai stood, then tilted his head and looked straight at her. He threw a wink at her, and the world began to crumble around her. She snapped her wings out with a startled croak as the limb beneath her disintegrated.

Then her wings fell off, and she plummeted to the desert below, barely avoiding sure impalement on a fishhook barrel cactus. She squeezed her eyes shut, trying to brace herself for the pain that would coincide with her impact with the cooling sand.

But the pain never came.

When she opened her eyes, she'd already sunk to her belly in the sand, and she squalled with terror. Off in the distance, another bobcat answered her with a squall of its own, but whether it was a cry of support or a warning to stay out of its territory, she couldn't begin to guess.

Besides, the sand was swallowing her with alacrity. She struggled, but it was no use. No use at all. She lifted her head and pointed her nose at the moon, wanting to draw as much air into her lungs as should.

When the sand blocked her view of the night sky, she panicked and thrashed in the sand.

That didn't work, either. In fact, she thought it might have made her sink faster.

After an interminable purgatory of darkness and sand and grit and no air to breathe, she sank through a three-foot layer of poured concrete and began to fall toward the cement floor. Again, she squeezed her eyes shut against the pain, and again, pain never came.

She spread her wings and buzzed back up toward the roof, not wanting to meet the business end of a fly swatter or the sole of someone's boot. She flew to the pale green wall and landed; wings poised to take her aloft in an instant if something threatened her.

*Something pulled her to the east, and she left her perch to fly across the hallway where she encountered more pale green blocks that barred her way. She buzzed in frustration and circled for a moment, not knowing what to do (*find a hallway that goes east and west, *said that tiny voice inside her). It was strange advice for a wasp, but she lacked a better one and flew south down the corridor, staying next to the ceiling of the strange cave (*the Compound*).*

Whatever.

*She found a branching hallway and flew east. About halfway down the corridor, she realized she'd gone too far and circled back. She flew to a big metal thing (*a door*) and landed on the wall above it, buzzing with frustration. She had no idea how to get inside (*crawl through the crack between the top of the door and the lintel*), how to get at the thing calling out to her from the other side.*

She explored the top edge of the door, and despite thinking her internal voice was as crazy as a bee, she found she probably could *slip through the space between the door and the wall.*

She did so, emerging into a rectangular room with six narrow beds along the far wall and six more on the near wall. Each of the beds had a woman sleeping in it. The one farthest from the door called to her, and she flew to it, then hovered over the foot of the bed.

After a moment, the bed's occupant sat up and stared right at her. She knew her, knew her name was Jamilla, and she could sense the sadness, the desperation, the fury in her mind.

As soon as their eyes met, she knew Jamilla for Kai's mother. Waspish anger roiled in her guts and…

8

3121 Newcroft Park, Rochester, NY
June 12, 1998, 11:18 pm EST

Adeline came out of her trance-like state, the fullness of the dream caught in her memory like a fly in a spider's web. She blinked the heavy feeling from her eyelids, and she knew there would be no more sleep that night. "Sweet Christ," she murmured. "Poor Jamilla and Kai."

She shook her head and looked down at her slack hands lying in her lap. "He did it anyway… But he *promised*! *He gave his word*!" One hand curled into a fist, her arthritic knuckles screaming.

She levered herself up and shuffled out to start making calls. She went down the stairs far too fast for a woman her age, but her feet still knew the trick of it, and miracle of miracles, she didn't fall. She stood next to the small round table in the parlor where she kept the only phone in the house. Despite the oppressive summertime heat in the house, she kept her windows closed, fearing a summer cold, and worse—a burglar or some other malcontent. She felt chilled, nonetheless, as she dialed the number she was only supposed to dial in an extreme emergency.

"Yeah?" drawled a man—a White man by the sound of his voice, and one who was barely awake. "Morty's Cab Company."

"I need to talk to him." Her voice took on the soft Southern twang everyone except her closest confidants expected of her.

"Talk to who, lady?"

"You know who, child. I have access."

"Oh. Give me a second."

Adeline bit back on her impatience as she heard the man put the phone down, then type rapidly on one of those new-fangled computers everyone fell all over themselves to get hold of. She stopped her foot from tapping and closed her eyes in a long, slow blink.

"You aren't supposed to call here."

"Yes, I am." Adeline's voice projected calm self-assurance.

"Only in case of a dire emergency." The man sounded a touch snappish to Adeline's ears.

"Listen here, child. I'm Adeline d'Clara, and—"

"I know that."

"—*and* I'd rather you don't interrupt me. If you know my name, you know my tag. You know all about me. What you don't know is that the Man and me have an agreement. Someone just broke that agreement."

The guy on the other end of the phone sighed, thunder in her ear. "Listen, Adeline—"

"Ms. d'Clara, if you please."

"Fine, fine. But listen, Ms. d'Clara. Your information is out of date. The Man is gone."

"He's… What?"

"It was pneumonia. Two months ago."

Adeline's heart sank to her nether regions. "The Man and I made an agreement. It don't matter if he's gone. He shook on it as the Director of Majestic."

"That's between you and him."

"But that's—" She shook her head. "No, never mind that. Hook me to the new one, then."

"I can put in a request."

"No, child. You put in a *demand*."

The line fell silent except for a faraway sounding clicking and a bit of static that fuzzed in and out. "Looking at your record, I know you know better than to make a demand," the man said at last. "Still, I'll put in the *request*. Expect a call by tomorrow evening."

"No sir. You tell 'em it's urgent. You tell 'em my name, and you tell 'em I said I got to talk to someone in the next ten minutes or—"

"Ten minutes? Have you lost your marbles?"

"—they might find me much less cooperative next time they need someone bird dogged. Turn your face back to that glowing screen, child, and this time, *read* it. I'm the best bird dog we've ever had. I can track farther and better than the best of the best under them Sonoran sands—better than anyone in the Special Operations Group, too. Unless I'm *distracted*, that is. Unless I'm *upset*, which, let me assure you, I *am*." She heard him sniff, then the line went quiet for another long stretch. "Do your job, child. You answer the phone; you relay messages. You *do not* decide who is allowed to do what."

"Fine!" snapped the man. "I'll relay your message. If you deserve a call back, you'll get one, but it will be at the P.D.'s leisure."

"I'll wait, but see to it I ain't got to wait too long," said Adeline, but the line was already dead. She frowned down at the phone as she cradled the receiver. "If he's really dead…" She shook her head, not wanting to follow that train of thought, not wanting the emotional payload that would come with it, not wanting to accept the truth of it. She turned and stepped into the dining room, snagged a chair, and dragged it back to stand next to the round table. She sank into the wooden chair and rubbed her aching knuckles.

9

U.S. Route 22, OH
June 12, 1998, 11:21 pm EST

Kai slumped against the wall of the van. It had almost worked. He sniffled as new tears rolled down his cheeks. His nose had stopped bleeding, but still, it throbbed and ached, as did the cut on his lower lip. The Pig—the name he'd given the driver of the van—hadn't made good on beating him unconscious. In fact, he'd only cuffed Kai twice, but his ham-hands were nowhere near as soft as the man looked.

He'd gotten out of the van, and he'd given in to the urge to look up at the limbs hanging over the van, but there was nothing there. Off in the woods, the animal—and he'd known better than to think was some bird—made another shrieking noise.

The Pig had taken a step closer to him, and in hindsight, that's what ruined Kai's escape attempt. When the giant man had turned his attention to the woods, Kai'd sprinted into the brush—or at least that had been his intent.

Taking one giant step, the Pig had reached out with one ham-sized hand and snagged the back of Kai's shirt. He'd jerked his hand back, and Kai's feet had gone flying out from under him. "Didn't I tell you this wasn't my first rodeo, kid?" asked the Pig, just as cool as you please. With his other huge hand, he'd bunched the front of Kai's shirt, then let go of his back. With a grunt, he'd picked Kai up and let him dangle there by his shirt. He'd looked into Kai's eyes with his flat doll eyes, then cuffed Kai with his free hand, first forehand, then again, backhand, and Kai's tears had come. "Now, you'll just have to piss and lay in it," the Pig said in a matter-of-fact voice.

He'd turned back to the van and stuck his hand into a storage bin, pulling out a length of thick rope. He pushed Kai face down on the van's floor and brought his hands around to his back without a thought for gentleness. The Pig had tied Kai's hands with deft efficiency, then looped the rope around his ankles and hog-tied him. Without another word, he'd given him a little shove and slammed the side door, almost crushing the boy's feet in the process. The van had creaked and rocked as the Pig climbed into the driver's seat. "Kid, I'm a real light sleeper, so let's not have a repeat of that foolishness. This time, take me at my word."

"I'm all tied up," Kai moaned.

"Sure, you are. But you listen to what I said."

Kai said nothing, only turned his head toward the back of the van so the Pig couldn't look in the rearview mirror and see him crying.

"I asked if you heard me, boy."

"Yes!" snapped Kai. "I heard you."

"Don't test me again." The driver's seat groaned as the big man shifted his weight. "I'll sleep about an hour, then we'll get back on the road. Lotta miles between here and where I'm to drop you."

"Whatever," mumbled Kai.

10

3121 Newcroft Park, Rochester, NY
June 12, 1998, 11:24 pm EST

The phone rang, jangling her nerves and making Adeline jump. She'd been dozing by the feel of her addled mind, but her hand snaked out and grabbed the phone. "Hello?"

"Ms. d'Clara."

"Yes?"

"You wanted to speak with me?" The voice was a dramatic bass. She recognized the voice, and it definitely wasn't the man she'd made her agreement with.

"Is this—"

"Don't use my name. This call is unsecure on your end."

Adeline sniffed. "You the new Program Director, then?" Sam McIntire hardly seemed suitable to the demands of the job.

"I am." He let the line hiss for a moment. "I want you to know that I only returned your call because of the esteem the Man—the previous one, anyway—held you in. This will be the only time."

"The Man and I had a deal, Director."

"Yes," said Sam in a non-committal voice. "He told me."

"Then…" Adeline shook her head. "I don't understand."

"What's there to understand?"

"The deal was that—"

"As I said, I know the details of your agreement with the Man, and your line is not secure."

Anger stirred in Adeline's belly. "If you knew, then why… Do you know who they grabbed up today?"

"Of course. I approved the operation."

A hint of her not-insignificant fury colored her voice. "Then why?" she demanded. "You knew the deal!"

"Ms. d'Clara…you and I have no deal. That agreement terminated when the Man drew his last breath."

"No. That's not how—"

"*Yes*. Besides, you know the rules. The boy tested at the top of the scale. You know he can't stay out in the cold."

"But the Man—"

"He's *dead*, Adeline. Things change." Sam's voice was firm, without a hint of wiggle. "And had he seen the results I've seen, he would have made the same decision. It's not safe to leave so much untrained power in the wild. Protocol One applies."

"Protocol One," Adeline repeated through numb lips. Simply stated, the protocol made a hard line in the sand. On one side, a budding psychic could either participate in the Program or have their powers stripped by a fixer. But on the other side of that line, the choice became training in the Program or death. "He tested that high?"

"He did. Some rules can be bent, others simply cannot." The Director allowed another long hiss to come between them. "I would have notified you once he was safely enrolled."

"And Jam—his mother?"

"She was offered a staff position. She represents no threat and will be treated by a fixer inside the Compound. It's the best we could do."

"I know," murmured Adeline. "But—"

"No buts, Adeline. You know the reasons behind Protocol One as well as I do. You've tracked any number of actives for us… Not all of them were of the proper age or mindset."

Heat rolled into Adeline's cheeks. She tried not to think about what might have happened once the operations team had contacted those out-of-spec targets she'd tracked. "Yes. *That* was also part of my deal with the Man." She left it there, certain Sam would take her meaning.

"Adeline, let's not—"

"As you said, *Sam*. The deal ended when the Man stopped breathing."

Another hissing pause passed between them.

"You're sure this is the course you want to pursue?" asked Sam in a cold voice.

When Adeline next spoke, white-hot fire backed her voice. "Are you sure of your own course?"

"The Protocols—"

"*The Protocols be damned*!" shouted Adeline. In her mind, she was already sorting through her meager possessions, deciding what she had to take and what she could leave behind.

"Goodbye, Adeline," said Sam with an air of finality. "I'm sorry you've chosen—"

Adeline slammed the phone down and started toward the stairs. The phone rang almost immediately, and she paused, her foot on the first step. She let the machine pick up but listened to the message.

"Adeline," said Sam. "Protocol One applies to *you* as well. Surely, you know that."

Adeline sneered at the machine lying next to the phone.

"Have it your way, then," said Sam. "I'll give you two days to think about it."

She knew that was a lie. Sam was probably signaling an ops team even as he spoke—or he might have activated them before he called. Adeline could afford to wait no longer. She did her best to sprint up the stairs—which amounted to more of a fast climb than a sprint—and began by doffing her nightgown and slipping on a light dress. She packed her things in a flurry of activity, then tempted fate again on the stairs. She flung the front door open, then paused, half-turning back to look at the little house the Program had provided her, remembering better times, family gatherings she'd hosted, playing with baby Kai on the sofa. With an unshed tear blurring her vision, she turned and walked down the concrete steps and curved around to the side of the house where her Oldsmobile Achieva sat. She'd have to change it somewhere first thing in the morning, but for the rest of the night, it would be safe enough.

11

Kai's head throbbed—the result of exhaustion, hours of sustained mental effort, and the two slaps delivered by the Pig, but he smiled to himself, nonetheless. The Pig, otherwise known as Jamison Capstrom—*my friends call me Reggie*—had slipped up, just a little, probably due to his own exhaustion, and Kai had wormed his way into the man's vile mind. He knew things about the man—*climb in the van, kid, and we'll play with the puppy in the back*—that made his skin crawl.

But he also had discovered useful things. First, Reggie was taking him to something he thought of as the Compound, and it was far, far away—at least another day's travel. The Compound contained the Program, which seemed like a school of some kind. Reggie himself had gone into the Program as a child, but there was a big wall of shame encapsulating those memories, and Kai hadn't had the strength to bull his way through all that emotion. The Pig hoped Kai was going to fail something he called "onboarding" and that he'd be allowed to take "ownership" of Kai's upbringing.

That scared Kai from his toes to the roots of his hair. The Pig's memories of getting children into the back of his van shouted at Kai, turning his stomach, making his skin crawl.

Reggie believed Kai's mother was dead—*rotting in a landfill by now*—but that felt wrong to Kai. The Pig also knew Adeline d'Clara, the old woman Kai and his mother had been on the way to visit. Reggie thought of her as a "bird dog" and was more than a little scared of her.

Kai's face throbbed with every beat of his heart, and his head felt itchy on the inside. The early morning sun was far, far too bright, even when he closed his eyes— a sure sign that his headache was only getting worse. "Can I have some aspirin?" he croaked but at such a low volume Reggie didn't hear. "Excuse me," he said, louder.

"What, kid? Don't ask for a bathroom break. You fucked that up."

"Reggie, do you have any aspirin?"

The tires shrieked as Reggie stood on the brakes, his glaring, angry gaze locked on Kai's via the rearview mirror. "*What* did you call me?" he shouted as the backend of the van slewed a little toward the double yellows in the middle of the road.

"Was it wrong?" Kai asked feigning distress. "I… It's just that I have a feeling that's what you want people to call you."

As the van came to a stop, the odor of abused rubber surrounded them. Other than his chest heaving as he almost panted for breath, the Pig didn't move. His eyes seemed to whirl in the rearview, and Kai dropped his gaze.

"I'm sorry if I got it wrong," said Kai in a little boy voice.

"No, you didn't get it wrong," said the Pig, and Kai raised his gaze to the mirror again.

Something akin to sinus pressure began to build in all the wrong places, adding to Kai's headache. At the same time, Reggie narrowed his eyes, and his breathing accelerated. Kai could feel the man's greasy mental touch but deflected it without much effort. He kept his face a careful neutral, innocence embodied. The Pig grunted and shifted so he could lean around the seat to stare directly into Kai's eyes, and the pressure mounted.

Even so, it took no heroic effort to keep him out. Kai grimaced and jerked at the rope linking his hands to his ankles, as though he'd forgotten the Pig had hog-tied him. "Ow! My head really hurts," he whined.

The pressure dissipated, but the Pig still stared at him through hostile eyes. He sniffed and tilted his head back to look down his nose—an assessing, probing gaze. Finally, he said, "I'll know if you lie to me, kid. I can see right inside that head of yours."

Kai did his best not to smile at the obvious lie. "Okay, but do you have any aspirin? My head is killing me."

"No aspirin," said Reggie, turning back to face forward. "If I ever get the feeling you're trying to scan me, kid..." He flicked his gaze to the rearview and stabbed at Kai with it. "Let's just say I'll make last night seem like two love pats. Capisce?"

"What does that mean? Capisce?"

"It means 'do you understand me?' And the answer is 'yes' if you know what's good for you."

"I don't know what you mean by 'scan you?'"

"Yes, you do." c and slammed the accelerator to the floor. The rear tires spun, and the van lurched forward.

Kai turned his face toward the back doors to hide his smile.

12

I-71, near Sparta, KY
June 13, 1998, 7:19 am EST

Adeline rubbed at her sore, gritty eyes. She needed sleep, but Kai wasn't sleeping, and neither was Jamilla. Anger seeped into her blood every time she thought of the conversation with Sam McIntire. Instead of waking her up, though, her rage wore on her, dragging her down like concrete galoshes.

She hadn't dared try to find Kai, not yet, but she didn't need to. The Compound was his destination, and old as she was, Adeline could still plan a route across the country. She knew the operative driving Kai, whomever he might be, would avoid the Interstate

Highway System, which meant she could travel faster on the Interstates, maybe intercept them *before* he delivered the boy into the hands of the Program.

She needed to change cars, to put distance between herself and her last knowns. She was the strongest bird dog in the Program, so she had no fear of clairvoyants tracking her the way she could have tracked someone, but the Program had access to other agencies, other ways of doing things—like a BOLO on her little Oldsmobile.

A sign advertised the town of Sparta, Kentucky— she wondered why every state seemed to have a Sparta—and Adeline piloted the car into the exit lane. She relaxed her grip on the steering wheel a little and almost gasped as the pain lanced up her wrists and into her forearms. She *was* an old woman and not used to the rigors of driving through the night. She needed to change cars, then find a place to sleep for a few hours— she knew the operative who had Kai would have trained himself to go without sleep for days at a time, and once she might have matched him, but those years were long in her past.

The exit lane dead-ended into a road called Sparta Pike, but there was no stop sign, no light. She nosed her car carefully forward to check the road was clear, then followed the signs that said Sparta was to the south. She rolled under I-71 and spotted a gas station and a motel sharing the same asphalt pad. She parked, went into the Speedway Motel, and approached the front desk. "I'll need a room," she told the front desk clerk.

"How long will you be staying?" asked the pleasant woman in a maroon jumpsuit.

"Oh, child, not long. I'm on a schedule, but this Interstate driving plumb wears me out." She'd slipped back into her old Southern woman voice, fitting into the clerk's expectations of an old Black woman like a well-worn shoe.

The woman behind the counter smiled and nodded. "Single occupancy rooms go for fifty-two dollars a day, but I believe we can extend the AARP rate to you." Again, she shot a guileless smile at Adeline. "How does forty-eight dollars sound?"

Adeline flipped open the worn black purse that had served her for so long, found her wallet, and counted her cash. "Lordy, me," she murmured. "I seem to have run off without my credit cards. Is there a discount for cash?"

The clerk glanced down at the wad of cash in Adeline's hand and no doubt counted it. She looked at the door set in the wall behind the counter, then leaned forward. "If you can keep it a secret, I'll give you the employee rate. Twenty-nine dollars."

"My, my, ain't you just a gem?" Adeline treated her to a broad, toothy smile. "I thank you so much, but you know what the Good Book says."

The woman's eyes sparkled. "Proverbs."

Adeline cackled and patted the woman's hand. "Your generosity will be repaid, sister."

"Amen," said the woman. She tapped away at her computer. "I'm giving you a room far from the elevator and the ice machine. It's the quietest we have."

"My, my. What a generous soul," Adeline murmured as she passed the cash across to the clerk and took her keycard. "I wonder…" she said.

The clerk looked at her attentively.

"Is there a used car dealer in Sparta?"

"Car problems?"

"More like age problems. My little car is fine for short drives, but I'm going clear to California, laws yes, and the little devil is wreaking havoc on my back and hips."

"Poor dear," said the clerk. "There's no car dealer, as such, but my cousin buys cars at the Cincinnati auctions, fixes 'em up, and sells them locally. He might help. I could call him if you like."

"Oh, thank you, thank you," said Adeline, pouring the sugar on with a liberal hand. "I'd like to trade even, or perhaps my car for one of his and some cash."

"Since you left your cards to home," the clerk said with a grin, "I'll whisper in his ear."

"Much obliged, my dear. My name is Clara—Clara Tracker. May I know yours?"

"Of course," said the clerk with a wide smile. "My name is Isabel. Isabel Masterson."

"Nice to meet such a fine Christian woman, Isabel."

"Likewise."

"I think I'll go to my room and catch a little sleep while you speak with your cousin."

"Get some rest, Clara. I'll speak to Jimmy and have an update for you when you wake up."

"Could you call me at noon? I'd still like to get farther on my trip before it gets dark."

"Certainly. Sleep well."

Adeline smiled and nodded, then turned and trudged to her room down a long corridor that looked like any other motel in the United States—weird carpet, bland beige walls, doors every thirty feet on both sides. Her room was standard fare for next-to-the-Interstate hotels, but there was a bed, and at that point, that was all that mattered. She lay her weary bones down on top of the comforter and was asleep in an instant.

13

U.S. Route 50, IN
June 13, 1998, 6:36 am CST

Kai lay on his side with his back resting against the rear doors of the van. He had his head tilted back and his eyes shut. Even so, he knew exactly what the Pig was doing at any given moment. Each time he touched the fat man's mind, it grew easier.

Reggie shifted in his seat and mumbled something Kai didn't catch, but that didn't matter. Kai knew why he was uncomfortable—he'd been tweaking the man's bladder for fifteen minutes.

"Dammit!" snarled Reggie. "Fetch me one of those plastic drink bottles."

"I would, but you hog-tied me, remember?"

Reggie's eyes snapped to the rearview. "You sassing me, boy?"

"No, sir." Kai jerked upward with his arms, pulling his feet with them. "See?"

The Pig grunted and gave his attention back to the road. "Need to find a place," he muttered.

"A place for what?"

"Never you mind."

Kai lay still for a few minutes, letting his head rock from side to side as the van jounced over the rough road. Then he said, "I'm very hungry, Reggie. Can we get Micky D's?"

The Pig snorted, keeping his eyes on the road.

With a grin, Kai put the image of a McDonald's bathroom into the man's mind.

"*Goddamn it!*" Reggie snapped. "We aren't stopping."

Kai dropped his chin and went to work on the man's bowels.

14

The van shuddered as the Pig laid on the brakes. Kai went flying toward the front of the vehicle, first sliding on his side, but as Reggie mashed on the brakes harder, he fell forward onto his belly. The Pig wrenched the wheel to the right, and the tires shrieked in protest.

"Whoa! Take it easy!" yelled Kai.

"Shut it, kid," said the Pig in a flat voice as cold as the grave. When the van came to a stop, Reggie killed the ignition, then swiveled his bulk in the seat to glare down at Kai. "Do I have to gag you?"

"What? Why?"

"Do I?"

Kai shook his head.

"Liar," said Reggie in that murderer's voice of his. He got up and squeezed into the back, standing over Kai, stooping as he did so to grab the length of rope connecting Kai's hands and feet. He picked him up with ease and carried him to the back of the van. The big man pulled a blue bandana from his back pocket and shoved it against Kai's lips. "Take it," he said, applying more pressure.

"Ow!" As soon as Kai opened his mouth to speak, the Pig shoved the nasty-smelling cloth into his mouth and clamped one cast-iron hand over the lower half of the boy's face. The Pig pulled another bandanna—red this time—from his other back pocket and wrapped it around Kai's head, securing the gag.

"No funny business, kid. Not this time." Reggie said the words in a stern voice, but his mind was already on the short run to the McDonald's restroom.

Kai was glad the red bandanna hid his smile as he nodded. All he had to do was wait.

15

Flying over the Midwest, USA
June 13, 1998, 8:05 am EST

Adeline's wings cupped the thermal updraft, the warm air lifting her, exalting her, propelling her, and she crowed with the pure joy of it. She soared higher until the wind pushed her past the invisible boundary between updraft and downdraft, and she plummeted earthward, her stomach dancing, eyes opened wide. She tucked her wings and increased her speed. There was somewhere she had to go…but where?

She scanned the ground below, looking for a clue, for a sign. Nothing in the green spaces seemed amiss. Without warning, the Earth began to spin beneath her faster and faster—far faster than she could ever hope to fly, even with the strongest wind imaginable at her back—*until it became a blur of colors that bled into each other. She could see nothing, and the wind ripped all the odors from her nose and thundered in her ears.*

As panic began to weigh her down, the spinning beneath her slowed until she could make out the shapes of forests and fields and the mess humans made of everything. She spotted one of the places (it's a town) *where humans had scarred the landscape with their foul-smelling black lines* (roads) *and the squat, ugly trees without leaves where they congregated* (buildings). *Her gaze speared downward as she began to glide over the town.*

Within moments, she spotted the white van sitting in a sea (parking lot) *of the foul black stuff* (asphalt) *the humans used to draw their* roads *on the skin of the Earth. She snapped her wings out, caught the air, and entered a gliding spiral toward the van. Trepidation filled her, growing and growing until she thought she must vomit it out and cover the Earth with its poison.*

A smaller White van (no, that's a car.) *bumped its way into the sea of black, belching poison and death, then pulled in next to the van. The* car *stopped vomiting pestilence into the already dreadful air, and its horrendous noise stopped. With a clunk, one of its sides* (door. That's a car door.) *sprang open, and a human got out and slammed the* door *closed again.*

The human had dark blue feathers (shirt) *over a lighter blue tail* (pants). *It put a dark blue covering over its fur (hair) and turned toward the garish yellow and red building. The human (that's a police officer—a cop) took a single step toward the garish red and yellow building (that's a McDonald's, over ninety-nine billion served), then stopped and turned to stare at the van, head cocked to the side in the manner of a fox listening for rabbits.*

Adeline's hearing was excellent, as good as any human's, at any rate, but she hadn't heard a thing.

The cop-human walked around the van, peering in the windows. The massive human she'd seen in the woods came out of the McDonald's and stopped short, his piggish eyes on the cop-human's back. He glanced around, then leaned his head back and stared straight at Adeline. His eyes narrowed, and something huge and invisible shoved her away.

16

McDonald's parking lot, Becker, IN
June 13, 1998, 7:08 am CST

Kai waited, and as the minutes ticked by, his anxiety built. He had never imagined a McDonald's parking lot could be so quiet, so empty. The Pig wouldn't be long—the feelings Kai had implanted in his mind had grown real to the man, but that didn't change the real amount of biological matter in the man's bladder or bowels. *Come on*, thought Kai. *Come on, come on*!

After another minute or so, the sound of a car turning off the road into the parking lot rewarded his chanting vigil. The rough purr of a big eight-cylinder engine crept toward the van and then pulled in the spot next to it. Kai wanted to shout with joy, wanted to cry out to get the person's attention, but the Pig's gag allowed him no more than a muffled slur of unintelligible sounds.

He heard a door open and close, and desperation wrapped its cold hands around his throat. He cast his mind outward, flailing for contact…there was nothing…nothing…*there*! He latched onto the mind of the female police officer walking toward the McDonald's.

Chapter 6
Just a Cigar

I

Gavin gave a sour laugh. "That's quite a story."

"For sure," said Maddie.

"And every single word of it is true," said Adeline.

"This Program and the compound you mentioned in the story—that's Majestic?"

"Part of it, in any case. There are also various operations groups. One of them kidnapped Kai and transported him."

"And you worked for them?" asked Maddie.

"Yes, child. I had no choice."

"We all have choices," said Gavin. "You could have refused."

"Could I?" asked Adeline without mirth.

"Why not?"

Adeline grunted. "Why not? I'll tell you in a single word. *Fixers.* If I had refused, a fixer would have sat behind me on a bus or next to me at the beauty parlor, and after that, I'd be back on board for finding the next psionic kid—or worse. And I'd have a failsafe stopping me from acting against the Program. Ever."

"A failsafe?" asked Maddie.

"A short-circuit in my brain. When one fires, it stops you dead in your tracks and sometimes triggers a series of actions—calling in, allowing a team to come pick you up, things like that."

"How do you know you don't already have one of those?" asked Gavin.

"Because I never gave the Man a reason to fear me. Though, after the new director invalidated his and my agreement, I did get a little rebellious, as I said." She yawned and then blew the breath out. "But I'm tired. Let's pick this up tomorrow."

"Okay," said Maddie. "Get some rest."

"I will. Thank you, dear."

After Adeline hung up, Maddie said, "Well? Is she a lunatic? Is she lying about Kai and Jamilla? About The Pig?"

Gavin got up off the bed. "I don't know. Maybe I have some documents to back it all up."

"Share them with me?"

"No safe way to do that, Mads."

"Then *read* them to me."

"I don't know, Maddie."

"Don't you think I'm already in this up to my neck? What harm could there be?"

"You could drown in it."

She laughed—a bright sound that lifted Gavin's mood immediately. "You're my ship, Gav, and I'll go down with you."

"Ship? I thought I'd at least be a sexy speedboat."

"Only men think speedboats are sexy. Tell me about the earlier memos, then read me the new ones."

"You sure?"

"As sure as when I said, 'I do.'"

With a sigh, he squinted at the file directory. "Ah. Here's a couple that seem on target."

2

From Program records
Marked June 11, 1998, 05:52 am

```
TO: gray_eyed_goddess@majest.ic
FROM: green_eyed_goddess@majest.ic
SUBJECT: Kai W.
```

Hey bitch,

You left your dirty clothes on the bathroom floor again. I know, I know: "You forgot." Your situational awareness is so bad it frightens me at times. Are you sure you should be out in the world running ops?

Anyway… The reports on the kid are damn impressive. Sending Reggie might be a mistake. How sure are you he can defend himself against the power Kai shows? We need the kid, so make sure it doesn't go sideways. And get the mom as well. She might be an asset for controlling the boy.

P.S. I put your sweaty clothes under your pillow. Should smell great by the time you get back.

3

From Program records
Marked June 12, 1998, 20:41 pm

TO: fieldops@majest.ic
FROM: operations.command@majest.ic

SUBJECT: BOLO Adeline d'Clara

Attention all field ops agents:

Adeline d'Clara has gone off the reservation. Her current location is unknown, but her known automobile is a 1992 OLDSMOBILE ACHIEVA, maroon in color (NY LIC: B1RD D06, registered: Clara Tracker). She is intimately familiar with our operations manual, however, and will likely change vehicles at her earliest convenience.

If observed, notify your operational commander immediately and await instructions. DO NOT APPROACH without orders.

4

From Program records
Marked June 12, 1998, 20:45 pm

TO: bird_dogs@majest.ic

```
FROM: operations.command@majest.ic

SUBJECT: Adeline d'Clara Supplemental

Attention all bird dogs:

As mentioned in the BOLO announcement,
Adeline d'Clara has eloped. Many of
you have a personal relationship with
d'Clara, but I expect you to act in
the best interests of the Program.

Find Adeline d'Clara. Do not attempt
contact—report her location to your
operational commander immediately. A
retrieval team is standing by. She
will not be harmed.

DO NOT DISAPPOINT ME.
```

5

Langfield Sun, Miami, FL
Wednesday, 10:54 pm

"At least we know Majestic is a real thing."

"Let's not call it that. Let's call it MJ."

"Yeah, because no one will figure that one out."

"Okay, okay. Call it the Program like Adeline does, then." Gavin chuckled. "Indulge your paranoid husband a little, eh?"

"Anyway, the Program *is* real. You have the proof right there."

"*If* those documents are credible."

Maddie laughed. "Good grief, honey. Maybe this is the Matrix and none of it's real."

"A little too paranoid?"

"A skosh."

"But these could be fakes. And Adeline herself admits the original Majestic 12 documents were shams created by the people in her Program."

"Gav, you can't use something the Program is supposed to have done to disprove the Program is real."

"Oh, sure. Bring logic into this." Gavin pursed his lips. "But Adeline arranged for a hack…the *person* who retrieved these records *before* I even told her about Pete getting shut down."

"Well, she does assert the Program is full of psychics… Again, though, we're right back at the same question: Why go to all this trouble to make the Program seem real? Why not—"

"Maybe she's doing all this to try to control the investigation. To steer it where she wants it to go. Maybe she's in league with the unsub."

"Okay, I can see that possibility," said Maddie. "But you have to admit the probability is slim. And if that's her goal, why not tell a mundane story—a *believable* story—to shift your attention elsewhere?"

"Like what?"

"Off the top of my head? How about this: Kai is a member of some cult, and they've brainwashed him. Or Kai is being set up by the real killer. If she knows about Manhattan, she'd know you were predisposed to believe that one. She knows the murderer, but he's a regular psychopath, not a psychic one."

"I see what you mean."

"And *someone* issued those BOLOs, right?"

"Yeah," he said, dragging the word out.

"And do they sound right? Official, I mean?"

"Sure."

"There you go, then. She went off the reservation when Kai and Jamilla were grabbed—when the Program broke her deal with the Man."

"Yeah," said Gavin, then sighed. "All of this cloak and dagger stacked on top of this ESP stuff… I'm used to supernatural themes when I'm reading your novels, but in the real world?"

"Sometimes the truth is stranger than fiction. Glacadairanam, for instance. And *I* couldn't have made all this up. It's too detailed, and at the same time, too ambiguous."

"What do you mean?"

"Look at what you just read. The first one talks about the blonde girl from the airport leaving her clothes on the floor. That's a detail. And the BOLOs have just enough detail to pique your interest, to grab you. I mean, an Olds Achieva with a custom plate? Who does that? At the same time, there's the veiled reference to someone named Reggie, to bird dogs—plural, mind—and field operatives. There's a jargon there, a common vocabulary that we don't have."

"Adeline told us about the bird dog thing."

"Right, because she's conversant with that jargon. Its use is casual, right? The messages don't feel contrived to me."

"No, me neither."

"And there's no mention of Maj...the Program except the name in the email addresses—as if everyone already knows about it. That's hard to fake. It's like writing realistic dialog."

"You write realistic dialog."

"Thank you, but you get paid to say nice things to me. Anyway, dialog is a mixture of natural talent and practice. A little knowledge of psychology helps, too. And it has to be casual to ring true. That's not quite the right way to say it, but you know what I mean. If it's stilted when it isn't supposed to be, it sucks. It rings a sour, false note."

"And you think these emails ring true?"

"I do. Could I fake them? Probably, given enough time and hard work. The question would then become: why?"

"To lend credibility to Adeline's story."

"Sure, but *why*?"

"To make us believe her."

"Why?"

"Because I'm an FBI agent, and she wants to influence my investigation."

"And why?"

"You're starting to sound like a parrot. We don't know her motives at present. Maybe the kid—"

"Kai."

"—is the one dropping bodies down here, and Adeline wants to protect him."

"Do I have to say it again?"

"Please don't. There's something between Adeline, Jamilla, and Kai. I don't know what. Maybe she's Jamilla's mother."

"Okay, let's say Adeline has ulterior motives along those lines. Let's say she has the juice to set up a fake hacker to feed you misinformation, that she wants to manage your investigation."

"All right."

"Do you agree she'd need a specific skill set?"

"Sure."

"Good. She obviously knows your mindset, Gav, so I've got to ask again: Why create such an elaborate fiction? She knows your first instinct is to question it all. And don't forget the test we gave her. And the stuff about your dreams. And knowing about that night in Hawaii. You can't just gloss over all that. If she's faking all this, how did she know all that?"

"Yeah, you're right. It's just that I have a hard time believing our government could keep such elaborate secrets for decades. And one thing we've skipped over."

"What's that?" asked Maddie.

"If she was active in that thing with General Walker, that was almost sixty years ago."

"So?"

"So, how old is she? She had the ear of the Man, right? She wasn't a new recruit."

"No, she said he included her in the original committee stuff, and that was before 1950."

"1947. *If* we're to believe President Truman set it up."

"You see? You just poked another hole. If she's got the skills to set all this up to fake you out, she's got the skills to tell a story without such obvious holes in it."

Gavin suppressed a yawn, then got up and crossed back to the bed to lie down. "It's more believable because it's unbelievable? That's your hypothesis? If she's so skilled, wouldn't she expect us to have a conversation like this? Wouldn't she know making it a little unbelievable would make it ring true?"

"Oh, I suppose," said Maddie. "But at some point, we need to believe there are limits to her powers of deception. We have to stop chasing our tails round and round."

"At the point where she makes us believe her with an unbelievable story? That's the limit of her abilities?"

"Maybe." The phone rustled against her cheek as she climbed into bed. "I'm just saying that at a certain point, paranoia becomes less of an asset."

"I know. But sometimes Adeline comes off like she's acting."

"We don't know her. She doesn't know us. A couple of nights ago, we'd never heard of her. And we all gild the lily a little bit, right?"

"I guess so."

"Just keep an open mind."

"I'm trying."

For a moment, silence hissed across the connection. Then, she asked, "How's the cop you're partnered up with? Good old Karl Santana?"

"No guitar licks, yet. He's good, but I rarely get someone who isn't."

"And the rest of them?"

"His lieutenant is willing and able to help us, so that makes it easier." He rolled on his side and looked at the bedside clock. "And speaking of that, I have a meeting at seven tomorrow."

"Enjoy it. I'll be sleeping," she said, laughing a little.

"Not if I call you when I wake up."

"You'd better not. Not if you want to come home and *not* find Frank in your favorite chair."

"Damn that Frank. He sure gets around."

"I'll let you get some sleep. Love you."

"I love you, too, Madeline Gregory."

They hung up, and Gavin plugged his phone into the charger, then he snuggled down into the covers, and minutes later, sleep overtook him.

6

A hotel room
Thursday, 1:54 am

Gavin snapped awake, heart thundering, thinking he'd heard something. But what? A scream? *He flung the bedclothes to the side and silently stood, ears straining against the cold silence. He froze—all except his eyelids going snick-snick-snick as he tried to blink the sleep from his eyes. He grabbed his duty weapon from the nightstand and pulled the slide back a quarter inch to check the chamber.*

He glanced over his shoulder, expecting Maddie nuzzled in under the covers, sleeping through his moment of terror. But the bed was empty, and his heart thudded all the more until he remembered she shouldn't *be there.*

This isn't Hawaii, *he told himself. With conscious thought, he turned and faced the draperies that hid the balcony, that hid Biscayne Bay, Miami Beach, and all points east. He walked over and drew the drapes back.*

The brutal Miami sun scorched his eyes, and he turned his head away. Daylight? *he wondered, but almost before he'd finished the thought, darkness descended on the bay like a B-movie monster falling on an unwitting blonde actress. He snatched the sliding glass door open, and the oppressive wet heat of South*

Florida in the summer embraced him, drowning him, and he gasped for air—a fish on the shore.

He stepped out onto the balcony, the gun held loosely in his fist. He closed the door behind him and froze as a chirp sounded from somewhere in the bay. This is a dream, he told himself. Only a dream.

An offshore breeze caressed him, and he breathed it in, expecting the scents of salt and sea and sun. Instead, the wind carried a darker scent, one of blood mingled with terror and rage and murder. He shook his head savagely. If this is a dream, it should go how I want it!

"Told you before, old hoss. Not sure I cotton to being told what to do." The smooth basso voice rolled around Gavin like thunder. "No, sir. Don't cotton to it at all." The wind-borne words smote him, drove him back and down, into one of the outdoor chairs stationed on the balcony. "You listen here. I'm going to tell you how it is, boy, and you're going to say, 'Yessir,' and hush your damn mouth and nod that bean you use to hold up your hats. Capiche?" The last word burned ragged on the wind. "This here is when you nod, cowpoke."

Gavin didn't nod, didn't acknowledge the voice roiling through the air above Biscayne Bay. What he did was raise the pistol.

Booming, cackling laughter split the heavens, and lightning danced across the white caps driven across the bay to pound on the sea wall thousands and thousands of feet below. The wind picked up—some vile dragon's *breath—bringing the scent of sulfur and burning stone and boiling acid.*

"You can't hurt me with that, old hoss," boomed the voice. "No, sir." Laughter echoed from horizon to horizon.

Gavin pulled the trigger, the report cutting through the laughter, killing it dead.

A scream of rage shook the basalt tower where Gavin sat, making it rock to and fro as if in the grip of a category five hurricane. With a horrible grinding noise, the tower lurched toward Biscayne Bay—except there was no water down there, only hot magma and open flame. Gavin grabbed the chair as gravity grabbed him, losing track of the pistol in the process.

With the shriek of aluminum on rough stone, the chair crab-walked toward the edge. Panic surged within him, bringing burning bile into the back of his mouth. He slammed his bare feet down to the stone, trying to hold the chair, to shove it back toward the slider to his room, but the basalt grew slick and wet, coated in a thick, viscous liquid—blood by the coppery smell and color of it.

The chair pitched off the ledge, and Gavin began to fall, a scream ripped from his lips.

7

Langfield Sun, Miami, FL
Thursday, 2:07 am

Gavin lurched up, his own tortured scream echoing in his mind. He blinked, then squeezed his eyes shut and lay back. *It was a dream*, he told himself. *Only a dream*. He glanced at the clock, yawning, then rubbed his eyes with the heels of his hands and settled back.

He rolled to his side—facing the slider—and closed his eyes.

8

1289 Welcrest Drive, Minnieville, VA
Thursday, 2:29 am

The chirp dragged Gavin out of a deep sleep like a fish pulled up from the deeps. His heart thundered, and he threw the bedclothes away, leaping from the bed, landing buck-naked in a fighting crouch. He stood there, eyes stretched wide open, not a hint of sleep left within him. He stared at the looming, twisting shadows draped around the room, willing his vision to penetrate the gloaming.

"Why are you just standing there like a big idiot?" Maddie asked him. "Get a move on, Gav, or you'll miss your chance to get a piece."

A smile stretched across his lips, following the sense of relief that washed through him. Home! I'm home! he thought exultantly. "No problem, babe! I'm ready!"

"Well, you'd better be, old hoss," said Maddie, her voice dropping through the registers as she spoke, ending in a deep basso roar that shook the house. "Say hey, sugar. I've been looking forward to fucking your soul by saving it. You ditched me for that brunette at LaGuardia, but I'm not too proud to put out."

Gavin spun to face the bed and took in the bedclothes mounded up on Maddie's side. This is wrong! he thought. Something's wrong.

"Why are you gawping at me like that, spark? Smile, it's prettier. You want a piece or what?"

The covers began to shift with a noise like that of granite sliding across granite. Fear rattled through Gavin, leaving him bereft of thoughts, of ideas, of the power to run. A peculiar chirp sounded right behind him, impaling his mind on a spike of pure terror, and still, Gavin couldn't move, couldn't even defend himself—all he could do was watch the covers shifting and sliding like chunks of butchered flesh, like burned corpses, like vast piles of teeth. He longed to squeeze his eyelids shut, longed to turn away, to run, to die, to wake the fuck up, but none of that was within his power. "Jesus Christ, will you get on with it?" he screamed.

Everything froze as his scream echoed around as though he stood in some vast cavern rather than his own bedroom. Silence fell on him like a ravening wolf.

"Told you once, spark. Told you twice. How many times are you going to make me tell you? I DON'T COTTON TO BEING TOLD WHAT TO DO!" The basso roar rattled pictures off the wall, photographs Maddie had taken on various holidays, various camping trips, vacations, and had then hung on their bedroom walls. The shout rattled the doors in their frames, rattling the glass in the slider that led out to the basalt ledge. With the horrible crack of a body dancing at the end of a hangman's rope, a massive crack zigzagged through the plane of glass. Gavin threw his arm to protect his face, wincing, expecting shards of glass to impale him, to bite into his skin, but nothing happened.

A hand fell on his shoulder, and Gavin jumped, barely holding back a shocked scream.

"Where we going, sugar?" asked the basso voice, the man's breath tickling his ear.

9

Gavin awoke, his pulse thudding in his ears, his breathing fast and shallow. *Where we going, sugar*? The question echoed in his mind. Cold sweat covered him, saturated the bedclothes, leeched into the mattress pad beneath. Disgusted at the cold, clingy feeling, he threw the bedclothes back and lurched out of bed, still half in the grip of the nightmare. *Where we going, sugar*?

Black velvet bathed the room, darker shadows shifting, rubbing, caressing the walls. He walked to the light switch and flicked it on with an angry swipe. "I will *not* go through this shit again," he muttered.

Another angry swipe lit the bathroom, and he stepped inside, spinning the shower faucet on to a skin-blistering temperature. He turned and stared at himself in the mirror, black bags already darkening his eye sockets. Steam laced the air behind him, and he turned and stepped into the stream of glorious hot water. He closed his eyes and leaned back, letting the water sluice over his head, caress his face, pound on his back.

Where we going, sugar?

Nowhere, motherfucker!

The heat did the trick—not only washing away the slick, cold sweat but also relaxing his shoulders and back. He heaved a sigh and stood with his eyes shut for a long time. When he finally emerged, he was clean, relaxed, and ready to try to sleep again.

But this time, he wouldn't go into battle unarmed. He fished the bottle out of his bag and looked down at it. The little yellow and white capsules beckoned, and he popped two Doxepin into his palm, then chucked them into the back of his mouth and swallowed. He flicked out the bathroom light but then switched it back on to provide some light if he woke again. He stepped into the other room and killed the lights there, then got into the other bed—the one that wasn't a sweat-soaked mess—and turned on the television to watch mindless shows until the drug took hold.

10

Langfield Sun, Miami, FL
Thursday, 6:43 am

Gavin rode the elevator to the lobby, fatigue steeping in his muscles. He hadn't dreamed again—not that he remembered anyway—but even so, the interrupted sleep, the stinging blast of midnight fear, and the adrenaline it evoked, left him feeling as though he hadn't slept much at all.

And dry-throated as if he'd run a marathon.

He stepped out of the elevator and crossed the lobby to the niche where the continental breakfast bar sat. He chugged a box of orange juice, then picked up a coffee and two pieces of buttered sourdough toast, wrapping the toast in a paper napkin. He walked toward the glass doors that opened on the portico, nodding at the front desk clerks as he passed by.

"Say hey, sir. Where you going, sugar?"

Gavin stopped and turned to face them. One was a tall Latino, wearing a bright smile and a happy expression. The other was possibly the palest-skinned person Gavin had ever seen, and the man stared at him, expressionless. "What did you say?"

"I'm sorry?" asked the Latino.

"One of you said something to me just now."

The clerks exchanged a glance, then the Latino turned back to Gavin and offered a little bow. "Our apologies, sir. You must have overheard our idle conversation." The pale-skinned clerk dropped his gaze to the computer screen hidden by the countertop.

"No, I don't think so," said Gavin. "It sounded like you asked me where I was going. And did you call me sugar?"

Again, the Latino leaned forward from the waist and inclined his head. "Sorry if we disturbed you, sir. It was not our intention to disrupt your morning. Please accept our apologies and allow me to make it up to you. Perhaps a free movie?"

Gavin stared at him for a few breaths, then shook his head. "No, it's fine."

"It's no bother, sir," said the Latino.

"I said it's fine," he said in a mild voice. "It struck me as odd is all." He turned and walked outside, marveling at the heat already burning away the day, and waited under the portico, trying to convince himself he hadn't heard what he was sure he had.

He turned to the east and stared at Biscayne Bay half a block away. The sun danced on the gorgeous blue-green waves, glistening like the midnight sweat of lovers. He sipped from his coffee and instantly regretted it—gaining an immediate understanding of why iced coffee seemed so popular with the cops in Miami. He ate his toast, gazing out at the bay.

A few minutes later, Karl pulled up behind him, and Gavin climbed in. "Morning," he said.

"That it is," said Karl. "Have a good night?"

With a shrug, Gavin sipped his coffee again. "I tend not to sleep well during cases. My brain doesn't shut off."

"I hate that," said Karl. He pulled out of the portico and headed back toward Biscayne Boulevard.

"How about you?"

Karl shook his head. "I had a quiet night."

"No Charger, then?"

"Nope. Nothing. And I watched my surveillance camera at the house for a bit." He glanced at Gavin. "Probably a coincidence."

"I guess so," said Gavin. They turned north onto Biscayne, and Karl began working his way toward the inside lane. As they approached First Street, Gavin pointed at the black Dodge sitting across the intersection, waiting for the light. "Then again, maybe not."

"I'll be damned," muttered Karl. He flicked on his red and blue lights and turned against traffic, blowing the horn. "I'll block him in."

"Right."

The driver of the Charger gunned it, spinning the tires and cranking the wheel to the right, shooting south on Biscayne before Karl could cross the intersection.

"Dammit," muttered Karl, spinning the steering wheel and grabbing the radio's microphone. "Mary Delta Five One Niner in pursuit of a late model Dodge Charger, matte black in color. Occupied times two." He punched it around the curve onto Second Street, the rear end of the Explorer swinging wide. "Get the plate?" he asked without taking his eyes off the road.

"Arizona plate…" Gavin squinted. "Get closer."

Karl closed the distance as the Charger ran into slow-moving traffic approaching the Third Avenue intersection. The Charger whipped onto Third, engine roaring, tires screaming. Karl whipped the Explorer around the corner and flipped on the siren.

"Got it! M-J-T-C-9-0-9."

"Good," grunted Karl. "Dispatch, the plate is from Arizona. Mike Juliet Tango Charlie Niner Zero Niner."

The Dodge blew through the light at First Avenue without slowing. Karl blipped the siren as he slowed, then shot through the empty intersection.

"Left on Flagler," said Gavin.

Karl slung the wheel left, and the SUV danced on the head of a pin for a moment, sliding through the turn onto Flagler, but then the tires caught, and Santana hammered the gas again. "See them?" he barked.

"Three blocks, braking hard."

"Shit," Karl muttered.

"Turning north."

"Dispatch, suspect vehicle heading north on First Avenue." Karl held out the mic. "Take it."

Gavin grabbed the microphone. "Dispatch, Special Agent Gregory on coms."

Karl pumped the brakes twice—hard—then cranked the wheel, pointing the nose of the vehicle at First Avenue, and the Explorer took the corner in a textbook controlled slide. Two blocks ahead, the Charger braked hard, leaving long ribbons of black, but shrieked through the intersection at Third Street. The driver floored it, and the car sped down the block, skidding through a tight turn onto the next street.

"Fourth," grunted Karl.

"Dispatch, suspect vehicle headed west on Fourth Street," Gavin said.

"Mary Delta One Niner," said a voice that sounded like Truxillo, "back off your pursuit. We have a rolling perimeter established."

"Shit," Karl muttered and slowed. By the time they reached the intersection of Fourth Street and Miami Avenue, the black Charger was out of sight.

II

742 NW Fifth Avenue, Miami, FL
Thursday, 7:23 am

Wearing grim expressions, Karl and Gavin watched the CSI team process the black Dodge Charger, saying nothing. They'd found the car tucked in behind the mint green liquor store on the corner of Eighth Street and Fifth Avenue—abandoned, of course, and probably wiped clean. The plates were gone, but there was little doubt it was the right vehicle.

A grey Ford Explorer pulled into the lot, red and blue lights winking, and nosed in beside them. Lieutenant Truxillo got out, shot a glance at the matte black car, then came over to stand next to Karl Santana. He nodded toward the suspect vehicle. "Fled?"

Karl grunted.

"On foot?"

"No one saw," said Gavin. "My bet is they had a clean car stashed here."

Truxillo nodded. "That's what I'd do."

"Me, too. We've got their plate number. We should be able to track them through that."

"Unless it's a stolen plate," said Karl.

"Or a rental," said Gavin.

"Still worth a shot. Two occupants?"

Gavin nodded.

"Two occupants…" said Truxillo. "Probably not our unsub, then?"

Gavin frowned. "No, probably not. I mean, there is precedent for a pair working together, but—"

"The Hillside Strangler," Truxillo said.

"Plus Bittaker and Norris, Lake and Ng, Gore and Waterfield, Lucas and Toole, Abel and Furlan in Germany, and others around the world."

Truxillo frowned. "Then…"

Gavin shrugged. "There could be two unsubs. One who stays back and watches, one who can mask his tracks." He jerked his chin at the black Charger. "I think they were following us—or me—yesterday."

"To what end?"

Gavin took a deep breath and let it hiss out between his teeth. "I have an informant who claims these crimes are linked to a black project."

Truxillo arched his eyebrows at Santana.

"First I've heard about it, Bobby."

Gavin nodded. "I'm not sure it's a real lead."

"Black project?" asked Truxillo.

"Secret. Off the books." Gavin fixed his gaze on the black Charger so he didn't have to see the expressions on Truxillo and Santana's faces. "The informant is a woman who claims to be a psychic."

"Uh… I didn't know the FBI went in for that," said Karl.

Gavin wagged his head. "Normally, we don't."

"What's special about this case?" asked Truxillo.

"She…" Gavin blew out another breath. "She sent me a letter. Before I was assigned the case. She said…" He shook his head. "She said she will help me find the unsub. She intimates that she knows him from way back, says she wants me to find him."

"And the name?"

Gavin shook his head. "We haven't got that far yet."

"Evidence? Have you checked her out?"

"She arranged for someone to send me some records. Computer files. So far, they don't relate to this case, but I've only read a tiny bit of them. And we ran her, but…"

"She doesn't exist?" asked Truxillo. "That's rich."

"Yeah, and that's why I haven't brought it up before. I don't know if it's worth anything yet."

"How'd you get the documents?" asked Karl.

"I'm not comfortable talking about that."

Truxillo and Santana exchanged a look, then Truxillo shook his head. "Sounds like whatever you have won't be admissible in court."

That's one way of putting it. Unless I'm the one on trial. Gavin nodded. "No, it won't be admissible, but I doubt very much you'd want it. It's not direct evidence at this point, more like proof she is who she says she is, that she might be telling the truth."

"You'll let me know if that changes—either for the better or worse. No matter what the source of the information is."

"Yes, sir," said Gavin.

Truxillo held his gaze on Gavin's face for a moment, then nodded and walked over to talk to the crime scene investigator in charge of the scene.

"That's why you needed the free Wi-Fi yesterday?" asked Karl in a low voice.

Gavin nodded. "Yes."

"Ah. So, the how of it is illegal."

"It could be."

Karl nodded. "Hacked?"

"That's how it was represented to me. You sure you want to know all this?" Gavin glanced at his face but couldn't read the man.

"Yeah, I guess I do."

Gavin nodded toward the Explorer. "Let's go grab a coffee. I missed breakfast." He glanced at Truxillo. "Should we include him?"

"Bobby? No, it's best we keep him clear of this."

12

Gavin and Karl sat at a little round table by the window overlooking the street—and the on-ramp to I-95 across from the building. Both had large cups of iced coffee, and Gavin picked at a raspberry danish. He'd just finished telling Karl all about Adeline d'Clara and her crazy stories. A few silent minutes had drifted by since he'd finished the tale.

Finally, Karl uncrossed his arms and took a sip of his ice-cold coffee. "That's quite a story."

"You'll get no argument from me."

"And you believe all this…hocus-pocus?"

"I'm not sure I do." Gavin shrugged and tore off a bit of danish. "But, so far, the documents seem to corroborate her story. And…"

"Go on."

"And my last case had a bit of hocus-pocus in it, too."

Karl nodded and took another sip. "I don't know you all that well, Gavin," he said, "but you seem like you keep your shit screwed together with long screws."

"Thanks, I think."

"What I mean is, you don't seem the type to buy into psychics or secret government training programs for assassins. Or hocus-pocus of any kind. That's so…so…" He shook his head.

"Jason Bourne? Project Treadstone?"

Karl shrugged. "Guess so."

"Again, no argument from me. But, like I said, so far the information seems credible."

Karl took another pull of his drink. "For now, we leave Bobby out of it, no matter what he said back there."

"You know him better than I do."

"All I want to do is stop the guy slicing up women. And Bobby needs to be able to say he didn't know what we were doing if it all goes south."

Gavin nodded.

"I don't care about this secret program, or psychics, or whatever the hell it is."

"I understand," said Gavin and popped the bit of danish into his mouth. "I feel the same way. And I don't think d'Clara wants us messing around with Majestic. She just wants us to—"

Karl snapped his fingers. "That license plate."

Gavin leaned back and closed his eyes. "M-J-T-C… Majestic?"

"Could be."

"Yeah. So maybe the car has nothing to do with the unsub?"

Karl squinted up at the ceiling for a moment, then heaved a sigh. "It would be stupid to come straight at us."

Gavin nodded once and took a sip of iced dark roast coffee. "Agreed. What do we do about them?"

"First, we have to figure out if they're here to stop us."

"What else could they be here for?"

Karl gave him a quick shrug. "Maybe to track the woman. You said she went rogue."

"In 1998."

Santana nodded. "Maybe they have long memories."

Gavin shrugged and popped another bite of pastry into his mouth. "Want to talk to her yourself?"

"Who? This psychic?"

"Sure. Two law enforcement reads are better than one."

After he mulled it over a minute, Karl asked, "Will she talk to me?"

"One way to find out. Let's head out to the car. We need some privacy."

Karl snorted. "No, we'll head back to the Langfield. Unless you'd planned on some kind of sweat-inspired vision from sitting in that car while the sun cooks you alive."

Gavin grinned. "The hotel it is." He finished the danish and washed it down with a slug of cold liquid mana.

13

They asked the concierge for a small meeting room and then ordered a pot of coffee and a pitcher of water. The room was small—perhaps ten feet square—but large enough for a good-sized table and four comfortable chairs.

Gavin set his phone down on the table. "I've been conferencing in my wife."

Karl arched an eyebrow as he sat down. "Part of your hocus-pocus on the last case?"

"Sort of. And she was there for the first call. She's interested in the woman's story." Gavin dialed her cell, and she picked up on the first ring.

"Phone sex before breakfast?" she said. "Why, Gavin! You dirty old lech."

"Uh, I have Karl here with me." He could almost hear her blush. "Karl, this crazy woman is my wife, Maddie."

Grinning, Karl said, "Hello, Maddie."

"Can we pretend the maid answered the phone?"

"Fine by me," said Karl.

"Mads, Karl and I had quite the conversation this morning."

"Oh?"

"About Adeline d'Clara."

"Oh."

"I offered to let him join the next call, and we have a bit of time. You game?"

"Okay."

"Conferencing her in." Gavin did the magic dance with his phone and got both calls stitched together. "Adeline, I have Maddie conferenced in, and Karl Santana with the Miami-Dade Police Department is here with me. I've already brought him up to date on what you've told us and the documents in my possession. Thanks for the help, by the way."

"Um, yes... Are you sure this is a good idea, Gavin? No offense, Officer Santana."

"It's detective, and none taken."

"Detective, yes."

"We have had an interesting morning, Adeline," said Gavin.

"I see."

"There has been a black car following us. We saw it twice yesterday and had a nice car chase with them this morning. Do you know anything about that?"

"How would I? I told you what my gift can and can't do."

"The license plate is interesting."

"Go on, then," said Adeline after a moment's hesitation.

"M-J-T-C," said Karl. "Majestic?"

"Or is it Mesa Junior Technical College?" asked Adeline with a chuckle. "Maple Junction Town Council? Miami Jumping Tent Corporation?"

"Yeah, those seem a bit far-fetched. The car following us is from Arizona but not associated with your group out there, and instead, it is part of some junior college? We can cross off the New England town due to the issuing state, can't we? And the last one? Well, it's just silly."

"Are you sure, Detective?"

"Are you denying the car belongs to your group? Would you know if they sent a couple of operatives to interfere?" asked Gavin.

"Why, child, I do believe I would. But if that was their aim, you wouldn't never have known. Ain't it probably more accurate to guess they've come to help you?"

"Help us?" asked Karl.

"Sure. If your killer is who I think it is, you'll need all the help you can get. Don't you want the help?"

"And who do you think it is?"

"I think it's a former student. A boy who had an extremely hard life. A boy so broken by his home life that we couldn't save him."

"Are you going to tell us his name?" asked Karl.

"In my own time, Detective Santana, but it won't help. Ain't no way he hasn't changed it around some since then. I want you to *understand* the boy, to see what made him. And, to be honest, if I led you straight to him—which, as I told Gavin and Maddie, I can't seem to do at the moment—you ain't equipped or prepared for such a meeting."

"And telling us your story will equip them?" asked Maddie.

"Yes, it'll help your husband and his detective friend."

"How so?" asked Gavin.

"For one thing, you might actually come to believe me. Going into a fight with someone from the Program without believing in their abilities would be worse than foolish. Like crawling into a bear's den without no rifle."

Gavin lifted an eyebrow at Karl, who shrugged and nodded. "Okay, Adeline. We'll play it your way for now. You left off with Kai in the back of a van, in a McDonald's parking lot. And you—"

"Yes, I remember." Adeline took a noisy sip of water. "Jamilla was already under the desert. Kai was feeling low, and his escape attempt had earned him a slap or two—not something the boy was used to, believe me. But Kai weren't like other children his age. He didn't give up, he just changed directions, and he'd had some success reading the operative driving him, even in making the man do what he wanted..."

Chapter 7
Breaking the Law

I

Bev Meredith got out of her cruiser and settled her navy-blue campaign hat at just the right angle. She hitched her duty belt, slammed the door of her patrol car, and turned toward the red and yellow mecca. *Hot coffee, a McMuffin with cheese, and* two *hash browns,* she thought. *Breakfast of champions.* She walked the length of her white cruiser and took a step toward the building, an anticipatory smile blooming on her lips.

But then she stopped and turned back toward the van, her head cocked to the side. Had a judge been handy, she'd have sworn on a stack that she'd heard a boy calling for help—muffled, like it came from the trunk of a car, or…

Or the back of a work van.

She advanced on the van, staring into the front window but seeing nothing. With one hand on the butt of her Sig Sauer .45, she walked around the side of the van. She peered in the driver's window, but the interior of the van was as dark as a grave. She cupped one hand to the side of her face, blocking the sunlight, and strained her eyes against the darkness inside the van.

Again, she heard a soft, far-away cry. "Is someone in there?" she called. She gave up on the driver's window and walked toward the back of the van, her hinky meter bouncing off its limiting peg. The skin on the back of her neck crawled, as though someone was staring at her. Or was creeping up behind her.

Bev had been a trooper for nine years and had been on thousands and thousands of calls. Each of those calls had taught her one thing over all others—to trust her instincts. She stopped near the rear tires and spun around, her Sig Sauer clearing her holster and arcing up to firing position, though her finger wasn't yet on the trigger.

A monster of a man stood near the nose of the van, blocking her path back to the parking lot, smiling at her—though she had a snap-image of him sneering at her as she turned. "Hey, don't shoot me," the man said.

"Hands!" she croaked. She'd never scared easily—one of the reasons why she was a great cop—but something about the man evoked a primal, knee-wobbling, belly-freezing fear in her.

The man lifted his hands, a smug little smile touching his lips. "Whatever you say, Officer." He jerked his head toward the van. "This is my rig. I didn't mean to sneak up on you."

"Yeah?" It wasn't much of a question, but it was all her mind could come up with. There was something about the man…something about his eyes? Whatever it was, it scared Bev half to death.

Wearing his obnoxious little grin, the man nodded. "Yeah. Is there something I can help you with?"

"Back up!" She was pleased to hear the snap of command in her voice.

"Sure, sure," the man said. "Like I said, I didn't mean to startle you."

Bev stared up at him, slowly letting her arms fall a little so the pistol pointed in the man's direction instead of at his chest. She was five-four and one hundred twelve pounds if she were carrying a five-pound weight. She guessed he was easily a foot taller and three times her weight. She opened her mouth to speak, but before she could, a boy's muffled voice rang out on the other side of the big sliding door set into the side of the van.

Look out! a boy's voice cried in her mind. *He's a kidnapper*!

Bev peeked sideways at the van, and when she did, the big man rocketed toward her. She tried to get her gun back up, back on target, but it was as if the pistol had gained fifty pounds. She could barely maintain her grip on it.

The giant of a man was half a step away, eyes bulging from his head. She tried to pull the trigger, but her finger couldn't get inside the trigger guard. Panic hit her like a brick to the back of the head. She thought of sending a 10-78, but by the time she thought of it, it was too late.

Something slammed into the side of her head—something that felt like a blacksmith's hammer swung in anger—and her head slammed into the door of the van with a hollow bong. Her pistol flew from her right hand. Dazed, she tried to backpedal, tried to put distance between her and the mountain of a man, but it was as if there were an invisible wall behind her.

The giant man balled his hand into a massive fist the size of a Sunday ham, then tensed, grunting with effort. Her left hand began to rise, and her baton edged into her peripheral vision.

Sorry! I'm so sorry! the boy's voice shrieked in her head.

Bev knew she should do something—knew she knew what to do—but couldn't move, couldn't scream, couldn't *think*. She watched her baton move upward in slow motion, her eyes bulging with fear. Then the man grunted, her left hand brought the baton crashing down, and she knew nothing else.

2

McDonald's parking lot, Becker, IN
June 13, 1998, 8:09 am CST

After a sound like a hammer thudding into a side of beef, something slammed into the side door of the van, and the vehicle swayed on its springs. Icy, undeniable fear settled in Kai's guts, stabbing upward at his heart. "No, no, no," he whispered, a mantra of denial. Another thudding blow, and the van rocked more, followed by the sound of something slapping down on the asphalt.

A key rattled in the lock on the side door. The door slid on its tracks, and there Reggie stood, glaring at him through narrowed, furious eyes. He squatted and when he straightened, he held a woman by her bicep and belt. Her head lolled, blood flowing freely from her gaping mouth. Reggie heaved her into the van—right on top of Kai, crushing the breath out of him. "You did this, kid," he snarled. The Pig stooped and grabbed the cop's baton and her pistol. He climbed in, tossing the gun to the driver's seat, and slammed the side door, then he stooped over Kai and his erstwhile savior. The big man glowered at him for what felt like an hour to Kai, and then a car idled by, headed for the drive-through, and Reggie glanced out the windshield.

The Pig went down on one knee, grabbed the police officer's radio, and tore it from her belt, ripping her blouse where the microphone had been clipped to her shoulder strap. He flung the radio to the front, then grabbed the cop by her duty belt and heaved her over, pulling her off Kai and letting him suck in a sweet breath. Reggie detached the cop's duty belt, flinging it to the front seat, then dug through her pockets and found her cell phone. He fixed Kai with a horrible stare. "You did this, and I'll deal with you later." He leveled a thick index finger at Kai. "That's a goddamn promise, you little fuck."

Kai shrank away, his gaze stuck on the Pig's face. A dull sheen covered the man's eyes—his *doll* eyes—and Kai could find no warmth, no humanity in them.

The woman groaned, and the Pig dropped a heavy knee onto her stomach, then leaned over and put her baton in her hand. The baton rose, then fell, striking the cop in the face—*hard*. Her head bounced off the metal floor with a hollow *thunk*. "Happy?" His gaze still pinning Kai in place, Reggie flicked his fingers and the cop's baton rose and fell, again bouncing her head off the floor. "You did this to her, you little fucker." Then, he glanced down at the cop, turned her head to the side, snatched the baton from her limp fingers, lifted it until it brushed the van's ceiling, and threw his weight behind a monstrous blow to the officer's forehead with a sickening *crunch*.

The cop began to jitter and flop, arms and legs flailing, and her eyelids rolled back, exposing all-white eyeballs. She seized for half a minute before the Pig flung the baton up front, then grabbed her chin and the back of her head. "You just murdered a cop, kid." He jerked her chin to the side with a horrible crackling sound, and the officer's gyrations stopped dead. "Enjoy the ride with your new friend," sneered the Pig as he moved to the driver's seat, then started the van. He rolled down the window a crack and dropped her cell out onto the asphalt. He took a moment to pick up her radio, turn up the volume, and put it on the dash in front of him. He jerked the vehicle into gear and drove out of the parking lot as though nothing had happened.

Kai's gaze rolled from the back of the Pig's head to the wide-eyed stare of the dead cop, and tears welled in his eyes. After a moment or two, he turned his face away from her brutal, cold, dead, accusing stare.

"I'm sorry!" he whispered. He could still feel her sightless gaze on his back.

3

Speedway Motel, Sparta, KY
June 13, 1998, 11:49 am EST

Adeline came awake in sluggish stages. First, came muddy annoyance. Overheated and sweating, she struggled under the mass of bedclothes, kicking her feet like a child, face screwed up into a grimace. Next, came an awareness of bright sunlight beyond her closed eyes, and she remembered where she was…and why. *The Speedway Motel, Sparta, Kentucky. This must be the worst queen bed ever built.* She rolled onto her side, a groan escaping her dry throat, to face away from the window, squinting at the reflected sunlight stabbing at her from the pale cream-colored walls. Then she slitted her eyes and groaned a second time. Her feeble kicking and inconsequential struggles with the covers hadn't accomplished a thing, and she felt weak and sick from the baking heat under the sheet, the blanket, the comforter, and both extra blankets she'd found in the small, foul-smelling closet. She fought her way out from under the mass of covers, flinging it all to the floor. Once the air hit her burning flesh, she remembered why she'd heaped all that on top of herself, to begin with. The room was freezing.

She glanced at the LED alarm clock on the nightstand—it read 11:23—and she groaned a third time as nausea assaulted her. Ire, her old friend and constant companion, coursed through her. Her doctor called it sleep maintenance insomnia, but she named it a curse. Her pique throbbed in her veins, adding to the heat, adding to the nausea, adding to the pounding in her sleep-addled head. She rubbed her eyes with dry, rasping palms and forced herself to sit up.

The room spun around her like a carnival attraction, and she pressed her eyelids closed, groaning yet again. She leaned back against the padded headboard and drew in a deep breath, then another, and another, through teeth clenched against the threat of sicking up what little she had in her belly.

She swung her feet off the bed, both arthritic knees popping as she put her feet on the God-awful purple and green carpet. She blinked her eyes a few times, then rubbed them again with the heels of her hands. She remembered her dream—her vision—and the fat man shooing her away as though she were nothing.

When the knock sounded on her door, she jumped and only barely stopped the scream that lurked in her throat. Her first thought was: *He's found me!* meaning the man from her dream, but she knew that thought for a lie. He was miles and miles ahead of her—and likely gaining more distance while she dawdled and pampered her old bones.

"Ms. Tracker? It's Isabel. The front desk clerk?"

Adeline opened her mouth to call her answer back but only managed a croak. She cleared her throat and took a sip of the water she'd left on the nightstand, grimacing at the flat taste of the water, and the sharp taste of sleep on her tongue. "One minute, if'n you please. I'm getting my old bones limbered up." She pushed off the bed and stood for a moment, staring at the bent-backed old biddy in wrinkled, slept-in clothes that stared back at her from the mirror on the wall. Then she shrugged and stuck out her tongue at the reflection.

She shuffled around the bed, down the short hall, then flipped open the privacy gizmo on the door. Pulling the heavy door open, she composed her face into what was expected—the glowing good cheer all old women were expected to display when younger people came by. "Why, hello, Isabel!" she said.

A tall barrel of a man stood behind the clerk.

"Hello again, Ms. Tracker. This is my cousin. The one I told you about. Jimmy, meet Ms. Tracker."

"Pleasure, ma'am," said the big man in a slow drawl. "I think I can help you. I've brought a couple of cars down for you to take a gander at."

"My, my. Ain't you a treat? And handsome as the Devil." Adeline chuckled, and Jimmy blushed.

4

*Beall Woods State Park, near Keensburg, IL
June 13, 1998, 10:27 am CST*

Kai sat with his face pressed against the metal wall of the van, crying in silence, no coherent thoughts in his head, only the enormous weight of guilt and the constantly replaying scene of the cop's brutal murder. She still lay behind him, staring her accusations at the back of his neck. Outside the van, he heard the vehicle's tires crunch gravel.

"You'd better hope no one is here," said the Pig. "Because if there is, I'll have to kill them, too. And if I have to kill someone here, that's on you, too."

Kai sobbed and snot coated his upper lip.

The van made a turn, and the suspension groaned as the vehicle began to bounce over a rough trail. Branches scraped and skittered and shrieked along the side of the van.

When the Pig stopped the van, he turned off the ignition and released a heavy sigh. "I hope they don't want you, rugrat. I hope they say I can have you." The van shifted as the big man turned and came back into the cargo compartment. "If they do, you better hope I get tired of you in a hurry, because I promise you this: I'll make every second *hurt*." He tugged off Kai's restraints and gag with a grunt.

Kai didn't turn, didn't peek, squeezing his eyes tighter instead.

The side door slammed open, then the van bounced as the Pig got out, dragging the body of the cop with him. "Get your pansy-ass out here!" he snapped.

Kai shook his head.

When Reggie next spoke, Kai shivered with fear. "If I have to get back in there and drag you out, something's going to be broken by the time the sun hits your bastard face."

Turning and forcing his eyes open, Kai wiped the tears from his cheeks. He slid on his butt across the floor, then dropped his feet into the gravel beside the van. He glanced at the dead cop's blood-stained uniform but couldn't bring himself to look at her demolished face.

The Pig thumped him on the head—just enough to smart—and pointed into the woods. "Get moving, you little asshole."

Shoulders slumped, Kai plodded in the direction the Pig had pointed.

"Since you're worthless, I'll carry this dead bitch," said the Pig. "And am I going to forget this? No, sir."

Kai didn't respond, tried not to hear the sound of the cop's dead hands slapping against the Pig's fat back. The forest would've seemed beautiful—thousands of shades of green, sunlight peeking down through the canopy, a thick blanket of fall's leavings covering the ground—if not for the Pig and his gruesome cargo.

They trudged on for ten minutes, going deeper into the woods, farther and farther away from the trail before the Pig called a halt. The remains of the cop slammed down beside Kai, scattering the leaves into the air.

"You're digging." Reggie put his back to a tree and slid down into a squat. "Get moving."

"I don't have a shovel," murmured Kai. He felt it almost instantly, the slightly greasy touch of the Pig's mind reaching out to his. His arm twitched, once, twice, and again, but he forced it still. They remained as they were for a frozen moment in time, then the Pig grunted, and Kai's knees buckled, pitching him into the leaves next to the woman.

"Then...use...your...hands," grunted the Pig, punctuating each syllable with a psychic shove.

Kai brushed the leaves away from a rough rectangle roughly the size of the woman. The soil beneath was black and rich and smelled like heaven. Kai dragged his hand through it, and it parted easily. "This is going to take time," he said in a quiet voice.

"Yeah? I'd advise against that, you little prick. I'm not exactly known for my patience."

On his hands and knees, Kai crawled into the rough rectangle of exposed earth and pulled great mounds of black earth toward him, flinging double handfuls through his legs.

5

Adeline flashed a smile at Isabel and her cousin Jimmy as she shifted the four-year-old Nissan Pathfinder into reverse. She let the clutch out too fast, and the SUV bucked like a bronco for a minute. She pretended to be a little flustered and grinned sheepishly at Jimmy, then waved a second time, as she put the car in gear and pulled out of the Speedway Motel's parking lot.

Her instincts had led her to the small deception of the two natives—her aw-shucks routine—as she looked over the cars Jimmy had brought, but she'd known the second she stepped into the parking lot that the Pathfinder was the car she needed. It had off-road tires that would be perfect for the Sonoran Desert.

She had the Pathfinder's title—signed over by Jimmy but not filed—a dealer's temporary tag, and over three thousand dollars in hard cash. She'd miss her little Oldsmobile, but things had gone beyond sentimentality.

As she pointed the Pathfinder toward the intersection of Sparta Pike and Boone Road, alarms started to clang in her head. A spurt of a soundless vision played in her mind's eye:

The hood of a blue Crown Victoria, the dash, the extensive radio setup, and an AR-15 standing in a mount between the two bucket seats. The Latino driver turned his head to the right and said something to the buzz-cut bull of a man riding in the passenger seat, and both men laughed. Then the driver turned his gaze back out the windshield, considered a sign for the Kentucky Speedway pointing right, and turned left off the I-71 exit ramp. He glanced down at the gas gauge, which hovered over the "E" and drove under the overpass.

In other words, coming between her and the on-ramp to I-71. She took an immediate left and drove down the wide dirt road into the heart of a massive lumber yard. Relying on instinct, she took the first right and stopped behind the sawmill. She pulled her purse into her lap and set her hands to rooting through it—paying the search no mind at all.

She stretched her senses, trying to latch onto the man she'd flashed on a moment ago. It wasn't easy, not knowing anything about the man and having to suppress her fear, but she was an old pro and found him quickly.

The driver turned left onto Boone Road, and the passenger pointed left. The hood of the Crown Vic slid across the road and into a parking lot, just as smooth as you please, angling for the pumps of the Marathon Gas station. The driver turned his head and—

The knock on her window made Adeline jump and let out a little cry. A sweaty White man in jeans, work boots, a hard hat, and what had once been a T-shirt, stood smiling at her, holding his hands up. "Sorry!" he said through the window. "I didn't mean to startle you."

Adeline rolled down her window and planted a smile on her face. "Lord's sake, child! You 'bout scared the dickens out of me!" She laid on the accent, fitting herself to the man's stereotype-derived expectations.

"I'm sorry, ma'am. I just wondered if you were lost."

She forced a chuckle. "No, but my spectacles are. I'm not 'posed to be drivin' without 'em."

"Ah," he said, nodding. "Well, this isn't such a safe place to park. We drive big machinery through here. I don't want you getting hurt."

"I'll be on my way in the shake of a hound dog's tail." She smiled up at him. "But thank you kindly, child. I'd hate to cause up a ruckus."

"No problem, ma'am. Drive safe, now, hear?"

She nodded, still smiling like a simpleton, and the man turned and walked back to a big yellow-orange Caterpillar with a monster claw hanging from the back of it. She pulled her glasses out of her pocketbook and waved them at the man as he settled into the cab of his machine. Dropping the Pathfinder into reverse, she backed up to the dirt road, then drove south, relying on her instincts, and followed the wide road as it bent ninety degrees toward the Sparta Pike.

Just shy of the road, she pulled to the side and found the man driving the Crown Victoria.

He stood next to the unmarked blue Ford, one hand on the roof next to the car's gas cap, one hand holding the nozzle of the gas pump. Mr. Buzz-cut was nowhere to be seen. The driver squinted at the Speedway Motel, and as he watched, Mr. Buzz-cut stepped out from the motel's lobby and beckoned.

"Well, shit," muttered Adeline. Her Oldsmobile had been titled and registered to her New York alias; she'd had no choice but to give that name to Jimmy. She had no doubt the men in the unmarked car would have that name. She had to hope that Jimmy had cleared out already and that Isabel was on her lunch break.

She resumed her approach to Sparta Pike, then hesitated. She could go right and hope the men didn't know she'd switched to the Pathfinder, she could take surface roads through rural Kentucky—to the next on-ramp or, perhaps, farther—or she could find a place to sit and wait a few hours, hoping to get back on the highway *behind* the men tracking her. All three options contained risks, and the last two increased the lead of the man who kidnapped Kai.

She pursed her lips, hoping for one of her insights, but nothing came. They never did when she needed them the most. She found and touched Kai's mind, then grimaced and cranked the wheel toward the interstate.

6

Kai rocked back on his knees, panting and dripping sweat. He'd managed to scrape out about six inches of dirt in an egg-shaped hole roughly forty-eight inches long and eighteen across. Rich black soil packed his fingernails and every crease in the skin of his hands and wrists. The dirt was ground into the thighs of his pants, and he thought he could feel it in his underwear.

The Pig still lounged against the tree behind him, Kai could feel his hard doll's-eyes on the back of his head. "You don't have time to lollygag, kid," the man grunted.

"I'm not. I'm *resting*."

"Sass me at your own risk, kid. I'm already in the mood to knock your teeth into your asshole."

"I didn't mean it that way."

"Sure you didn't, brat. Get back in there and dig faster. We have a schedule to keep, and this fucking stunt you pulled has put us way behind."

"If I had a shovel—"

"Well, you don't, so stop bitching about it."

"I'm not—"

"*Dig*!" snapped Reggie. "Because if I have to get down in that hole and finish it, it'll be because you have a broken arm to be followed by a broken jaw when you get back to the goddamn van. Hear that, you fucking punk?"

Kai frowned at the hole in front of him, then shifted down into it. "How deep do I have to go?"

"You go until I tell you to stop or I crack that little noggin of yours."

Still facing the dirt, Kai pushed at the Pig's mind a little. Just a little wriggle against his defenses, wondering if the man could even feel his presence. Reggie said nothing, and Kai pushed a little harder, worming his way deeper.

When Reggie didn't react, Kai's face split in an evil smile. He started digging with renewed energy.

7

The Compound, under the Sonoran Desert, AZ
June 13, 1998, 10:54 am MST

Jamilla's head *hurt*. Pain lanced from behind her left eye, back over the top of her skull, and down into her neck. It felt like someone was pulling razor wire through her skull. Any move she made set her head to thumping and her neck to buzzing.

On top of that, she hadn't slept more than ten minutes in any one stretch. She kept waking up in a panic, Kai's name on her lips, echoing in her ears, tugging at her heart. She'd even had some screwed-up dream about a wasp that wasn't a wasp.

No one had woken her. She'd half-expected some kind of hazing—something like the bootcamp she'd endured in Parris Island. And if not that, then a boring day of indoctrination and HR nonsense.

She blinked against the buzzing overhead fluorescents, exploring the foul-tasting pit her mouth had become in the long, sleepless hours of the night. Her mossy teeth tasted like pond scum, and she grimaced.

Jamilla rolled up on one elbow, turning to the narrow nightstand that was "hers," and looked around. The dorm held eleven other cot-like single beds, barely wide enough to lie flat on. The other beds were made with military precision, bedclothes squared away and proper. Other than her, the room was empty.

"Great," she muttered. She grabbed her new toothbrush and toothpaste and headed into the seafoam green hall. Each step thudded into her brain, jarring her thoughts out of alignment. She looked left and saw a ruler-straight corridor that stretched a hundred yards before another hallway intersected it, then continued beyond. She turned her head to the right—the direction she thought she'd come from the previous night. Fifty yards away, her hall dead-ended into one that ran on a perpendicular course. Doors dotted the corridor in both directions, but they were all closed, all unmarked except for numbers painted on the walls above the doors. "Great," she repeated.

She turned right and trudged toward the corridor, arms flopping at her sides, toothbrush in her right hand, toothpaste in the left. After she'd taken ten steps, though, she stopped and turned back, peering up to read the number above her door: 3813. She repeated the number silently as she trudged to the intersecting corridor.

When she reached the intersection, she looked both directions, hoping to see something familiar, but there was nothing but more numbered doors and the stupid rainbow of colors. Try as she might, she couldn't remember what that blonde bitch had said about the colors. She slumped against the wall, searching her befuddled memory for the path from the previous night.

"How can this be a real place with no one in it?" she muttered. She turned and looked back, past her room, to the other intersection and the corridor beyond it. Nothing moved, nothing made noise, nothing did *anything*. "Barbie, where the fuck are you, bitch?"

Barbie? Oh, that's funny! Bethany didn't say you were funny.

Jamilla froze, mouth hanging open, gaze flicking back and forth, back and forth.

Laughter burbled in the back of her mind. *Don't worry, girlfriend. You're not going crazy. My name is Beatrice.*

Get out of my head!

Where's the fun in that? Stay where you are, I'll be right down.

Jamilla shook her head, turned, and walked the other way. "There has to be a bathroom around here somewhere," she muttered.

Yeah, there is, Agent Recalcitrance. You're going the wrong way. Go back toward your dorm, look for room 3822. It's communal, but this time of day, it should be empty. I'll meet you there.

"What the fuck?" Jamilla murmured, but she turned and walked past her room, checking the numbers as she went. Room 3822 was a large rectangle, triple the size of her dorm room, containing sinks, toilet stalls, and a slew of shower stalls. Lockers ran along the wall opposite the sinks, and an over-stuffed laundry cart sat in the corner. Another laundry cart was near the showers, filled with white towels like you'd see in any motel. Opposite it was a rolling shelving unit stacked with clean towels and washcloths.

She stepped to the first sink and turned on the cold tap, running her toothbrush through the brisk stream of water. She applied a healthy dose of toothpaste and set to work on the garbage pit that had replaced her mouth in the night. The door opened, and Jamilla grimaced as the blonde bitch sauntered into the room wearing a little, *knowing* grin. "Tell me that wasn't you."

Oh, it was me, alright. The blonde woman's green eyes glinted. *But I'm not Bethany.* She chuckled and held out her hand. *I'm Beatrice, Bethany's sister.*

Jamilla narrowed her eyes, toothbrush hanging from her hand, half-forgotten. "You're twins?"

Beatrice nodded. *I got the good looks.* She tapped a perfectly manicured nail next to her left eye. *Green, not gray.*

"You sure the world can stand two of you?"

The woman looked down at her empty hand and let it drop, then laughed. *So far, anyway. Sorry I wasn't there when you woke. I was distracted by a problem over in the academy.*

"Can't you talk out loud? I don't want you in my head."

Tough titty, little kitty. Beatrice flashed another smile. *You'll need to get used to it sooner or later.*

"How come Barbie doesn't talk in my head?"

The blonde threw back her head and laughed. *Oh, I bet she loved that! Mind if I steal it?*

Jamilla shrugged and went back to brushing her teeth.

I'm going to like you, Jamilla. And don't worry about me in your head. I'm speaking to you, not poking around in your head. That's bad etiquette around here.

Jamilla grunted and spit, then sucked water from the tap, swished it around, and spit it out. "Bad etiquette from a bunch of kidnappers and murderers?"

Beatrice sobered a little, then, as though she'd made a conscious decision to do so, laughed. *Bethany so likes*

*to play badass, doesn't she? You know about good cop-
bad cop?*

Jamilla rolled her eyes.

Well, I'm the good twin, Bethany's the bad twin.

"You both work for the people who kidnapped my
son."

Yes, we recruited *Kai. But after he arrives—*

"Where is he?"

*He's in transit. As I was saying, after you see how
much he grows, you'll stop thinking of it as a
kidnapping. We have his best interests at heart.*

"Right." Jamilla rolled her eyes.

*People as powerful as Kai don't do well in the outside
world. Here, he'll thrive. He can learn from the mistakes
of others—teachers, guides, and the older students. Out
there, his power would overwhelm him, destroy him.*

"Powers." Jamilla scoffed. "What kind of powers?"

Beatrice smiled and reached out to touch Jamilla's
arm. *Powers like Bethany's. Like mine. We don't know
what form they will develop into, not yet.* She cocked
her head and pinned Jamilla with an intense gaze. *You
have some, too. Not much, mind. Just enough that your
intuition is almost always right, that things just work
out for you. I wonder why…*

"Why, what?"

Pursing her lips, Beatrice shrugged. *I'm wondering
why you weren't inducted. You could have been
developed into a pusher or a snoop, surely.*

"A pusher? A dealer?"

No, no. In the Program, a pusher is a telekinetic—like Bethany. A telepath, we call a snoop.

"You're a telepath?"

Beatrice chuckled. *No, in addition to the good looks, I also got most of the psi. I'm what we call a fixer.*

"What, like a hitman?"

Pushers or puppeteers usually handle the black bags. I'm a teletechnitic.

"Yeah, okay. Sure." Jamilla rolled her eyes.

Beatrice laughed and touched her arm again. *You're so funny! I love it. A teletechnitic, from the Greek. Tele for remote, technitic as in mechanic or artisan.* She cocked her head. *Think of us as psychic brain surgeons.*

"Okay..." Jamilla put the cap on her toothpaste. "I'm going to pretend that makes any kind of sense."

Grinning, Beatrice patted her arm. *It's a lot to take in all at once. Psionics are classified by what they can do*—she flapped her hand—*and by their strength. But mostly you'll hear the function tags. Snoop, pusher, puppeteer, fixer, and bird dog.*

"What are puppeteers and bird dogs?"

Telecheiristirics are called puppeteers because they can control the motor centers of others. The word telecheiristiric means remote controller. Bird dogs are telezitonic—remote seekers. Like Adeline d'Clara.

Jamilla jerked her head back as if Beatrice had slapped her. "Adeline?"

Beatrice nodded. *She finds people. Operational targets.*

"What's that mean?" Jamilla demanded, a sinking feeling dragging her stomach toward the floor.

New students, runaways, others.

Jamilla shook her head.

It's true. Adeline is the best of the bird dogs. Beatrice shrugged and grinned. *She found both Bethany and me, and if she hadn't, I'd have gone nuts, for sure. I owe her my life.*

Headache flaring, Jamilla stumbled a step back. "No."

It's true. Beatrice shrugged. *Oh! She had nothing to do with Kai, if that's what you're thinking. We'd never ask anyone to—*

Jamilla lashed out, palm slashing across the space between them. Beatrice's eyes blazed a moment, and Jamilla knew a moment of real fear.

Don't ever do that again. Beatrice's mental voice was as cold as deep space. She didn't attach a threat or consequence to it. She didn't have to.

Not knowing what else to do, Jamilla nodded and dropped her gaze.

8

Adeline's gaze darted to her rearview mirror for the umpteen hundred and third time since leaving Sparta. Like the times before, she scanned the cars behind her, looking for the distinctive front end of a Ford Crown Victoria, looking for a blue hood and push bars. And like all the times before, she didn't find them. The traffic had gotten progressively thicker as she passed from rural Kentucky into the Louisville metropolitan area, but not so much that they could sit back and surveil while remaining hard to see themselves.

But, of course, if they had more than one car…

She shook her head—it didn't pay to borrow trouble. She'd seen *one* car with two goons in it, so she'd assume she needed to watch only for it.

Worry for Kai also bit at the edges of her mind—a pack of terriers going after the mailman's ankles. That bastard who had him had managed to drive her sleeping self away—a feat he'd never have been able to accomplish had she been awake and directing her far-seeing. She didn't recognize the operative, which meant exactly nothing since she'd always tried to keep all the induction operations at arms-length—though nagging familiarity hounded her. She couldn't abide the type of person who could transport a new student across the country prior to admission, and what's more, she didn't *want* to—despite what the Program required of her.

She couldn't afford to send her whole consciousness on walkabout, not unless she wanted to wreck her new ride, probably killing herself in the process. But she could touch the boy's mind, just enough contact to keep tabs on his location. She couldn't communicate— and if the Program wanted him, he'd have power, and she didn't know if he'd *allow* her to communicate with him. She wouldn't force her way in, not with him, and in her experience, untutored psionics defended themselves out of survival instinct.

What bothered her was that the boy wasn't on the move. Operations had schedules, *tight* schedules. He was still in the same location as when she'd left Sparta. Given the content of her dream, she didn't think Kai was in the company of the Indiana State Police. That meant the operator had decided to stop…maybe to make Kai pay for the trick he'd pulled in that McDonald's parking lot.

She grimaced at the thought and ratcheted the Pathfinder up another ten miles an hour.

9

I understand you're upset, sent Beatrice. *I'm making allowances for your rudeness but striking me is a quick way to becoming brain-dead. Understand what I'm saying?*

Without looking up, Jamilla nodded. "You can really do that?"

You bet your ass I can. Are you going to shower? If so, get to it. I have other things to do than babysit you. Her mental tone had drifted miles away from the friendly, bantering tone she'd projected in the beginning.

"Look, I..." Jamilla shook her head, angry with herself for having the urge to apologize, to smooth things over with one of the blonde bitches keeping her from her baby.

Yeah, sent Beatrice. *Shower or no?*

"I don't have any clean clothes."

Beatrice pointed at the linen cart. *Smocks are over there. Above the washcloths.*

"Then, I guess I would like a shower."

Fine. I'll be back in five minutes. Be ready. She whirled around and strode out of the room. Jamilla followed her out, then went to her dorm and got the supplies she'd need.

Five minutes later, Jamilla was ready. Her hair was wet, but she'd at least washed away the grimy feeling left on her skin from the many miles of travel she'd put in the day before. She grabbed her supplies and returned them to her nightstand. When she straightened and turned, one of the twins stood in the doorway, looking at her through narrowed eyes.

"Which one are you?"

"*Barbie!*" snapped Bethany.

Jamilla flew backward onto her bunk, as if propelled by a giant invisible hand—or an explosive concussion. Her nightstand rattled for half a heartbeat, then rocketed across the room to slam into the wall, disgorging Jamilla's things as it flipped over. Her supplies began a frenetic mid-air dance, cavorting like fairies, then dove at her, moving fast and hard. She tried to scoot to the edge of the bed, and instantly, that giant invisible hand was back, pressing her down, compressing the mattress, making the bed creak and groan.

"Don't hit her again. Even if she lets it slide, I *won't*," growled Bethany.

Jamilla returned her steely-eyed gaze without flinching. "I'll make you a deal. Return Kai to me and let us go, and I'll promise never to touch either one of you."

Bethany's jaw worked, and her nostrils flared, but all she did was turn her back and walk away, leaving

Jamilla to follow or not. "Clean your shit up. Hurry up. Administration is waiting."

Jamilla glanced around the empty room and shrugged. She retrieved her nightstand and all her worldly possessions, then she followed Bethany into the hall.

10

I-64, near Elberfeld, IN
June 13, 1998, 2:18 pm CST

Adeline kept her gaze dancing back and forth between her mirrors and the road ahead, and the stress and constant vigilance had taken their toll in the guise of monstrous, heavy-lidded fatigue that circled through her mind like a vulture checking out a bit of roadkill. Even so, she felt *close*.

Her intuition told her that Kai and his captor were somewhere to the northwest. Maybe sitting in a park somewhere off U.S. Route 41 or U.S. Route 45. Maybe she hadn't made enough headway to do any good, but she'd spent the last several hours gaining on the van transporting Kai—she was certain of that much.

She snapped a glance at her side-view mirror, and her heart skipped a beat. A blue Crown Vic sped toward her in the fast lane.

II

Jamilla's head still pounded, and her mouth still tasted of ash and worse. If anything, she felt worse than she had in the morning. She'd spent the first few hours of her day filling out paperwork as though she'd *wanted* a job in the Program, then more wasted time listening to some HR wonk explain benefits she had no intention of being around long enough to earn. The only positive was that she hadn't seen the Barbie twins since the morning.

But as she stepped out of the administration section, one of the blonde bitches smirked at her from where she leaned against the concrete block wall. Jamilla shook her head and grimaced by way of a greeting.

I feel the same way, sent Beatrice. *But we have to work together—at least for a little while.*

"Do we? Why? Do you plan on cleaning or cooking or whatever the hell I get assigned to do tomorrow?"

Hardly. The woman's chiseled features smoothed from the smirk, taking on a practiced neutrality. *Let's get this over with in as little time and with as little unpleasantness as we can.*

"This?"

Beatrice nodded. *I need to evaluate your strengths.*

Jamilla narrowed her eyes. "Why? I'm not in your damn Program."

You're here, aren't you? Beatrice's green eyes danced. *Besides, everyone is evaluated.*

After a half-minute staring contest, Jamilla broke her hard-eyed glare. "What's this 'evaluation' amount to?"

You'll see. We can't do it here in the middle of the hallway. Follow me to my office.

"I'm tired. Exhausted. Headachy. Can't this wait until the morning?"

Beatrice flashed her a fake smile. *Rules are rules, Jamilla. Your physical malaise won't influence the test results.*

"First, it was an evaluation, now, it's a test," Jamilla grumbled.

Call it what you like best. The point is, we're going to do it now.

"And if I don't cooperate?"

Then I call someone to make *you cooperate.*

Jamilla glanced back at the door she'd just emerged from. "I wonder what the HR people would think about that?"

They will think whatever I tell them to think. As will you. A bit of fire touched Beatrice's eyes.

"This is because I slapped you, isn't it?"

Hardly. I could care less about what's in the past.

But Jamilla thought the woman harbored a grudge, that this test or evaluation or whatever would contain pain—unnecessary pain.

Beatrice rolled her eyes. *No. I told you—it's just an evaluation. No special treatment. Besides if I wanted revenge, Bethany would have delivered it this morning.*

"Is that how it works? You say jump, and Barbie number one asks how high?"

One side of Beatrice's mouth curled up in a grin. *Barbie number one? Does that mean I've achieved Barbie status?*

"Let's just get this over with!" snapped Jamilla.

Beatrice's half-grin evolved into a full-fledged smile, exposing a mouthful of perfect white teeth. *That's the spirit.*

12

Beall Woods State Park, near Keensburg, IL
June 13, 1998, 2:18 pm CST

With leaden arms, Kai sat back and looked down at the hole. It wasn't pretty—its edges weren't crisp and square like they showed in the movies, but it was another half a dozen inches deep. He puffed out his cheeks and peeked over his shoulder at Reggie. "Is this deep enough?"

The Pig lifted his chin and looked down his nose at Kai, narrowing his eyes like the bully he was. He sniffed, then rolled to his hands and knees, his pendulous stomach swinging, before he struggled to his feet. He stepped closer and looked down into the hole. He hawked and spat in front of Kai. "I should make you dig it deeper, but the schedule clock is ticking." He glanced at Kai and jerked his chin to the side. "Get up, kid. Go drag that pig-bitch over here."

Kai stood and dusted off the seat of his jeans. He climbed out of the hole and took a quick peek at the police officer. He couldn't stand much more. "I can't move her. I'm only eleven."

The Pig rolled his beady eyes and shoved Kai out of the way—hard enough to send him ass-over-teakettle—then crossed to the cop, took her belt in one massive hand, and heaved her toward her shallow grave. She landed with a gross plop—a barrel full of slop hitting concrete—as her body hit the dirt a yard-and-a-half short of the hole. Reggie repeated the one-handed throw and planted her face down. "Get this pig-bitch covered up."

Kai didn't argue, though he hated the thought of burying her face down. He stood facing the pile of dirt he'd created digging, spread his legs wide, bent at the waist, and started flinging the dirt into the hole with both hands.

"Christ, kid," grumbled the Pig, "we don't have all day." He came over and shoved Kai out of the way, then started bulldozing big piles of the black earth into the hole with his foot. "You start smoothing it out."

Kai shrugged and did as he was told, shoving dirt around the police officer's body first, then covering her. When they'd finished, there was an obvious mound.

"Go get some leaves and fallen branches and junk like that. And you'd better be Johnny Nimble, if you catch my drift," said Reggie as he stepped onto the grave and started jumping up and down. "But don't get any ideas about running off. I'm a fat ass, but I'm still faster than you."

Kai turned away and started searching the ground, happy for a task that took him out from under the Pig's thumb for a minute so he could let his smile of satisfaction dance on his lips. His slow progress on the grave had kept them stationary for far longer than he'd believed the Pig would allow. He darted a glance up into the trees, then, when he didn't see her, he turned his head toward the southeast as if he could see her driving on the interstate.

"What the *fuck* are you doing? Didn't I tell you to be quick?"

Hot red pain exploded in the small of his back, and Kai went flying. He landed face down in the thick carpet of leaves—and right on a tree root, which stole his breath. He couldn't even moan as the hot tears sprang from his eyes and rained on the rotting leaves.

"I guess you need a lesson," said the Pig. "This should do."

Kai turned his head and saw the Pig coming toward him with murder in his eyes and a thin switch he'd pulled from a nearby tree. He tried to get up and run, tried to push himself away from Reggie, but the man's long strides made short work of that.

The Pig grabbed him by the ankle and jerked him closer, and from the feel of it, he nearly dislocated his knee. He ripped Kai's pants down and went to work with the switch.

Chapter 8
Easy Fixes

I

Karl slapped his hand on the table. "Hold on. Just hold on a damn minute. Are you saying this Reggie character—"

"Jamison Capstrom," said Adeline.

"Whatever. You're saying he attacked that police officer in the parking lot? That he somehow took control of her body? That he made her hit herself with her own nightstick? That he killed her and forced Kai to bury her?"

"Yes," said Adeline. "That's exactly what he did."

"And then what?" asked Maddie in a voice that made it sound as though she didn't want to hear the answer.

"That comes next, child."

"No, I mean, he pulled Kai's pants down…"

Gavin and Karl exchanged a sickened glance.

"He just beat the tar out of the boy," said Adeline in a tone as hard and cold as steel. "*Nothing* more."

"How can you know that?" asked Karl.

"You said yesterday that Kai found out Reggie had been in the Program, but the memories were wrapped in a wall of shame. Is that where Reggie got his training?" asked Maddie.

"Some, I guess," said Adeline. "Reggie was a very broken man—but you already done figured that out, I bet. Even as a teenager, he was too interested in the younger students. He was a what-do-you-call-'em…a pedophile, to be sure. Unsuitable for advanced training, so he was let go."

"But he still worked for the Program," said Gavin.

"Yes, he found contract work with the operations group. They often take them failed students—the ones we can fix so they's safe, that is. It makes it easier—they already know about the Program, y'see? When a student flunks out for whatever reason, a fixer crawls around in their heads. Takes their power down a few notches, even deletes memories of techniques too advanced. Reggie was one such. He'd shown promise as a puppeteering student, but as I said, his mind was warped like one of them funhouse mirrors. They kicked his fat ass out, and a fixer took after his thinking and his psi abilities."

"But you let him go on molesting kids," said Karl, his disgust evident in his voice.

"He was *fixed*, Detective, as I said. But urges like that need an outlet. They—"

"You are complicit in every kid that twisted monster abused!"

"No, Detective. I had no part in Compound administration, not back then. And as I said, he needed an outlet. What Kai read in his mind, that weren't nothing but pure fantasy—his real desires, yep, but his fixer reset his brain so that he fantasized the acts, and those fantasies became memories. He *thought* he actually did those things. He got pleasure from it, to be sure, but he didn't never touch a child after the fixer readjusted his brains. You follow? And the children he was interested in inside the Program were watched over, protected. He never molested a single child. So, if you want to lay blame on my shoes, I'll take it. But we *saved* countless children from his abuse, not the other way 'round."

"And we're supposed to believe you?" demanded Karl.

"Why wouldn't you, child?" Adeline asked in a soft voice. "I wouldn't condone any abuse of a child. I promise you that."

"We should believe you because you told us to believe you? That's your argument?"

"I deserve that," said Adeline with a rueful chuckle. "That's not much of an argument, I guess. But how can I prove a negative? How can I prove that Reggie never molested no one? All I can do is tell you we have no reason to believe he did, that we took steps to ensure he wouldn't."

Karl puffed out his cheeks, shaking his head.

"We could pull his sheet," said Gavin.

"Okay, but where? Arizona? He drove all over the country."

"True," said Adeline, "but always on a tight timeline, always under observation."

"Observation by you?" asked Maddie.

"No, child, but by people like me. People we trained to monitor psionic emanations. To monitor and make a record of 'em, I should say. Gavin, see if you can find observation reports on Reggie. See if he ever tripped his failsafe or broke his programming."

"You talk about him like he's some kind of computer," said Maddie.

"Well, what's a brain but an organic computer?"

"And your fixers can overwrite whatever programming is there? Even down to limiting psychic powers?"

"Yes," said Adeline. "To both questions. And more when they take it to mind."

"How?" asked Gavin.

"For that, you'd need to ask a fixer. All I can say is I seen the results. Countless times. It works, however they do it." Adeline took a drink, slurping it.

"Is that what happened to Jamilla there at the end?" asked Maddie. "Beatrice reprogrammed her."

"Yeah," said Adeline in a dead voice. "That was the first time."

"The first time?" asked Gavin.

Adeline hesitated for several breaths, then said, "I need a potty break. I'll be back in a minute."

"Me, too," said Maddie. "And lunch."

"Fair enough," said Gavin. "Let's all take a break. Karl, can you get us some food? I'll look for those records."

"Sure. Subs?"

Gavin shrugged. "Your choice." He held out an American Express. "FBI's buying."

Karl grinned, then took the card, turned, and left.

Gavin ran an NCIC search on Jamison Capstrom, Reggie Capstrom, and on a whim, Reggie Jamison, but he struck out under all three names. Then he set to work digging through the Black folder, looking for reports on Reggie. He found five and opened them.

"Gav, you there?" asked Maddie.

"Yes, hon," said Gavin.

"Did you find the records Adeline suggested?"

"Five of them."

"What about in the NCIC database?"

"He's clean."

"At least that part was true."

Karl shouldered the door open, balancing two Styrofoam containers in one hand and two massive cups of sweet tea in the other. "Burgers," he said. "The line for the sub place was ridiculous."

"And all I've got is Kashi Go Lean," said Maddie.

"My wife is addicted to cereal," said Gavin with a smile. He turned his Bureau laptop toward Karl. "Nothing in NCIC."

Karl shrugged and sat. "That just means he never got caught. If d'Clara thinks that puts her in the clear—"

"I'd prefer you call me Adeline or Miss Addy, but if you must use last names, it's *Miss* d'Clara."

"Welcome back," said Maddie. "Gavin didn't find any criminal records on Capstrom."

"Mmm-hmm," said Adeline.

"But I did find some Program records." Gavin accepted a white Styrofoam food box from Karl and a sweet tea and set them next to his laptop. "I'll read these documents aloud."

"Yes, do," said Adeline.

2

From Program records
Marked April 14, 1986, 16:07

```
TO: operations.command@majest.ic

FROM: observer_67@majest.ic

SUBJECT: Jamison Capstrom Initial
Field Observation report

Subject observed by observers 67 and
83, in twelve-hour shifts, constant-
scan.

Initial     24-hour     impressions:
reprogramming  appears  successful.
Fantasy    substitution    modeling
effective.

Log:
00:00 to 12:00: Subject entertaining
morose thoughts. Appears depressed,
```

unable to sleep, mind awhirl. He perseverates on Program dismal. Fantasized about the two blue-suiters he targeted in the Compound. Fantasy to memory circuit activated, sex drive reduced.

12:00 to 00:00: Subject lethargic. No activities of daily living performed, including sustenance and hydration. Spent most of the day staring out the window—but he has been in the Compound for four-and-a-half years, so this observer ranks the behavior as normal.

Recommendations:
1. Continue daily field observations, one-week report interval.
2. Step down from constant-scan to periodic-scan after a four-week period free of failsafe trips.
3. Monitor for failsafe trips.
4. Monitor F to M circuit activation and impact on libido.
5. Consider giving subject tasks to complete to aid in overcoming his negative affect re: dismissal.

Report ends.

3

Adeline cleared her throat. "You see?"

Karl swallowed and took a sip of water. "One report, from persons unknown. That doesn't put you in the clear any more than not finding a police record does."

"There are four more reports," said Gavin. "Let me read them all, and we can discuss it after."

4

From Program records
Marked April 28, 1986, 16:07

TO: operations.command@majest.ic

FROM: observer_67@majest.ic

SUBJECT: Jamison Capstrom Week 2 Field Observation report

Subject observed by observers 67 and 83, in twelve-hour shifts, constant-scan.

Week 2 impressions: All circuits firing as described and to good effect. No failsafe trips noted in the past seven days. No inappropriate behavior. Fantasy life appears rich. Memory formation continues.

Log:
Day 1: Subject up early, performed all activities of daily living required to get him to assigned workspace on time. Eating well—perhaps too well. Near-continuous fantasies while awake, but these do not appear to interfere with his duties.
Day 2: Similar behaviors as with Day 1. In addition, subject started initiating conversations with other contractors in the hub. Has expressed an interest in operational logistics.
Day 3: Subject continues to improve. Has requested a driver's education program.
Day 4: Subject not scheduled for work in the hub but showed up anyway. Subject volunteered his time to assist other contractors in daily tasks. Affection for teammates and friendship-building mechanisms noted.
Day 5: Similar behaviors as with Day 4. No anomalies noted.
Day 6: Subject up two hours early, reported to hub ninety minutes before schedule. Requested time on the simulator. Supervisor granted the request and stuck around to critique subject performance—which was received in a positive manner. Note: no fantasies while engaged with simulation, though they restarted after the practice session.
Day 7: Subject reported to work ninety minutes early again. Requested sim

time and put in eighty-three minutes.
Supervisor noted improvement and
offered praise. Subject took great
pleasure in doing well. Note: no
fantasies while engaged with
simulation, though they restarted
after the practice session.

Recommendations:
1. Continue daily field observations,
   one-week report interval.
2. Enroll subject in independent
   contractor operations training,
   including: driver's education,
   pursuit and evasion, physical
   restraints, improvisation, as
   available during off-hours.
3. Monitor for failsafe trips.
4. Monitor F to M circuit activation
   and impact on libido.
5. Allow subject to use simulator
   when not otherwise engaged, even
   outside of hub operation hours.

Report ends.

5

From Program records
Marked May 17, 1986, 17:18

TO: operations.command@majest.ic

CC: fieldops@majest.ic

FROM: observer_67@majest.ic

SUBJECT: Jamison Capstrom Periodic
Field Observation report

Subject observed by observers 67 and
101, in twelve-hour shifts, periodic-
scan.

All circuits continue to function as
prescribed. No failsafe trips noted.
Periodic scanning shows a well-
adjusted individual with a rich
fantasy life. Addition of work duties
has drawn subject out and given him
confidence again. He appears happy and
well-adjusted. April 13 reprogramming
successful. Subject is ready to move
into full-time independent contractor
training.

Recommendations:
1. Continue periodic scanning on
   Fibonacci schedule as per
   operational guidelines.
2. Cede primary observation to Field
   Operations.
3. Promote subject to full-time
   training program—we can find
   someone else to push that broom.
4. Annual fixer assessments and
   adjustments.

Report ends.

6

From Program records
Marked April 14, 1987, 09:07

TO: operations.command@majest.ic

FROM: matteson@majest.ic

SUBJECT: Jamison Capstrom Annual Psych/Fixer report

Psychiatric impressions: Subject willingly submitted to examination by this fixer. Sedation unnecessary. Subject seemed interested in my findings. Conversant, well-groomed, positive affect. No inappropriate behavior or speech noted.

Teletechnitic impressions: Failsafe circuit active and functioning, with zero trips. Fantasy-to-Memory circuit functioning at peak efficiency. Adjusted personality traits show no signs of rejection. Subject remains (and will remain) loyal to the Program over all others. Motivation implants remain effective: praise from Program personnel, efficient and effective completion of duties as described by supervisory personnel, developing skills as necessary to complete independent contracts for Field Operations Group—namely package logistics and delivery, or as assigned by supervisory personnel—and taking initiative for such skill development. Psionic reduction continues as planned. Memory wipe of full telecheiristiric potential secure and reinforced by this fixer.

Recommendations:
1. Continue intermittent monitoring by Field Operations.
2. Allow subject solo contracts.
3. Reinforce positive results with additional perks (apartment upgrade, new clothing, better vehicle) at Field Ops admin team's discretion.

Report ends.

7

From Program records
Marked April 14, 1988, 09:07

TO: operations.command@majest.ic

FROM: matteson@majest.ic

SUBJECT: Jamison Capstrom Annual Psych/Fixer report

Psychiatric impressions: Significant mental fatigue and stress noted. Subject willingly submitted to exam, no sedation needed, but affect negative, mood dark. Subject trying to cope with lighter workload while confronting the reality of his personal life (loneliness).

Teletechnitic impressions: Failsafe circuit active and functioning, with zero trips. Fantasy-to-Memory circuit functioning at peak efficiency. Adjusted personality traits show no signs of rejection. Subject remains (and will remain) loyal to the Program over all others. Motivation implants remain effective. Added motivational implants: physical fitness, friendship development. Psionic reduction continues as planned. Memory wipe of full telecheiristiric potential secure and reinforced by this fixer.

Recommendations:
1. Continue intermittent monitoring by Field Ops admin team.
2. Assign subject friends.
3. Encourage physical activity, diet maintenance.
4. Fixer examinations at increased frequency (quarterly).

Report ends.

8

"That's it," said Gavin. "I couldn't find anything else on Capstrom."

"Do you need more?" said Adeline with a chuckle.

"Seems to me that there is a lot of language in those reports about rejection of these 'implants' and the like," said Karl. "Plus, it seems too easy. Pedophilia has no cure. Pedophiles *can't* change. What's to say he hasn't rejected the programming in the time since?"

"The rest of my story, that's what." The words came out snappish, in the tone of an exhausted mother whose children were trying her patience.

"There's more? How does all this help us?" asked Karl.

"It helps you to understand the man killing those women."

"What do you know about him?"

"For one thing, he obviously has psionic abilities, what with them girls cutting on themselves like that."

Gavin held up a hand to stop Karl's response. "How do you know that?" he asked quietly.

"You must have told me."

"I don't think I did."

"Do you want my help? If so, kindly shut up and let me help."

Gavin nodded. "You're saying that Capstrom has the ability to make our victims cut themselves."

"You remember I told you about puppeteering, don't you?"

"Yes, but—"

"Don't get all excited, Gavin. There are hundreds of puppeteers in the Program. Besides, Reggie ain't in Miami. He ain't your killer."

"How do you know that?" asked Karl. "How can you—"

"Because I know where he is, and it ain't Miami. The person in Miami, I can't see, can't locate."

"Where is Reggie?" asked Maddie.

"Arizona," said Adeline in a matter-of-fact tone.

"This dream you told us about, the one where you flew like a bird…"

"Yes, dear Maddie?"

"How come Capstrom could push you away? If I understood that gobbledygook in that psych report, Reggie isn't a puppeteer anymore?"

"He isn't—or I s'pose it's more accurate to say his psi rating doesn't warrant his inclusion no more. Anyhow, many of us have multiple gifts," said Adeline. "For me, it's augury. For others, it's TP or TK. Reggie had a bit of TP. That's how he saw me, how he sent me packing. I was dreaming. He wasn't."

"And Kai?" asked Gavin. "He had to have some TP to pick at Capstrom's mind, right?"

"Yes."

"And this TC, the puppeteering thing?" asked Karl. When Gavin shot a questioning glance at him, he said, "He made Capstrom need the toilet. He…did stuff to the man's body, his bowels."

"Very good, Detective," said Adeline with the air of an approving teacher. "That's exactly right. Also, a touch of TK. Gavin, you'll find a report on Kai's psi rating. It has his gifts spelled out."

"Haven't seen that one yet."

"Well, you'll have to look for it."

Gavin narrowed his eyes. "How do you know what documents I have?"

"It's just a guess, child. Don't get that paranoia a-going again."

"Why didn't Kai use his power to stop Capstrom?" asked Karl.

"Detective, he was a child. Eleven years old! And Reggie was grown and had had some training. Kai ain't had nothing but what he intuited. If he'd had even a little training, things would have gone different."

"The point of these stories… Are you saying that our unsub is a puppeteer, Adeline?"

Static crackled across the call for a few moments. "My, ain't you the clever one, Gavin?" she murmured. "But I ain't saying that. Not yet. Let's leave it at: he *might* be a puppeteer, but if he is *only* that, I should be able to spot him."

Gavin sighed and glanced at Karl and asked the question with one lifted eyebrow. Karl rolled his finger.

"All right, Adeline. Go on with the story."

"Where was I?" she muttered. "Oh. Illinois. The blue Ford. Little Kai in the back of the van, sore butt and a bruise or two but *unmolested*."

Chapter 9
On the Road Again

I

Adeline bit her lip as the blue Ford drew closer and closer. She slowed, flicked on her blinker, and changed to the inside lane, tucking in between an old pickup and a semi. She slouched lower in her seat and wished she'd thought to bring a hat, a scarf, or any kind of disguise.

She peered at her side-view mirror, heart in her throat, right hand gripping the wheel hard enough that she felt sure she would leave dents in the plastic, left hand fluttering toward her throat. The car slowed a couple of car lengths behind her, then the right turn signal flashed to life, and the Crown Vic slid into the lane behind the old pickup.

"Dammit!" she snapped in a harsh whisper. She glanced at the exit sign ahead. "I-69 North ½ mile," it read. *Maybe they're going to take the exit*, she thought. "Or maybe *I* should." She dithered, gaze darting back and forth from the exit ahead and her side mirror.

Every now and then, the Crown Vic slid toward the inside lane—not changing lanes, just poking out to peek around the battered chevy farm truck separating them. Adeline fancied she could feel the eyes of the driver on the back of her head.

Take the exit? she asked herself. *Or put the hammer down and run?* All the saliva in her mouth seemed to have boiled off when she wasn't paying attention, and her dry tongue stuck to the roof of her dry mouth. Her right hand began to throb with each fast heartbeat, and her wrist got that sick feeling that forecast one of her bad arthritis attacks. Her neck and shoulders ached with tension.

Behind her, the old chevy put on its turn signal. *Decision time*, she thought. The pickup drifted into the exit lane, and behind it, the blue Crown Vic straddled the line between the exit lane to I-69 and the westbound lane of I-64, as though leaving her space to cut in front of them.

She locked her gaze on her rearview mirror, watching the blue car to the exclusion of anything else—traffic, her lane, the exit lane. It just sat back there, passenger tires in the exit lane, driver's side in the westbound lane.

Decision time, she thought again, without realizing she'd just thought the same thing half a minute before. *Exit or floor it?* she asked herself. The only problem was, her mind wasn't answering any of her questions. Panic throbbed through her as adrenaline flooded her veins.

I-69 takes me away from Kai, and they'd just follow me. They know it's me. They know! Those thoughts brought with them the metallic taste of terror as the tempo of her heart lurched into a higher gear.

The Ford settled back into her lane and accelerated toward her, closing the distance left by the pickup. The gaze of both occupants of the car seemed to meet her gaze in the rearview mirror. Her heart thudded, seeming to flutter every few beats, and she was huffing air like a steam engine.

Now or never! a voice screamed in her mind as the exit lane began to curve away from the westbound lanes of I-64. *Decide*! *NOW OR NEVER*!

In the Crown Vic behind her, the driver smiled.

2

State Road 1, approaching Cowling, IL
June 13, 1998, 2:31 pm CST

Kai sat with his back against the rear door of the van, his knees up, and his hands dangling from his knees, leaning toward the left in an attempt to keep his weight off the mass of cuts and bruises the Pig had given him with the switch. He was near exhaustion from the physical labor, the stress, and his attempts to get inside the Pig's head, but his spirit was buoyed by the success of his stalling tactics back in the woods.

And the fact that he suspected the Pig had made a grave tactical error.

In his haste to bury the cop, Reggie had forgotten the woman's gun and baton, which Kai could see lying in the passenger footwell. He also seemed to have forgotten the police band radio on the dash.

The only problem was that, try as he might, Kai couldn't work out how to get to the police officer's weapons, and even if he did, he didn't know how to use a gun, and he doubted he was strong enough to do damage with the baton.

But the police radio…he could make that work, he thought. At least until the Pig took them out of Illinois.

He stared at the back of the Pig's head through eyes squeezed to the narrowest of slits. He poured all his energy into his effort, wriggling through Reggie's defenses, worming through the top layers of his mind—despite the disgust he felt at touching the man, even if the contact was only mind-to-mind.

Reggie grunted, his gaze crawling to the rearview mirror.

Quiet, now, Kai thought at him. *Nothing going on back here.*

The Pig sniffed as his doll-eyed gaze crawled away from the mirror.

The radio.

Reggie's gaze dropped from the roadway ahead to the police band radio lying on the dash under the rearview mirror.

It's in your way, isn't it? It's distracting. You keep looking at it, taking your eyes off the road. It's worse than distracting, it's dangerous!

The Pig cleared his throat, cracked his neck with a violent jerk of his chin, darted a glance at the rearview, then gave the road his attention. After a moment, he leaned forward and slid the radio a little more toward the passenger seat.

Wow, that's even worse, right? You should put it on the floor between the seats.

Moving as if in a dream, Reggie leaned forward and hooked his fat fingers around the radio's antenna, then sat back, pulling the radio toward him. He sat still after that, left hand on the steering wheel, radio dangling from his right hand held down by the side of his seat.

Almost! sent Kai. *Doesn't that antenna feel funny?* Kai had visited a reptile house the previous school year and had volunteered to hold a python. He recalled how the snake's body had felt while it writhed and moved in his hands. *Feels like it's alive, right? Feels like a* snake!

The Pig tore his gaze off the road and glanced down at the radio, mumbling something to himself.

Ick! Drop that disgusting thing!

Reggie's hand spasmed, the muscles in his forearm writhing beneath his skin, and the radio slipped an inch closer to the floor.

Kai slid away from the back doors of the van, moving toward the front with as little noise as he could manage. The Pig's gaze snapped to the rearview, nonetheless, boring into Kai's. Pumping his shoulders up and down, the boy shifted position to lean against the sidewall of the cargo box. *I'm not doing anything suspicious,* he sent. *I'm just a kid moving around to take his weight off the ass-beating you gave me.*

The Pig sniffed again and returned his attention to driving.

That's right…give the road your full attention. In fact, you need both hands on the wheel.

Reggie lifted his right hand toward the wheel, and when the radio slapped against his leg, he let the antenna slide through his fingers. It bounced off the Pig's meaty thigh, then fell between the seats.

A sense of power surged through Kai, and he clenched both fists in mute victory. *Keep your eyes on the road. I'm not making a sound.* Kai shifted his weight forward and pulled his knees under him. He crawled toward the back of the Pig's seat, his gaze riveted to the radio lying on the metal floor. *You don't notice anything inside the van. That's because nothing is happening. Keep your hands on the wheel—*both of them—*and keep your attention on the road.*

Reggie grunted softly, and Kai crawled into the cloud of the man's stench—body odor and spoiled meat. His own gaze switched from the back of the seat to the radio, and he reached for it. The antenna felt cool and slick as he curled his fingers around it.

Watch those cars! he sent at the Pig. *What's that idiot doing?*

Reggie slammed his left hand on the horn. "Idiot!" he muttered.

At the same time, Kai pulled the radio to his chest, cradling it like a teddy bear. He slipped it inside the collar of his T-shirt, clipping it securely. He reversed himself and crawled toward the back of the van. *You must pay attention to those crazy drivers. Watch them like a hawk.*

Kai twisted around and put his back to the side of the box, just past the wheel well, and unclipped the radio. He set it on the floor next to him so that his thigh hid the thing—just in case the Pig stole a glance back at him. He keyed the mic to see what would happen, and his heart thundered at the sound it made through the radio's speaker. He stared at the knobs on the radio's top, found the volume, and turned it all the way down.

He'd done a report on Morse Code in the last year in school. He didn't know how to send a distress call in cop-code, but he knew how to send SOS. He tapped the mic button three times in rapid succession, then made three long, slow presses, then three more short and fast.

He hoped someone was listening.

3

The Compound, under the Sonoran Desert, AZ
June 13, 1998, 1:37 pm MST

Jamilla blinked hard and tried to lift her hands to scrub the hot tears out of her eyes but something held her still—something she couldn't see or feel. Confused and disoriented, she twisted her head to first one side, then the next, but saw nothing—*could* see nothing—as though shrouded by black felt—a perfect, velvety blackness. "What the hell," she muttered in a voice that warbled and cracked. "Kai? Kai, where are you, baby?" Her voice sounded flat, muffled, to her ears, and she detected no echo. "Hello?"

She blinked rapidly, trying to clear her vision, but the matte black shroud stayed put. She tried to stand but couldn't straighten her legs. She threw herself to the side, expecting to strike something, to feel *something*. She heard nothing but her own voice, and even that seemed muffled. It was as if she floated in deep space or a sensory deprivation chamber.

Her body felt chilled—as cold as a corpse. "What the *fuck*?" she shouted.

Relax, tough girl.

The mental voice seemed familiar, but Jamilla couldn't place it. "Who's that? What's going on? *Why can't I move?*"

It's almost over. Be quiet and it will go quicker.

"Who are you?" Jamilla shouted. "What is this place?"

Though she couldn't hear it, she had the distinct impression that whoever owned the voice in her head had sighed. *You will understand soon, Jamilla. For now, just relax.*

Something inside her head seemed to wrench sideways, and she screamed. It wasn't that it hurt, not exactly, but it felt…*wrong*.

Oh, come on. You're tougher than this, Jamilla.

"I'm not. I-I-I'm not!"

Again, something seemed to shift, as though some giant had rotated the room that she couldn't see—as though the room had flipped on its side or perhaps rotated around her ninety degrees.

She gasped and threw herself against whatever held her there, but she couldn't feel any restraints. "Help me!" she cried. There was another wrenching sensation, and when she opened her mouth to scream, there was no sound, not even the sensation of exhaling breath.

Terror took her mind in its oh-so-untender grip and shook it to the edge of sanity. In full-blown panic, she thrashed against whatever held her—or thought she did, anyway. She opened her mouth wide, and had she been able, would have screamed and screamed and screamed.

Goddammit! The voice snapped in her head like a whip crack, something lurched sideways again, and Jamilla knew no more.

4

Adeline chewed her lip, staring at the rearview, at the ice-cold gaze of Mr. Buzz-cut as he reached forward and wrapped his hand around the AR-15 mounted by the dash. Even though the rifle's barrel pointed straight up, the threat was clear, and her heart skipped a few beats as the Pathfinder thumped across the concrete bridge over I-69.

The blue Ford edged closer yet, well inside a single car length.

"Didn't nobody teach you not to tailgate?" Adeline whispered. She didn't see a flasher on the dash of the car, and the license plate was out of Ohio. *Not cops then*, she thought. *Operatives.*

That was worse than cops, though—it meant they had no compunction against using that rifle if she gave them even a hint of trouble. Then again, the way she'd left the conversation with Sam McIntire, Mr. Buzz-cut's orders might be to terminate the chase at the first opportunity. *Shouldn't have snapped at him. Shouldn't have gotten angry. I could've disappeared quietly.* Adeline chuckled sourly, still watching Mr. Buzz-cut. *Little late for shouldas, woman, as usual.*

The Crown Vic came even closer, and Adeline considered brake-checking them, but she wasn't sure of the Pathfinder's brakes, wasn't sure the man driving the Ford wouldn't take the opportunity to bump her off the road. *What else can I do?*

Mr. Buzz-cut dropped his hand off the fancy rifle, and the blue car darted out into the fast lane and accelerated. The man with the buzz-cut stared at her as they rocketed up next to her.

Going to run me off the road! Heart thudding, Adeline jerked the Pathfinder's wheel to the right, her passenger tires thudding through the wake-up markers scribed into the lane's outside edge and onto the paved shoulder. She jammed both feet onto the brake pedal, her tires locking up and the whole vehicle shaking as the Pathfinder skidded toward the grass.

Mr. Buzz-cut made a finger gun and shot her, then winked and the car was gone, speeding ahead like she was standing still.

She let up on the brake, puffing out her cheeks in relief.

But there was only one thing that could make operatives shift their attention elsewhere. *Kai!* she thought.

She brought the SUV to a halt, put on the emergency flashers, and sent her consciousness to find the boy and his repugnant captor.

Kai sat toward the rear of the van's cargo box, holding something out of view, fiddling with it. The driver's attention seemed fixed on the road ahead, and he cursed and blatted the horn, even though there was almost no traffic. Kai wore a self-satisfied grin as he pressed the microphone button on what looked like a police band radio.

"Sweet Christ!" Adeline cried. She took her foot off the brake pedal and floored the accelerator. "Kai! Don't do that!"

Her face set in a rictus that was half-worry and half-determination, she set off after the blue Crown Victoria, urging the three-liter V6 in her Pathfinder to match the Ford's eight cylinders.

Adeline cursed her calling, cursed her lack of ability to influence the events she could view remotely. The boy was in serious trouble and had no idea he was already caught.

Chapter 10
Sightseeing

I

"You can't talk in someone else's mind like the kid can?" asked Karl.

"No," Adeline said with a sigh. "Things might have been different if I could."

"You mean you would have stopped him signaling for help?" asked Maddie.

"Yes. The Program…the field operations team, anyway, monitors the police bands. Can't have no one chasing one of our vans, now can we? And they're brighter than them cops was. *They* figured out Kai's messages."

"Are the people in the black Dodge part of your field ops teams?" asked Gavin.

"Didn't we talk about that already?"

"You said they were here to help," said Karl.

"I said *probably*, Detective. How would I know who they are? I ain't in Miami any more than Maddie is."

"Are you going to answer me, Adeline?" asked Gavin.

"Haven't I done that?"

"So far, you've responded to his questions with questions of your own. Ones designed to deflect attention," said Maddie.

"Have I?"

"There's another one," said Karl. "You must really want to keep something from us."

"Like what, Detective? And I *know* that's another of them questions—I simply can't fathom your line of thinking."

"Two men in the Charger, Adeline, just like your blue Ford."

"Not every car with two men in it works for the Program. You and Karl's for instance."

"Tell me about the people in the Dodge, Adeline. Do I have something to fear?" Gavin kept his voice low, making her *listen* to what he said.

"Okay, child. Okay. *If* they are Program operatives, the driver will probably be a physical so he can protect the passenger. That one can react to situations as they develop, but not physically, if you ken my meaning. Most likely that passenger would be a puppeteer or a fixer."

"Puppeteers are the guys who can possess your body?"

"Yes, Karl. One of those," said Adeline.

"Why would they help us? Wouldn't they want to take the unsub back to have him fixed?" asked Gavin. "Why wouldn't they fix him like you keep saying they'd do to me—without his ever knowing?"

"Now, you're asking me to put on the robes of an oracle. I can't read their motivations. How could I know why?"

"You know the Program. It's evident you worked in Field Ops from that first story."

"Back then, it weren't called Field Operations, and it was far less organized than today. But you're right. I did fieldwork," said Adeline. "I ain't had no choice, but that's neither here nor there."

"Speculate," said Maddie.

"What, child?"

"Guess why the Program would send agents to babysit Gavin and Karl."

Adeline let out a long sigh. "Maybe they are there to protect them from the killer. If I can recognize his nature, they can, too. They might even know who it is."

"Don't you know that?"

"Maybe," she said. "If I can expand my answer to knowing the only people it might be, my answer changes to yes."

"Names," said Karl. "Give us their names."

"I can do that, Detective, but it won't help none. The names I know ain't out there in the world. They're using aliases hidden behind aliases."

"I give up," Karl muttered.

"I don't mean to be persnickety and contrary, Detective. I'm an old fool, is all. But I really can't give you any names that would help. What I can give you is the story, so you can recognize him when you see him."

"Why not just give us the descriptions?"

"Because, child," Adeline said with an air of harried patience. "It's been years since I've seen them, more than twenty of 'em, and they ain't look like they did then."

"There's always an answer," said Karl. "I'm going to check in with Truxillo." He got up and walked out into the hall, pulling his cell phone out as he did so.

Adeline heaved a deep sigh. "Give me strength," she muttered. "Can't make him drink."

"He wants to catch this guy before another young woman gets cut up," said Gavin. "He hasn't had my...*experiences*. This is all new to him. Psychics, secret government programs. Hell, it's new to me, too, but..."

"But then there's Glacadairanam," said Maddie in a voice that shook.

"Yes."

"Don't fret, dear Maddie. That little beastie is occupied with a new project."

"A new string of murders," grumbled Gavin.

"Mayhap so, mayhap not."

"How come you can find him, but you can't find the killer in Miami?" asked Maddie.

"That's a simple one. He doesn't know I exist, and I wouldn't know he existed, except for my sightseeing in your husband's dream."

"Are there—"

"Others like him?" Adeline asked. "I can't know. I don't understand his nature, not fully. But I know someone who might—probably does, in fact."

"Who?" asked Gavin.

"Fry."

Gavin shook his head. "I don't understand."

"The hoodoo man?" asked Maddie. "Why would he know anything about Glacadairanam."

"Call it intuition. I just got me a feeling he knows about that little devil."

"Is that why I'm having dreams with the weird chirps and someone who talks a lot like the guy you described in your Dallas story?"

"Mayhap," she said in a speculative voice. "Mayhap, indeed."

"You've had a repeat of the dream from Tuesday night?" asked Maddie, concern coloring her speech.

"Not exactly. It's not like in New York."

"Then what's it like?" she asked.

"Well…in the second one, it started out like the dream about Hawaii, but I wasn't in Hawaii. I was here, in my motel room. You weren't here. I go out on the balcony, like in the first dream, and the onshore wind brings me foul odors. I say—or *think*—I should be able to control the dream since it's my head that's doing the dreaming. The cowboy voice says he doesn't cotton to being told what to do…except it's like he's half-cowboy, half-mafioso. He even says *capiche*."

Adeline gasped.

"Does that mean something to you?" Gavin asked.

"No, shadow on my grave is all. Go on with your dream."

"He's telling me that when he says 'jump,' I should say 'how high.' I don't know how I ended up doing it, but I think I shot him. He screamed, and I was no longer in the Langfield Sun—the hotel. I was in a big black tower like in the *Lord of the Rings*. His scream breaks the tower, and I fall into Biscayne Bay, only it's lava or something instead of saltwater. That's where I woke up."

"Next?" said Maddie with a little snap in her voice.

"It was just last night, honey. I wasn't keeping it from you, I just haven't had a chance to tell you about it."

"I know, Gav. I'm worried, not angry."

He shrugged, even though there was no one to see it. "It starts like the others—something spooking me out of a deep sleep. I think it was a chirp. I jump out of bed, and you are there. You say something saucy, and I grin, knowing I'm home, that I'm safe. But then you say something, call me 'hoss' or something like that, and as you speak, your voice goes low—really, really low. I can't see you, you're under this mound of covers—you know, like you sleep when I run the fan during the winter. The blankets start to slither and shift, and it's like the slowest reveal in the history of reveals. Glacadairanam is right behind me, but I can't move, can't see him, only *feel* he's there. It's like I'm hypnotized by the slithering bedclothes. I scream 'hurry up,' and the crazy cowboy goes off on me—screaming, breaking stuff. I'm facing the slider and it cracks. I put my hands up to shield my face, and he...and he...puts his hand on my shoulder and says, 'Where we going, sugar?' right in my ear, like he's right there behind me." Gavin swallowed convulsively and heard Adeline gasp for the second time. "Then I woke up."

"Why do those things bother you, Adeline?" asked Maddie. "'*Capiche*' and 'Where we going, sugar?'"

"Ain't nothing, child. Déjà vu, maybe."

"Oh?" Maddie said in that tone Gavin knew meant she didn't believe the old woman. "Are you sure?"

"Yes!" snapped Adeline, but then she blew out a long breath. "I'm sorry, child. I don't know why those things spook me, but they do."

"Is Gavin in danger?"

"Mayhap they're just dreams."

"His dreams about Glacadairanam in the alley weren't."

"No, they weren't. I can't say if he's in danger, dear. I don't know."

"But you would say if you did?"

"Of course."

"Is he in danger from the men in that car?" Maddie demanded.

"No, I don't think he is."

"But you don't know for sure?"

"How could I, child?" Adeline sipped her drink. "This is making me cranky, all this distrust, all these questions. At the same time, I know how hard it is to believe what I'm saying. I've been in similar situations—as my story illustrates—but *I* am telling you the truth as best I know it."

"Okay," said Maddie. "Okay. What can he do to protect himself?"

"From the bogey in his dreams? That's easy."

"Then?"

"Stop dreaming."

Gavin chuckled. "It's that easy? If only I could stop myself from dreaming."

"They ain't got doctors down in Miami?" asked Adeline. "They got medicine to stop you dreaming, child."

"Great. First, I have to take something to get to sleep, and something to keep me sleeping, and now I need another pill to stop me from dreaming."

Adeline giggled. "Well, you asked."

"What else can I do?"

"I ain't sure you *need* protection from your dreams—true or not. That dream in New York, that one was a prophetic dream all tied up with the darkness you was in the middle of. That's all. And nothing *hurt* you in that dream, right?"

"I suppose not."

"There you go. Maybe some of 'em even helped," said the old woman. "Now, where's that detective? Let's get this show on the road."

"I'll get him." Gavin got up and opened the door, but Karl wasn't in the hall outside. He stepped out and looked down the hall toward the lobby. Karl came around the corner, phone pressed to his ear, his face set.

"We've got to go," he called. "A new one."

"Shit," muttered Gavin. "Is it fresh or one he hid better?"

"I don't know."

"Shit," Gavin repeated. He went back into the meeting room. "We'll have to finish later, ladies. Duty calls."

"Another one?" asked Maddie.

"Yes. Just found. I've got to go." He powered down his laptop and shoved it into his laptop bag.

"Be careful," said Maddie.

"I will. Call you later." He cut the connection to Maddie and Adeline, then turned and sprinted down the hall.

2

Everglades National Park, west of Miami, FL
Thursday, 4:47 pm

Karl let the Explorer idle past the few civilian vehicles already parked in the Mahogany Hammock Trail parking lot. He gave it some gas to take them past the news vans and sweating, on-the-scene reporters doing promo bits for the six o'clock news. He pulled up to the end of the ring of law enforcement vehicles blocking the Mahogany Hammock Trailhead.

They hadn't spoken much on the trip out, and when they did, they both steered clear of Adeline d'Clara as a subject. For his part, Gavin felt a vague embarrassment, as though he'd done something stupid. Plus, he still didn't know what to think of her stories, backing documentation notwithstanding.

Gavin got out and ducked under the yellow crime scene tape, Karl following behind. He grimaced at the earthy, rotten-cabbage stench and loosened his tie in a futile attempt to battle the hot, wet blanket of afternoon heat.

Karl found the duty officer and logged them both in. He strode over to Gavin, glancing down at his shoes, then at the trailhead. "The duty officer said we can make it most of the way on the boardwalk, but the rest is a bit of a muddy slog.

"Great," said Gavin. "And we're going to sweat right through our shirts."

Karl treated him to a quick shrug. "You get used to that. I've got spare shirts in the car for normal duty. After this, though, we'll both need to head home and change."

"I have no doubt," said Gavin.

"Come on. We might as well get out there before dusk sets in. If we have time, I'll take you sightseeing— show you the largest living mahogany tree in the States." Karl led him down the weather-beaten and age-grayed boardwalk that bridged the sawgrass marl between the parking lot and the island of hardwoods, itself. When the boardwalk forked, Karl took the right side, ducking under Fig tree branches, Gumbo Limbo boughs, and shoving aside palm fronds that didn't get the memo to stay clear of the boardwalk.

The deeper they went into the hammock, the more the rank odor intensified—rot, decay, and wet mud—and despite the shade provided by the tall trees growing right up against the railing of the boardwalk, it seemed hotter than the parking lot. The slats creaked a bit under their weight, but Karl paid it no mind, and Gavin tried to emulate him.

After a few minutes, they came to a bit of crime scene tape tied around the handrail. "I guess this is it," said Karl. He stepped up on the mid-rail and swung his other leg over the top, then shifted his weight to the other side, climbing down the handrail like a ladder. When he dropped to the ground, his feet sank an inch or so, accompanied by a wet squelch. Gavin followed him over, while Karl surveyed the area, looking for the next breadcrumb. "There," he said, pointing at a tree twenty-five yards distant that wore a yellow ribbon around its trunk. They followed the strips of crime scene tape, trying to avoid the worst of the muck, and after a few minutes' walk, they came to a cordon marked by a ring of yellow tape—the crime scene itself.

Truxillo, dressed in calf-high tactical boots, old jeans, and a faded T-shirt advertising something called CLAW & WARDER, which appeared to have a werewolf dressed up like Sherlock Holmes and a succubus cop fighting a hellhound. He nodded at

Gavin, then beckoned them both forward. "Welcome to the real Florida, Agent Gregory."

"Hello, Lieutenant," said Gavin.

"Call me Bobby."

"Then I'm Gavin, not Agent Gregory."

Truxillo's mouth curled in a half-smile. "Like a couple of old hens." He chuckled and shook his head. "You'll never guess what we found in that Charger this morning."

"Let me crank up my psychic powers," said Gavin. "Nothing?"

"Wow, telepathy really works!" Truxillo grinned, then turned to Karl. "Thought you'd change, at least."

Karl shook his head. "We came right here."

"Well, if the suit gets ruined, you can expense a replacement."

"Thanks, Bobby."

"What have we got?" asked Gavin with a jerk of his chin toward the group of CSI technicians.

"Another woman. All cut up, just like the rest of them. But she's been out here exposed to the magic of the Glades."

Karl grimaced. "Ugly, then."

Truxillo nodded. "And something's been at her. Adolescent gator maybe."

"Or a panther," said Karl.

"Or that," said Bobby with a nod. "Took a chunk out of her thigh, whatever it was."

"Does she show the same kind of mutilation as the others?"

"Yeah, probably," said Bobby with a sigh. "The ME estimates three months of exposure, but he saw signs of freezing. Possible signs, at least. And that estimate is a rough one. He was very clear on that."

"That fits the timeline. It puts this murder first, a month to a month-and-a-half before the South Point body," said Gavin.

"Yeah," repeated Bobby. "Want a look at the scene?"

"Yes, I think I'd better. This isn't the murder scene if she was frozen, but maybe he left us a message."

Truxillo called everyone away, then nodded to Gavin.

He strode forward, looking at the position of the body, penetrating glances bouncing from her to the ground around her, then up to the low hanging branches above her. As horrific as the others in the series, she bore deep wounds in various places, wounds caused by a very sharp instrument. He squatted next to her and examined the worst of the wounds—a deep gash that traversed the tops of both breasts—and saw no signs of hesitations, no shallow starts and stops, no scrapes—and a quick look at the other wounds confirmed she hadn't hesitated on any of the cuts…just like the rest of the victims. "Does this mean what Adeline wants me to believe it does?" he asked her. "What are you trying to tell me? That you have power over these women? More power than it takes to kidnap, rape, and kill?" Maintaining his squat, Gavin turned in a slow circle, gazing into the trees around the body.

"You didn't spend any time here, did you? Just dumped her and walked away." He turned his gaze back to the victim, noting her orientation, the position of her head, the position of her limbs. "Didn't care about her at all, eh? She was nothing to you alive and worth even less dead. You don't play with them, do you? Your corpses?" Another quick scan of the scene, this time with his eyes unfocused, looking for anything that stood out.

He shook his head and stood up, then did one last circle before rejoining Karl and Bobby. "This unsub is strange," he said. "It feels like he's a new kind of serial killer."

"How so?" asked Bobby.

"I get the distinct impression that the corpses are just garbage to him—a chore, something to dispose of. He doesn't come back and visit them. He has all his fun in their last few hours." Gavin glanced back at the victim, draped over a root, arms flung out, legs splayed, but not in a sexual way, hair hanging across her face. "He *wants* them found. He wants *us* here, confused, lost."

"You can tell that by the body position?" asked Karl with a half-grin.

"I can guess that. Look at her." He turned back and flicked his fingers at each body part as he explained. "She's sloppy. Hair any which way, arms lying where they flopped to when he dropped her, legs apart, but the pose isn't a sexual one. It's less a pose than a final orientation after he cast her aside like something he'd finished with. He doesn't need to humiliate her. He wants us to find her, for the media to know, like scorekeepers, but it isn't about shock value or degradation. It's confirmation of his prowess, of his power. We already know he's not scared of *us*, so it's not like he's worried we'll find something out here that will lead us back to him." He shrugged. "But why he's so confident, I can't say. This isn't an exact science. I could be wrong."

Karl glanced at him and nodded.

"You can have a team search the woods, but I doubt there's anything here to find. Except her."

"After three months? I'd say not," said Truxillo. "And even if we find something fifty feet away, how can we know it came from the killer."

"Barring a knife, I'd agree with that. Even evidence found on her body is suspect unless we get something up under her nails." Gavin turned back to Truxillo. "Or inside her."

"Then again, this is the first victim in the series, right? He might have made mistakes," said Karl.

"Maybe," said Gavin with a shrug. "But we don't know this is his first vic. There may be others out here in the swamp, or he might have fed the sharks with some. It's all guesswork."

"When should we expect a fresh one?" asked Truxillo in a quiet voice.

Gavin grimaced and folded his arms. "If he follows his accelerating schedule, tonight."

"Tonight," murmured Truxillo. "Great. Get out of here and get some food. Take a rest."

3

Karl pulled under the portico. "I'm going to head home. Change. Eat with my wife for a change."

"Sounds like a good plan. If I end up talking to d'Clara again, do you want me to conference you in?"

"Want? No." Karl scratched his chin, staring straight ahead. "But I think it's best. It saves the time it would take you to repeat it." He turned to face Gavin. "And I get to hear it from her, in her voice, her own time."

"Right. Filtering her stories through the perception of two law enforcement officers is better than one, like I said this morning. I'll give you a call." He got out, then turned to the rear door and got his laptop out. When he straightened, he noticed an old white Chevy Caprice with dark tinted windows creeping into a parking space across the street. He couldn't say why, but the car made him uneasy. He stepped into the open front door, then bent down and said, "See that white Chevy?"

Karl glanced at it and nodded.

"Feel hinky about it?"

"Hinky?"

"Uneasy. Spooky."

Karl took another look. "Thousands of those things in Miami, Gavin. It's probably a decommissioned county vehicle sold at auction."

"See if you can get a plate as you go by. I want to see if it's following us. Plus, that bouncer at The Olive said the unsub drove an old white Chevy."

Karl nodded, and after Gavin swung the door shut and stepped back, pulled back onto Chopin Plaza. Gavin gave the car another look, then turned and went inside.

His suit was waiting for him, freshly dry cleaned and pressed—luckily since his second suit was now a mess. He took a cold shower, then changed into a pair of jeans and put his dirty suit out for pick up, then bent to cleaning his shoes. The whiff of swamp still lingered around them, even after they were spotless, so he walked to the balcony and set them outside the sliding door.

He set up his laptop, intent on doing some reading after he ate. Then, he ordered some dinner and called Maddie while he waited for it. "Dinner?" he said by way of a greeting.

"That depends. Do you have any strange-to-me men lurking in the background or is it safe for me to flirt?" she asked.

Gavin chuckled. "You didn't give me a chance to warn you."

"You'll notice I learned from my mistake. I'm very circumspect now. A veritable conversational nun."

"Let's not get crazy."

"I mean, did you ever wonder what they wear under those penguin suits? Could be *nothing*."

"And you call me a lech."

"Hey, a girl can't be a lech. Ever hear anyone say 'she's a dirty old lech of a woman?' No, because no one says that. It's patently ridiculous."

"I concede my argument."

"That's a much better attitude. What happened with the body?"

"Did you know the Everglades stinks?"

"Well, I mean it *is* a swamp."

"Right. The body was pretty far gone, too. We won't get much from it."

"And your Spidey-sense? How'd that work out."

"She wasn't killed there, just dumped. Not much to see. Plus, the scene was three months old."

"Ew."

"Yeah. Ew. Is that all you, the big-time writer, can come up with?"

"I save all the good stuff for my characters. Are we going to call Adeline now?"

"You want to?"

"Yeah. Your buddy left us on a cliff-hanger, interrupting her like that."

"A cliff-hanger, eh?"

"You bet. Dial."

"All right, all right, but I've got to add Karl to the call as well. Have you said all your smutty words?"

"Very funny. Dial, stud, while I put on my leather teddy."

Grinning, Gavin called both Karl and Adeline, then linked all three calls together.

"My, it's getting crowded, ain't it?" mused Adeline.

"Do you mind?" asked Karl.

"No, child," she said gently. "Not at all. I always thought Gavin would tell you anyway. This-a-way, you get to hear it straight from the horse. But, if it's all the same to you all, let's keep it at three. If I have to go through all that distrust and arguing and such-like again, I might burst me a blood vessel—though I do understand the impulse. This story ain't easy to believe if you ain't seen it yourself."

"But we want to hear it," said Maddie.

"Of course, child. Of course." She paused and hummed a little. "Let's see… Kai was busy transmitting his Morse code, right? And the blue Ford had just ripped on by me. It was difficult, but I kept them in sight, all the while trying to figure a way out of the mess."

Chapter 11
Westbound and Down

I

I-57, northeast of Charleston, MO
June 13, 1998, 6:38 pm CST

Adeline's hands and wrists ached from driving for such a long stretch without a break. She'd done her best to keep the blue Ford in view, though she'd lost them many times, necessitating a brief stop in the breakdown lane to find them remotely and ensure she was still on their trail. Her brain ached from the stress, from the concentration required to bird dog the pair of operatives, from keeping track of Kai, from avoiding killing herself and the drivers around her as her fatigue had grown and grown and grown, scattering her thoughts like a runaway freight train. Her eyes burned from the harsh summer sun reflecting off the windows of the cars around her, the meaningless chrome accents on the fancier cars, even the concrete roadway itself. Her mind was as sluggish as if she'd just woken from the nap she direly needed, but if she wanted to have a chance of rescuing Kai, she had to keep going, to marshal her strength, to utilize her gift in ways that allowed her to gain any advantage she could. She couldn't quit, couldn't rest, had to keep going, to keep chasing the blue car, hoping against hope she could intervene when they caught up with Kai.

The sun winked at her from the rear window of the Crown Vic so far ahead. She kept an eye on it, kept track of it every few seconds. She couldn't afford to lose sight of it again.

At the same time, she struggled to plan, to think of a strategy that would result in Kai's freedom. She could talk Jamilla free of the Program, but if she couldn't free Kai, what was the point? Jamilla wouldn't come, wouldn't stray from her child, and that would mean a fixer would make adjustments to her mind, her memories, her personality. Once that happened...

Adeline shook her head and tightened her expression into a thin-lipped grimace. *That will not happen. I* will *rescue Kai,* will *rescue Jamilla.*

Despite the strong, self-assured mental voice she used to tell herself that, deep in the back of her mind, a voice wailed and cried at the hopelessness of her quest.

2

U.S. Route 60, west of Sikeston, MO
June 13, 1998, 6:43 pm CST

Kai's thumb ached from transmitting his signal, his SOS, almost without pause for four hours. What's more, his brain ached from keeping the Pig distracted. Fatigue circled through his mind, distracting him, making him lose count of his dits and dahs. His eyes burned to close, to rest, his brain felt muddled, wrapped in cotton batting, but if he wanted to have any chance of being rescued, he had to keep sending out his distress call.

Reggie's mind felt muddy, too, far more exhausted than he'd been before, and Kai suspected the man was fighting him—at least on an unconscious level. The Pig's attention kept drifting from his driving, his dead eyes darting toward the passenger footwell and the cop's weapons jostling around in it. He kept fiddling with the air conditioning, muttering and grunting to himself.

It's okay, Kai sent. *Everything is* fine. *There's nothing to worry about.* For the first time, Kai felt a kind of pressure resisting his thoughts, something pushing back, and he glanced warily toward the Pig, losing count of his dits. He sucked his teeth with irritation and started over. *Dit dit dit dah dah dah dit dit dit,* he thought as he tapped out the code on the radio.

"You say something, brat?" murmured Reggie.

Never mind. It's nothing.

"Don't distract me, these idiots are trying my patience."

I won't, sent Kai, clamping down on his thoughts, trying only to send what he wanted Reggie to hear. His back hurt from jouncing against the painted metal wall, and his butt had gone to sleep hours before.

Reggie bolted up in his seat, his gaze locked on his side-view mirror. "Holy Christ," he muttered, throwing another glance at the passenger footwell.

"Kid, if you want to live out the week, keep your damn trap shut."

"What is it?"

"Cops, I think," said the Pig. "Just keep quiet back there."

Kai's spirits soared, and he took his hand off the radio, rubbing it with his other hand. *Here's my chance,* he told himself. *Don't blow it. Wait for the right time. Wait for it…*

3

I-57, east of Sikeston, MO
June 13, 1998, 6:45 pm CST

Up ahead, the Crown Vic swerved into the exit lane for I-55, still moving quite a bit faster than the legal limit. Adeline flicked on her turn signal and got over into the outside lane, maintaining her speed. Gritting her teeth, she swerved onto the shoulder and whipped around a slow-moving car. She couldn't afford to lose the Ford because she didn't drive fast enough.

The blue sedan swerved out of the exit lane, evoking a symphony of car horns and shrieking tires. "What are you doing now?" she muttered, regaining the outside travel lane.

But then she saw it—the nondescript white van bumping along in the slow lane. Her heart swelled even as her stomach shrank with fear and anxiety.

The blue Crown Victoria arrowed straight toward the van.

4

U.S. Route 60, west of Sikeston, MO
June 13, 1998, 6:47 pm CST

Unease wrapped its cold arms around Kai's guts and squeezed. The Pig had slowed down, had started driving carefully, making sure to signal, to perform every action as smooth as cream. If the cops had found them, they weren't closing in. But if they hadn't, why was the Pig acting that way? Kai put his hand on the police-band radio and began to tap out SOS with the microphone button again.

"Motherfuck!" shouted the Pig. He floored the accelerator pedal, and the van's engine roared.

No, no, sent Kai. *There's nothing behind you. No cops.*

Reggie tore his gaze from the road ahead and peered into the wing mirror. He lifted his foot off the floor.

You want to get out and stretch your legs. You want to pull over to the side of the road.

Flicking on the turn signal, the Pig glanced across at the other side view mirror, then began to pull to the shoulder. "Got to stretch my legs," he muttered.

That's right. There's no one behind us, no one chasing us. This is the perfect time to pull over and rest.

The Pig put his foot on the brake pedal and brought the van to a rocking stop. He shoved the gear selector into park, then turned off the ignition. The van rocked as a car sped past, then tires shrieked.

Kai jumped up and stared out the front windshield. A blue Crown Victoria was parked at an angle in front of the van, and a gigantic man with a crew cut had the passenger door propped open, a wicked-looking black rifle pointed at the van. The Pig had his hands up, his door open, one leg dangling.

"Driver!" shouted the man with the rifle. "Step out of the van and keep your hands where I can see them!"

Kai froze in place, his mind a complete blank as the Pig nudged the door wide open and slid out of his seat.

"Turn around! Walk backward toward the sound of my voice!"

Reggie edged around the door and backed toward the blue car.

Are they cops? Kai asked himself. *Looks like a cop car.*

"Stop there! Down on your knees!"

"Hey, man, I can't get down on my knees without putting my hands down. I've got a bad back."

"Down! Now!"

The Pig's gaze skipped over to Kai's, and his expression was so dark, so hateful, that the boy knew if Reggie somehow talked his way out of the situation, Kai was unlikely to make it to wherever he was supposed to be going. He backed toward the rear of the van, feet scuffing across the metal floor.

The guy with the rifle stood up, still pointing the gun at the Pig, and walked toward the van. The driver of the blue car also got out, but his focus was on the van, not Reggie.

For some reason, that scared Kai more than the thought of the Pig beating him up.

5

U.S. Route 60, west of Sikeston, MO
June 13, 1998, 6:52 pm CST

Adeline let the Pathfinder idle up the shoulder, her foot hovering over the brake, her heart in her throat. The van sat idling on the side of the road, and the fat man driving had gotten out and backed around the front with his hands up. She could see the tail of the blue Crown Vic sticking out at an angle from in front of the van.

She brought the Pathfinder to a jerky stop, then put on the parking brake and took it out of gear. Her hands were shaking so much she could hardly get the door open. Without checking for traffic, she stepped out and immediately hunched over.

"Don't you move, big man."

"Where would I go? I haven't done anything, Officer."

Trying to make as little noise as possible, she crept forward toward the van's rear doors. She put her hand on the door handle and pulled.

6

U.S. Route 60, west of Sikeston, MO
June 13, 1998, 6:54 pm CST

Kai backed up until his shoulder blades brushed against the rear doors. His heart thudded in his chest, his gaze locked on the man on the far side of the blue car, and the inside of his head feeling funny...*itchy*. The police-band radio dropped from his hand and clunked on the floor of the van, but Kai didn't notice.

He wanted to try his new trick on the man—what he'd done to the Pig, to tell the man he wasn't interested in Kai at all, but a curious blank—a strange apathy—had stolen over him.

When the door behind him sprang open, he fell backward, enervated and uncaring.

7

Adeline pulled the door open, then squawked as Kai fell toward her. She threw out her arms, grabbing the boy under his arms and keeping him from going headfirst onto the pavement. Pain exploded through her lower back as she took his weight.

"The boy!"

She knew who the voice belonged to—sometimes it happened that way after a remote viewing through someone else's eyes. It was Mr. Buzz-cut's partner, the driver. "Kai!" she whispered. "Get to the truck!" She pulled him, but his legs dragged out behind, and his eyes rolled in his head. She jerked on him, hard, and her back sang out again. "*Help me, boy*!" she cried.

"Forget that idiot! Get back there!"

"Hey, I'm—" That came from Kai's tormentor.

"Shut up!"

Adeline heard feet pounding on pavement and another set thudding through grass on the shoulder. A burst of adrenaline gave her the strength to wrench Kai up and around, setting him on his feet, pointing him at the Pathfinder, then giving him a strong shove toward the passenger side. "Get in! Get in, Kai!"

She hustled to the driver's door and jerked it open, throwing one terrified glance toward the van. Mr. Buzz-cut stood at the back corner of the van, his gaze drilling into her own, the AR-15 halfway to his shoulder. She threw out a hand, palm up and toward the man, commanding him to stop, then jumped into the SUV.

A thunk came from the passenger side, and she threw a glance that way. Kai stood there, staring at her intently. Then he jiggled the door handle again.

"Oh!" She pressed the unlock button with her left hand and reached for the gear shifter with her right. Her gaze jumped from Kai toward the back of the van. The driver of the Crown Vic sprinted from the shoulder-side of the van, his gaze burning a hole in Kai as the boy slung himself into the vehicle.

Adeline slammed the gas pedal to the floor, then popped the clutch. The Pathfinder's tires shrieked as the SUV launched itself backward.

Both men from the Crown Vic sprinted toward them, both lifting their firearms to fire. Behind them, standing by the passenger door of the van, stood Kai's ersatz captor, pistol in hand.

"Get down!" she shouted at Kai and wrenched the wheel. The Pathfinder slid into a J-turn, leaving the front of the SUV pointed at the grassy median separating the westbound and eastbound lanes. She thumped the shifter, putting the Pathfinder into first, and popped the clutch while still moving backward. The tires shrieked and smoked but then caught, and they rocketed across the westbound lanes of U.S. Route 60 before bouncing into the median.

The men shouted behind her, but she didn't wait, cranking the wheel instead and keeping the gas pedal on the mat.

A shot rang out, and Adeline ducked out of instinct, then turned to look behind them. Mr. Buzz-cut was sprinting alongside the van, his AR-15 at port arms. Kai's captor stood at the rear corner of the van, smoke curling from the cop's pistol. The driver of the Crown Vic stood a handful of paces away, one arm extended, fingers curling into claws, his other arm flared from his side. The pistol began to shake, its business end wavering back and forth, up and down.

Ever so slowly, the gunman's elbow flexed, and as it did, he torqued his wrist in an attempt to keep the gun pointed in the right direction. But as his elbow passed ninety degrees, the pistol snapped up and back as if on its own. The van driver cried out as he rammed the pistol into his cheek below his right eye. He shook his head frantically, then red mist exploded out the back of his head, and the pistol's report crashed through the air as the fat man collapsed like a ragdoll. The driver of the blue Ford relaxed, his arms dropping to his sides, though his gaze never left the pulp, blood, and bone-flecked brains that fanned across the shoulder of the road. He took an exaggerated step, careful not to put his feet in the gore.

"Who…" muttered Kai.

"Shh, now, baby," said Adeline absently. Her attention was on the blue Ford and the men running toward it. Mr. Buzz-cut had sprinted around the back of it, going for the driver's door, just as the other man emerged from the van's shadow.

"That man…" said Kai. "He… Is he a cop?"

"No, baby, he's no cop."

"Then—*LOOK OUT!*"

Adeline jerked her head around, just in time to see the ditch, but not in time to avoid it. The Pathfinder plowed down the slope, then slammed into the opposite bank, hitting so hard that the rear tires leaped skyward, and the engine stalled. Her head snapped forward, smashing her into the inflated airbag, and everything went black.

8

U.S. Route 60, west of Sikeston, MO
June 13, 1998, 7:28 pm CST

Kai moaned as he regained consciousness. His face burned, and his neck felt like a gorilla had stepped on it. Something warm and sticky coated his lips and dripped from his chin. For a moment, and exactly one moment, he thought he was at home, that he'd woken from one of his special nightmares and had a nosebleed, but then he remembered the Pig. He raised his hand to wipe away the blood but couldn't lift his arms.

"Kid's waking up," said a gruff voice.

"He's a tough one," said another, higher, and sounding like it came over the radio. "But he won't be any trouble."

Kai froze and tried to control his breathing, listening hard. When he identified the familiar rumble of the van's engine, of the vehicle's heavy-duty tires on pavement, his heart sank to his guts. *Something happened*, he thought. *The Pig… That doesn't sound like his voice.*

It's not Reggie, Kai, said a voice in his head.

He couldn't say why, but he associated that mental voice with the second man who'd spoken—the one with the high voice.

That's correct. And you needn't worry about the Pig. Not anymore.

"What…" His own voice in his ears started a cacophony of thudding pain in his head, and he groaned.

Shh, now. You've had a rough go, and the old woman slamming head-on into that embankment hasn't helped matters.

Miss Adeline! Kai thought and panic followed.

It's okay*, Kai*, said the voice in his head. *She's fine. She's right next to you back there.*

"I'm telling you, he's waking up," said the rough voice.

The radio crackled with static for half a heartbeat. "Anton, listen to me. I've got it under control."

"You're not the one he's going to squash if he gets it in his mind, Chavez."

Chavez, thought Kai. *That's you?*

Yes. I'm in the car following the van.

And Anton?

Adeline called him Mr. Buzz-cut. Don't worry about him. He's muscle—purely physical. The radio crackled again. "Listen to me, Anton. Kai's a good kid. Operations fucked up sending Reggie. He was...*weak.* The kid called him 'the *Pig.*' Can you believe it?"

"Out of the mouths of babes," said Anton with a low chuckle. "Glad you scratched that waste of flesh out."

He's... Reggie's...gone?

Gone for good, Kai.

Wuh... Kai swallowed hard. *Why?*

You think I should have let him go on living? An untrained eleven-year-old took control of his mind— what possible use could we have for him now? Besides, you were inside his head. You know *what he was.*

Yeah. Kai sighed.

You're not going to make a liar of me, are you? asked Chavez.

What do you mean?

You'll stay out of Anton's head. It wasn't a question, rather a command. *You'll leave him alone and let us deliver you to a place of safety.*

Where?

A school. A special school for special kids—kids like you. Like I was back in the day.

Kai sniffed and opened his eyes. Adeline lay trussed up on the floor next to him. *Why is Miss Adeline all tied up?*

Sometimes, Kai, adults can lose sight of what's best for a child they love. Especially someone as sweet as Adeline. What she was trying to do—to hide you away from us, to keep you from attending the school I told you about—would've been very bad for you in the long run.

Bad? Bad how?

You'll learn all that later on. For now, can you trust me that I'm working in your best interest? That I'm your friend?

Kai felt a strange pressure building behind his eyes. *Don't push.*

He had the sense Chavez was laughing as he answered. *No, I won't push you. You're a gem, Kai. I can't wait to start teaching you.*

You're… You're a teacher? In the school?

That's right. Adeline was too, in years past.

Kai looked at the woman he called Miss Adeline, and for the first time, he wondered about her past. White-haired, and covered in more wrinkles than a prune, she never seemed able to give consistent answers about her age, about when, exactly, she'd grown up. It seemed there were other things she kept secret.

He didn't know what to think about that.

I'm too tired, he sent to Chavez.

Too tired?

To make trouble with Anton. I think I'll sleep some if I can.

Do that, champ. And don't worry. Anton and I won't let a thing happen to you. To either of you.

Yeah, okay, sent Kai, his eyes already drifting shut.

9

Sonoran Desert, Southwestern AZ
June 14, 1998, 11:27 am CST

Kai grumbled and tried to roll away from the insistent hand that shook him gently. "Lemme 'lone," he murmured, his mind sluggish with sleep.

Come on, champ. Time to wake up.

"Let me sleep," he groaned.

Can't do that, champ. We're here. We're home.

The scene from the roadside flashed through his mind's eye. The man from the blue car holding a claw-hand out toward Reggie, the gun in the fat man's hand twisting around, then slapping against his skull before it went off, scattering everything Reggie was in the wind. Shaking his head, Kai blinked his eyes open, seeing only the wall of the damn van he'd spent the last couple of days in, then scrubbed his eyes with the palms of his hands. He drew in a deep breath and flopped over.

Adeline was gone, and the side door was open. The ineffective dome light burned, but it couldn't penetrate the darkness outside. Chavez squatted beside him, smiling a little.

"Where's Miss Adeline?"

Don't worry about her, Chavez sent. *She's being seen to. Come on, sleepyhead. It's time to get moving. Lots to do, lots to learn.*

Kai grunted and sat up. "What time is it?"

Almost noon.

"Wow, I really slept."

Chavez grinned down at him and patted him on the back. *You exerted a lot of energy.*

"How did you…"

Chavez lost his pleasant grin. *How did I make Reggie shoot himself?*

Kai shrugged and looked down.

I'm a telecheiristiric—as I think you may be.

"A telecheri…" Kai shook his head. *I don't know what that means.*

Chavez took his arm and pulled him to his feet. *It means my gifts allow me to control other people remotely. It means I can make their bodies do what I want, regardless of what* they *want.*

Oh. And you think I'm a telechair… He blew out a frustrated breath, and Chavez laughed.

It is a mouthful. All it means is "remote controller." He tilted his head to the side and smiled. *Have you ever seen a puppet show?*

Of course, said Kai.

Chavez nodded. *My power is like the rig a puppeteer uses to control the puppets. You know, the funny-shaped handle with strings that connect it to a puppet's body.*

Kai nodded. *Telecheiristic.*

Not quite. Telecheiristiric. Chavez grinned. *But other members of the Program call me and people like me puppeteers.*

Oh, I get it. Kai cocked his head and looked at Chavez askance. *And you think I'm a puppeteer? Why?*

I don't know *that's your calling, not for sure, but the way you manipulated fat Reggie Capstrom makes me think so.*

Kai couldn't help but think about the Pig, about the things he'd made Reggie do.

You're a good judge of character, champ. The Pig, that's priceless.

My name's Kai, sent Kai, bristling a little. *The Pig never called me by name. He was always calling me 'kid,' or something.*

No offense, Kai, sent Chavez. *I'm not much like old Piggy. You'll find that out as we go.* He glanced through the open sliding door. *We need to get moving, cha—Kai. People are waiting to meet you.*

What people?

Other people from the Program. People like me, like you. *In the Program, you won't have to hide your talent.*

Here, almost everyone is like you and me, at least to some degree. The untalented are the minority around here. With one hand on his shoulder, Chavez led Kai to the door, then urged him forward.

Kai stepped out of the van and looked around. Other vehicles—some vans, some cars, some big rigs, some 4x4 trucks—hulked in the shadows around the Pig's van. The blue four-door Ford stood nose to nose with the van. The floor beneath them was concrete, as was the ceiling, and massive concrete pillars dotted the large area. *It's…it's a garage?*

You got it, Kai. Chavez came to stand behind him once more and rested his hand on the boy's bony shoulder.

Who owns all these cars and junk?

The Program. We use them as we need to.

To bring in more kids like me?

Sure, sent Chavez. *And other things. This is a school, like I said, but graduates of the school do other things for the people who provided all this to us.*

What people? asked Kai.

President Truman started the Program way back in ancient history. We call it "the Program" because the official name is beyond top-secret. Only the President and a few trusted advisors know the name these days. Well, and all of us.

Kai's brows bunched. *I've never heard of President Truman.*

Chavez shrugged. *It doesn't matter. All that happened like fifty years ago.* He started guiding Kai through the shadowy garage. *When it started, the government controlled what the Program did. In the fifties, the Central Intelligence Agency took control of the program, but after the MKUltra fiasco, people like us took over.*

People like us.

You got it, Kai. People with talents like yours, like mine.

Puppeteers?

Chavez shook his head. *Not all of us are puppeteers. Didn't Adeline ever talk to you about all this?*

Kai shook his head, eyes downcast. *None of us talked about my episodes.*

Chavez stopped and pulled Kai around to face him as the man knelt. *Listen to me, Kai. That shame you feel when you talk about your gift is the vestige of the jealousy of so-called normal people, of a society of talentless people, of physicals. You have nothing to be ashamed of. Your talent is your best asset, not something to hide under a bushel.*

"Okay," Kai said without looking up.

Chavez hesitated a moment, kneeling in front of the boy, both hands on his shoulders, then stood and walked Kai into the Compound.

10

Jamilla bent to wring out her mop, and when she straightened, she saw Kai through the one-way glass. A man she'd never seen before walked by his side, though he looked familiar, one hand on his shoulder, his grip seeming possessive to her. For a moment, she bristled, but then the feeling faded, replaced by a sense of dull interest.

Kai was her son, yet she felt curiously flat at seeing him. Her emotions barely twitched, and mostly it was surprise. She cocked her head as she watched him walk down the brilliant white hallway on the other side of the mirrored glass. She felt no motivation to bang on the glass, no instinct to run to him, no urge to find a way to reach him, no desire to speak to him. Instead, she felt a vague sense of satisfaction that Kai had arrived, that he'd finally be able to start his real education.

She watched the boy for a moment longer, then turned her attention to her mop and got on with her work. She never saw him glance her way.

11

Kai felt a vague tickle as they walked down the hall, Chavez's hand on his shoulder. He couldn't place the feeling, though he felt drawn to look at the floor-to-ceiling mirror on his left. He saw nothing there but Chavez's and his own reflections. After a moment, he shrugged and turned his attention toward the front, though he couldn't help but feel a vague sense of loss, and his eyes teared up a little. *Silly*, he thought. *You're tired from the past couple of days, that's all.*

Chavez gave his shoulder a squeeze, a small smile on his face. *Feeling a little overwhelmed?*

Kai nodded. *I guess so.*

You've been through a lot these past two days. You've seen and heard things that might have broken most eleven-year-olds. But you've come out the other side of your trials. You are stronger for it, Kai.

Again, the boy nodded.

Chavez's hand left his shoulder as they reached the door at the end of the bright white hallway, and Kai found himself missing the man's touch. After punching a code into the keypad set in the wall next to the door, Chavez smiled down at him, then ruffled his hair. "Are you ready to get on with the *best* part of your life, Kai?"

Kai smiled in return and nodded.

Chavez pushed the door open and waved Kai through.

12

The Compound, under the Sonoran Desert, AZ
June 14, 1998, 11:47 am MST

Adeline d'Clara groaned and brought her hands up to bookend the throbbing mass of pain and sick that sat atop her shoulders. She sensed a bright light through her closed eyelids, and the last thing her aching head wanted was bright. Besides, one eyelid seemed matted shut. She turned her head to the side, gasping at the burst of fiery pain that raced up and down her spine.

Leaving one hand to cover her eyes, she put the other behind her neck and prodded it tenderly. Wherever she touched, she felt a horrible hot zing of fiery shock radiating away. She drew in a breath and hissed it back out. Her head felt stuffed as though she'd come down with the nastiest flu the world had to offer, and her hissing breath sounded far away.

The air smelled…*different*. Drier. Spicy. She refused to accept what that implied.

"Kai?" she croaked. "Child? Are you there?"

When the boy didn't answer, Adeline groaned again. She rolled to her side, moving one body part at a time, at a snail's pace because every movement, no matter how small, sent waves of hot agony shivering through her head and neck. That done, she lay there a moment, doing nothing but breathing while the pain crawled back down to its original level. She rubbed her eyes with her thumb and forefinger, brushing away the crud that held her eyelid shut with the gentle pressure of a woman who had raised three children. She opened her eyes the barest of slivers and winced at the onslaught of light that seemed to surround her. She blinked and blinked as her eyes watered and ran.

Hello, Adeline. The voice cauterized her mind like white-hot metal.

"Speak aloud, Beatrice. You're hurting me."

A door opened across the small square room, and the blonde woman entered, letting the door swing shut behind her. "I guess you've had an exciting couple of days." She blinked down at Adeline for a moment. "For all the good it did you."

Adeline sniffed and closed her eyes. "I had an agreement with—"

"Not my concern, Miss Addy."

Adeline tried to sit up, but the room swam and spun, and she lay back, groaning.

"Concussion," said Beatrice. "Airbags saved your life."

"Kai?"

"Not *your* concern, Miss Addy."

"He's—"

"*Not your concern.*"

Adeline sighed. "Is the boy hurt?"

The sound of Beatrice's heel clacking on the concrete floor hammered at Adeline's ears. "He's fine. Jamilla's fine."

Adeline groaned and peeked under her lowered eyelids. "Has she been…"

"That's also not your concern, Miss Addy."

"They're family," insisted Adeline.

"*We're* your family. Have you forgotten?"

"Blood. They're blood-family."

Beatrice sniffed and tossed her hair to one side. "Does that mean so much? Poor Bethany fell to pieces when she heard what you tried to do."

The chuckle escaped Adeline before she knew it was coming. "Bethany has never fallen to pieces about anything in her life."

"She cried, Miss Addy."

Adeline scoffed. "No, she didn't."

Beatrice shrugged, and one corner of her mouth curled up. "She said she *should've* cried, but you're right. No tears fell."

"The Man promised me that—"

"Miss Addy, stop. You know that even if I knew all the details, there's not a thing I can do."

Adeline tried to sit up again, and this time, Beatrice helped her. "But there are things you can do. You and Bethany, both."

"Like?"

Turning to look the younger woman in the eye, Adeline said, "For one, you can stay out of Jamilla's head."

Beatrice's gaze flicked away. "Jamilla chose to come. Bethany gave her—"

"A choice between death and coming on staff," said Adeline. "I know how it works." She put a finger under Beatrice's chin and turned the woman's face toward her. "And I know what it means when you look away. You could reverse it."

Pursing her lips, Beatrice shook her head once. "Stop this, Miss Addy. You know the rules as well as any of us."

Sudden fury flamed in Adeline's veins. "That's right, I do. And I'll tell you what else, I was there when President Truman formed the working group tasked with investigating, and ultimately developing, psionic ability. I was there when the CIA wrenched control from the MJ12 committee. I watched in horror as they took the Program and warped it to suit them. I watched them start with the drugs, with the *mind control* experiments, and I watched them blunder their way into the public eye. I was there—I *helped* pick up the pieces. I've always been here, girl. I know the guidelines, the protocols, because I helped *write* them. The Man knew just as well as I do. That's why he made our agreement." Beatrice tried to turn her face away, but Adeline grabbed her chin and held her fast. "Kai *doesn't* have to be a part of the Program. *I* can help him through his awakening. Jamilla *doesn't* have to be here. She's lived this long in the wild, she can go on just as she was. You *can* help. It *is* your concern. It is because you have the position, the authority, the *power*, to help me get them away from here before it's too late."

Beatrice stared back at her as Adeline chased her breath. Her green-eyed gaze seemed empty—empty of compassion, empty of pity, empty of empathy.

"And that look you're giving me, child," Adeline said softly. "That's the perfect proof of why you should be helping me. Kai's a good boy, a kind, helpful, loving child."

The blonde woman wrenched her chin out of Adeline's hand and straightened, rising to her full height. "Did you have these second thoughts when you found *us*? Where was your concern twenty-three years ago, Miss Addy? Did you insist the Program leaders at that time leave *our* parents alone, or did they come here to work in the shadows, always hidden away from Bethany and me? Or did you allow their assassinations?"

"Child, I—"

"I haven't been a child for a long time, Adeline d'Clara. For about twenty-three years."

"Fine. Beatrice, I can't argue with you. I can't justify everything I've done in my life. I can't—"

"No, you can't," said Beatrice in a voice devoid of emotion. "But do you know what? I *can*. You did the right thing when you bird dogged Bethany and me.

Whatever happened to our parents, you did the right thing. I've been through the Program, Miss Addy. I remember the day I walked down that bright white hallway and stepped through the door. I remember, and I *approve*. So does Bethany. *All* the graduates of the Program approve. Would you like to know why?"

Adeline struggled against the hopelessness, against the enervation that assaulted her. "Why?" she croaked.

"Because you were *right*—you and the others—when you developed the protocols and the rules and the guidelines. *You were right, Adeline d'Clara.*"

Eyes sliding shut, Adeline released a pent-up breath she hadn't realized she was holding. Her shoulders slumped, her head sagged forward, and her arms flopped to her lap. "No, Beatrice," she whispered—*begged*, "I was wrong."

"Miss Addy…" Beatrice put her hand on Adeline's shoulder. "This—your actions, this passionate entreaty, everything you've done in the past two and half days—is nothing more than *fear*."

Adeline shook her head.

"It *is*, Miss Addy. You fear for Jamilla, you fear for Kai. But we do too, Bethany and me. We want what's best for them, even if you disagree as to what is best. *We* aren't hampered by emotions, by the sense of family that drives you. We know the Program is our family. And Jamilla does too, I've already made sure of that. Kai will learn it on his own."

"No. *Please*, no."

"Yes, Miss Addy," said Beatrice in a curiously tender voice. "The question is what happens to you. You know we can't allow you to pivot away from us. You're too strong, too powerful, too skilled, too *knowledgeable* about our practices. You know all this. As you said, you helped write the protocols, including Protocol One."

There it is, thought Adeline sourly. *The stick... Next, she'll trot out the carrot. She says she understands my role in this wretched place, yet she doesn't seem to understand I know what she's doing, that I authored the strategy she's following.* She shook her head.

"Adeline, we *need* you. You are the last surviving member of the original MJ12. You are the longest active operative in Program history. We can't afford to waste you."

Go on, girl. Stop pussyfooting around and dangle it.

"I've spoken with the Man—with Sam." Beatrice chuckled a little. "He was very hard to convince, but I managed. I'm still not really sure how I convinced him." She shook her head and flashed a little half-grin at Adeline. "I told him how much we could use you— here, I mean. Here in the Compound. Think of the young people you could help with your knowledge, your expertise, your *experience*. You could continue to help operations—the great thing about your gift is that you can bird dog from anywhere." Beatrice squatted in front of her again. "And Adeline, if you are *here*, you can still be a part of Kai's life. You can see Jamilla, talk to her. If you make Sam take the other choice, both will be on their own. You know that."

Adeline sighed, feeling defeated. *Maybe she does know what she's doing.*

13

A dark place
June 14, 1998

As if someone flipped a switch, Kai opened his eyes, regaining consciousness in one mad rush, rather than in gentle stages the way he usually woke up. He lay on something cold and hard—like concrete or maybe natural stone. He opened his eyes, but impenetrable darkness surrounded him. He glanced upward, looking for stars or a ceiling or *anything*, but could see only more darkness. The last thing he remembered was meeting a blonde woman with green eyes, Chavez smiling down at him, his hand on Kai's shoulder.

"Hello?" he said. No one answered him, not even the echo of his own voice. He lifted a hand in front of his face but couldn't see it. "Hello!" he shouted. "Mommy? Chavez?" When no answering call came, Kai sat up, fighting a sudden vertigo. His head pounded with each beat of his heart, and a tinge of nausea undulated in his guts.

He rolled to his hands and knees, then had to stop and wait—eyes pressed shut, head hanging, mouth open and sucking in cool air—for the dizziness to subside. When he could, he crawled in the direction he faced. The cold surface below his hands and knees felt smooth and regular. *Concrete, then,* he told himself. "Turn on the lights!" he yelled. "I can't see anything!"

Again, no one answered him.

He kept moving forward, hoping to find a wall he could follow around to a door or a light switch. His mind kept wandering back to the green-eyed woman and her somehow captivating gaze. Her eyes had drawn him with the irresistible pull of a magnet, but after meeting her gaze, everything was blank until he woke up. *What is this? Some kind of test? Am I supposed to find my way out?*

He put his right hand out in front of him, expecting more cold concrete but feeling nothing. He sat back on his knees and dropped his hand onto the concrete immediately in front of him. He pushed his hand forward, moving at a slow, steady pace until he found the edge.

He leaned over it carefully, stretching his hand down, hoping to feel a staircase or a ladder but feeling only cold air. His brows knotted, and he sat back on his knees again. "Hello? I found the edge over here. What am I supposed to do now?"

He began moving even as he spoke the last couple of words, no longer expecting an answer. He turned and crawled parallel to the edge with more care than he had originally, counting each time he moved his knees forward. He'd reached six when he felt another edge that ran perpendicular to the first. The corner where the two edges met was sharp and crisp. He backed up, turned around, then lay flat on the cold surface, inching his way back, holding his legs stiff behind him, feeling for another platform with his toes. When he couldn't hold his legs straight any longer, he bent at the hip and reached downward, but there was nothing below that he could reach.

He turned to his left and began crawling again, this time confirming that the edge was arrow straight on his right. He counted his "steps" again and reached fifteen when he found the next corner. He tested the corner as he had the first one, then moved on, following the new edge. He repeated the process twice more—the concrete made a rectangle ten by fifteen "steps" and a chasm he couldn't feel the bottom of by reaching down surrounded it.

At the final corner, he plunked down on his rear, hanging one leg off on each side of the platform, the well-defined corner between them. "What do I do now?" he called. *Chavez?* he sent. *Miss Adeline? Mommy?* he sent, putting a little more effort behind the words. He listened with both his ears and his mind, but no answer came.

With a loud sigh, Kai crawled back to what he judged was the center of the platform and curled up on his side.

14

A dark place
June 14, 1998

Kai rocked in the rear of the van, his shoulder blades rubbing against the bloody metal walls. In the front of the van, the Pig hummed some old song from the sixties—snapping with both hands rhythmically. The tires hummed along on the asphalt, an accompaniment to the Pig's song.

Kai couldn't get a sense of the length of his imprisonment, but the Pig knew. The knowledge was just sitting inside his fat head, but Kai rebelled at the thought of touching his sick mind.

"People are strange…" sang the Pig. His gaze snapped to the rearview mirror, and he narrowed his eyelids at Kai. "What did you say?"

Kai shook his head. "Nothing."

The driver's seat creaked as the Pig swiveled his fat-jowled face around to peer into the back. As his head turned, the back of his skull fell off and clattered to the floor between the seats. Kai couldn't help but look down, a sick fascination momentarily overcoming the morbid dread the chunk of bone evoked. When he raised his gaze again, the Pig had somehow moved from the driver's seat into the rear compartment and stood three feet *away, breathing hard, face contorted with rage, mouth agape to show off the black-ringed hole in the top of his mouth.*

"If you pull any funny business, I'll make you pay and pay and pay," said the big man.

"I—" Kai's voice turned into a squeak as the Pig bent at the waist, shoving his forehead into Kai's.

"Don't you make me run, you little shit," growled the Pig.

"I'll be good," said Kai. "I promise."

"Yeah, we both know that's bullshit. You're going to get me killed."

"I—"

"Nah. Don't bother lying. The proof is right here." With that, the Pig shoved a pudgy index finger into the hole in the roof of his mouth.

Kai turned his face away, squeezing his eyes shut. "I didn't do that to you, Reggie."

"I didn't do that to you, Reggie," the Pig said in a ragged singsong. "Well, who the fuck do you think shot me in the mouth, rugrat?"

"You did," said Kai in an almost inaudible voice. "With the cop's gun. You pulled it on Chavez and—" White-hot pain exploded across his face, and for a moment, his vision faded to a dull red. Bright red blood exploded from his nose and coated the wall.

"Now you'll just have to bleed and lay in it," said the Pig. As he spoke, his voice dropped through the registers, ending in a basso growl so low that Kai felt it rumble in

his guts. "Don't you ever say his name to me! Do you hear me, boy?"

Kai forced his eyes open, forced his gaze up, up, up to meet Reggie's hot glare, forced his mind inside the Pig's head.

"Yeah, that won't work, you little bastard." The Pig pirouetted on one pointed toe, stopping with his back to Kai. "Don't you remember?" He lifted a ham-sized fist over his shoulder and stuck it inside his head through the massive hole left by the back of his skull.

Kai opened his mouth to scream...

15

A dark place
June 14, 1998

Kai awoke, his heart thundering in his ears, the image of Reggie standing there with his fist inside his skull lodged in his mind like a cherry pit swallowed by accident. He shuddered at the memory of the nightmare, knowing it for a dream but still trapped in the reality of it.

"Chavez! Where are you?" he cried with all his might.

After thirty seconds without an answer, Kai rolled over to his other side, his head cradled on his arm. "Fine," he muttered. "I'll just lay here."

16

A dark place
June 14, 1998

Kai rocked in the rear of the van, his shoulder blades rubbing against the bloody metal walls. In the front of the van, the Pig hummed some old song from the sixties—snapping with both hands rhythmically. The tires hummed along on the asphalt, an accompaniment to the Pig's song.

"Hey, kid?" rasped a voice from behind him.

Kai turned toward the sound, then screamed at the top of his lungs. Eye to empty eye socket, he screamed in the female police officer's bloody, bone-flecked face. He shoved himself away from her, but she advanced an inch for every inch he scooted away.

"Why'd you do this to me, kid?" the dead cop asked. "Why'd you pick me?"

"People are strange, when you're a stranger..." sang the Pig.

"I-I-I thuh-thought you'd rescue me. I—"

The Pig's gaze snapped to the rearview mirror, and he narrowed his eyelids at Kai. "What did you say?"

As though she hadn't heard Reggie, the cop asked, "Yeah, I know, kid, but my question is, why'd you pick me? What did I ever do to you?"

"I didn't pick you," whispered Kai, darting a peek over his shoulder at the gaping hole in the back of Reggie's head. "I called for help, and you heard me."

The dead cop sucked her split and broken teeth, then spat blood on the wall. "Well, shit, kid. You pulled some funny business, and he made *me* pay for it. Where's the justice in that?"

"I'm sorry," said Kai.

"What did you say?" asked Reggie, so close his fetid breath tickled Kai's ear.

Kai jumped and tore his gaze away from the dead police officer, turning his face toward the front. Reggie's eight-ball eyes seemed ready to swallow him, to drown him in blood. "Nuh-nothing. I was talking to her, not you, Reggie."

Like an animated figure in reverse motion, Reggie ambled back to the driver's seat. "Oh. Sorry to interrupt," he said.

When Kai turned back to the police officer, her face had rotted off and fallen into her lap. Utter blackness filled the holes in her skull—eyes, nose, and, except for the cracked, split teeth, her mouth.

"I don't think she's up for conversation anymore," said Reggie in a ragged singsong. "It's just you and me, champ."

Before his eyes, the police officer began to come apart, skin sloughing off her bones like water off a rain slicker, her already exposed skull crumbling to dust.

"I'm sorry!" Kai screamed. "I'm so sorry!"

17

A dark place
June 14, 1998

Kai came awake, cheeks wet with salty tears, a sob wrenching itself loose from his chest, the nightmare image of the female cop disintegrating replaying on a loop in his mind's eye. "I'm so sorry," he muttered. "I didn't know he'd come out. I didn't know he'd kuh-kill you. I th-thought you'd arrest him. I th-thought yuh-you'd *save* me." He cried for a few minutes, then swiped his tears away with angry jerks of his arms. "Anyway, I'm the one who should be mad. I'm *eleven*! I was kidnapped! You're the damn cop! Why didn't you rescue me?" He sat up, pulled his legs up under him, wrapped his arms around himself, and rocked— as he had done so many times when he dreamed about his father who had died in Iraq.

A thought struck him—one that drilled through his sadness like a hot bit through ice. *Maybe,* an evil hiss of a voice whispered within him, *this is your punishment for the cop. Ever hear of just desserts, Kai? Do you think that cop, buried in that park, dirt over her eyes, feels like this?*

He rejected the voice, rejected the thought, but even so, a part of him believed just that.

"Mommy! Miss Adeline!" he shouted as loud as he could. "Chavez!" Frustration sang in his mind, leaked into his blood. *Chavez!* he sent. *You promised to* help *me!*

But as before, no one answered him. The sobs came, then, rolling through him with the force of a hurricane. He *hated* being alone, *feeling* alone. *Where is everyone? If it was so damn important to get me here, why have you left me to rot?*

Inside, in the very back of his mind, something reptilian rolled over. A small voice said, *There's an easy way out. You know what it is.*

"No!" Kai screamed.

18

A dark place
June 15, 1998

Kai didn't know how long he'd been sitting there, but it felt like hour upon hour upon yet more hours. He thought it was late—his stomach had that borderline queasiness he associated with three in the morning, and his eyes felt gritty—but he'd decided not to sleep. Not now, not ever again.

Sleeping led to dreams. *Dreams can just suck it*, he thought miserably. *Mommy*! *Mommy, where are you*? he broadcast the thought as loud and as far as he knew how, but as with his shouts, the sending felt funny—as though something absorbed it as soon as he sent it out.

He balled his fists and pounded the unyielding surface he sat on, striking out at the concrete, again and again, until his hands burned, his wrists throbbed, and his elbows ached.

Chavez! he sent, again using as much power as he knew how. He wanted to break things, to bring down the walls of the strange prison he found himself in. He wanted to destroy, to rend limbs, to scratch out eyes, to scream in someone's face the way Reggie had screamed in his in the dreams. He bottled those feelings up, held them tight, poured more anger, more frustration, more loneliness into the ball of fury he held, and when it was full, when he could pack nothing else inside without choking on it, he imagined it exploding like a bomb, wave after wave of force expanding outward from him in concentric circles.

Chavez! he screamed in his mind.

But none of it worked. No one answered. No one cared that he was hurting. Not the green-eyed woman, not Chavez. Not his mother, not Miss Adeline.

No one.

19

A dark place
June 16, 1998

Kai stood staring into the utter absence of light that surrounded him, arms crossed over his chest. He'd stopped listening for any noise a long time ago, and he'd stopped trying to raise the alarm. *Have to face it*, he told himself. *I'm all alone. No one cares that I'm lost in this…this…fucking place.* He didn't waste energy on feeling bad for his language. "Fuck, fuck, fuck, fuck, fuck," he sang. No one could hear him.

Or if they could, they didn't care enough to listen.

"*CHAVEZ*!" he thought-screamed.

His stomach felt as though someone had stuffed glowing coals down his throat, which had become so dry it hurt. He'd stopped trying to gauge the length of his imprisonment, had given up on figuring out what they wanted from him—whoever they were.

If Chavez won't talk to me, I'll make *him come get me the way I made Reggie do things. I can do it.* He painted a picture of Chavez in his mind, ignoring the friendly smile that arrived with it—obviously, he was "handling" Kai to make him compliant—then animated it. He moved the man's legs faster and faster, imagined him running to Kai's rescue, flinging open the door to wherever Kai was trapped, turning on bright white lights, then falling to his knees and begging for Kai's forgiveness.

He waited, not actually hoping but giving the magic time to work. When he ran out of patience, he imagined a generalized puppet running to his rescue and poured as much mental energy into the image as he knew how. And again, he waited.

Anger built for every second, every microsecond, every nanosecond he waited, becoming hot, then incandescent, then a raging torrent of uncontainable fury. He lashed out at the darkness, mustering every bit of himself to do it. He didn't plan what he did, didn't imagine anything specific, he just vented his ire into the darkness.

But that too, failed.

Something deep inside him broke, just popped open like a cheap plastic toy, and rage, loneliness, miserable despondence, and wretched heartsickness poured into and over him, consuming him, drowning him, scalding him with terrible desperation.

He wanted it to end. He wanted it all to end, wanted to go back in time and stop his mother from taking him to Rochester. He wanted peace.

He nodded once to himself, then again, a half a minute later. He sniffed and uncrossed his arms.

Kai Washington gave in to his despair and took a single step forward, his body plunging into the dark abyss.

Chapter 12
Nightmares Walking, Psychopath Stalking

I

"That poor kid!" said Maddie with tears in her voice. "And what cruel people would do something like that to a child?"

"That's how they got me. How they twisted me back into the fold. That carrot—Beatrice knew I couldn't resist it—protecting both of them with my presence, and the stick of what might be done to either Kai or Jamilla if I drove them into killing me. Kai was already there, already in *processing* as they call it. Jamilla had already had her first psychic surgery, and I didn't have the skills or the gift to set her back to right. Without me there, in the Compound, nothing would change. The Program had Kai and Jamilla both, and Beatrice could alter them both for perfect loyalty to the Program. Oh, I didn't have no illusions that I could free them. No, I knew it was too late for such thoughts. But I thought I could protect 'em, shield 'em from the worst the Program had to offer." She sighed across the phone line, and the harshness gave Gavin the chills. "So, I fish-flopped. I gave in. I let it happen, all of it, thinking I could still help in some way. That I could save that darling boy." She sucked her teeth and made a peculiar noise—half snort, half moan.

With a start, Gavin realized the old woman was crying—doing her best to hide it but crying, nonetheless. "I'm sorry, Adeline. I know what it is to lose a child. The helplessness, the…the horror of it."

"Yes," said Adeline with a sniff. "Yes, you do. I'm sorry to dredge that up." Her voice sounded stronger, more in control. "So, after enough time to be sure I meant to be good, they let me out of my cell, let me have free rein in the Compound. Oh, I couldn't leave, and many a time that rankled, but it was passable, being with my own people as I was. Time did what time does and put a distance between those emotional times and happier ones."

"And Jamilla didn't fight back?" asked Maddie.

"She couldn't, child. Beatrice—"

"Hold on a second," said Gavin. He pulled his laptop closer. "I think I have three records under the heading 'Controlling Jamilla W.'"

"Let's hear them," said Maddie.

Gavin cleared his throat and started reading.

2

TO: gray_eyed_goddess@majest.ic
FROM: green_eyed_goddess@majest.ic

SUBJECT: Controlling Jamilla W.

Hey Barbie-bitch,

I really like that. I think that's your nickname from now on. Got a problem with that, Barbie-bitch?

So, anyway, I was right, you were wrong (duh), AGAIN (again, duh). Jamilla's reprogramming is a success. I gave her the task of cleaning the intake hall observation area when I knew Kai would be coming in. Know what she did?

Nothing. She glanced at him, then went back to her cleaning. Know why?

Because your sister is a complete badass.

Don't you forget it. :P

3

From Program records
June 16, 1998, 11:37

TO: green_eyed_goddess@majest.ic
FROM: gray_eyed_goddess@majest.ic

SUBJECT: RE: Controlling Jamilla W.

Hey Barbie-bitch,

So, in case you forgot, we're goddamn twins, and if Barbie-bitch works for me, it works for you—just like those shitty paisley shirts Mommy made us wear all the time.

As for Jamilla, it is entirely possible that she's playing you for the bimbo you are. I wouldn't put it past her to play docile for a time— the time it takes her to find a way to *speak* to Kai.

I hope I'm wrong, I really do because I already think you're a badass, Bea. Then again, maybe you reprogrammed me to think that way?

Ha ha. JK, Barbie-bitch, calm down. Geesh.

Maybe we should set an observer team on Jamilla. Just to be sure?

4

From Program records
June 16, 1998, 23:54

TO: gray_eyed_goddess@majest.ic
FROM: green_eyed_goddess@majest.ic

SUBJECT: RE: RE: Controlling Jamilla W.

The Man said do it. Hey, even a broken clock is right twice a day. Get it set up, bitch.

Oh, and BTW, Jamilla is a latent TP, psi rating 3.8, and TK, psi rating 4.1. She has no idea, and after my reprogramming, she never will.

BUT…I know what you're thinking. I put in a failsafe. Oh, I also put failsafes on non-productive thought lines. If she trips them, we'll know, but she won't.

BTW, did you see Kai's psi rating?? Good God. TC psi rating 9.9. He's fucking eleven!! TP psi rating is 8.9 and TK is at 6.3. Again, he's fucking eleven, the little twerp. I think you were twenty-seven before you hit 6.3.

Just kidding 8P, I also think my sister is a complete badass.

5

"My, ain't them a pair?" asked Adeline with a rusty chuckle. "And how they did talk!"

Gavin didn't think she found them all that funny. To him, her chuckle sounded false—a cover for some other emotion.

"Can fixers interfere with a mother's love? Her maternal instinct to protect and nurture?" asked Maddie in a voice that shook.

"Oh, child, I'm so sorry to bring this pain up again—for both of you, I know." The line hummed a moment, then she went on, "But to answer your question, a fixer can manipulate *anything*. Some changes are physical, some chemical, and some electrical or some such. I don't understand any of that, I just take it to mean they can do what they want to whoever they want whenever they want."

"What did she mean that if Jamilla tripped them, they would know, but Jamilla wouldn't?" asked Maddie.

"A failsafe is like a string tied to a bell but inside your mind. If you trip one of 'em, a psychic observer will know. Mostly, tripwires have a specific action tied to them—a memory wipe of the incident or a psionic command, something like that. I told you all of that before, but this here example, they wired up that failsafe to zap out her memory of whatever she was a-doing to set it off."

"That's horrible!"

"*Horrible*," said Adeline. "Yes, Maddie, that's the best word for it."

"That sounds like a lot of power for any one person to have," said Karl. "What these fixers have."

"It is, Detective," said Adeline. "And you know that old saying? 'Power corrupts?'"

"That's just what I was thinking."

"Well, this tale will get around to a fine example of the truth of that adage before we're done."

"Can one of these fixers undo the reprogramming?" asked Karl. "Or is it a case of done-bun-can't-be-undone?"

"It's possible to reverse a reprogramming," said Adeline, "but the risk is generally considered too great."

"The risk?" asked Karl. "Of what?"

"Going mad," said Adeline. "There's a risk with each alteration and stacking one reprogramming on top of another increases that risk."

"So she left Jamilla…" said Maddie, "that green-eyed one…the fixer…she just…"

"Yes, child," said Adeline in a voice that made her sound old and tired, then she drew in a deep breath and sighed. "I don't know all of the details, but at that time, Beatrice loosened Jamilla's maternal instinct. She also implanted the thought that Kai *needed* something she couldn't provide, that without the influence of the Program and its instructors, Kai would self-destruct. She also wired Jamilla up with failsafes that stole away her short-term memories if she even thought about trying to contact him, but she did far worse before it was all over," said Adeline in a grim, funereal voice.

"And you couldn't stop her?" asked Karl.

"To my shame. Oh, I *tried*, but I failed. I ain't no fixer, Karl. I have to *convince* people to see things my way. At that time, because I'd run off and done what I did trying save Kai, my political position in the Program wasn't the finest. In their eyes, I'd betrayed their trust. The Man and I had—"

"Is that the Man you loved or the new one?" asked Maddie.

"Loved, child?" Adeline said with a laugh. "What makes you think I loved him?"

"It's obvious."

"Well, I *respected* him, to be sure, but he was White, and I was Black."

"And you loved him anyway. Right?"

Adeline took a breath as if to argue, then let it out. No one spoke for a few moments, waiting for her to answer. "It's been a long time," she said at last. "If I ever did love him, that's long over. Besides, my Man is the one who died of pneumonia in 1998. The Man I'm talking about now was the one who took over. Sam McIntire, his name was."

"Why don't you call them by name?" asked Gavin.

"Yes, I suppose I should. But it's habit. In the Program, we don't use the director's name. We just call him 'the Man.' That's a security measure, and we use it exclusively, so we tend to *think* of him that way, so we never accidentally give his identity away."

"And they're all men?" asked Maddie.

"Let's leave women's lib out of this and get back to my answer. I had to be very careful—any little slip-up would've been used to get rid of me for good. What help would I have been then?"

"But what about the authorities—"

"Detective, if you think there *are* any authorities outside of the Man, I haven't told you the story right," said Adeline with a rueful laugh. "And seeing as Beatrice was one of the Man's—drat, I mean Sam McIntyre's—favorites, her word was right up there next to God's."

"The same way the previous director thought about you," said Gavin.

"Well, I s'pose so, now that you mention it."

"Am I understanding all that crap about psi levels to mean that Kai was something special?"

"He was that without no psi at all," said Adeline in a quiet voice.

"You know what I mean," said Gavin.

"I do, and he was. That's probably why McIntyre decided to grab him up in the first place."

"But…" started Maddie.

"How do they know?" Adeline gave a sour chuckle. "Bird dogs like me set out to find others with potential. We tag them, and a field team gets close enough that their fixer can assess the potential—usually they give the kid a nightmare and then assess their dream-actions and guesstimate the psi power from that."

"I'm starting to hate your Program, Adeline."

"Ayup," said Adeline. "It's an easy thing to grow to hate."

"Adeline, what are these observers?"

"Well, they're just what the name says. We have observers in the program—snoops, mostly—who are tasked with watching over things. They watch individuals, looking for broken thinking, misbehavior, and the like. Then, they communicate their findings to the relevant parties."

"Babysitters," said Karl.

"Well…yes, I suppose that name works as well as any other."

"And those two women put one of those observers on Jamilla to track her emotions, her thoughts? A psychic observer?"

"Yes, and to monitor the failsafes Beatrice installed."

"So it worked?" asked Maddie.

"The reprogramming? Yes, child. For a while it did."

Despite his best efforts, a jaw-cracking yawn escaped Gavin. He rubbed his eyes and muttered an apology. "If I understand you, his power exceeded expectations during his…test?"

"Yes," said Adeline. "Keep his age to mind. He was eleven—he hadn't even hit puberty, yet he was broadcasting with more power than some of our students ever achieve. As the twins would later carp about, he was a prodigy."

Though he tried not to, Gavin yawned again, and this time Karl did too.

"My, but you boys are plumb worn out." Adeline chuckled.

"It's been a long, hot day," said Gavin.

"Should we stop for the night?" asked Maddie.

"Yeah, I'm beat," said Gavin.

"And so am I," said Adeline, "though I haven't done anything like what you two got up to today. Let's pick this up tomorrow."

Karl and Adeline said their goodbyes and disconnected.

"And now, I've got you all to myself," said Maddie with what sounded like forced brightness in her voice.

"Mads, I love you," he said. "I really am beat."

"I know. I can hear it in your voice. Are you worried about dreaming again?"

"I…" He sighed heavily. "I need rest, but I don't want to dream."

"First thing tomorrow, I'm calling Dr. Tremaine. I'll ask him about the meds."

"You know I don't like—"

"To take medicine. Yeah, I know, but you need rest, Gavin. You're not twenty anymore. You can't keep pushing yourself like this."

"I know."

"Then, tomorrow, you will go buy whatever Dr. Tremaine recommends."

"Yes, dear."

"And for tonight, you'll leave the lights on."

"How am I supposed to sleep—"

"The bathroom lights then. So, if you do dream, it won't be pitch-black when you wake up."

"Good idea," he said.

After he hung up, he turned on all the lights in the bathroom, then climbed into bed.

6

A hotel room
Thursday, 11:39 pm

Gavin bolted awake, lurching up, bedclothes pooling around his waist, his heart pounding, his breath coming in a kind of rasping pant, a woman's scream ringing in his ears. Sweat ran from his scalp, down his forehead, and into his eyes, his eyelids snick-snicking as he blinked the sweat away. He swiped his hand across his eyes and forehead, then peered into the grave-dark room. He widened his eyes, once, twice, and again, but it didn't help, it didn't help him penetrate the darkness, and it didn't leave him calm the way it was supposed to. He rested a hand on his service weapon.

"Who's there?" he asked, his voice not much more than a child's squeak. He shoved the covers away and swung his feet to the floor. Didn't I leave the bathroom lights on? His gaze went to the short hall that led to the bathroom but could see nothing more than pitch-black gloom.

Beneath his soles, something cold and scaly wriggled away—back under the bed. Gavin stifled a cry and launched himself up and away, then spun around and froze, staring at the inky darkness under the bed he'd slept in. He thought he could see a shape there, one darker than the rest of the shadows, the rest of the room—a lumpy shape that undulated and twitched.

"Who's there?" he repeated, not knowing why, not sure he wanted an answer.

"Caught me, spark," said a woman's voice.

He squeezed his eyes shut, denying the shape, denying his over-active mind.

"You think squeezing your eyes shut will protect you?"

The pitch-black room seemed to breathe at a silent, inexorable rhythm, and he felt compelled to match it. He backed away a few steps, his eyes dancing toward the door to the hall with despair—to get to the door, he'd have to pass by the creature under the bed, and as if reading his thoughts, a scaled tentacle slithered out from the foot of the bed. He glanced over his shoulder at the sliding glass door and the yawning abyss outside.

Trapped! I'm trapped in here with…with…it!

A gurgling came from under the bed. "Oh, sparky, you're in trouble now. I told you once that the Lord Gawd would pound and pound and pound you. You didn't believe me, but now, you've woken him up."

"Leave me alone!" Gavin cried.

"Told you so many times, old hoss," said a horrible male voice in his ear. "I DON'T COTTON TO YOU TELLING ME WHAT TO DO!" The sheer volume of his shout cracked the mirror above the cheap fiber-board dresser and shattered the sliding glass door. "Me or that stupid bitch under the bed. Don't you do it no more, spark."

Deaf in one ear, Gavin jerked away, sprinting for the door. He leaped over the tentacle, but it snapped up, lightning-quick, and batted him to the floor, and another tentacle snaked out from under the bed and scaly flesh slithered around his ankle, capturing it, caressing it, squeezing it.

Rolling onto his back, Gavin cried out in disgust and fear. He kicked at the rubbery gray tentacle with his other foot. "Get off! Get off!"

"Are ya'll fucking stupid, hoss?" The voice came from the walls, from the carpet beneath him, from the tentacle, the bed itself—everywhere at once, pounding his eardrums, pulsing from the walls.

With one more mighty kick that peeled the tentacle away, Gavin scrambled on his hands and knees toward the slider, toward the balcony and the long drop into the black bay below.

A heavy tentacle fell on his shoulder, and Gavin jerked away from the touch with a cry.

"Where we going, sugar?" Fetid breath tickled his ear, and a long, slimy tongue caressed his cheek.

Screaming and screaming, Gavin bolted up like a sprinter coming out of the blocks and ran for the balcony's edge.

8

Langfield Sun, Miami, FL
Friday, 12:03 am

Gavin bolted awake, lurching up, bedclothes pooling around him, his heart pounding, his breath coming in a kind of rasping pant, his own screams ringing in his ears. Sweat ran from his scalp, down his forehead, and into his eyes, and he swiped it away while his eyelids went *snick*, *snick*, *snick*. He shot a glance toward the hall and sighed in relief at the warm yellow light shining from the bathroom.

His cold sweat had soaked the bedclothes—the bulk of which had wrapped around his feet, and a corner draped over his shoulder—and he shivered in the air conditioning.

He got up, grimacing down at the wet bed, then walked to the bathroom and turned on the hot water. He rinsed the sweat from his skin and luxuriated in the hot water cascading over him. He didn't think about the dream—consciously avoiding it. In fact, he tried not to think at all. Steam swirled in the bathroom, condensing on the mirror.

After a long, hot soak, Gavin turned off the water and grabbed a plush bath towel, using it to give his skin another scrub. As he rubbed it through his close-cropped hair, he thought he heard a peculiar chirp, and he froze a moment, listening hard. "Just your imagination, Gav," he murmured. After a minute or so without a repeat, he took another dose of Doxepin and then climbed into the bed he hadn't already soaked.

9

A hotel room
Friday, 1:28 am

Gavin stood staring out the sliding glass door at the swirling abyss, his face cold, his stomach roiling, his hands itching to open the door, his feet inching forward, bringing him closer and closer to the cold glass. Behind him, an unnatural silence choked the room.

A heavy hand fell on his shoulder. "Where we going, sugar?" asked a grating voice in his ear.

"Nowhere," said Gavin in his most commanding voice. "This is a dream."

"Is it? Is it really, spark?" Laughter capered just beneath the words.

"Bathroom light is out," he said, hooking a thumb over his shoulder. "That's how I know."

"Well, I hate to be the one who tells you this, old hoss, but that light is on."

"No, it isn't," said Gavin, but he turned his head to check, nonetheless.

A nightmare vision stood behind him—orange-eyed, dressed in an old army jacket, a hoody up over his skull. The man grinned at him, and the fires of Hell danced in his gaze. "Oh, you wanted to see the bathroom light. How rude of me." He stepped to the side, keeping his taloned hand on Gavin's shoulder.

Warm yellow light stabbed into the dark hallway from the bathroom door.

"See there? Light's on, like I said."

Gavin shrugged. "You turned it on."

The man laughed. "No, sir."

Again, Gavin shrugged. "It's still a dream."

"Is it, spark? Is it really?"

Gavin wrinkled his brow and grimaced into the orange light of the man's stare. "You're not her."

"Who, old hoss?"

"The woman on the plane. Back at LaGuardia."

A large, toothy grin split the nightmare man's face. "No, that stupid bitch is still recovering. Call me Fry."

"Recovering?"

Fry chuckled. "You got her arrested. My dinner was late. I beat that bitch down, *partner. I pounded and pounded and* pounded *her. A lesson she won't never forget." He nodded solemnly.*

Gavin recalled the strange thing she'd said: The Lord Gawd needs his dinner and hates it if it's late. The Lord Gawd knows I don't want a smack in the chops for not having dinner ready. *He frowned and stared into Fry's glowing orange eyes. His irises looked like molten lava.*

"Careful, old hoss," he crooned. "When you gaze long into an abyss, the abyss also gazes into you."

Gavin stared a moment longer, then cut his eyes away. "You're not God."

"Oh, how the fuck would you know, hoss? Could be I'm as close as you'll ever get."

Gavin shrugged. "I don't believe in God, anyway. Too much evil in the world. Too many men like you."

Fry threw back his head and laughed, and the mirror over the fiberboard dresser shattered. "I like you, son. You've got spunk."

"What's your name?" Gavin asked. "Your real name?"

"How's it go?" asked Fry as he scratched his chin. "Oh, right." He cleared his throat and straightened out

of his perpetual slouch. "My name is Legion, for we are many," he said in a growling Halloween voice.

Gavin shook his head. "I don't believe in demons, either. Or angels. Or the devil."

Again, Fry laughed, louder this time, cracking the slider from floor to ceiling. "Who gives a fuck, old hoss? How'd you get this opinion of yourself? That what you believe matters at all, to anyone? For fuck's sake, boy. Get over yourself."

"Says the figment of my imagination. The ugly spot in my id."

This time, when Fry laughed, the slider exploded out into the night, but instead of the glass shards falling toward the bay, they floated in midair for a moment before sliding skyward. They ascended until they became indistinguishable from the stars.

"So, should I call you 'Fry' then?"

"Fry, Furfur, the Nightmare Man, why would I give a solitary fuck what you call me, son? You're nothing to me."

Gavin chuckled, but nothing cracked or exploded. "Maybe, but you're sure spending a lot of time in my dreams."

"Am I? I thought I was a figure of your imagination? The dark stain on your id?"

"Ugly spot, I said."

"You may have said that, old hoss, but you meant dark stain."

Gavin shrugged. Upon reflection, Fry was right. "What do you want from me?"

"From you, spark? Nothing." He leaned close. "But my son is another matter."

"Your son?"

A peculiar chirp sounded from the balcony, and before Gavin could turn to look, Fry's hands shot out and gripped his head. A three-fingered clawed hand fell on his shoulder. Breath as cold as the void tickled his ear. When it came, the piping, chirping *voice seemed to drill into his flesh, through his skull, and nestle inside the deepest, most reptilian part of his mind. The words, when they came, hit like a thirty-thousand-amp bolt of purple-white lightning, frying his brain, cooking his spinal cord, shorting his nerves.*

"Where we going, sugar?"

10

Langfield Sun, Miami, FL
Friday, 1:58 am

Gavin clawed out of his nightmare, a scream on his lips, Glacadairanam's piping, *chirping* voice ringing in his ears. Terror twisted in his guts, fear froze him in place as he waited for that horrible voice to come again, for Glacadairanam to ask him that horrid question.

Where we going, sugar?

He forced his head to move, forced his eyes open, shot a glance at the hall to confirm the bathroom light still burned. *Where we going, sugar?* Again, he lay in a sodden mess of bedclothes, sweat still dripping from him. He flopped back into the bed's cold embrace and closed his eyes.

"You think squeezing your eyes shut will protect you?"

His eyes flew open, his heartbeat galloping. For a moment, he panicked, thinking he'd heard the words aloud, rather than in his mind.

He glared at the alarm clock as if it were to blame for his lack of sleep, then shoved the sodden mass of blankets and sheets away and got up. He stood there, swaying with exhaustion and the dregs of his slumber, then turned and walked to the balcony. He lifted a hand to pull back the drapes, but then stopped and let his hand fall.

Where we going, sugar? The very air itself seemed to ask the question, whispering to the reptilian brain deep inside his skull. *Where we going, sugar?*

Trepidation cooled his guts, but he had to know if black basalt and fiery magma awaited him outside, had to *know* whether this was all part of another nightmare. He took a deep breath and pulled the curtains back…

And stared out at Biscayne Bay, the lights of Miami Beach shining across the intercoastal.

Where we— With a grimace, he banished the voice, banished the question, stopping it cold, stopping it dead.

Shaking his head, he turned and surveyed the destruction he had managed to reap on both beds, both sets of bedding. A shaky sigh escaped—a sigh that was almost a sob. He walked to the hall and opened the closet across from the bath and felt a little less wretched after finding the extra blankets and pillows. He turned his back on them and returned to the room proper, pulling the sweat-soaked sheets and comforter from both beds, dumping them on the floor in front of the slider. That done, he returned to the bathroom and stepped into the shower to rinse away the dream. He opened his mouth and sucked the water into his mouth, healing his parched throat.

Ten minutes later, his skin a rosy hue from the towel, he grabbed the pillows and blankets, piling them at the end of the bed. He grabbed the spare towels from the bathroom and covered the wet, body-shaped spot on the mattress, then drew one blanket over them and tucked it under the mattress. He threw a fresh pillow toward the headboard, then climbed into bed.

"Don't fucking dream, asshole," he whispered.

As if that would work…

11

Bayfront Park, Miami, FL
Friday, 3:17 am

Gavin stood in a copse of oak trees, wearing a cloak of shadow, shielded from the road by more trees, by the amphitheater, shielded from the bay by a pile of rocks and the darkness and his nature. He raised his gaze for a moment and took in the grandeur of Biscayne Bay in the platinum moonlight. The woman—a brunette with too much makeup on and not enough clothes—lay in the manicured grass. She looked up at him with bright, round eyes, then shifted her gaze to the knife he showed her.

He lifted the hand holding it—a beautiful Damascus blade—then turned it around with a practiced flick of his wrist. "Here," he said. "You take it. Then you don't have to be scared. That's the last thing I want."

She narrowed her eyes at him, and a line appeared between her brows. "I thought you wanted to fuck."

"Oh, I do," he said. "But first, I want you to be comfortable. I mean, we just met, right? I could be crazy or a rapist or something. Or that Bogeyman fella all the talking heads are yammering about all day, all night. I want you to feel comfortable."

"And you think pulling out a sword will—"

"It's not a sword. It's a Bowie."

"—make me comfortable? Buddy, you need to work on your technique."

Her words irked him, but he kept the smile on his face and even managed a chuckle. "Yeah, maybe I do, but this ain't over yet."

"Does this knife-thing work with other girls."

He shrugged. "You'd be surprised, sugar."

She looked up at him for a few more moments, then held out her hand. "Fine. Give it to me." As he slapped the hilt into her hand, she said, "You'd better be good after all this."

"Oh, I think you'll have a grand time," he said, stepping back into the shadows.

"Hey, I'm over here," she said.

"Yeah, I know. Will you do something for me?"

"You mean besides fucking you?"

He chuckled. "Yeah. Something to make it more fun."

She shrugged. "What? I'm not into kink."

"Cut yourself."

"What?" She glared at him, pushing herself up on her arms, the knife still held in her right hand.

"You know," he said, gesturing at her. "Blood is a natural aphrodisiac."

"Listen, buddy, you're not that cute. I'm out of—" Her mouth snapped shut as her right arm twitched, then raised the knife. Her left arm buckled, stretched out to her side, and she fell back, eyes wide with terror.

The knife hovered over her face, its tip dancing back and forth between her left and right eye. She opened her mouth to scream, and when she couldn't, terror came to roost in her eyes.

Behind him, a phone rang.

12

Langfield Sun, Miami, FL
Friday, 3:28 am

His phone rang again, and Gavin grabbed it and swiped to accept the call. "Gregory," he said.

"It's Karl. How fast can you get down to the lobby?"

"Five minutes."

"Make it two. Another one dropped, and you're going to love where it is."

"In the park across the street?"

Karl hesitated a moment. "How'd you know? I thought your room looked out on the bay."

"It does. Be down in two." He disconnected before Karl could say anything else. He grabbed a pair of jeans from where they lay over the chair and pulled them on. He put on the T-shirt hanging over the other arm of the chair, then slipped his feet into his shoes. He slid his Glock into his waistband and his shield into his back pocket.

The lobby was like a crypt—cold and deserted—and he pushed out through the double glass doors, his gaze already tracking to the copse of trees from his dream. He stepped out into Chopin Plaza without looking and started across.

Karl stood next to the Explorer, parked across the street, and Gavin changed his course a little to meet him. "How'd you know?" the detective said when Gavin was close enough.

"Dreamed it," said Gavin without batting an eye.

"Yeah, that's *real* funny," said Karl, falling into step. "She's over there past the fountain."

"I'll follow you."

They took the wide concrete path that angled toward the rocks lining the bay, then looped around the fountain and into the trees, stopping outside the yellow tape. "Not a bad spot," said Gavin as he peered toward Biscayne Boulevard. "Good cover from the street."

"And those rocks shield the body from the bay. He could stand back there in the shadow of the trees, and as long as he didn't move, no one out on the water would even notice him," said Karl. "Not that many boats would be out this time of night."

Gavin signed the scene log, then ducked under the tape and approached the body. "Don't be brunette," he whispered.

"What's that?" asked Karl as he signed the log.

"Nothing," said Gavin. The woman lay under a white sheet that seemed too bright for the night, a beacon against the dark shadows. He squatted next to her head and peeled back just enough of the sheet to see her hair color. "Shit," he muttered. He moved around the body, lifting the sheet, gazing at horrible, self-inflicted cuts, growing wearier and wearier with each new atrocity.

"Like the others?" asked Karl as he came to stand next to Gavin. "Self-inflicted?"

"I'd say so," said Gavin. "But not really."

"You want me to pull everyone back for a minute?"

"No need," Gavin said, then sighed. He stood and walked out of the circle of tape, stopping eight feet from a clump of oak trees. "He watched from here. We need to expand the crime scene."

"Uh…how do you know?"

"Trust me," said Gavin, his tone oozing confidence and disgust. "He stood next to that oak. In its shadow. Watching her cut herself, *making* her cut herself." He turned and stared toward the concrete parking lot across the small, man-made stream at the edge of the trees. "He parked over there. We might find footprints on the other side of the stream."

Karl turned and looked toward the parking lot for a moment, then corralled a uniformed officer to add another, bigger ring of crime scene tape. When he turned back to Gavin, he arched his eyebrow.

"Good," said Gavin, coming closer. "What if he gives her the knife to make her feel comfortable?"

"Then he's insane," said Karl. "Leave the knife out of it and she'll feel better."

"Yeah, I know, but he *wants* her holding the knife. The 'feel more comfortable' bit is artifice. He wants the knife in *her hands.*"

"So, what, then? Hey, look at this cool knife. Want to hold it so you feel safe?" Karl shook his head.

"I know it sounds ludicrous, but I'm sure that's how he does it."

"I mean, he's already talked her out of a club somewhere, got her here in the dark of night—no one around, nowhere to run for help—and for what? The promise of sex?"

The woman's voice in his dream came to Gavin: *I thought you wanted to fuck,* she'd said. "That would be my guess."

"He'd have to find the right woman for this. One who likes the idea of doing it in a public place."

Gavin nodded and looked at the sheet-draped corpse. "One who didn't mind a one-night stand."

"One who'd done something like this before."

"Nightclubs around here?"

Karl pointed at the Bayside Marketplace. "There's a mojito place right there. And a daiquiri bar."

"Let's go."

Karl shook his head. "It's half-past-three. Bars around here close at two."

"So, they hung out in the parking lot for a bit?"

"I bet they came straight here. Dispatch got the call at quarter to three. The bar closes, they come here, he does whatever magic he does to make the women cut themselves up. That takes, what? Half an hour?"

"Maybe quicker," said Gavin.

"That's a lot of cuts. And it's not as though the women would want to do it."

"No hesitation cuts, remember? Quick, steady strokes."

Karl shook his head and shrugged hopelessly. "I can't figure it."

"Whatever it is," said Gavin, "it's more like the killer is doing the cutting than the victim. As though the victim were a *puppet*."

Karl cocked his head to the side. "Adeline's story?"

Gavin nodded.

Karl's phone chirped, and Gavin jumped. "Easy there, FBI. It's just a text." He looked down at his phone, the screen lighting his face. "Truxillo. The anonymous caller used his cell phone. If we head over to the phone company's main office, we can pull the billing address. I just need to make a call and wake up a friend who works there."

"Let's go," said Gavin.

13

Karl turned onto Michigan Avenue, then idled down the street. Gavin pointed to the third house, a white single-story home with an overgrown lawn. "Dark," said Karl. "Sleeping or not at home?"

"One way to find out."

With a grunt, Karl nosed the SUV into one of the angled spots across the street from the house. They got out and walked to the front door. Gavin rang the bell three times before a light came on inside. After a moment, the bare bulb above the door lit, washing them with yellow light.

"Who's that?" an old man asked in a querulous tone. "Don't you know what time it is? Didn't your mother teach you—"

"It's the police, sir," said Karl. "Detective Santana and Special Agent Gavin Gregory."

"Police? I didn't call no police. You got the wrong goldang house. I swear to—"

"Sir, please open the door so we don't have to shout and wake up your neighbors."

The man said nothing for the space of a few angry breaths, then the three deadbolts rattled, and he opened the door an inch-and-a-half. The man wasn't much more than five feet tall, dressed in worn boxers, a sweat-stained white T-shirt, and a pair of white socks with worn-out elastic. The only other thing he wore was a belligerent expression. What little hair he had left glistened white and hung to his collar. "Well, ain't that goldang great? You're worried about waking the neighbors, but not about waking me? You're as bad as that dang islander next door! Ain't my sleep worth nothing? For Christ's sake, I—"

"I don't want to interrupt your tirade," said Gavin in a voice barely above a whisper, "but we have reason to wake you. Do you own a cellular phone?" Looking past the man, Gavin noted the stacks of newspapers lining the walls, the old duct-tape-patched recliner, and the foul odor of rotting meat and garbage.

"What? Cell phone? What the hell are you talking about?"

Karl cleared his throat and took Gavin's lead on lowering his voice. "We received a 911 call earlier. When we ran the number, this address came back as the billing address on the account?"

"Well, you got sold a goldang bill of goods. I ain't got no fancy cell phone. I ain't *never* had none." He narrowed his eyes at them. "I want to see IDs." Karl showed his badge, and the man nodded. "That's Miami-Dade heard from. Now you." He glared at Gavin.

"That's no problem, sir," said Gavin as he pulled his leather ID wallet and flipped it open, showing his badge and FBI identification. "Now, let's see *your* ID."

"My ID? I didn't come ringing your goldang doorbell at the ass-end of goldang dawn. I don't have—"

"Sir," Karl said. "We can do this nice and neighborly." He left the rest unsaid: We can also do this hard, but we *will* do it.

"May we come in?" asked Gavin. "This will go better if we can all relax."

The man's narrowed gaze flipped back and forth from Karl to Gavin, then he blew a raspberry, turned, and walked deeper into the house.

Gavin pushed the door open and, after taking an appraising glance around, stepped onto the white tile. Karl followed him in.

"Close the goldang door. Air-con costs me plenty, and I ain't made of money."

With a glance at Gavin, Karl swung the door closed gently. "Now, about that ID."

"Yeah, yeah," the man muttered. He walked around a pony wall that was missing its counter-top and opened a drawer.

"Whoa, partner," said Karl. He rested his hand on the butt of his service weapon.

The old man raised his gaze and sneered. "For Christ's sake, make up your goldang mind!" he snapped.

Gavin walked around so he had a clear view.

"There!" snapped the man. "You got your faggot feeb watching me. Is it okay for me to get out the goldang ID you're goldang pestering me about?"

Without waiting for an answer, he dropped his gaze to the open drawer and rooted around inside. "Where's that bastard got to?" he muttered. After a moment, he pulled out a canvas wallet with a screen-printed picture of a shark surfing on a huge wave. He flipped it over in his palm, grabbed the flap, and ripped open the Velcro strip. He withdrew a laminated card and flipped it at Karl. "There's your goldang-monkey-shittin' ID. I can't have no driver's license no more so that had better do."

Karl bent and picked up the card by its edges. "Yes, sir. A Florida ID card is fine. Mr. Fannin, is it? Charles Fannin?"

"Your goldang right. Ain't that what it says on the dang card? 'Cept it's Chuck, not Charles. Chuck ain't no goldang-short-for."

Karl glanced down. "So it is. My apologies."

"Come out of there, now," said Gavin quietly.

The old man glared at him, then turned to the refrigerator and got out a beer. While the door was open, Gavin caught the foul odor of rotting food. Fannin cracked open the beer and took a long pull, then wiped his mouth with the back of his hand. "I don't cotton to being told what to do. I ain't gonna be ordered around in my own goldang house, youngster."

After a momentary fear inspired by his dreams washed through him, Gavin held up his hands in supplication. "We have a few questions, then we'll get out of your hair." He exchanged a glance with Karl and saw the detective was thinking the same thing he was: *No way Chuck Fannin is the killer, but he might still be part of it.*

"Let's get back to your cell phone. It was—"

"Goldang it, son, don't you *never* listen? I said I ain't got one, and I ain't *never* had one. Ain't got no goldang use for the goldang things. Nothing but a goldang nuisance if you ask me—like the goldang cops. Got to plug it in all the goldang time or them goldang batteries will be goldang flat when you want to make a call."

"Then we have a problem," said Karl. "The phone company says you *do* have a cell phone, and that they've been billing you at this address for the past nineteen months."

"Ha! Then them goldang liars is having fun with you." Fannin walked into the living room, sank into his recliner, and scratched his groin. "I ain't never had no monkey-shittin' phone, nor no goldang bill."

Karl and Gavin exchanged another glance.

"And y'all can just stop sending each other kissy looks. What are y'all, queers?" He slurped another mouthful of beer, spilling it on his already-stained shirt.

"The records are clear, sir." Karl's voice contained a harsh edge.

"Yeah? Them records can kiss my White ass."

"There's an easy way to solve this," said Gavin.

"Yeah? What's that, FBI?"

"Let us take a look around. If we can't find any bills or a phone, then you're in the clear."

"I'm already in the goldang clear, sonny. And you ain't looking at nothing without that goldang paper."

"Paper?"

He waved his hand. "One of them things signed by a judge. A warren."

"Warrant," said Karl. "And we can surely get one, Mr. Fannin, but while we're waiting for the paperwork, we have to secure this residence. That means you have to take a ride downtown, and we put a uniform right where you're sitting."

Fannin's expression darkened from irritated to enraged. "Ain't no one taking me nowhere," he said. "*I* ain't no goldang-monkey-shittin' wetback you can just push around!"

Karl didn't so much as twitch, but his eyes hardened.

"Just let us take a look," said Gavin. "Why inconvenience yourself further?"

Fannin's beady, angry-eyed gaze flicked back and forth between them for a moment. "Fine!" he snapped. "But if you find any goldang Mary Jane, it's goldang medicinal. On account of my anxiety."

"We have no interest in your marijuana," said Karl. "We're working a homicide."

"Then look. But be monkey-shittin' quick, goldang it!"

"You go ahead, Gav. I'll just stay out here and keep Mr. Fannin company."

Gavin nodded.

"Don't do me no goldang favors," muttered Fannin.

Gavin took the narrow path through the stacks of newspapers and magazines into the kitchen. He started with the drawer from which Fannin had taken his ID. It was like a typical junk drawer on steroids. It seemed Fannin deposited all his mail in the drawer unopened, and it overflowed with envelopes. More hung over the back panel of the drawer, and no doubt the cabinet underneath it was packed with them. He scooped out a double handful and lay them atop the newspapers stacked in front of the lower cabinet, shuffling through them. He repeated the process seventeen times, then shook his head at Karl before picking his way through the little kitchen and into the hall running toward the back of the house. It, too, had towers of yellowed newspaper stacked along both walls—only the stacks went all the way to the ceiling.

The first door he came to opened onto a rank-smelling bathroom. He flicked the light on and saw why—a five-gallon bucket filled with human waste sat next to the toilet. Holding his breath as long as he could, Gavin flicked open the medicine cabinet, glanced inside, then backed out to the hall.

The next door led to a narrow laundry room equipped with a Jalousie door that led outside. The washer and dryer looked positively ancient, and catalogs made miniature mountains on top of them both. The last door led to Fannin's bedroom—also stacked to the ceiling with even more newspapers in every conceivable space except for a narrow five-foot section of exposed, stained mattress.

If he has a cell phone, Gavin thought, *I'll never find it. Not without a CSI team and a full clean-out of this mess.* He shook his head, arms akimbo, then turned and made his way back to the front room. He shook his head at Karl. "All right, Mr. Fannin. This is what we're going to do—"

"You said y'all would leave me alone if you couldn't find nothing."

"And we will," said Gavin. "As soon as we can figure out why someone has been paying for a cell phone at this address for the last nineteen months. Do you have grandchildren that might've used this address to keep the bills from mom and dad?"

"Ain't got no kids to give 'em to me. And…" His brows knotted as he slurped the last of his beer. "Grab me another cowboy," he said to Gavin. "And one for yourselves if y'all want it. I think I can solve this bastard right'chere."

Gavin went back to the kitchen and braved the refrigerator for another cold can of Schmidt's. He returned to the front room, holding the beer. "Solve it how?"

Fannin held out his hand and snapped his fingers. "Beer."

Gavin shrugged and handed it over.

"Nineteen months, y'all said?" He cracked open the beer and took a noisy swallow. "That's when that goldang brown bastard moved in next door." He jerked his can of suds toward the next house to the north. "Cubano or Jamaicano or goldang Puerto Ricano." He grunted and waved his beer around. "Y'know, some such 'ano with dirty brown skin. You know," he said leering at Santana. "A *darky*."

"What's his name?" asked Karl in a mild tone.

Fannin frowned and took a desultory pull on the Schmidt's. "Julio. Jorje. I don't know. Juan. Some shit like that."

"Last name?"

"What do I goldang look like? Monkey-shittin' information? Go ask the man. Wake *him* up and order *him* around in his own goldang house. Leave the White people alone."

Karl shook his head and flipped his notepad closed. "I'm surprised you lived to this advanced age with that racist attitude."

"A lot you know about anything. Back in the day, people like you knew better than to confront a White man, let alone apply to the cops. People like you knew *your place*."

"Oh, the 'good old days.'" Karl laughed. "Times change, old-timer. Now, *I'm* the Man." He turned to Gavin and jerked his head toward the door. "Let's get out of here before he gives me a reason to arrest his tired old ass."

"If I was twenty-goldang-years younger, I'd—"

"Get your ass kicked and then take a ride downtown," said Karl without looking back at him.

"But things being how they are, be content that you're just an old bigot worth about as much as a fart." He walked out the front door, and Gavin turned to follow him.

"Why would a good White man like you put up with working with a goldang Spic? All that PC shit too goldang hard to fight?"

Gavin chuckled sourly. "I'd rather work with Karl than a 'good White man' like you, you decrepit piece of shit."

"Well, la-dee-goldang-da," said Fannin as Gavin closed the door.

Outside, Karl stood staring at the dark house next door. Newspaper covered the windows they could see on the side of the house, and there was no car in drive, but the lawn was kept nice. "Knock or sit on it?" he asked.

Gavin had that hinky feeling he hated—like a bear or a big cat watched him from the shadows. Like he was prey. "No car," he said.

Karl jerked his thumb at the house they'd just left. "No car for Mr. Personality, either."

"True," said Gavin. "What's your gut telling you?"

Karl nodded. "He's in there."

"Yeah, watching us. I think so, too."

"Backup?"

"At this time of night? It'd take a patrol car ten or twenty minutes to get out here."

"Safer," said Gavin.

Karl nodded. "So, what do you want to do? We go sit in the car, maybe Mr. Bigot drops a dime, and our tipster takes a powder."

"Him call the 'darky' living next door? Helping him?" Gavin shook his head.

Karl shrugged. "I got the feeling he hated one thing more than people with brown skin."

"Yeah," said Gavin with a sigh. "Cops." He took a deep breath. "Let's go, then."

A thigh-high brick and wrought-iron fence stood on the lot-line all the way around the house next door. They walked around to the front, having to step out into the street, just in time to see a white Chevy disappear around the next corner. Karl grunted and nudged him with an elbow. Gavin nodded, and, as he did so, his sense of foreboding deepened. He didn't like the idea of an unknown in front *and* at his back.

Karl opened the gate in the middle of the lot, and it squealed on its iron hinges. They stood for a moment, staring at the bleak house. "Hell of a warning system," Karl muttered. He squared his shoulders and walked up the concrete path leading to the front door. An awning shrouded the door itself, piling shadow on top of shadow. Iron bars secured all the windows across the front of the house. He climbed the three steps to the door and rang the bell.

Gavin waited at the foot of the steps, slightly to the right of Karl, his body turned at an angle, right hand on his pistol, and split his attention between the street and the big curtain-shrouded window. He strained his ears but could detect no movement within, nor a car pulling up behind. "Try it again," he whispered.

Karl grunted and lifted his hand as though to pound on the door, then stopped, as still as a statue. A frown formed on Gavin's face as he spared Karl a glance. "What's up?" he whispered, but the detective didn't answer, didn't speak, didn't even grunt. "Karl?" He tore his gaze from the front window—where nothing moved in any case—and gazed up at Santana. Karl's arm shook with tension, but he didn't move, didn't even blink. Stepping closer, Gavin tapped him on the shoulder. "What's up, Karl? What are you doing?" he hissed.

Karl made a strange noise—somewhere between a choked gasp and a grunt—and jerked around a quarter turn, arm still up, a white-knuckled fist held ready to pound away at something, eyes still locked on the space before him.

Gavin took a step back, the hair on the back of his neck standing up. His gaze darted back and forth between the windows on the front of the house and Karl's strange behavior. "You okay?"

Another awful, gasping grunt, and another ninety-degree turn, and then Karl's fist came down at Gavin like a hammer's blow but missed by a country mile. The detective jerked down a step, then another, his movements getting more and more fluid with each step. His right hand dropped to the holster he wore on his hip and jerked his Glock out.

Gavin side-stepped and put his hand out to ward away the pistol, but Karl batted his arm down with his other hand. His wide-eyed gaze fell on Gavin's face, and Gavin could read the terror in Karl's eyes. He shoved Karl off the steps and into the hibiscus bush beside them, then turned and kicked the door hard— once, twice, and a third time before the jamb splintered around the deadbolt, and the door banged open.

He snapped his pistol out and moved into the dark house in a running crouch, wincing at Karl's zombie-like footsteps thudding up the stairs outside. Gavin ducked into the front room, sweeping the room with his pistol. Shadows painted the walls, but nothing moved in response to his entry. Karl reached the top of the steps, and Gavin plunged through the only other door and into the formal dining room, bumping his hip on a tall, straight-backed chair and sending it scuttling into the wall.

He cataloged the room with a hurried glance: table, six chairs, a china cabinet, a rolling service tray—all covered with a thick film of dust. No dark forms lurched toward him from deeper in the house, but Karl stomped into the living room behind him, and again, Gavin raced through the only door and into the kitchen.

Shadows danced across the floor, nothing more than vague shapes, but enough to kick Gavin's fight or flight reflex into high gear. Hands shaking with the rush of adrenaline, Gavin swept his pistol from dark corner to shadow and onward. Covered with newsprint as it was, the window allowed enough light to bleed through that he could see the room was empty—except for a rickety card table and a single folding chair.

He darted a glance back through the door to the dining room, saw the glint of Karl's eyes halfway through the room, and threw himself back, even as the detective's Glock thundered. "Karl!" he shouted. "It's me! Hold your fire!"

Karl increased his pace by way of an answer, and Gavin dashed toward the dark hallway on the other side of the kitchen. Karl's pistol thundered again, and he felt the wind of the round's passing on his cheek. He ducked and careened into the hallway leading to the back. He ran hunched over, waiting for the searing pain, for the hammer blow of a hollow point slug driving through his flesh.

Ahead of him, glass shattered, and there came a flurry of sound—scrabbling, thudding. He sprinted down the hall, gun held ready in front of him.

He threw himself to the side and slid into a crouch, his shoulder scraping down the wall. Three pitch-black doorways faced him—and he thought the noises came from the middle door. He duckwalked forward, throwing glances back toward the kitchen every other breath.

He reached the first darkened door and peeked inside—a bathroom. He rocked forward and stole another glance inside and found the room empty.

Gavin pushed past it, listening hard, peeking over his shoulder, trapped between whatever was going on with Karl and whoever was in front.

"Gavin!" Karl croaked from the darkness behind. "I'm… *Jesus Christ.* What the fuck was that?"

He reached the middle door and stopped, trying to slow his heartbeat, to control his breathing. He glanced back and saw Karl coming toward him in the darkness, his pistol pointed at the ceiling, his gaze frantic, assessing.

Looking for bullet holes, Gavin realized. He shook his head, then pointed at the door, and Karl nodded.

Gavin dove across the yawning blackness defined by the door frame, then spun back into a crouch, facing Karl with the door between them. He held up three fingers and counted down. When he dropped the last finger, he plunged into the room, Karl standing, giving him cover from above.

The room was empty, save for an antique desk set missing its chair—obviously used to shatter the window set at chest height in the wall. Karl ran to the window and glared out into the dark night. Then he looked at Gavin and shook his head.

"Christ, Gavin, I—"

Gavin shook his head and said, "It wasn't you, was it?"

Karl swallowed hard. "I couldn't do anything. I tried to stop, but…"

"Puppeteering," Gavin said, and Karl swallowed again, then nodded.

"He had me, ran me like a toy robot, but then…"

"He let you go?"

"That's not… I mean…" Karl shook his head. "That's not what it *felt* like."

"What did it feel like?"

"Like someone else forced him out."

14

1089 Michigan Avenue, Miami Beach, FL
Friday, 5:49 am

By the time Lieutenant Truxillo rolled up, the CSI team was already inside the house, taking it apart atom by atom. He looked at Karl first, then approached Gavin on the other side of the front yard, a sour, stern expression on his face. "Tell me," he said.

Gavin looked him in the eye and told the lies he and Karl had come up with to explain the "shots fired" call for backup. "We were next door"—He hooked his thumb at Fannin's house—"at the billing address for the phone used to call in the body this morning. He's a grumpy old bastard, and a bigot to boot, but he didn't make the call. He claims he has never owned a cell phone, and I believe him. He told us the guy living in this house had moved in at around the same time the cell phone account was created. Karl and I decided to check the house. It—"

"No backup? No call to me?"

"The house looked empty, Lieutenant. Paper on the windows." He gestured to the side yard. "Completely dark—no car, no signs of life."

Truxillo nodded but still wore the sour expression on his face. "Then what?"

"Karl went to the door to knock, and I provided cover on the windows. A commotion kicked off inside, and Karl stepped aside from the door, trying to take some cover in case someone came barreling out the front door. He stepped wrong and fell into the hibiscus." He pointed at the crushed plant. "Then, I thought I heard someone scream—"

"You *thought* you heard someone scream or you *heard* someone scream, Gavin?"

Gavin shrugged and jerked his chin toward the door. "At the time, I was sure, but now… It might have been the guy we were looking for trying to trick us. At any rate, I kicked it in and told Karl to follow when he could."

"You kicked it in?" Truxillo sent a glance Karl's way. "Not Karl?"

"That's right," said Gavin. "Karl was still fighting his way out of the hibiscus."

"Okay."

"I moved inside, but I had to go slow. The papers on the windows and the drawn drapes out front let in very little light. I called out, identifying myself and commanding anyone inside to come toward the living room, hands up, and all that." Gavin glanced across the yard. "Karl came in as I did that. He took cover behind some furniture, and I nodded toward the next room— which is a formal dining room. I moved inward, and Karl covered me. The room was obviously empty— you'll see it when you go in. As I looked around, an unsub came out of the kitchen, pointing something at me. Karl yelled, I ducked, and he fired but missed. The unsub turned and ran back deeper into the house. I followed, with Karl supporting, and moved into the kitchen. The unsub ducked out from the corner where the hall meets the kitchen. I missed it, but Karl saw him point something at us again. He told me to get down, and I dropped. He fired once more, but the unsub had already turned and taken off down the hall. He ducked into the second door back there. We heard the crash of broken glass, but I thought it might be another trick. You know, to get us rushing into the room where he waited in ambush."

"Like he did in the kitchen," said Truxillo with a nod, his expression softening.

"Yeah. We made a careful approach, and by the time we'd determined there was no one waiting, the unsub had escaped through the window. We checked the yard, but he was gone. That's when we called it in."

Truxillo nodded. "You separated to wait for us?"

"Not at first," Gavin said with a shrug. "We were worried the unsub might come back, so we blocked the kitchen door with the dining room table and set up in the living room. We stayed there until the first patrol officers arrived and secured the scene."

"And Karl's going to tell me the same story?"

"I don't know," said Gavin, "we didn't talk about it."

Truxillo grunted and said, "Stay here." He crossed the yard to hear Karl's version of events—which would be different enough in minor details to make both accounts seem reasonable. The lieutenant glanced at Gavin several times during Karl's account, and Gavin met his direct gaze with one of his own.

Finally, Truxillo nodded and headed inside. When he emerged onto the stoop, he beckoned both Karl and Gavin. "No blood, and the techs found both slugs," he said to Karl. "They've got something on the unsub. I should take Karl off the case, pending the formal investigation, but I'm not going to. He's my best detective, so policy can suck it. I'd rather catch this freak than stick to the letter. I'll handle the shoot team. I want both of you focused on The Bogeyman." He bounced a stern gaze between them, then held up his index finger. "But…no more stunts. No more cowboy policing. Am I absolutely clear?"

"Lieutenant—"

"Am I clear?" His steely glare bored into Gavin's.

"Yes, Lieutenant."

Truxillo looked at Karl, who nodded. The lieutenant glanced over his shoulder, then stepped closer. "Now that I've officially chewed you out, if it takes cowboy tactics… Well, we need results, gentlemen. *Lo entiendes*?" He looked at them until they both nodded, then he turned and stepped into the house. "Come on." He led them to the back of the house, past the room with the broken window, into the last door. A long folding table was set up along one wall, and cardboard file boxes lined the opposite wall. A folding chair that matched the one in the kitchen sat neatly tucked under the table.

Truxillo grabbed a translucent evidence bag and handed it to Gavin. It was a cell phone bill, addressed to the old man next door. When Gavin passed it to Santana, Truxillo handed him four other bags—each containing a credit card statement under four different names.

"We have names, gentlemen," said the lieutenant. "I'll get a track on these credit cards." He took back the evidence bag and handed over a list with four names on it.

Gavin nodded, then scanned the list. "Xavier Frire, Rayson Friogais, Dylan Steke, Javier Freir."

"I've already put out the APBs," said Truxillo. "Now, get out there and get the bastard."

15

The concierge gave them a strange look when they requested a meeting room before most of the guests in the hotel were up but shrugged and unlocked the one closest to the lobby. Gavin brought down his laptop and connected it to the hotel's Wi-Fi, then remoted in to his desktop back in Quantico. He pulled up the NCIC database, ran the four aliases against the violent person file, and found nothing. He also tried ViCAP on the off chance that the names showed as suspects to an unsolved violent crime. "All four are clean," he said with a shake of his head.

Karl grimaced. "That would have been too easy, anyway. But I might as well try the FDLE while you get the old woman on the horn." He got up and stepped into the hall.

Gavin called Maddie first and, by the muddled quality of her voice, woke her up.

"What time?" she mumbled.

"Seven," he said.

"I am *not* in the FBI, Gav."

"Yeah, but I am. We almost had him, honey."

Bedclothes rustled in Virginia, evoking a small smile in Miami. Gavin could imagine her bolting up and kicking the covers off as she often did on the weekends. "Tell me."

"Unfortunately, the thing started with a new body. But the unsub made a mistake and called it in using a cell phone. Karl tapped a buddy at the phone company and got—"

"The billing address?"

"Got it in one. But he was half-clever about it. He used a neighbor's address."

"And he was home? The neighbor?"

"The neighbor and the unsub both. There's more, but I want to tell Adeline, too."

"Get her on the line while I get coffee, then."

Gavin switched over and dialed the old woman's number, then conferenced the calls together.

"It's early," said Adeline with what sounded like a stifled yawn.

"Right?" said Maddie.

"We almost had him this morning. There's—"

"Another dead girl, and they worked out the unsub's address. He was there, evidently," said Maddie.

"Right. He took control of Karl," Gavin said. "Ran him like a remote-control car."

"A puppeteer, then," said Adeline.

"Yes. That's what your stories have been building up to, right?"

"Yes," she said.

"We also found four credit card bills under bogus names."

Adeline chuckled, "My, my. Ain't he clever?"

"Then you do know who it is?" asked Gavin with an edge to his voice."

"No, child," she said. "I meant 'whoever he is.'"

"These four names—

"Let me tell my part first. Is Detective Karl there?"

"Yes, but he's out doing a search on the four names in the FDLE database. The Federal databases had nothing."

"He won't find nothing, either. Any more dreams?" asked Adeline.

The door opened, and Karl came in.

"Yeah, but let's get into that later. Here's Karl."

"Morning, Karl," said Maddie. "You'll note I didn't say 'good morning.'"

Karl chuckled. "Sorry about the early call, but we've had a big break."

"About that," said Adeline. "Ain't none of those four going to be *real* names. But the names he chose is clues, I'll bet. Tell me them names."

"Xavier Frire, Rayson Friogais, Dylan Steke, Javier Freir," said Gavin.

"Ayup," she said. "As I figured. Three of them first names, I know—Rayson, Dylan, and Javier. All three were students of the Program. Xavier is the French form of the name Javier. Three of them last names are the same word in different languages, so I'm willing to bet the one I don't know is too."

"Where are these students now? Miami?" asked Karl.

"I don't know. The last time I saw any of those boys was in the dawn of the year 2000."

"What are the names of those former students?"

"Javier Dela Cruz, Rayson Fergus, and Dylan Jepson."

Gavin ran the names through NCIC. "No records on any of those, either."

"No, there wouldn't be, even if he was arrested for something. Just like you found nothing on my name, I'll warrant." When Gavin didn't answer, she cackled. "That's okay, child. Of course, you had to check on me. I knew you would, and I knew you'd find nothing."

"Are these three students in the group of people you suspect could be The Bogeyman?"

"Yes, all three."

"Didn't you say there were four men in that group?" asked Maddie.

"Ayup. I bet you can guess who number four is."

"Fry," Gavin murmured.

"Yes, my hoodoo man, as your lovely wife named him. If I could only guess once, I'd pick him. Them last names? Frire, Freir, Steke, and Friogais?"

"Yes?"

"Frire is French, Freir is Spanish, Steke is Norwegian. All of them mean 'fry.' If I had to bet, I'd put my money down on the line that Friogais is Gaelic for the same word."

"But is it Javier Freir—"

"Dela Cruz," said Adeline. "Javier Dela Cruz is his real name."

"Fine. Is the person using the names Javier Dela Cruz or your Fry?"

"Your guess is as good as mine. Javier was a nasty piece of work, even as a child. He was the first student Kai spoke to once he was processed in, and Javi was responsible for what happened to Jamilla, too, in his own way. When Kai woke up that first morning, it was to the sound of what we called 'the pacers.' Students who wasn't allowed leave the dorm at night but who couldn't sleep neither. Javier Dela Cruz was the poster child of the pacers.

Chapter 13
The Blues

I

The Compound, under the Sonoran Desert, AZ
June 17, 1998, 5:57 am MST

A scuffing sound awakened Kai, dragging him from a deep, restful sleep. *A* healing *sleep,* he thought. *But healing from what?* He rolled onto his side, jerking the covers up to cover his ear, all the while keeping his eyes shut, hoping to fall back into the blessed warmth of unconsciousness.

…scriff…scruff…scriff-scruff…scriff…

The sound never stopped, pausing for a heartbeat at a time, only to restart an instant later. The more he tried to ignore the sound and go back to sleep, the harder he listened for the next noise. He grunted with frustration and opened his eyes.

He lay on a cot-like bunk in a room full of other cots. The one closest to him was empty—in fact, it looked unslept in. The cot beyond that bore a mound of blue topped by a crop of auburn hair.

The dimmed lights overhead showed a room swathed in blues. Blue blankets, lighter-hued blue sheets, blue painted walls, and blue frieze carpet. Kai shoved his own blue bedclothes aside and rubbed his eyes. A loose baby blue jumpsuit hung from his frame. On the floor next to the cot rested a pair of blue slip-on athletic shoes—not a name-brand, but rather something he expected from one of those cheap shoe stores. Behind him, mirrors stretched from floor to ceiling, and opposite that, in front of him, was a huge archway that spanned the width of the room and opened onto a concrete-block hall painted sky blue. Another row of bunks lay against the opposite wall, the two rows separated by a six-foot aisle. Four or five blue-suited figures paced back and forth, back and forth, back and forth down the length of the aisle, and that's where the *scriff-scruff* noises came from—the legs of their oversized blue jumpsuits.

Kai sat up, rubbed his eyes again, then swung his legs out of the bed and slipped into his shoes. The chilly air raised goosebumps down his arms as he stood and stretched.

Another boy—one of the pacers—came toward him in the aisle. His lips moved to the rhythm of his footsteps, but Kai couldn't hear what he was saying— if anything. The boy had dark hair, dark eyes, and pale skin. His gaze drifted over to meet Kai's, but no friendship showed in the gaze, only hostility and disdain.

He looked away and stood up, throwing his arms in the air and stretching until his back crackled. When he opened his eyes again, the boy stood in front of him, a quirky smile on his face.

"I'm Javi," he said, sticking out his fist.

Kai glanced down and bumped his fist. "Kai."

"Looks like we're neighbors," said Javi with a grin. "I hope you don't fart a lot." The open hostility he'd shown Kai a moment ago was gone.

"Where's the bathroom?" He had to cant his head back a little as Javi had him by about six inches. He looked a few years older, to boot.

"C'mon, I'll show you, *chamaco*," said Javi. "What's Kai short for? Javi is short for Javier."

"Nothing," said Kai with a shrug.

Javi chuckled. "Yeah, you people are always making up names." He turned and strode into the aisle, taking a moment to glare at another pacer who'd come to their side of the room.

"Uh...that's a little racist, don't you think?"

Javi shrugged, his smile undiminished. "Listen to you, talking all White and everything."

"Anyway, it's not made up. It's Hawaiian. It means 'sea.'"

"Oh. Cool, I guess," Javi's tone made it clear he thought anything but. "Maybe I'll call you 'Seaman.'" He chuckled at that, but Kai had no idea why. "Javier means 'my dad's an asshole who let my Mexicano mother pick the name.'"

"Oh. Uh..."

Javi laughed and thumped him on the arm. "That's supposed to be a joke, *cuate*."

"Okay," said Kai, dropping his gaze and looking away.

"Shitter's this way," said Javi, thumping him on the arm again. He turned and led them to the big arch that connected the room to the hallway. "There are a lot of rules in this dump, Kai. One of the stupidest is that during sleepytime—and yes, that's what they really call it—blues are supposed to stay in the dorm. But—and get this—the bathroom is down the hall, between the blue section and the yellow dorm section."

"Yellow?"

"Yeah." He tweaked Kai's nipple. "Blue. B for baby. We're on the lowest rung of this place. Yellow is the next rung up."

"How many steps are there?"

"Blue, yellow, green, charcoal, white, and red. Try to stay away from the people in red—real bunch of assholes."

"Oh."

"Ah, *mierda*. I forgot my toothbrush." He leaned out into the hall and pointed. "Bathroom's right down there. The only door on the block."

"I can wait for you."

"Nah, you go on and do your business. I don't want to smell it, anyway. I'll meet you there in a few minutes."

Kai shrugged as Javi turned back and strode off down the aisle. He glanced down the hall in the direction Javi had pointed, then shrugged again and stepped into the hall. He walked at a brisk pace—truth be told, he couldn't have waited long for Javi anyway.

When he stepped out of the bathroom, shaking his hands to dry them, a tall boy in a red jumpsuit was waiting for him. "First day here, and you're already a rule-breaker."

"Um, what?"

"What color are you wearing?"

"Blue," said Kai, looking down.

"And what's the rule about sleepytime?"

"I just woke up. No one's told me—"

"Javier Dela Cruz told you the sleepytime rule, kid. Don't make it worse by lying."

"But—"

"No buts." He grasped Kai's shoulder and steered him up the hall in the other direction from the dorm he'd woken up in. "Take it like a man, that's my advice."

"Take what like a man?"

He got no answer. Instead, the boy in the red jumpsuit marshaled Kai through a ten-minute walk and a maze of corridors, then planted him in a row of chairs like those found outside the principal's office at school back home. He told Kai to sit there until he was called in.

Kai sat and fidgeted, and the red jumpsuit went into a room across the hall. After ten or fifteen minutes, a guy who didn't look old enough to be in charge of anything stuck his head out and hooked his finger at Kai. Inside the office, the guy went around a desk that had multiple computer monitors set up on it and sank into a chair.

"Guess you screwed the pooch this morning, eh, kid?"

"I just woke up in a place I've never seen before and had to pee. One of the—"

"Nah," said the guy, and Kai wound down to a halt. "We don't deal in excuses in the Program, and you need to reconcile yourself to that. We hold each other accountable. We police *ourselves*, Mr. Washington, so that *no one else* needs to do the job." The guy chuckled. "Not that anyone else could."

"I don't know what you—"

"Yes, you do. I just told you."

Kai bit his lip and looked around the small office. It was bereft of decoration or personal items. There wasn't even a nameplate on the desk. "Who are you?"

The guy leaned forward. "Who I am doesn't matter. The question is: Who are *you*, Kai Washington? Are you a guy who blames others for his own misdeeds, or are you an upright guy who can be trusted to take responsibility when he screws up?"

Kai took a deep breath, then squared his shoulders like his daddy had taught him to. "I went to the bathroom. Javi told me where it was, but it's not fair to hold me accountable for rules when no one's bothered to tell them to me."

The guy's chair creaked as he rocked back in it and steepled his fingers in front of his face. "Who promised you fairness? Was that your mommy and daddy?" He leaned forward and fixed Kai with an intense stare. "Do you see your mommy and daddy here?"

Kai dropped his gaze and shook his head.

"Yeah, I don't either. Everything they taught you to expect from the world is wrong. Compassion, fairness, everything like that, it all amounts to one thing, Kai."

He narrowed his eyes at Kai. "*Weakness.* There is no place for weakness here in the Program. Let's see if we can teach you that in a way you'll remember, eh, Kai?"

2

The Compound, under the Sonoran Desert, AZ
June 17, 1998, 6:25 am MST

Jamilla wet the mop, then squirted some cleaner on the rough textured floor of the observation hall that ran between the mirrored back walls of the dorms. She slopped a little water out of her bucket with the mop, then went to work spreading the cleaner around. She stole a glance to her left as she worked the mop, glancing into a blue dorm, noting the walkers in the center aisle and scanning their faces. None of them, however, looked familiar.

A pale-skinned kid came down the aisle, muttering or talking to himself, and stopped less than a hands-breadth from the mirrored glass. He cocked his head to the side and smiled. He made a slow, exaggerated wink, letting his mouth hang open as he did so.

Jamilla knew he couldn't see her, that he was just clowning, hoping someone would be there to catch his act. She looked down at the mop and worked the cleaner into the corner at the bottom of the mirrored wall. She jumped and dropped the mop when the kid knocked on the glass.

She lifted her gaze and found that the kid had followed her movements. He still stood a few inches from the mirrored surface, staring at her, seeming to meet her gaze head-on. She bent to retrieve her mop, and the kid knocked again.

She stood straight and turned to face him. She stuck out her tongue, and he smiled and shook his head. She stepped to the side, and he followed her. She lifted her hand and waved, and so did he. She tilted her head to the right, and again, he mirrored her movement. "You can't see me," she murmured.

The boy nodded.

"No," she said, and again, the boy nodded at her. Then he half-turned and pointed at an empty bunk. Jamilla looked where he pointed, but it was just an empty bunk, like the one next to it. She lifted her shoulders and let them fall.

The kid turned back to face her and mouthed the words, "That's Kai's bed."

Kai, she thought. *Now, I know where he lives.*

The boy flashed a one-sided grin at her, but it seemed to Jamilla that it wasn't a pleasant smile, not a smile to share, but a smile at someone else's expense.

Jamilla narrowed her eyes, and the boy winked at her, then pointed at the archway.

3

The Compound, under the Sonoran Desert, AZ
June 17, 1998, 6:29 am MST

Tears streaked down Kai's cheeks, and a little snot bubbled in his right nostril every time he exhaled. The kid in the red jumpsuit walked beside him, taking him back to the blue dorms. He'd tried to put his hand on Kai's shoulder, but Kai had shrugged him off and scowled at him through his tears.

As soon as they turned onto his hallway, Kai bolted away from the kid and ran, stealing glances at the dorms he passed. When he recognized the pacers, he ducked through the arch and trotted down the central aisle to his bunk.

Javi stood at the back of the room, next to the mirrors, half-turned so he could look at Kai. As he reached his bunk, Javi nodded at him and winked, then turned back to the mirror.

"You're an asshole!" Kai snapped, more tears spilling from his eyes, though these came from frustration and anger.

"Yep," said Javi without turning, his gaze shifting from his own reflection to Kai's and then back. "But, *chulo*, don't blame me. *You* were the one who broke the rules." Javi chuckled. "And I'd just *told* you the rule, you little idiot." He turned his attention back to his own reflection. "Don't act like a *mama's boy!*"

"Shut up, Javi!" Kai yelled. He flung himself onto his cot, rolling up on his side, presenting his back to Javier.

4

Jamilla watched her son come running into the dorm, tears streaking his cheeks, and shook her head. He ran to the bed the pale-skinned kid had pointed to, then yelled at him. The boy at the mirror said something back, then laughed and turned back, locking his gaze on her.

"Don't act like a *mama's boy!*" the Hispanic boy said, though he looked anything but angry. In fact, he looked like he was enjoying himself.

"Shut up, Javi!" Kai yelled and flung himself on the cot.

Javi's grin stretched and stretched—a Cheshire grin if Jamilla had ever seen one. He stepped to the side, turning away from Kai and using his body to block Jamilla's view. He winked at her, then laughed again.

Jamilla grimaced and narrowed her eyes. Javi was a world-class bully in her estimation, and a conman to boot. *Kai isn't prepared to deal with a boy like Javi,* she thought without emotion. *He's been surrounded by good people his whole life, not people destined for a prison cell.*

Javi thumped his fist against the glass, drawing her gaze back to his own. His face was a study in rage, lips twisted, teeth exposed, but it was his eyes that scared her. Fury danced there, mixed with hate and a promise of pain to come.

Without meaning to, Jamilla stepped back until her shoulders bumped against the glass wall on the other side of the hallway. She couldn't look away from Javi's enraged, hateful stare. The inside of her skull began to itch and throb and ache, feeling like her brain had swelled against it, had cracked it, had shattered the bone into a thousand pieces. Her right bicep jumped under her skin once and again, then twice in rapid succession. Her whole right arm twitched, then bent at the elbow, her fingers curled into a tight ball, and her fist rocketed up into her cheek. Pain and shock and fear all vied for possession of her mind, then her fist rammed into her face as hard as she knew how to hit, then again, and a fourth time. Her vision swam, and her cheek and knuckles traded throbs.

Javi continued to stare at her, her hand locked into a fist, her arm tense, ready to go another round. The boy lifted his hand and stabbed his finger at the mirror, pointing at her, then he whirled around and stomped toward Kai's back.

Jamilla felt a momentary urge to pound on the glass, to warn Kai, but it passed. Her thoughts seemed clinical where the boy was concerned.

5

The Compound, under the Sonoran Desert, AZ
June 17, 1998, 6:31 am MST

Kai lay curled on his side, back to the mirrors, back to Javi, his knees drawn up and his thumb in his mouth. He stared toward the arch, ignoring the cadre of pacers, the other kids who were sitting in their bunks, looking around bleary-eyed.

White-hot agony erupted in his spine, and the force of the blow to the small of his back shoved him forward, toward the edge of the cot. Kai cried out and slapped one hand to the area that hurt the most. One of the pacers had stopped dead in his tracks and was staring past Kai.

Kai rolled to his back—just in time to take another of Javi's kicks to his side, catching it on the pelvis. "Stop it!" he shouted, but Javi's face bore a twisted, malicious expression, and his eyes… His eyes showed no mercy, no compassion, and a promise of more pain to follow. He stepped closer, balling his hands into tight fists. He sneered at Kai and raised his fist.

6

The Compound, under the Sonoran Desert, AZ
June 17, 1998, 6:32 am MST

Jamilla tried to step toward the one-way glass as Javi kicked Kai in the small of the back, but her body seemed frozen stiff. *Someone should stop this*, she thought, and seemingly of its own accord, her gaze flicked to the arch and hallway beyond. Her mind felt as though she were in the eye of a storm, perfect calm amidst chaos. She watched as Kai rolled to his back, and Javi delivered another kick. *Who will stop this*? *Where are those red-suited proctors*? Her gaze leaped from the two boys closest to the mirror to the archway and back again, but she saw only blue shades. She opened her mouth to yell for help, unsure if her sudden paralysis extended to her voice box.

"Help! Send help to"—she glanced at the words stenciled on the glass at the top center of the wall—"Blue Dorm Seven!" She had no real idea of who she expected to hear her, let alone follow her commands. Her mind felt detached, so much driftwood whisked away from shore by a strong current. She took a breath to call out again, but Javi twisted his head around to the mirrored glass, then spun to face it, his gaze seeming to snap to hers. He mimicked pulling a zipper shut across his lips. The ragged itch inside Jamilla's head doubled, and her mouth snapped shut. Her right fist squeezed tighter and tighter until her knuckles blanched. Then it slammed into her cheek again, hard enough to bring stars to her eyes. Her fist came again, this time colliding with her jaw under her chin, and she staggered to the side.

In the dorm on the other side of the glass, Kai launched himself at Javi's back—leaping from atop his cot. Javi staggered into the glass with a hollow clamor, and his control of Jamilla faltered. She turned and ran.

7

The Compound, under the Sonoran Desert, AZ
June 17, 1998, 6:32 am MST

She flew through corridor after corridor, trapped underground, unable to find the sky, unable to soar among the clouds. She became aware of an insubstantial tug, of a pull like the force that tried to pull her from the sky—except the pull was to the side instead of down.

She banked in a tight circle in an intersection of two halls, fixing the direction of the pull in that special navigational sense she had. She followed the pull, followed the tug on her mind, sliding right through the rock-like walls of the corridors, blipping through closed caves (rooms) behind fixed slabs of steel (locked doors), even sliding through solid stone (concrete) for a time.

Then she was there—a place painted the color of the sky, an artificial cave (dorm) in a hall of artificial caves. A raucous commotion roared in the back of the cave (dorm! Dorm!) and without her bidding, her body banked into the dorm and glided toward the back wall of falling water (mirrored glass).

Two boys in ridiculous blue plumage (jumpsuits) fought one another like bobcats—rolling on the floor, kicking, hitting, biting. She found herself floating effortlessly above them, watching as the bigger boy slowly gained purchase on the smaller one (Kai! Kai!), pinning him to the floor.

The bigger kid smiled the smile of a mad wolf and sat back on his haunches, knees on either side of the boy-child Kai's ribs. He glared down at the boy-child Kai, then the muscles of his face tightened, and a look of intense concentration burned in his eyes.

She opened her beak to scream at the bigger kid, to scare him off, to do anything she could to protect the boy-child Kai. She drew air into her lungs and…

…screamed Kai's name, jerking up from her cot, heart and mind in overdrive, adrenaline smoking through her. Eyes wide, she stumble-danced to the phone on the narrow desk across the room. She stabbed an extension into it with a swollen-knuckled finger.

"Night ops," said a bored-sounding man.

"Blue Dorm Seven," Adeline rasped. "There's going to be a bad fight."

"Yeah? And you know this how?"

"I'm Adeline d'Clara, child, and you'd better get moving. If anything happens to Kai Washington, you'll answer to me." She could almost hear the man coming to attention.

"Yes, ma'am. I'll get right over there."

"See that you do." She snapped her finger up and down on the hook, then dialed another extension. It rang four times before anyone picked it up.

"What?" Bethany demanded in a sleep-blurred voice.

"Kai's in trouble."

The blonde woman sighed. "Miss Addy, you know that he will endure a certain amount of punishment—"

"Listen to me, child! One of the other boys is going to beat him senseless in a few minutes. Or maybe it's already started. I sent the night watch, but we may need a puppeteer!"

"Chavez," said Bethany, all vestiges of sleep gone from her voice. "Beatrice is sending for him."

8

Kai leaped from his cot, arcing through the air to land on Javi's back, one arm snaking around the older boy's throat, the other arcing around to smash into his nose. Javi cried out—sounding every bit the enraged bear—and spun in circles, one hand rising to peel Kai's arm from his neck, the other trying to ward off the boy's blows.

Their dormmates stared at them, no one moving, no one making so much as a peep, no one trying to stop the fight. Kai kicked his legs around Javi's waist and hammered away at his face. The pair lurched around in circles as Javi spun and spun, trying to peel away Kai's arm and legs, ignoring the blows that rained down on his face. After a few moments of that, he gave up on trying to dislodge Kai and charged at the wall next to Kai's bunk, twisting around at the last minute to slam Kai into the wall and *hard*.

Kai's breath whooshed out of him, and the air in the dorm seemed to evaporate. Javi flicked his arm away, and he fell to the floor, gasping. Javi delivered a savage kick, then dropped on him, driving punches into his face, his torso.

Kai rocked side to side, but the blows still found him, either the impacts or the lack of breath making his ears ring while spots danced in front of his eyes. After an eternity of that, Javi put his knees to either side of Kai's chest and sat back, showing a mean smile.

Javi's eyes seemed to spin as his gaze bored into Kai's, and a foul itch developed inside Kai's head. The muscles in Javi's face tightened into a grimace of rage, and his gaze grew harder and harder.

Kai wanted to look away, willed his head to turn, but could not. The irritation in the center of his mind grew worse and worse with each second that passed. He could feel Javi asserting his will over Kai's muscles, could feel the intrusion into his mind like a hot poker. His arms flopped at his sides, out of his control. He pushed back against the mental pressure in his mind, imagined constructing brick walls, imagined giant earth-moving machines pushing Javi out of his mind with their giant Caterpillar engines and wide steel blades.

Javi grunted and narrowed his eyes, and the itchy pressure increased. One by one, Kai's imagined earth-moving machines crumpled as though constructed of wet cardboard.

He constructed giant stone walls, concrete barriers, brick walls, giant basalt cliff faces, but no matter what he tried, no matter how much they slowed the other boy's assault initially, Javi eroded their foundations and slipped past them. All it took was time.

Panic wrapped icy fingers around Kai's bowels. *Someone help me*! he sent with as much force as he could muster.

Javier grinned, his eyes crinkling with pleasure. He pushed harder and harder and harder, pouring energy into his advance.

"What's going on here?" cried a male voice.

Javi didn't pay him any mind. He kept right on, forcing his advance deeper and deeper into Kai's mind. Fighting force on force, Kai had to give more and more ground, had to retreat—slowly, sure, but still retreat. He needed something else…

"Get off him!"

A second later, Javi's weight disappeared, and at the same time, the mental assault faded. Kai sucked in a deep breath. He pushed himself to a seated position, his back sliding up the baby-blue wall.

A man Kai didn't recognize stood next to his bunk, holding Javi down with one hand and staring into his eyes. He threw a glance at Kai and said, "You okay, kid?"

Kai nodded, but even as he did, the man's eyes grew unfocused, and his gaze drifted back toward Javi's. The hand planted in the middle of Javi's chest twitched, once, twice, and again, then his arm jerked back, hovering an inch above the boy's chest. The man grunted, and his face twisted into an expression of desperation and fear. His arm began to shake as he tried to make it return to Javi's chest, but it continued to rise.

A nasty smile grew on Javier's face, and he sat up on the cot, gaze burning. He grunted, and Kai's prospective rescuer lurched into motion, moving like one of those automatons Kai had seen at Disney World.

The man groaned, and spit bubbled past his lips as he spun into a drunken dance, jigging left and right, taking lurching steps, his arms cocked at his sides, snapping to some unheard beat. His eyes rolled in his head like that of a panicked horse.

It dawned on Kai that Javier was doing the same thing he'd done to the Pig.

He attacked, circling Javi's mind, looking for a way in, a weakness he could exploit, but the boy's mind was as unlike the Pig's as his body was. Still, Kai pressed in, probed, poked, and he could sense Javi's focus slipping. He struck at the boy's mind like a snake, a quick hit, then pulling back to ready the next strike.

"Stop, you little fuck!" Javi groaned.

But he didn't let the man go, didn't stop his manipulation, so Kai continued his attack.

The guy who'd broken them up started to spin in place, his arms wide, feet fast blurs on the blue carpet. Javi leered at him, spinning his finger in time to the man's frantic pirouettes.

Kai chiseled and punched and bore down on Javi's defenses with increasing pressure and furious savagery. He lost track of anything else, focusing only on getting inside. He imagined a big M1 Abrams tank, turbine screaming, slamming into the walls around Javier. He pictured a battleship ramming a fiberglass sailboat, painted a medieval ram slamming into a castle's wooden gates. He imagined Javi had made his defenses from glass, imagined them cracking, the cracks spreading like lightning, imagined large chunks falling to shatter on the ground. He applied more and more and more pressure, bearing down until his pulse thundered in his ears, and his vision blurred.

Javier moaned and let go of the staffer, twisting his head to stare at Kai. He attacked, swarming around Kai, crushing him with the sheer number and rapidity of his attacks. Kai cried out, trying to fend him off.

STOP! DELA CRUZ, STOP! The mental voice rolled through Kai's mind like thunder.

Kai built and built and built walls, only to have them shattered by Dela Cruz in a matter of moments. His breath came in gasps, spots danced in his vision. He began shaking his head back and forth, pouring all his energy, all his focus, all his power into the defense.

And then, it ended, and Kai sagged sideways, leaning against the leg of his cot, not seeing, not hearing a thing. After a moment, he opened his eyes to find Javi pinned to his own cot, lying flat and staring at the ceiling. A single tear rolled from his eye and dripped down to his ear.

Chavez stood at the foot of Javi's cot, staring at the boy, frowning. The other staffer sat on a cot across the main aisle, his head in his hands.

9

The Compound, under the Sonoran Desert, AZ
June 17, 1998, 6:43 am MST

Adeline trotted down the hallway, her slippered feet aching with each step, her knees threatening to give out, her hips screaming, and her back burning as if afire. Beatrice jogged at her side, Bethany a step behind, neither woman speaking. They rounded a corner, raced through the next three intersections, then turned again.

We don't need to go in person, sent Beatrice again.

"That's right," said Bethany. "Chavez has it under control."

Adeline kept trotting at the same speed, not answering because, to speak true, she didn't have the air to spare. A rictus of suffering locked her face in a rigid grip.

A door down the hall slammed open, and Jamilla burst into the hallway. She looked at the two sisters before locking eyes with Adeline. "Blue Seven," she cried. "There's a fight."

The three women stopped, Adeline huffing for air. "It's being taken care of," said Bethany. "You can return to your work."

"Kai is…" Jamilla's face went slack for a moment. "The other boy is older. Powerful."

"We know, child," said Adeline, returning Jamilla's gaze without blinking.

"You…don't…speak   to…"   Jamilla's   gaze wandered, then snapped back to Adeline's, her eyes blazing.

"Oh, child," said Adeline with a sigh. "I'll come find you. Later. I'll explain."

"Don't bother!" Jamilla snapped.

Bethany shot a glance at her sister and smirked.

Go back to your assigned duties, Jamilla, sent Beatrice. *Every moment you delay, delays* us *from getting there.*

Her gaze left Adeline's and twitched toward Beatrice without quite touching the blonde's eyes. She turned and opened the door. "Can I watch?"

Through the mirror, yes, but don't interfere.

Jamilla stepped into the hidden hall and let the door swing shut behind her.

Adeline glared at Beatrice.

It's for her own good. You know that.

Adeline resumed her trot toward Blue Dorm Seven. "Did you have to put my room all the way across the Compound?"

10

Jamilla leaned against the door, her chest heaving, air whistling between her teeth. *Almost lost it,* she thought. *Seeing her...here.* She shook her head once, violently, and took a deep breath. *But why? This is where Kai should be. She did the right thing.* Her eyebrows knitted, and her mouth drew down into a frown. Those thoughts, those ideas, seemed so foreign, yet she could not deny the truth of them.

She pushed herself away from the door and turned to retrace her steps to the observation hall behind the back wall of Blue Dorm Seven. Her expression darkened as she ran. *If anything happens to Kai, I'll kill that gray-eyed—*

Jamilla came back to herself a moment later, standing in the middle of the observation hall, hands hanging loosely at her sides. *What am I doing here?* she asked herself. *What was... I was doing something a moment ago...but what?*

She shrugged and looked at her surroundings to orient herself, then headed back to her assigned duty.

11

The Compound, under the Sonoran Desert, AZ
June 17, 1998, 6:47 am MST

Hands shaking, Kai sat at the foot of his cot, a baby-blue blanket wrapped around his shoulders. Exhaustion swam in his veins, and white noise filled his mind. Chavez stood at the opposite end of the room, under the archway, speaking with Adeline and two blonde women he didn't know. He wanted Chavez to come over to him, to ask how he was doing, to ruffle his hair, even.

He wasn't sure if he wanted Adeline to come over or not.

One of the blonde women had put Javi to sleep, then a gaggle of six wearing red jumpsuits carted him away. No one had spoken to Kai, not even to ask if he was okay. He sighed and shook his head.

He kept catching other kids from his dorm staring at him, then looking away quickly when he looked back or pretending to look at the mirrored wall behind him. He didn't know what that meant, but he didn't like it. He didn't want the attention, didn't want to scare people. He didn't want to become a bully like Javi.

When next he glanced back at the adults standing in the arch, all four had turned to face him. Chavez met his gaze and smiled, but Kai didn't smile back. He could feel Adeline's gaze on him, but he refused to look at her.

Are you okay, Kai? sent Chavez.

Kai nodded and released a sigh.

Want to speak to Miss Adeline?

NO.

12

The Compound, under the Sonoran Desert, AZ
June 17, 1998, 6:49 am MST

Jamilla found her mop, her bucket, and her spray bottle of cleaner lying scattered between Blue Dorm Seven and Blue Dorm Twenty-one on the other side of the hall. She stood ten yards away, staring down at her materials. She remembered what had happened, but like the events had happened to someone else—like a memory of a movie.

She glanced at Blue Dorm Seven, noting the silent, frozen kids in blue jumpsuits, noting Chavez, Bethany, Beatrice, and Adeline standing in the arch. The kids stared at Kai as though he'd done something that scared them.

She wondered what he'd done. Anxiety bubbled in the back of her mind, but she couldn't say why. She shook her head, then retrieved her tools and got back to completing her task.

13

Kai studied Chavez for a moment, and the man seemed to welcome it, to open to Kai's scrutiny. He gave every appearance of friendliness, and yet he hadn't responded when Kai had called for help during the psi rating. Now, he was here, acting like nothing had happened.

Chavez said something to the three women that Kai couldn't hear, then he advanced down the center aisle until he stood looking down at Kai. *Are you sure that you're okay?*

Kai shrugged and looked away.

Ah. So, no, then.

Again, Kai shrugged.

Want to tell me how all this started?

Do you want *to know?*

Yes, of course.

Why?

Because I'm your friend.

You're my friend? Kai couldn't keep the bitterness to himself, and several of the kids nearby gasped.

Kai, sent Chavez, a gentle tone to his mental voice, *I am* your friend.

"Yeah?" Kai demanded, suddenly furious. "Are you?"

Yes, of course. What have I done to make you feel otherwise?

Kai narrowed his eyes, then looked away. One of the blonde women had come closer but was far enough away she couldn't overhear their conversation. "I woke up alone, in the dark and alone. I called out to you." He snapped his gaze back to Chavez's face. "You *ignored* me!"

Ah. Can I explain?

Can I stop you?

Yes, Kai, you can. If you say so, I'll leave you alone.

Kai shrugged. "Explain, then."

What you experienced, waking up in the dark, alone, trapped on that raised plateau, we've all been through it. It's called the Sensory Deprivation test—that's why it's too dark to see, why it's soundproofed. That's why I couldn't respond. You had to think yourself utterly alone.

What the hell for? Kai demanded.

Chavez nodded. *Because the whole point of the sensory deprivation is to encourage you to use your abilities with as much power as you can muster. The test allows us to evaluate your psi rating, to assess its maximum power.*

Why do you need to know that?

Because, Kai, we need to know what your strengths are. What you're good at, you know? What are you good at, Kai?

Xbox, Kai sent instantly, hopefully.

Chavez laughed. *Nice try. Another reason is that some people have abilities that span functions. We—*

What's that mean?

Chavez sat beside him. *Well, like you expressed telepathic abilities—as did I, which is allowing us to speak this way. You also expressed telekinetic ability. But you were strongest when using telecheiristiry, or TC. That's important, because if you are a natural puppeteer, as I suspect you are, then it doesn't matter how much we train you in TP or TK, you will always be stronger in TC.*

And why couldn't you let me know it was okay?

Chavez nodded slowly. *Like I said, we needed to know your maximum psi.*

Yeah? Well, your stupid test sucks donkey balls.

The man chuckled and bumped Kai with his shoulder. *Yeah, it does, but it's over, isn't it?*

Why didn't you come once I was out of the test?

We all need sleep, buddy. Chavez grinned at him. *Not all of us wake at the asscrack of dawn and start breaking all the rules.*

Kai frowned. *What about Javi?*

Chavez shrugged. *He's an example of why we do the testing. You, better than most, know how dangerous he can be. He saw through the test and held back. He kept his power secret.*

How?

Never mind that. But rest assured that Javi will be dealt with.

Good, sent Kai. *He should get in lots of trouble.*

Speaking of getting into lots of trouble, do you want to talk about it?

Anger stirred in the back of Kai's mind. *Do you know what that...that...that* asshole *did to me?*

Chavez shrugged. *I can guess.*

He hurt me—all over and all at once.

He stimulated the pain centers of your mind, that's all. Yes, I know it hurt—I felt it myself when I was a student here. Looking back, I know each instance was exactly *what I needed at the time.* Chavez put his arm on Kai's shoulders. *When you're older, you'll think the same thing.*

Kai's expression crumpled. "Never!" he hissed.

Chavez chuckled and ruffled his hair. *Wait and see, Kai. In the meantime, I'd suggest letting it go so you can concentrate on your studies today.*

Kai turned his face toward the archway, not wanting Chavez to see the tears shimmering in his eyes. One of the blonde women said something to Adeline, then turned and walked away. Adeline took a step toward him, but the other blonde Barbie put her hand on Miss Adeline's arm, then hissed something in her ear. Together, the two women turned and walked away.

Rage blossomed within him. Fury at Adeline for setting both his mother and him up in the Rochester airport, indignation at the man who'd punished him earlier, and outrage that Chavez had taken the matter so lightly.

"Fine," he said and shook Chavez's arm off. For a moment, Kai thought he saw hurt in the man's eyes. "I'm going to shower—that is if it's not against the rules."

Chavez looked down at his watch. *Better wait four more minutes. First bell rings at seven.*

"Fine," Kai repeated. He walked toward the archway, leaving Chavez sitting on the bunk, frowning.

14

The Compound, under the Sonoran Desert, AZ
June 17, 1998, 6:55 am MST

Jamilla squirted cleaner on the floor, hit it with the damp mop, then squirted more cleaner and mopped again. She knew she was mopping the same section of floor, again and again, but was helpless in the face of the compulsion to stay near Blue Dorm Seven. Her behavior confused her. Her head spun every time she tried to get on with her work assignment.

She squirted cleaner on the floor, then straightened and stared at the man with his arm around Kai's shoulders. The man's skin was the golden color of wet beach sand, and his hair was a glossy black. Jamilla felt certain she'd never seen him before, but all the same, a familiarity tugged her gaze to him, again and again. *He's beautiful,* she thought, but that tidal tug didn't come with the taint of lust. *Did I know him in school?* She shook her head and used her mop to spread the cleaner around, then without even thinking about it, sprayed more cleaner on the already wet floor. *One of Kailan's friends?* She wondered, then froze for a moment as grief, both familiar and well-worn, washed through her like a storm surge. Kailan Washington, her husband and Kai's father, had died in 1991 in the sands of Iraq.

She added more cleaner to the puddle already shining on the tiles, then moved to rewet her mop. She wrung out the ropey cotton strands, then straightened, looked at the cleaner on the floor, and dunked the mop again. Once more, her gaze drifted to the golden skin and sable hair.

What are you doing, Jamilla?

The question rang through her mind, but she didn't process it. Instead, she wrung out her mop, then plopped it into the center of the puddle of cleaning fluid. She began to spread the cleaner around, stealing glances into Blue Dorm Seven.

Jamilla!

She started and dropped her mop, then froze, eyes wide, arms splayed to her side as though she'd lost her balance. Her gaze never left the golden man.

A warm hand came to rest on her arm, and Jamilla startled again, this time drawing in a gasp of air and its overpowering odor of cleaning chemicals. Another hand edged into her field of vision, moving ever so slowly, then turned her head away from the man in Kai's dorm.

"Oh! Beatrice!" said Jamilla, her tone that of a sleepwalker who'd just woken up.

What are you doing here?

"Uh…" Jamilla's gaze darted around, then settled on the mop lying at her feet. "Work. Uh, my detail is to…"

Mop?

"Yeah. Yes, to mop this observation corridor."

And are you almost finished?

Jamilla shook her head, and her eyes rolled toward Blue Dorm Seven. "Just…uh…I'm…"

Again, Beatrice took her by the chin and turned Jamilla to face her.

"Who *is* that man?" Jamilla murmured.

His name is Chavez. Hector Chavez. He's a senior instructor here.

"Oh." Jamilla nodded. "Oh. Okay. Uh…"

Beatrice grimaced, staring at Jamilla with an almost brutal intensity. Returning the blonde's gaze made Jamilla feel faint and scared at the same time, but she couldn't break away. Her eyes began to burn, to tear up and leak, but none of that mattered. The only thing that mattered were those green eyes, spinning and shining from the darkness that had descended on her.

15

Jamilla drew a deep breath in through her nose, and the stench of cleaning fluid assaulted her, burning through her sinuses, scalding the back of her throat as though she had her face in a giant puddle of the stuff. But when she opened her eyes, she found the cleaning fluid sealed up and back on her cart. Likewise, her mop bucket and mop were stowed away, and she stood in the middle of a seafoam green hallway.

She turned and looked behind her, but the hall was empty. "What am I doing here?" she murmured. "I was just…" She couldn't finish the sentence. "I need to…"

Jamilla shook her head as she sometimes did after waking from a nightmare, trying to clear the cobwebs, but it didn't help. "Something happened, didn't it?" she muttered.

Did something happen? she asked herself. Her mind showed her a brief glimpse of a Black boy about the age Kai would have been, had he lived, and a pang of old grief raced through her.

Chapter 14
Making
Memories

I

Langfield Sun, Miami, FL
Friday, 10:11 am

"That *bitch*!" Maddie cried. "She made her think her *own child* was dead?"

"Yes," said Adeline in a voice that was half-angry, half-graveside-hush. "And worse. And worse, child. But I…"

"This Javi kid attacked the mother?" asked Karl. "That was puppeteering?"

"It was," said Adeline in a subdued voice.

"And Kai fought him. I don't mean just physically."

"He did, Detective."

"Why isn't Kai one of the group of people you suspect of committing these murders here?"

She drew in a quick breath that sounded half-a-sob. "I need a break. Just a few minutes."

"That's understandable," said Maddie in a quiet, motherly tone. "Take your time."

"Yes," said Adeline. "There should be a psi rating for Javier Dela Cruz, and a report after the fight. Read those while I…" Her voice trailed away into a mournful sigh.

"Yes," said Gavin. "I have them."

"I'll…I'll be right back," Adeline said.

"Poor woman," said Maddie.

"Seems a convenient time to take a break," said Karl.

"I think they are related," said Gavin. "Her and Jamilla and Kai."

"That's why this is so hard on her." Maddie's voice dipped to almost a whisper. "Imagine having to tell three strangers about—"

"Yes," Gavin said.

"We have to consider Kai Washington as another suspect."

Gavin nodded and ran his name. "Nothing on him, either."

"Of course, there isn't," said Karl with a shake of his head.

"Let me read these files about Javi. See where all this leads. The first one is from a week or so before the fight."

2

From Program records
Marked June 6, 1998, 15:06

```
TO: blue_team@majest.ic
FROM: observer_11@majest.ic

SUBJECT: Javier Dela Cruz Psi Rating
Report

Sensory Deprivation test administered
as per guidelines. Initial field
reports suggested the possibility of
awakening abilities of significant
```

power. Additionally, the reports
indicated the subject has experienced
significant trauma at the hands of his
mother, at least two different step-
fathers, and various psychiatric
facilities. This observer is unsure if
salvaging the child is an option,
though an attempt should be made. Both
TP and TC expressed during the
procedure and at significant psi
levels. All expressions of psionic
power successfully blocked, but this
observer wonders if the limits of Dela
Cruz's power remain unknown despite
the procedure. Take note of the fact
he was aware of my psionic presence
during the test. Also of note: the
control of his psi power, and his
precision in the last hour before the
test was terminated (subject sent TC
bursts of psi 8.0 every 8 minutes).
Additionally, each instance of psi
ability was rated at a whole number.
This one could be dangerous to himself
and others. The subject is older than
we'd like to accept into the Program
but still within the guidelines.

Psi rating: 8.0, though it may be
significantly higher.

Recommendations:
1. fixer evaluation, earliest re:
   PTSD, psychiatric mistreatment,
   lack of trust.
2. close surveillance by qualified
   personnel, to wit, people with the
   strength to contain subject's
   emotions—should have a psi rating
   9+.

3. self-control, anger management curriculums.
4. Given high psi TC, recommend further evaluation re: telecheiristiric mastery by puppeteering faculty.

Report ends.

3

From Program records
Marked June 17, 1998, 08:01

TO: blue_team@majest.ic
CC: admin_team@majest.ic
FROM: observer_23@majest.ic

RE: Javier Dela Cruz Behavior Report

Please see:
1. Kai Washington Discipline Report
2. Javier Dela Cruz Psi Rating Report
3. Night Watch Incident Report
4. Blue Dorm Seven Incident Report

Subject continues to show antisocial behavior during mandatory sleep periods, as previously reported by this observer. Psi communication noted between JDC and staffer behind the mirror-wall. Please note that I suspect TP between the two, though it was not detected, let alone blocked. Behavior continued to decompensate this morning before first bell, leading to a full psionic altercation between JDC and KW. During this altercation, JDC successfully deployed TC at a psi rating of 10.4 against two adult staffers and KW. Senior puppeteering instructor Chavez sent to intervene and reported that containing JDC required his complete focus (note Chavez is psi rated 18.7) and significant effort.

Given observations reported above, allow me to make the following recommendations:
1. Adjust JDC psi rating to 10.4.
2. Significant fixer intervention for JDC
   a. If intervention is unable to curb destructive antisocial behavior, suppression of TC is advised.
   b. Failing that, advise discharge of JDC and application of Protocol One.
3. KW and JDC (should he remain) should be re-dormed away from one another and should follow different schedules.
4. Fixer evaluation for KW re: PTSD from attack, potential for negative ideation and power-seeking behavior.

Report ends.

4

"If only they had heeded them recommendations," said Adeline in a weary voice. "So much might have changed." She scoffed. "But they had to have their little contest between them two boys, had to try to make 'em both stronger. It was foolish."

"Are you okay?" asked Maddie.

"I am. Thank you, child. The wounds are old, but they still bleed from time to time."

"Are you ready to tell us why Kai isn't on the list?" asked Karl. "Just because he's a family—"

"Can we leave it at: 'it isn't possible?'"

"Uh, that's not generally how we do things."

"I know, but the reasons it isn't possible will become apparent as I continue the story."

Karl spread his hands. "That's convenient."

"I'm sorry, Detective, but you couldn't have it any more wrong. This is hard for me to relive."

"We understand," said Maddie, a fierce undercurrent in her voice. "Why did Beatrice do what she did?"

"Jamilla began tripping her failsafe circuits. She had prescribed thoughts about Bethany, me, all of us, really. Her instinct to protect Kai hadn't been assuaged as Beatrice had thought, merely corrupted."

"I'm not sure what that means."

"She became obsessed with Chavez because Kai looked to the man like he was his daddy. That triggered something in Jamilla that short-circuited her. Beatrice thought making her believe Kai was dead would alleviate the issue." Adeline sighed. "It didn't. Of course. Gavin, look for reports that mention Jamilla's failsafe trips. Also, I had me an email exchange with Beatrice about that time."

Gavin looked at his laptop screen, scanning the names of the documents. "I have them."

"Read them out, child, so I don't have to tell it."

5

From Program records
Marked June 17, 1998, 06:47

```
TO: green_eyed_goddess@majest.ic
CC: gray_eyed_goddess@majest.ic
FROM: observer_42@majest.ic

SUBJECT: FLASH ALERT: Read soonest JW
failsafe trip

ALERT ALERT ALERT

At  06:45,  17  June  1998,  subject
Jamilla Washington tripped one of her
failsafes—specifically  harm  ideation
```

(Bethany). Triggering thought: KW coming to harm. Automatic redress fired successfully. Post-redress, subject showed minimal confusion, and flash-term retrograde amnesia as intended by failsafe design.

Recommendations:
1) Continue constant-scan observation
2) fixer evaluation of failsafes and current reprogramming to determine if strengthening is advisable

Subject remains focus of constant-scan, twenty-four-hour observation by observers 37 and 42, in twelve-hour shifts.

Report ends.

6

From Program records
Marked June 17, 1998, 07:19

TO: observer_42@majest.ic
CC: gray_eyed_goddess@majest.ic
FROM: green_eyed_goddess@majest.ic

SUBJECT: RE: FLASH ALERT: Read soonest JW failsafe trip

First, thank you for notifying me as to the failsafe trip, though I was already aware of it. As to your recommendations for fixer

intervention, there is no further
need. I've seen to her and made
adjustments at the time in question,
though the failsafe did exactly what
it was designed to do, and it
performed perfectly. If I were to
perform sufficient reprogramming to
eliminate any possibility of negative
thoughts, she'd be worthless—probably
catatonic.

Continue constant-scan observations
until further orders from me.

7

From Program records
June 18, 1998, 12:37

TO: green_eyed_goddess@majest.ic
FROM: missadeline@majest.ic

SUBJECT: WHAT DID YOU DO??

I just came from having lunch with
Jamilla. What in God's name did you do
to her? SHE THINKS KAI DIED WHEN HIS
DADDY DID!

You can't just change a person like
that! It's BARBARIC! That's her baby
you just erased!

You'd damn well better be able to undo this mess, young lady, or there will be consequences!

8

From Program records
June 18, 1998, 13:02

TO: missadeline@majest.ic
FROM: green_eyed_goddess@majest.ic

SUBJECT: RE: WHAT DID YOU DO??

What a pleasure to hear from you, Miss Addy. Yes, I'm doing well, thank you for asking. What's that? Bethany? Oh, she's…well, she's Bethany, isn't she? :)

As to your concerns about Jamilla, rest assured all is well, and all manner of things are well. She's fine.

No, she's better than just fine. She was broken before—broken by worry and fear and concern about Kai. She wasn't able to live a productive life—she was caught in a mobius compulsion—and she'd already had a failsafe trip. I took steps to ensure the chance of another failsafe going off was close to zero. You, better than anyone, know what can happen when a person experiences too many failsafe trips. I did what I did to protect Jamilla.

And I did the same for Kai. He has memories of his mother dying in a car accident when he was six. He has memories of dealing with the grief in a healthy manner and living with his father's parents until he applied for enrollment at our school. He's well adjusted, motivated, and, best of all, *strong*.

In other words, Miss Addy, I did my job, and I did it well.

P.S. Mind your own goddamn business and take your threats and shove them deep inside—maybe they'll keep you warm. They won't do anything else for you.

P.P.S. You're not too old for reprogramming, you know. Maybe that would be best? You can't seem to handle things as they are.

9

From Program records
June 18, 1998, 13:08

TO: green_eyed_goddess@majest.ic
FROM: missadeline@majest.ic

SUBJECT: RE: RE: WHAT DID YOU DO??

Oh, sweetness! Did you just threaten
me? Surely, I must have mistaken your
meaning.

I'm a formidable enemy, little girl.
Read my personnel file if you doubt
it—I'm sure it's accurate and
complete, even if you might have to
read between the lines in a few
places.

I'll make my own assessment of Kai. I
know him far better than you do. As to
Jamilla, if you think the walking
zombie you turned her into is for the
best, I seriously question your
ability to judge matters objectively.

I shall speak with the Man about this
and about your conduct.

10

Langfield Sun, Miami, FL
Friday, 10:27 am

Adeline sighed. "I should have followed through on
that threat. There's so many things I can see so clearly
now."

"Hindsight is always twenty-twenty," said Karl.
"You can only do your best at the time."

"Ain't that the truth," said Adeline. "But the cost of
my weakness was high. So high."

"What happened?" whispered Maddie.

"They pushed him. They pushed Kai and Javi both, using different levers to move each boy how they wanted." She sighed again. "Poor Kai had no one to turn to—not Chavez, not Beatrice, certainly not Bethany—and Beatrice made him think he was all alone in the world despite Jamilla's and my presence right there. They set up this policy that if any of those three bullies confronted Kai, ain't no one was to intervene. Worse than that, over the next fifteen months, they pushed Kai through his exams while they held Dela Cruz back. That set it up so their conflict would come to a boil—all to make Kai 'strong and confident.' Never mind that what they did turned Kai into a monster." She paused and took another drink. "Oh, hell. They might've done that on purpose. I know they wanted a cold-blooded assassin because that's exactly what they were making."

Chapter 15
Some Kind of
Monster

I

The Compound, under the Sonoran Desert, AZ
December 2, 1999, 8:52 pm MST

Kai walked out of the practice room, exhausted and sporting a big headache from his four hours of running a rat through a maze. He didn't particularly like puppeting rodents, but the puppeteering instructors forbade the yellow cohort from attempting control of anything more complicated. Some of his classmates couldn't even handle a rat and had to settle for mice or hamsters, but for Kai, rats presented no challenge.

He threaded through the human-sized maze of corridors, looking forward to a shower and then a late supper. As he caught sight of the section devoted to the yellow dormitories, he heard a herd of footsteps behind him, and his stomach took a dip toward his knees.

"Hey, Javi, look who it is."

Kai increased his pace, pretending not to have heard.

"Oh, look, fellas. Poor little Kai is running away," said Javi.

Kai plastered a grin on his mug and glanced back over his shoulder. Javi Dela Cruz, Rayson Fergus, and Dylan Jepson—all older and bigger—trailed five or six steps behind him. "Nah. It's just that the smell of you animals precedes you."

Javi nodded as though he agreed. "See that? That's why we like you so much, Kai: your winning personality."

Kai felt heat rising up his neck and cheeks. "I'm only joking."

Javi shrugged. "I'm not."

Kai faced forward and increased his pace again.

"Look at him scurry," said Dylan with a caustic giggle.

"Running away like the little rat-lover he is," said Rayson.

"Did you have fun fucking your rat, rat-lover?" asked Dylan.

"Why so antisocial, Kai? Are you too good for us?" asked Javi.

"I think he's intimidated, Javi."

"Is that it?" asked Javi. "Do we intimidate widdle Kai?"

Kai shook his head. "Nah. I want a shower and some food, that's all."

"Then slow down, big dog," said Rayson. "We just want to ask you about something. Won't take a minute."

"Yeah," said Dylan. "We'll walk with you."

"See, we're tired of the hamsters, Kai," added Javi. "We want advice about what we're doing wrong, and since you're the best puppeteer in the yellow cohort…"

Kai glanced back in time to catch their mischievous grins and sped up, walking as fast as he could. "Leave me alone."

"I'm bored with this shit," Javi said. "Get him, Dylan. Quick, before the watchers catch on."

He broke into a run and heard Dylan pounding toward him, using his longer stride to catch Kai up. Dylan grabbed him from behind, wrapping his arms around Kai's torso, pinning his arms to his sides. "Look, I caught a little rat," said Dylan.

Kai struggled, but he couldn't loosen Dylan's grip. Javi and Rayson jogged up, and Dylan spun Kai around to face them.

"Nothing to the face," said Javi, then slammed his fist into Kai's guts, driving the breath from him.

"What are you boys doing?" called Chavez, coming around the corner in the intersection they'd just passed.

Dylan dropped his arms, and Kai fell to his knees, holding his belly.

"Kai was choking. We were trying to—"

"Bullshit, Javi. All three of you report to Discipline. If you take more than five minutes, I'll send some reds after you."

"Come on, man," said Javi. "We're just playing around. Right, Kai?"

"Don't even try it," said Chavez. "Discipline. Now."

Kai glanced up in time to see Javi's cheeks color with fury, and his eyes narrowed to slits. "*Pinche chamaco*," he whispered.

"*¿Neta, pendejo? ¿Con un nombre como* Hector Chavez *crees que no hablo español*?"

"I don't care if you do," said Javi, spinning to face him. "You think I give a shit about Discipline? You think I haven't had it worse?"

"Get moving."

"Javi," said Dylan in a small voice. "Don't make it worse, bro."

Javi sniffed, gave Kai one last glare—a promise of things to come—then turned and stomped down the hall.

Chavez watched him until he disappeared around the corner, then turned and squatted next to Kai. *You okay?*

Kai rubbed his belly. *I'm just perfect. Why does Javi hate me?*

Nodding, Chavez put a hand on his shoulder. *Jealousy is an ugly master, Kai.*

I make good grades because I work hard. I can't help my psi rating.

I suspect Javi is jealous of something else.

Kai flopped his hands over in his lap. *What?*

Never mind. He stood, pulling Kai up with him. *I was on my way to see you.*

Kai looked up at him. *Really? Why?*

Because, Kai Washington, you're wearing the wrong jumpsuit. The corners of his mouth turned up.

Kai looked down at the pale-yellow cloth, then back up at Chavez. *Huh?*

Chavez started walking, pulling Kai along. *Let's go get your things. You're in the wrong dorm, too.*

Kai's brow knitted. He'd heard of boys being dropped back down to blue, but they were the fuck ups. *What dorm am I supposed to be in*?

Green Dorm Five, sent Chavez with a grin.

Green?

Chavez nodded. *By unanimous vote.*

Kai smiled, and Chavez put his hand on his shoulder.

2

The Compound, under the Sonoran Desert, AZ
December 26, 1999, 10:52 am MST

Jamilla watched the teenagers in forest green jumpsuits work in their practice room. One of the kids seemed too small, but at the same time, he seemed inconsequential. Her gaze wanted to zip right past him, but there was something she—

She shook her head and blinked a few times, her eyes stinging and tearing as if she'd stood there like an idiot who forgot to blink. She stood facing the empty practice room, wondering what she'd found fascinating about an empty room. She shook her head again and turned back to her cart, glancing down at her duty sheet.

After one last glance at the room, she shrugged and set off to clean the admin wing.

3

The Compound, under the Sonoran Desert, AZ
January 5, 2000, 3:52 am MST

Kai roamed the halls, wide awake despite the early hour. His forest green jumpsuit meant no one cared whether he slept or not. In fact, he could do just about anything he wanted to, so long as he kept up with his work—and that wasn't something he struggled with.

But everyone else in the green cohort had the same privilege, which made finding a place to be alone difficult. He turned and walked into the blue section, seeking a quiet he'd never find in the green dormitory section. He enjoyed the solitude of early morning, the chill in the air, the relative darkness, the silence. He walked with his neck bent, his head down, and his arms behind his back, lost in his own thoughts.

No one in his new cohort picked on him because of his age, and in the past few months, he'd grown an inch, so his size wasn't that far off the others. Some of the girls giggled at him when he spoke, but he didn't know if that was necessarily a bad thing. Chavez said being funny was the easiest way to "get" a girl.

Sometimes in his nocturnal wanderings, Kai wished that his parents had survived to see him doing so well. He wished that somehow, someone besides Chavez paid attention to him.

"Hey, *pendejo*."

Kai stiffened, the hair on the back of his neck standing up. He lifted his head and looked around. Dylan stood just inside one of the blue archways, wearing a blue jumpsuit and staring daggers at him. "Oh. Hey, Dylan." He cut his gaze away the second he could, embarrassed as though he'd caught Dylan doing something nasty.

"Yeah, you should feel bad. Did you plan it with your ass-buddy, Chavez?"

"Um. Plan it?"

"Don't be stupid, asshole!" Dylan snapped. "Don't pretend you didn't get me dropped back to blue on purpose!"

"Shut up!" someone called from inside Dylan's dorm.

Dylan winced and looked around, then went on in a quiet voice. "Don't think we've forgotten you. Don't think *Javi's* forgotten you."

Kai's mouth went dry. "Javi's back in blue, too?"

"Right, go on playing stupid. Rayson, Javi, and I were all dropped back. Because of you."

Anger sparked and his brows knitted. "No, you got dropped back because of *Javi*, because you followed him around like a dog and did whatever he said, no matter how stupid it was."

Dylan growled and took a step forward, the toe of his blue sneakers touching the line between inside the dorm and outside. "I'm gonna fuck you up. I'm gonna beat you until even Chavez won't want to look at you. I'm gonna—" He stopped speaking, mouth open, eyes wide and staring as his hand snapped up to cover his mouth.

"No," said Kai in a rough voice. "You're not going to do a thing to me. *Ever*." He made Dylan's other hand come up and tweak the boy's nose. "Know why, dummy?" He made Dylan's head shake back and forth. "Then I'll tell you. It's because I'm *better* than you will ever be. At just about everything." Kai stepped closer. "*And* because you're in blue. Your next demotion is out of the Program, and I know something you don't. Would you like me to tell you?" He made Dylan nod. "More than two-thirds of the idiots who get themselves thrown out of the program become plant food in the desert up there." He made Dylan's hand rise toward the ceiling, his index finger extended. "But most of all, *pendejo*, because you're scared of me, now." He released his control of the other boy, then shrugged. "And you should be. You very much should be, Dylan Jepson." Kai took another step, his green-shod toes touching Dylan's. "*I fucking guarantee it!*" He spit the words right in the other boy's face.

Dylan stumbled back a step, then another. His gaze bored into Kai's for a moment. "Fuck you, nigger."

Kai threw back his head and laughed. "Not on your life, *cracker*." Not for the first time, he silently wished there was a word for White assholes that hurt them as much as "nigger" hurt and infuriated him. He tangled Dylan's feet together and made him fall on his ass. "Enjoy your life, Dylan, and don't ever speak to me again."

4

*The Compound, under the Sonoran Desert, AZ
January 5, 2000, 9:47 am MST*

Jamilla pushed her cart to the next intersection and turned left. She had the theme song from The X-Files on a seemingly infinite loop in her head. She couldn't shake it, couldn't even replace it with an equally annoying theme song like the one from Knight Rider, with its early 80s synthesizer crud. She reached the next intersection and plodded around to the left, dull-eyed, expression slack.

She drifted to a stop, staring straight ahead, head leaning toward the wall as though she were too exhausted to hold it upright. *What would he have been like*? she wondered for the umpteenth time that morning. *Would Kai have been tall and lanky, like his daddy? Would he have been smart?*

She startled at nothing and started pushing the cart again. Jamilla shivered a little as a cool breeze found the back of her collar and snuck past it down her back. At the next intersection, she paused, watching a group of green-garbed students walking away from her two blocks down. One of them sent a pang down to her belly. He was shorter than the others, dark-skinned like Kai had been, and there was something about the way he sauntered along next to his friends that—

With a start, Jamilla realized she was staring at an empty hallway. *But they were there. I'm sure of it. The Black kid who—*

Again, she twitched, standing next to her cleaning cart in the middle of an intersection of hallways. Her assigned cleaning area was down the left hall. She was sure of that much.

She turned the cart to the left and began to walk down the hall again. *What was I doing back there?* Whatever it was, it felt *important* somehow, but why in the world would she have something important to do? *I'm a maid, not a boss.*

She reached the next intersection and turned left. *Almost there*, she told herself. *At the next intersection, I need to go left, and the medical office will be halfway down.*

5

The Compound, under the Sonoran Desert, AZ
January 5, 2000, 10:09 am MST

Adeline sighed and pushed away from her narrow desk, rubbing her sore knuckles. Fatigue nibbled at her, harried her, stealing away her resolve, her strength, her patience. Her head pounded and throbbed. *Things with little miss green-eyes are getting out of hand*, she thought for the fifth or sixth time since she'd gotten Beatrice's last email and fired off her own angry reply. She rubbed at her temples, knowing what she *should* do, but not liking it one bit.

She crossed the room and laid down on her little cot, wrapping the wool blanket around herself. She shut her eyes and tried to still her racing thoughts.

She might as well have been trying to hold back the rising tide with a toothpick. After a few fitful minutes of tossing and turning, she got up and went back to her desk. She lifted the phone and hit zero three times.

"Yeah?"

"I need to talk to him."

The line buzzed like a dying fly, then the sound faded to silence. "Is it important?"

"I wouldn't bother him otherwise."

"Yeah," said the man with a sigh. "Give me a minute."

Adeline hung up the phone and pulled out her chair to sit. She pulled up the academic and practical reports for the green cohort. She told herself she was interested in the cohort as a whole—that she wasn't buzzing through everything until she found mention of Kai.

When it rang, she snatched the phone from its cradle. "Adeline," she said.

"Hello, Adeline," said Sam McIntire.

"Sorry to bother you. I know you're probably up to your elbows in alligators."

"Then let's dispense with the pleasantries. What's wrong?"

"It's… Well, I sense a problem coming. Between Beatrice and me."

After a moment of silence, Sam said, "You *sense* a problem, or you think there might be one?"

"I don't need no augury to predict this tussle. I can forward you a couple of emails—"

"I'm not a couple's counselor."

"No. I know that, but—"

"Send me a couple of emails?" he demanded, then sucked his teeth. "You and Beatrice are grown damn women. You're old enough to be her grandmother. Surely one of you is mature enough to get along?"

"It's not—"

"Surely neither of you need me to remind you of the stakes. Then again, maybe *you* do, given…well, *everything*."

"No," said Adeline. "I know how important the Program is. I know because I was one of the first to join up."

"Right, back in 1947. Do you mean to tell me that in all that time, you never butted heads with someone you had to work with? Do you mean to tell me you don't know how to work this out on your *fucking own*?" By the time Sam reached the end of the last question, he was shrieking into the phone, and Adeline held the receiver away from her ear.

After a moment of silence, she put the phone back to her ear. "If you're going to wash your hands of it as a problem, then you can't bitch about my solution," she said evenly.

"Want to bet, d'Clara? I'll *bitch* whenever I want. I'm not the previous Man. I'm not wrapped around your little finger by a bunch of chivalrous nonsense. And you…you seem to be overvaluing your contribution to the cause."

"I see," said Adeline in a frigid tone.

"And don't call me with the internal bullshit of the Compound. I can't afford to let you interrupt me—to *distract* me. Especially with piddly little high school girl's locker room bullshit! Am I making myself clear?"

"Crystal!" snapped Adeline. She cradled the receiver and stared at it balefully. She'd expected it to go badly, to get reamed out, but she hadn't expected a complete and utter disaster. *If I'm such a bother, you conniving bastard, why are you forcing me to stick around? Not that I'd leave Kai and Jamilla…*

The pain in her head multiplied until she thought her skull would break. She went to her little bathroom—not much bigger than a shower stall—and opened the medicine cabinet to get out her aspirin. Then she remembered using the last two doses. She'd planned to go to medical and get another bottle, but it had slipped her mind. *Ain't life just grand*, she thought bitterly.

She fished her slipper-shoes out from under her bed and slipped them on, gingerly avoiding tweaking any of her toes. Then she headed out the door.

6

The Compound, under the Sonoran Desert, AZ
January 5, 2000, 10:13 am MST

Jamilla turned left at the intersection, then paused and looked around. When she was seven, her parents had taken her to the state fair, and she'd begged and begged until her father gave her permission to try the House of Mirrors on her own. She'd gotten turned around, then lost. Her panicked screaming resulted in the lights coming on and one of the attraction's minders coming in and leading her to the exit—all while wearing a disgusted look. He'd called her father a spade and spit between his feet.

She remembered the look on her daddy's face—the anger, the hurt, the shame. Of course, living in rural Mississippi in the 1970s, her father had bitten his tongue, and the disgusting redneck cracker sumbitch had scoffed and told her daddy to mind his "monkey."

Why am I thinking about this? she wondered. *What in the world does that memory have to do with* anything? She walked down to the next intersection, thinking she needed to go left. She paused there and peered down all four hallways, including the one she'd just walked through. They all looked the same—concrete blocks painted seafoam green, polished cement floors and ceilings, steel doors with cryptic numbers painted above them.

The memory of that state fair came rolling back, thundering through her mind like a runaway freight train. She shook her head and tried to banish both the song that had been running through her head for what felt like a month and the memory.

Neither obliged her.

She took the hallway that led to the left. *Almost there*, she told herself. *At the next intersection, I need to go left, and the medical office will be halfway down.*

7

Adeline walked at a slow pace, her slipper-shoes scuffling on the polished concrete. She came around a corner a few blocks from medical just in time to see Jamilla pause in the next intersection, then go left. "Jamilla!" she called, but the younger woman seemed lost in her thoughts.

She picked up her pace and made for the intersection. She went left, again just in time to catch Jamilla going left at the next block. She walked as fast as she could with aching, mincing strides, and when she rounded the next corridor, she found Jamilla standing in the center of the hall, arms limp by her sides, mouth hanging open, eyes empty.

"Jamilla," she said, laying a gentle hand on her shoulder. Jamilla didn't so much as twitch. "Child? What's wrong?" She gave her shoulder a gentle shake. "Baby?"

Jamilla remained still for the next half-minute or so then jerked like a person coming out of a dream. "Left," she muttered. "Then halfway down." She put her hands on her cart and gave it a push without acknowledging Adeline's presence.

"Jamilla?"

She gave another twitch, then turned her head ponderously. She narrowed her eyes and peered at Adeline as though she were a hundred yards away rather than mere inches. "Miss Adeline? Is that you?"

"Yes, baby. What's wrong?"

"Wrong? Noth—" Her eyes went to that far away empty place for a few moments. "That man at the fair. That *fucking* bigot redneck *asshole*!"

"Child," said Adeline, lifting her other hand to take one of Jamilla's. "Are you feeling sick?"

"He shamed my daddy. For what? Because a little seven-year-old got lost in his maze-house?"

"Shh, now," crooned Adeline. "Why don't you take a little rest? Here, sit next to the wall."

A series of twitches shuddered through Jamilla. "Can't. Can't. I've got to…" Her eyes glazed again. "Can't. Can't. Left. Left."

"Shh, baby. I think we should go on over to medical. I was heading there anyway."

Jamilla's eyes lit up. "Left! Left at the next intersection!"

"No, child," crooned Adeline. "But don't you worry your pretty head. Miss Adeline knows the way. Here, you just come with me."

"Left?" murmured Jamilla.

"No, baby. Hold onto my hand, now. There, that's better, isn't it?"

"My cart! I need to…" Her voice drifted away, maybe echoing in that empty place she kept falling into.

Adeline pulled her gently. "You just walk with me, child. Miss Adeline's old and weak. I can't carry you like I used to could."

"Left…" Jamilla whispered.

They retraced their steps to the first intersection Adeline had seen Jamilla in, then turned left. She walked along like a docile child, holding Adeline's hand in a tight grip that hurt the old woman's knuckles. "Another left, then down halfway," Jamilla muttered.

"Shh, baby," said Adeline. "Rest your mind, now, hear?"

8

The Compound, under the Sonoran Desert, AZ
January 8, 2000, 07:28 pm MST

Kai put his metal dining tray in the bin and tossed his napkin in the trashcan next to it. He mused about the time he spent in the blue cohort and how many times he'd been tasked with washing the dishes and trays in the bin. A wry grin split his face. In the green cohort, he had almost no chores—giving him more time to master the practicals and study for the academic tests.

"What the fuck are you grinning about?" asked Rayson Fergus.

"None of your fucking business," said Kai, pleased his voice didn't even warble.

Rayson stood a head and a half taller than Kai—which made sense since he was sixteen, and Kai was only thirteen—and he moved a step closer, so Kai had to crane his neck back to look up at him. "Maybe I want to make it my business, twerp." He wore one of the rubber aprons provided to students on kitchen clean-up.

"Then I'd suggest you go see a counselor about your frustration at being denied." Kai turned to go, but Rayson's hand shot out and dragged him back.

"Oh?" he asked in a deceptively reasonable-sounding voice. "Let's talk about that."

Kai wanted to look around, to find the closest staffer or red jumpsuit, but he knew that would be a mistake—besides, the staff and red-suiters never seemed to be around when the bullies came at Kai. He couldn't show fear. He sniffed and made his face harden. Then, in a pleasant voice, he said, "Good. Let's talk, Rayson."

Fergus narrowed his eyes and glowered at Kai.

"Oh, nothing to say?" He shrugged, hoping to pull off a casual cool he didn't quite feel. "Then I'd like you to take your dirty paws off me." He bore down with his mind, pushing past Rayson's meager defenses and *made* his hand open and fall to his side. "Thanks for not making this weird." He cocked his eyebrow and waited a moment before spinning on his heel to walk away.

"Kai! Look out!" yelled one of his classmates.

Too late, Kai tried to turn back to Rayson. One of the metal trays whistled down and pain exploded through the back of his head. He spun around, and so did the entire world, and he stumbled, arms pinwheeling. The metal tray went up over Rayson's head, and he screamed like a barbarian in a fantasy show.

Kai lashed out, snapping Rayson's defenses away like mere twigs in the path of a tornado. His head hurt, and he was as dizzy as he'd ever been in his life, but pain and shame and rage and vengeance roared through him in rapid succession, leaving him even dizzier than before. He locked Rayson's arms where they were—just starting the downstroke for another blow to Kai's head. He'd never wanted to actually *hurt* someone before, but he did in that moment—and *badly*. He moved Rayson's right foot behind his left, then pushed the bigger kid—hard, his own scant strength augmented by adrenaline and fury and frenzied bloodlust.

With a squawk, Fergus went ass-over-teakettle, landing flat on his back with a thud and a clang from the metal dining tray he'd been using as a weapon. He opened his pig mouth to speak, but Kai snapped his teeth together, catching the tip of the boy's tongue between his incisors. A moaning howl rumbled from his chest as blood spurted over his chin, and Kai grinned at him.

"We're just getting fucking started here, Ray-ray. Save some of the screaming for what's to come." The jagged, ferocious tenor of his voice surprised Kai, even scared him for a moment before that writhing berserker of wrath inside him shrieked its war cry, overriding any mercy or benevolence or charity or humanity within him.

He glared down into Rayson's wide-eyed stare, and for once in his life, saw fear in there—a fear Kai had manufactured and put there. A warm rush of emotion filled him from the inside-out, a delight of pride and pleasure, a beatitude of blissful intoxicating power over another human being. His features shifted, a large smile splitting his face, showing his teeth, his eyes round and blazing, nostrils flaring, and Rayson's fear increased.

He tried to speak, and Kai stilled his tongue, sticking it to the roof of the boy's mouth as surely as a mouthful of peanut butter. Kai stilled the boy's lips, made his cheeks go slack, but kept Rayson's eyes open—refused to let them slide shut. Oh, yes, he wanted the kid to see him transformed, a great red dragon—just like that Blake painting they'd studied in class—with seven heads and ten horns and seven crowns on his head. His name was ire, his name was furor, was rampage, was wrath.

He made Fergus's right hand release its white-knuckled grip on the metal tray, one slow finger at a time. He brought his arm out straight, poking up as though Rayson had a question to ask, then, with great deliberation, curled the boy's fingers into a tight fist. He moved the fist around in a circle of ever-increasing diameter, drawing out the movements, making each muscle flex and relax in its turn, moving with leisure, with heavy purpose, all while staring into Rayson's terrified eyes.

Rayson tried to close his eyes again, and again, Kai forbade it. He tried to roll his gaze away, and Kai forbade it. He tried to jerk his head to the side, and Kai forbade it; he tried to stop his fist making its circles, and Kai forbade it.

No, Kai sent at the boy. *No, there is no escape for you, Rayson. I gave you a chance—don't say I didn't. I gave you* every *chance, again and again and again, and at each step, in each instance, you rebuked my generosity. Fine, that was your choice to make, but don't come whining and crying to me* now. *Now, it's too late. Now, you're going to get your just desserts. Know why, you ponderous, slothful, asshole? I'll tell you since I won't allow you to speak:* I am become wrath, destroyer of worlds. *I'm so fucking sick of you dumb pricks, I can hardly see straight. Well, guess what? All that ends. Right fucking now.* He brought Rayson's fist arcing down at blurry speed right into the kid's groin, using every single muscle fiber, using all Rayson's considerable strength. The blow struck with the sound of a butcher's maul, and the boy's eyes shot open, big and round and swimming in agony. Kai made the fist jerk upward, activating muscles and nerves as he needed them, shooting that fist as high as he could get it, then slammed it down in the same place. He did it a third time, and again, and a fifth—while the noise in the room fell to terrible silence.

Rayson gargled with agony, screamed with it, shrieked and howled and squalled, while Kai intercepted every impulse to give voice to his inchoate dissonant symphony of nightmarish torment and denied him the power to articulate it. The boy screamed inside a mouth that Kai owned, tried to form words with a tongue Kai owned, tried to call for help and beg Kai to stop, all with a voice Kai owned.

An intense satisfaction flooded Kai's mind. Rayson was his property and would remain so until Kai freed him. The breathtaking puissance of it, the competent, confident potency of it, shivered through him from head to toe, and Kai smiled. He smiled like a maniac, like a cold-hearted executioner, a maven of sadism and domination.

And it felt grand. He felt like a king, like a vengeful god. He relished the pure rapture of holding Rayson in limbo, in a hell of Kai's own design. Again, he brought Rayson's fist up and froze there, threatening another blow. He made the boy's left hand bring the tray up to meet his fist, made the fist open and take a firm grip on the tray. Kai froze Rayson's muscles there, an unadulterated exhibition of his power and control, a tableau of torture.

Then he brought the tray down on the boy's face— once, again, three times—and watched the blood splatter across the concrete floor. Blood rained on his shoes, spotted the pants legs of his green jumpsuit, painted Rayson red.

Kai paused a moment, then, wondering if he'd made his point, knowing he had and not caring. He didn't want the feelings to end. He didn't want to give up his utter domination of another human being.

So, he didn't.

He made Rayson discard the tray and used the boy's fingernails to carve into his cheeks, his fingers to rend his hair. Loud, harsh slaps rang out in the room that had gone as quiet as a grave, and Kai relaxed Rayson's neck muscles so that his head rocked from side to side with each blow of his open hand. Rayson boxed his own ears, moaning deep in his chest.

When he tired of violence, Kai's mind turned to degradation. He made Rayson roll to his hands and knees, then stagger to his feet. He was as unsteady as a life-long drunk in a whisky mill, but Kai forced him to keep his feet. With laggard care, he made Rayson work the zipper of his jumpsuit, then shrugged the boy's shoulders until it became a puddle of blue entwining his ankles. Underneath, he wore blue boxers, and Kai made him drop those as well. Then, in shuffling steps, he made Rayson walk among the tables of the dining room, making sure everyone got a good view of his swelling testicles.

Tears washed blood from Rayson's cheeks, but there was plenty gushing from his wounds. He made a continuous wailing sound deep in his chest, and his eyes rolled like a terrified animal. Kai made him do another lap of the room, this time dancing a shuffling, staggering jig.

Kai faced the dining room, meeting any gaze that pointed his way, one eyebrow arched. He waited to see if anyone would argue his right to do what he wanted to Rayson, but no one did. Many of the students wouldn't meet his gaze, but that was okay. If he wanted them to, he could *make* them.

And everyone in that room knew it.

Kai finally tired of hurting Rayson. He finally ran out of ways to humiliate him. He grew tired of the silence, of the stares, of no one daring to move or speak or challenge him. He relaxed all of Rayson's muscles, letting him flop to the floor like a discarded rag doll.

He swept the room with a narrow-eyed gaze one more time, then walked down the aisle and out the door. Rayson lay in a heap, not even trying to move.

9

Adeline stopped outside Beatrice's quarters and took a deep breath. *Calm. Be calm. Don't let her push your buttons, old woman,* she thought. She knocked and stepped back to wait.

And wait.

After a few minutes, she stepped forward and knocked again. One good thing about being a bird dog is she always knew when people were home. She cocked her head at the door and crossed her arms, drumming the fingers of her right hand on her left elbow.

Another few minutes trickled by, and her nerves began to sing with frustration and ire. She made a fist and pounded on the door. *Don't get angry, woman. Catching flies goes better with honey than vinegar and all that happy horse manure.*

Beatrice snatched the door open to fix Adeline with a glare. "Do you know what time it is?"

"About half-past seven," said Adeline with a brash air. "We need to talk before the day gets a-moving."

"Talk?" sneered Beatrice. She wore a long T-shirt—and possibly nothing else—and raked her hand through her mussed hair. "What would you imagine we have to talk about that we haven't already covered?"

"Child," Adeline began in an annoyed tone but then shook her head and held up her hands in surrender. "Please, Beatrice. We can't go on like this—at each other all the time."

"You think?"

Adeline ignored the sarcasm and nodded. "I do. For my part, I reacted badly to Jamilla and Kai's reprogramming. I'm too close to them for objectivity, and I know that. But that's no excuse for how I snipped and snapped at you. Will you accept my apology?" She stuck out her hand, offering to shake.

Beatrice narrowed her eyes and glanced down at Adeline's open hand. "Well…" She heaved a deep breath in and out, then nodded. "I'm sorry, too. I don't handle challenges to my work very well. Never have." She grinned and took Adeline's hand. "Remember Nora Cranston?"

Adeline chuckled. "Until this moment, I didn't. But seeing you and hearing her name…" She laughed. "Yes, I recall."

"Come on in, Miss Addy," said Beatrice stepping back. "Want some java? I'm making it either way." She turned and walked to the wall adorned with a row of cabinets, a small stove, and a sink, then filled the coffee machine with water and coffee.

Adeline entered Beatrice's quarters and closed the door behind her. "Coffee would be grand," she said despite already needing the bathroom to get rid of the two cups she'd had with her breakfast. She sank down onto the couch and looked around. The usually immaculate room looked as if a tornado had crashed through the living room area, and Adeline noted the clothes flung willy-nilly.

The door to the rear of the flat opened, and Bethany stomped in. Her irritated gaze swept from Beatrice to Adeline and back, and she quirked an eyebrow. Like Beatrice, she wore only a long T-shirt. Like Beatrice, her first instinct was to glower at Adeline. "What's she doing here?"

"Relax, bitch. She came to make up. She says we need to talk."

Bethany turned her gaze on her sister, and something passed between them, unsaid. Then she shrugged. "I'll have a cup, too. And make one for Hec." She turned back to Adeline. "Is the subject good for all three of us or just for the bimbo making coffee?"

"Mostly it's between Beatrice and me, but I do want to touch on Kai's program goals and pass an update along about Jamilla."

Bethany nodded. "I'll get Hec. He'll want to be part of the conversation."

"Uh, Hec?"

Bethany turned and went into the bedroom. She returned in a few moments, with Hector Chavez trailing behind her. Adeline arched one eyebrow at him, and he colored nicely. "Not my business, Chavez," she said.

Bethany glanced his way and laughed. "Are you ashamed of us, Hec? You'd better answer no if you want to keep seeing us."

Beatrice sniggered in the kitchen.

Adeline lowered her gaze to her lap.

"I'm not ashamed," said Hec, though he sounded a little contrite. "What I am is surprised. Good morning, Adeline."

"Miss Addy says we need to talk about Kai's program goals and that she realizes she can't be objective about either of the Washingtons."

"That's right," said Adeline with a nod. "I'm too close to see past my love of them."

"You said you had an update on Jamilla?" asked Beatrice.

Bethany frowned. "I haven't heard a peep from medical."

Adeline nodded. "I wouldn't have if I hadn't gone over there last night. The medics began weaning her off the sedation drip yesterday, but as soon as Jamilla regained consciousness, she became confused and agitated. The medics have had to restrain her. There was talk about a psychiatric commitment."

Beatrice shook her head. "No, that can't happen. I'll take care of that."

"Good," said Adeline. "Ain't nothing good in one of them places."

"How did she respond to you?" asked Bethany.

Adeline dropped her gaze. "She didn't seem to recognize me, but they had her pretty doped up."

"Would you like me to take a look?" asked Beatrice. Her voice was pleasant enough, but there was an edge to it.

"Or one of the other fixers," said Adeline, nodding her head, "if your schedule is too tight. I think a familiar face would do her good, though."

"Of course, I'll go," said Beatrice. "Anything for a friend."

Chavez glanced at Bethany and raised one eyebrow. Bethany shrugged. "I told you they made up."

"What do you want to know about Kai's program?" Chavez asked.

"You may think I'm a silly old bird for how I acted, but—"

"No," said Chavez. "Everyone knows how close you were with Kai in the outside world."

Adeline smiled. "Yes. And with Jamilla, but she made her own choice to follow Bethany that day."

Bethany nodded.

"Where I'd like to start," began Adeline, "is with the high-level goals in Kai's plan. Academic and otherwise."

Chavez nodded. "As you already know, Kai's a strong psi puppeteer. The high-level goal is to prepare him for operations. Academically, that means languages, law, polisci, economics, high-order math including formal logic, a basic understanding of biology."

"And on the practical side?" asked Adeline in a voice that shook a little.

Hec glanced at first Bethany, then Beatrice, and when she nodded, he took a deep breath. "He'll begin an advanced puppeteering track immediately, given the prowess and increased psi rating he displayed last night. That will include long-range telecheiristiric techniques, psi assault and defenses, and perception manipulation."

Adeline nodded.

"Now, look, Miss Adeline," began Chavez, "we know how you feel about Kai. Will you accept that I've grown close to him as well?"

"I know that's true," said Adeline in a small voice.

"It is. Can you also accept that I wouldn't want him to come to harm of any kind?"

Adeline nodded again, staring into his eyes.

"You know how it goes, Miss Adeline. The staffing needs of Operations depends on the geopolitical landscape and the state of things domestically. Sometimes they need snoops to bolster their spying capabilities. Sometimes they need bird dogs to help track individuals of interest. Sometimes they need pushers—either to destroy technologies in enemy states and—"

"And to stop the clocks of enemies," said Adeline.

Chavez nodded. "And to work on black bag teams. According to the legends, you've participated in teams like that, yourself."

"Yes," Adeline murmured. "In the sixties and seventies."

Chavez nodded again. "At present, the Operations wants puppeteers who can…" He glanced at Beatrice again. "Who can work solo black bag jobs…and make them look like suicides or accidents. You know, walking someone off a roof, making them slit their own wrists, or swerving into oncoming traffic on the highway." He shrugged. "Or something along those lines."

Adeline lifted her hand to cover her mouth. "Then they want killers."

Chavez shrugged again. "My training was no different."

"Yes," Adeline said in a dead voice.

"And Kai is a natural. If you could see him perform… Watch him work, Miss Adeline," he urged. "Watch the videos. Watch how fast he picks up new techniques and integrates them. Hell, Miss Addy, none of us taught him the kind of proprioceptive control he displayed last night. He expanded on his practicals to do that, and he did it as though born to do it. He's a prodigy, Miss Adeline. A real prodigy."

"Yes," she repeated in the same dead voice. "A prodigy." She lifted her gaze and pinned Chavez with it. "How soon will you start him?"

"Start him?"

"Don't play coy!" Adeline snapped, eyes blazing.

Chavez glanced at Beatrice once more.

"Within the year," she said. "He'll advance to charcoal within the next three to six months, according to instructor evaluations and my own examination of his psyche. After a month or so to settle in, he'll start the Covert Ops course. Once he completes that, he'll move to the Special Activities curriculum."

Adeline looked down at her lap. "He'll be *fourteen* when you start teaching him to kill, Chavez. He won't even be able to get a driver's license."

"Miss Addy, he won't need a driver's license. You know that. And it's not like he'll go straight into the field. There are the training courses, and he still needs to advance to red before he can start field training. He'll probably be an adult by the time he's ready."

Adeline shook her head. "He's a prodigy, remember?" she murmured.

Chapter 16
Children of the Damned

I

Adeline sucked her teeth. "They wanted a prodigy. Heh, they wanted *two* prodigies, but all their manipulation, all their cruelty, led to zero prodigies."

"I'm sorry, Adeline, but that story does nothing but confirm that Kai Washington has to be one of our suspects," said Karl.

"No," said Adeline. "He ain't in Miami. He ain't your killer."

"But—"

"They pushed Javi until he broke—or until Kai broke him's more like it—then Beatrice put him back together again. But even that wasn't enough. No, not for them three. Then they made them become friends, put Kai in the mouth of the beast for sure. I've told you how Kai"—Adeline's voice cracked—"changed, became violent, callous, and Chavez and Beatrice were to blame. And me. I should've stopped 'em. I should've taken Kai and Jamilla out of there, consequences be damned. I could've kept 'em safe, I could've hid us away. Alaska or South America. I could've watched for their agents. Watched for 'em and stopped 'em cold. I should've *done something*." After a moment of silence, Adeline sighed and took a sip of water. "Anyway, I didn't do nothing. I guess it's more accurate to say I did all the *wrong* things I could think up. I tried to reason with 'em. Heh. I'm as guilty as the others for not heeding them observer reports."

"What happened to Dela Cruz?" asked Karl.

"He…escaped. There's probably a slew of records about it all. I…" She took a deep breath then blew it out. "I don't think I can tell any more right now. It's too…"

"We understand," said Maddie. "It's cost you a lot, telling us these stories."

"Not as much as living them cost Kai," said Adeline.

"And the others on your list?" asked Karl. "Dela Cruz, Jepson, and Fergus?"

Adeline grunted. "I ain't sure."

"You said Kai became callous, violent. You just recounted a tale where he physically tortured a kid—"

"Rayson Fergus."

"—then moved on to psychological torture and degradation. And he made Fergus inflict his own wounds. Just like our killer. Plus, the manipulation he suffered there…that sounds like the perfect recipe to make a serial killer," said Karl.

"Not Kai," Adeline repeated. "Not Kai."

"Well… Why not?"

"Kai is…" The old woman drew in a ragged, rasping breath. "Kai died the night Dela Cruz escaped. Murdered…murdered by Dela Cruz, Jepson, and Fergus. They did it to make 'em an opportunity for escape, and"—Adeline sobbed once—"it *worked*. They escaped. They *murdered* sweet little Kai and escaped.

Jamilla went after them and…and they killed her, too. And then Javier turned on the other two." She made a choking sound. "I can't. I can't tell you anymore. It's too *hard.*"

A rattle and click sounded on the line, and Gavin glanced down at the screen.

"That's okay, Adeline," said Maddie. "We—"

"She's gone, hon," said Gavin. "She disconnected."

"Oh."

"But is all that…" said Karl.

"True?" asked Gavin. "Has she given you a reason to doubt her?"

"Sometimes I get a read on Adeline that I don't like," said Karl.

"What kind of read?"

"The kind you get in an interrogation room when the skell across the table is feeding you some gilded bullshit making himself look good while pushing the blame on the others in his crew."

Gavin nodded. "Yeah, I get that from her at times. But I've got more records. Let's find out if she's on the up and up."

"Can we afford the time?"

"Can we afford *not* to make the time? More information is better than less. Six hours ago you got a taste of what's possible for this unsub. Do you feel ready to confront him again?"

Karl loosed a flat, humorless laugh. "No, but I'm not sure more stories will help that."

"We won't know until we have all the information," said Maddie. "Go on, Gavin."

2

From Program records
Marked January 5, 2000, 03:59

TO: green_team@majest.ic
CC: admin_team@majest.ic
FROM: oversight@majest.ic

SUBJECT: Kai Washington Behavior Report

In reference to the altercation between Kai Washington (green) and Dylan Jepson (re-blued), it is my finding that KW acted appropriately. Please consider the following.

Recommendations:
1) Dismiss re-blued student (Dylan Jepson) from the Program with Protocol One check performed by a fixer.
2) Reinforce subject's superiority over re-blued students (Chavez?).
3) Consider no-intervention order re: subject confrontations with peers.

Report ends.

3

TO: admin_team@majest.ic
FROM: chavez@majest.ic

SUBJECT: RE: Kai Washington Behavior
Report (attached)

I've cut oversight from the
distribution list so we can discuss
it. I'll relay our decision to the
oversight team in person.

First point: I haven't given up on
Jepson. Without the influence of his
buddies, we might still turn him
around. I vote we keep him a while
yet.

Second point: I'm happy to atta-boy
Kai about his responses and actions.
I'm tempted to tell him he didn't take
it far enough. Thoughts?

Third point: The no-intervention
order is doing what we hoped. I see no
reason to terminate it. Just look how
Kai has progressed—this interaction
with Jepson is proof of concept. It
will be interesting to see if Kai is
able to stand up to the other two.
Should we perhaps arrange a
confrontation?

4

From Program records
Marked January 5, 2000, 07:21

TO: admin_team@majest.ic
FROM: green_eyed_goddess@majest.ic

SUBJECT: RE: RE: Kai Washington Behavior Report (attached)

Christ, doesn't anyone sleep around here anymore?

My two cents: Hec is right. On all points. I wholeheartedly agree with initiating a confrontation with Dela Cruz and the Fergus kid—but maybe one at a time. It will either prove we are on the right track with Kai's development or underscore his unsuitability for all this extra attention.

5

From Program records
Marked January 5, 2000, 07:33

TO: admin_team@majest.ic
FROM: missadeline@majest.ic

SUBJECT: RE: RE: RE: Kai Washington Behavior Report (attached)

First, let me say two things: 1) I congratulate the team on Kai's rapid advancement through his studies. You've all done a marvelous job getting him on the fast track. 2) I am very pleased that Kai is standing up to these bullies.

With that said, I feel I must ask if you've *lost your fool minds*?

Regardless of his rapid advances, Kai is a thirteen-year-old boy. Do you really think he's ready to take on the world? Do you think his actions (especially the belittling of Jepson through puppetry) are appropriate? What kind of person do you wish to create? A psychopath? A killer?

6

From Program records
Marked January 5, 2000, 07:34

TO: admin_team@majest.ic
FROM: green_eyed_goddess@majest.ic

SUBJECT: RE: RE: RE: RE: Kai Washington Behavior Report (attached)

Good, we're all in agreement.

Proceed, Hec. Unless you want me to set it up?

7

From Program records
Marked January 5, 2000, 07:49

TO: admin_team@majest.ic
FROM: chavez@majest.ic

SUBJECT: RE: RE: RE: RE: RE: Kai Washington Behavior Report (attached)

Beatrice, you slay me at times.

I think it might be best if the manipulation is unconscious for all involved. Go-go Superfixer.

8

From Program records
Marked January 5, 2000, 07:57

TO: admin_team@majest.ic
FROM: green_eyed_goddess@majest.ic

SUBJECT: RE: RE: RE: RE: RE: RE: Kai Washington Behavior Report (attached)

Aw, you say the sweetest things, Hec.

Consider it done.

9

From Program records
Marked January 5, 2000, 08:21

TO: admin_team@majest.ic
FROM: missadeline@majest.ic

SUBJECT: RE: RE: RE: RE: RE: RE: RE:
Kai   Washington   Behavior   Report
(attached)

Did my last reply not go through?

10

From Program records
Marked January 5, 2000, 09:06

TO: missadeline@majest.ic
CC: chavez@majest.ic
FROM: green_eyed_goddess@majest.ic

SUBJECT: RE: RE: RE: RE: RE: RE: RE: RE: Kai Washington Behavior Report (attached)

You mean the one where you got all holier-than-thou and accused us of making psychopaths?

Nope. It must've gone right to spam (where it deserves to be, imo)

II

From Program records
Marked January 5, 2000, 09:08

TO: green_eyed_goddess@majest.ic
FROM: chavez@majest.ic

SUBJECT: OMG your fuckin' killing me

Still ROFL. You are as funny as you are sexy, and that's quite a lot.

I've half a mind to come by right now and…well, you know what ;)

I thought you adored "Miss Addy?"

12

From Program records
Marked January 5, 2000, 09:11

TO: chavez@majest.ic
CC: gray_eyed_goddess@majest.ic

FROM: green_eyed_goddess@majest.ic

SUBJECT: RE: OMG your fuckin' killing me

What's stopping you? I'm here, I'm waiting. Bethany can come play with us, too, if she's not too busy.

Fuck Adeline—but me first. Then, me again. And again. Oh, look, I've just freed my whole calendar for the day.

Barbie-bitch, are you cuming?

13

From Program records
Marked January 5, 2000, 09:13

TO: chavez@majest.ic
CC: green_eyed_goddess@majest.ic
FROM: gray_eyed_goddess@majest.ic

SUBJECT: RE: OMG your fuckin' killing me

Cuming? Barbie-bitch-2, I'm already naked.

Hec, where are you, stud? Get in her. Oops. Typo :D

14

From Program records
Marked January 5, 2000, 10:31

TO: green_eyed_goddess@majest.ic
CC: missadeline@majest.ic
FROM: medical@majest.ic

SUBJECT: Jamilla Washington evaluation

Custodial staffer, Jamilla Washington (JW), brought to medical by Adeline d'Clara. JW found wandering the halls by Adeline, perhaps lost, perhaps after suffering a seizure that left her befuddled.

On examination, I found sufficient evidence to conclude the patient is suffering from Frontal Lobe Epilepsy with possible Temporal Lobe Epilepsy co-morbidity. Patient shows marked cognitive decline, a fixation with the word "left," perseveration on a memory from childhood, and significant confusion. It is our opinion the patient suffered from multiple complex partial seizures in the frontal lobe and possibly in the temporal lobe as well. Due to the plethora of connections between the frontal and temporal lobes, it is difficult to determine beyond any doubt which lobe(s).

Blood tests reveal both white blood cells and neutrophil granulocytes are significantly elevated—indicating sleep deprivation, which almost certainly contributed to the problem this morning. Depriving the body of sleep has a similar effect on the brain as a large dose of alcohol. Neurons are robbed of the ability to effectively function. Chronic sleep deprivation poses a significant risk to physical and mental health, and there may be a psychiatric component to the patient's general state of confusion.

I am not a fixer. I'm only a doctor, but I do have teletechnitic tendencies, and I can sense significant reprogramming in the patient. At this point, I wonder if it isn't doing more harm than good. I believe continued fixer manipulation will worsen the problem.

As of five minutes ago, I have sedated the patient and admitted her to my care for an unspecified length of time. Notification to custodial management sent. I plan on keeping the patient sedated for at least a day or so to allow her to rest.

I will keep you apprised as to the patient's recovery.

Report ends.

15

From Program records
Marked January 8, 2000, 22:47

TO: green_team@majest.ic
CC: admin_team@majest.ic
FROM: oversight@majest.ic

SUBJECT: Kai Washington

I don't know what to say. Oh, wait, yes, I do. Here it is:

For fuck's sake, I warned you this could happen. I'm at a complete and utter loss why you've left the no-intervention order in place. He might've killed Fergus! As it is, the kid has a broken nose, chipped tooth, and maybe a fractured eye socket—and that doesn't include any lasting damage to his genitals, which is possible.

I do not want to be assigned to KW anymore. You've turned him into some kind of monster…a killer in the making. I don't want to touch the mind of a budding sociopath. Find someone else. Find anyone else. Keep me assigned to him, and I'll quit.

Recommendations:
1) Fixer to neuter KW
2) Find someone else to watch this bastard—I won't do it anymore.
3) Continue suicide watch for RF.

That's right, he tried to kill himself at 21:29, so add 28 stitches to the butcher's bill. He fought the medics treating him and required physical, chemical, and psionic restraints. He didn't want the medics to save him. That is my considered opinion. Not after what that little psycho did to him.

You know what? Forget assigning me to someone else.

I fucking quit.

Report ends.

16

From Program records
Marked January 8, 2000, 23:07

TO: admin_team@majest.ic
FROM: missadeline@majest.ic

SUBJECT: Have you seen the latest report from Observer 31?

I don't even know where to begin. Perhaps you should all take a look at my email from the other day—especially the last two lines.

I'm sad and disgusted and angry that I was right. Now, can we please set some appropriate behavioral guidelines around here? This isn't a gladiator school. Our job isn't to produce unfeeling assassins.

I'd be saying this even it wasn't Kai.

17

From Program records
Marked January 8, 2000, 22:07

TO: admin_team@majest.ic
FROM: green_eyed_goddess@majest.ic

SUBJECT: RE: Have you seen the latest report from Observer 31?

>> Perhaps you should all take a look at my email from the other day—especially the last two lines.

No thanks. Once was enough.

>> I'm sad and disgusted and angry that I was right.

Who said you were right? I must've missed it.

>> Now, can we please set some appropriate behavioral guidelines around here?

We already have them.

>> This isn't a gladiator school. Our job isn't to produce unfeeling assassins.

You sure about that? I've read your personnel file, Adeline. The Program has always been about producing assassins, and you've done your best to find us the *right* people. Right?

18

From Program records
Marked January 8, 2000, 22:18

TO: admin_team@majest.ic
FROM: chavez@majest.ic

SUBJECT: RE: RE: Have you seen the latest report from Observer 31?

>> >> I'm sad and disgusted and angry that I was right.

>> Who said you were right?

Sorry, Miss Adeline, but I agree with Beatrice.

>> >> Now, can we please set some appropriate behavioral guidelines around here?

>> We already have them.

And again. Our guidelines are created for each individual student with the intent of maximizing their personal growth. Kai had no confidence, no backbone.

If anything, tonight's altercation has proved we're on the right track.

19

From Program records
Marked January 8, 2000, 22:23

TO: chavez@majest.ic
CC: green_eyed_goddess@majest.ic
FROM: gray_eyed_goddess@majest.ic

SUBJECT: Don't feed the troll.

Adeline doesn't get it. She's too close to the Washingtons to see things clearly. You know it, I know it. Adeline doesn't know, but that's tough shit for her. Don't feed into her bullshit.

Hec is right. This is proof that the non-interference policy is dead nuts on (no pun intended) for Kai.

Besides, we *do* plan on starting him in covert ops training, soon, right?

Who gives a fuck what Adeline thinks?

Hey... I get hot every time I think about our play date. When are we doing it again?

20

From Program records
Marked January 8, 2000, 22:25

TO: gray_eyed_goddess@majest.ic
CC: chavez@majest.ic
FROM: green_eyed_goddess@majest.ic

SUBJECT: RE: Don't feed the troll.

What was it you said to me the other day?

Oh, yeah. Barbie-bitch, I'm already naked.

And guess who just rang my bell? (Hint: it isn't Miss Adeline.) I'm going to let him in. Maybe he can ring my bell before you get over here.

21

From Program records
Marked January 19, 2000, 06:25

TO: blue_team@majest.ic
CC: admin_team@majest.ic
FROM: oversight@majest.ic

SUBJECT: Kai Washington Interaction Report

Re-blued subject Javier Dela Cruz eloped from Blue Dorm Thirteen prior to first bell (05:43 hours). Subject made a beeline between Blue Dorm Thirteen and the Green Study Hall, where JDC confronted Kai Washington.

JDC made aggressive advances toward KW, and KW employed TC (psi 15.2) to subdue him. KW practiced similar techniques as with Rayson Fergus, though inflicting less physical damage and no humiliation in front of peers as none were present. Note: JDC didn't suffer these things without resistance—he fought, and he fought hard, employing TC (psi 12.8) and TK (psi 8.3). No-intervention order noted, no red-suiters or staffers dispatched.

KW showed remarkable proprioceptive control—leaving JDC frozen inside the study hall room as KW walked to his dorm, took a shower, then attended morning meal in the dining hall. After second bell, KW released JDC.

JDC marked tardy for his first class of the day and detected in the incorrect dormitory section after first bell by a red-suiter interning with the oversight team. JDC took his punishment without comment, though this observer believes this is not the end of the confrontation. JDC just doesn't think that way.

Recommendations:
1) Fixer intervention to remove JDC's fixation on KW.
2) Assign suitable male figure to JDC—he needs guidance, or he will require discarding.
3) Consider fixer intervention for both subjects to create a positive relationship. Perhaps KW can become an example to JDC?

Report ends.

22

From Program records
Marked January 19, 2000, 06:25

TO: blue_team@majest.ic
CC: admin_team@majest.ic
FROM: charlie_fixit@majest.ic

SUBJECT: Javier Dela Cruz Reprogramming

As requested, I brought Javier Dela Cruz in for reprogramming. His records indicate a strong TC ability, as well as average TK ability. After sedating JDC, I went digging.

Wow, this kid has a long history of abuse by male role models—both at home and in the various psychiatric institutions his parents dumped him in. JDC has no trust in him. He will never accept the guidance of a male role model without significant deep-trait reprogramming—which comes at significant risk to the subject. He has no motivation to succeed—believing instead, that if he succeeds, he will only draw the attention of another abuser.

It gets worse.

The echthrocentric fixation on Kai Washington is the result of JDC's twisted accomplishment drive. JDC feels no joy in success. He feels no satisfaction in reaching goals. Instead, he feels joy in the failure of others. He achieves satisfaction via derailing his peers, fixating on those who show the most potential. He feels no remorse for these actions. He feels pleasure.

In short, he's a budding serial killer, folks.

I was able to successfully correct his accomplishment drive and eliminate his fixation—not only on Kai Washington, but also on three new blue-suiters.

I reworked his memory center to increase the cognitive load of remembering negative scenes from his past to blackout-levels, while at the same time lowering the cognitive load of positive memories. It is my hope that these adjustments will yield a more compliant student and give him a few positive reasons to succeed.

It is important that we provide a positive role model immediately. Likewise, JDC will require praise and positive experiences related to academic and practical successes. We should consider bumping him out of blue the second he begins to perform on target.

I recommend isolating JDC from both of his "friends." I have created an aversion sensation tied to both boys. Recommend fixer reprogramming for both of them as well. Do with it what you will.

On a side note, do we know who his biological parents are? There's something…strange about the psionic expression. In a fully-trained adult, I might think he's creating a smokescreen.

Charles

Report ends.

23

From Program records
Marked January 29, 2000, 18:23

TO: admin_team@majest.ic
FROM: green_eyed_goddess@majest.ic

SUBJECT: Observer 53's report on Dela
Cruz: Decision time.

If you haven't read it, go read
Observer 53's 10-day report, but
here's a summary.

Great news—we've salvaged JDC when his
demise seemed so certain. I was glad
to see that a snoop determined his
behavior is a true representation of
his mindset. Should we pass that on to
Charlie?

His psi ratings look great—TC: 13.1,
TK: 8.9, TP: 6.7. Interesting to note
he was able to hide his TP from
everyone. That bears thinking about.
Perhaps we need to transfer JDC to the
experimental section?

What to do about giving JDC a mentor?
Kai was suggested, but I'm not
comfortable adding additional levels
of reprogramming on top of the
necessary and minimal reprog re: his
parents I've already made. I don't
want to risk him as his psi—which we
all agree—is quite frankly amazing.

Is JDC worth the risk? I don't know the answer to that.

Thoughts?

24

From Program records
Marked January 29, 2000, 18:23

TO: admin_team@majest.ic
FROM: missadeline@majest.ic

SUBJECT: RE: Observer 53's report on Dela Cruz: Decision time.

Beatrice, I agree that Kai's power is too great to risk. Another reprogramming would lie atop the current implementation, correct? I'm not the expert here, but I believe that kind of doubling increases the risk of psychotic rejection by at least double?

We should leave Kai out of this. He and JDC have significant history. Throwing them together is irresponsible.

Great news about the Dela Cruz boy. Should we consider similar fixer intervention with the other two? Fergus and Jepson?

25

From Program records
Marked January 29, 2000, 18:23

TO: admin_team@majest.ic
FROM: green_eyed_goddess@majest.ic

SUBJECT: RE: RE: Observer 53's report
on Dela Cruz: Decision time.

The risk of PR isn't quite double but
close enough. A layered reprogramming
creates a *significant* risk of PR.

Are Fergus and Jepson worth the
effort? Neither is anything special in
terms of psi rating.

Irresponsible, Miss Addy? Can we have
one discussion where you don't lapse
into hyperbole?

26

From Program records
Marked January 29, 2000, 18:23

TO: admin_team@majest.ic
FROM: chavez@majest.ic

SUBJECT: RE: RE: RE: Observer 53's report on Dela Cruz: Decision time.

IMO, Fergus is a run-of-the-mill student. Middle of the pack. Jepson, on the other hand, shows some promise. He may be worth the effort—his TC psi is decently high if you aren't comparing him to JDC and Kai.

As to whether JDC is worth risking Kai, the answer is an absolute no. Even without considering attitude and drive, Kai's psi is astounding for his age. JDC's is good, but I would never agree to risking a prodigy to gain a merely good puppeteer. I will talk to Kai. I'll explain what was wrong with JDC and ask him to forgive and forget. He's a good kid. He'll probably do it for me.

And, Miss Addy, irresponsible would be like letting a promising student wither on the vine because of a *personal* tie with another, right? If Kai weren't a part of this conversation, you wouldn't have even replied. We all know it. Can't you see how much these constant burrs under

our saddle blankets are wearing us all
out? Please stop.

27

Langfield Sun, Miami, FL
Friday, 12:37 pm

"It's just like she said. They *reveled* in what Kai was becoming," said Maddie. "They…they *taunted* Adeline with it."

"It seems so," said Karl, "but those three grew up in that place. How could they be anything but broken?"

"Were *they* manipulated like they manipulated those boys?"

"They do seem like psychopaths to me," said Karl. "I'd guess they were."

"Right out of *Children of the Damned*, all of them. And that's not even the end of it," said Gavin. "There's a lot more."

"Do we need to hear them?" asked Maddie. "I mean, those you've already read have backed up everything Adeline said."

"You don't have to hear anymore, Mads. Not if it's… Not if it's too upsetting."

"You'll go on, though. Right?"

"I have to, Mads," said Gavin. "I can't leave it alone. Not now. Not with one of these people down here in

Miami killing people as a result. There might be something in these damn reports that leads us to him, and it seems like Adeline is done telling us stories for now. But now is when we need the information."

Maddie sighed. "I know."

"Want to take a break? Get some lunch?"

Karl's phone buzzed where it lay on the table, and he swept it up. "Truxillo," he said and put the phone to his ear. "Hey, Lieu, what's up?" He listened for a moment, then waved at Gavin's gear. "Got it. We're on our way."

"What?" asked Gavin. He snapped the lid of his laptop closed and shoved it into his bag.

"We got a credit card hit on Xavier Frire. Car rental place by the airport."

"Go," said Maddie. "Call me later. After you've got him."

"Right." Gavin broke the connection and shoved his phone into his pocket. "It's insane, Karl. Why would he use a card after knowing we were in the house and most likely found his little stash of credit card aliases? Why wouldn't he assume those names and cards were burned?"

"Stupidity? Crazy? Take your pick." He stood and put his hand on the doorknob. "Or maybe he has no other choice."

"Or another ambush?"

"Or that," said Karl in a grave voice.

28

3900 NW 25th Street, Miami, FL
Friday, 1:18 pm

Karl pulled the Explorer into the lane marked "Authorized Vehicles Only" then up onto the sidewalk near the main doors for the MIA Rental Car Center. Both he and Gavin got out and entered the building. Inside, everything was sleek and lit with colorful signs for various rental companies. Rows of black seats identical to those inside the airport itself crowded the center of the floor, bordered by roped-off serpentine lines leading to the various counters. Karl grunted and jerked his chin at the counter lit by yellow signs of the Axis Rental Car company.

"Got it," said Gavin. He skipped the line, walking around the roped off queue, and approached the counter.

"Hey! We're all in line here," said a gentleman trapped behind the yellow ribbons.

Gavin ignored the man and walked to the closest agent. "Excuse me."

"No, sir," said the woman behind the rental counter. "The lines are there for a reason."

"Yeah, buddy! You ain't special. Wait like the rest of us."

The chances that the unsub was still in the building were slim—the credit hit had taken place forty minutes before, but Gavin didn't want to risk alerting him. Karl walked up to the loudmouth in the line and began a low volume conversation. With a frown, Gavin pulled out his credentials and stepped up to the agent's workstation. "Get your manager. Now." He gave the agent a peek inside his badge wallet. She nodded and picked up the phone.

Gavin turned his back to her and scanned the sea of tanned faces nearby. None of them matched the composite sketch they'd gotten from the cook at Tequila Jack's, and none of them took special care to avoid his gaze. Karl glanced his way and cocked an eyebrow. Gavin shook his head.

"Can I help you?"

Gavin turned back to the counter. "Yes. I need a copy of the rental agreement for Xavier Frire. He secured a car within the last hour. Here's the credit card number he used." He slid his business card to her with the credit card number written on the back.

She took the card and rattled away on the keyboard of the closest terminal. "Yes," said the manager. "The issuer notified us that there was a problem with the card. They asked us to delay the transaction."

"And did you?"

"We did. He was very understanding. He said he'd get some coffee and come back."

Gavin rolled his finger. "And?"

"He hasn't returned."

"I see." He took the composite sketch out of his inner breast pocket and unfolded it. "Is this the man?"

The manager glanced at the sketch and shook her head.

"Look at it again, please," said Gavin. "Take a good look. He may have been wearing a disguise."

"That isn't the man. Not unless they have disguises that can turn a man Black."

Gavin brows furrowed. "Black?"

"Yes. The man was Black. Very dark skinned." The manager shrugged. "Attractive."

"How old?" Gavin pulled out his little leather notebook and his pen.

"Youngish. Thirties, maybe a little older."

"What else do you remember about him?"

"His eyes…" She blushed. "They were beautiful."

"What color?"

"Sort of amber, I think. I've never seen eyes quite like his."

"Hair? Build?"

She shook her head. "Shaved bald. He had an athletic build. You know, like he worked out a lot."

Gavin scratched his chin. "As tall as me? Shorter?"

"A little shorter."

"And you're absolutely sure the man with that credit card said his name was Xavier Frire?"

She nodded. "He had to, right? The name was imprinted on the card."

"Did you ask for another form of ID?"

"I did. Driver's license out of New York. He smiled at me as he got it out. Flirty, you know?"

Gavin nodded. "I assume the name matched."

"Of course."

"And the address on the driver's license?"

She rattled away at the computer again. "Here it is. 3121 Newcroft Park, Rochester, New York, 14624." She picked up a pen and a square of paper emblazoned with the Axis logo. "Here's the license number." She wrote it down and passed it over.

"Thank you," said Gavin. "If he returns, please call 911, and do what you can to stall him."

"That sounds serious. What is he, a serial killer?"

"Have a good day, ma'am." Gavin turned and walked over to meet Karl near the black seats. "It's not him," he said.

"What do you mean it's not him? He used one of the cards."

Gavin nodded. "The manager back there took a five-second look at the sketch and said it wasn't him. The man that used the card is Black. 'Very dark-skinned,' she said."

"Black?" Karl frowned. "I was so wrapped up in Fannin's bigotry." He shook his head. "Didn't he say the guy next door was Cubano or Puerto Rican?"

"You forgot one. He said Jamaicano, too. And then there's the endearing 'darky' comment. And originally, he called him an islander."

"But that's nonsense."

Gavin gave him a single slow nod. "And he always said the neighbor was brown-skinned. He led us astray with the name and the 'ano business."

"I should go back and bust him," muttered Karl.

"Fannin's not worth the sweat, Karl. He's a small-minded bigot lost to ignorance."

"Yeah." He pinched the bridge of his nose with his thumb and forefinger. "So what now?"

Gavin blew out his cheeks. "All of the witnesses that tied the composite to the victims... We have to believe the sketch is accurate enough to tell a pale-skinned man from a deep pigment."

"Then he's not the one producing victims." Karl's face twisted into a grim rictus. "This was a wild goose chase."

"Maybe not," said Gavin. "Remember how we got these cards. We went to the billing address of the person who called in the anonymous tip about the last victim. I just assumed it was the unsub. But what if the man who called it in is also hunting the killer?"

"Like another cop?"

Gavin shook his head. "Maybe a vigilante."

"Or, the two killer theory is right," said Karl. "And this is the guy no one sees."

"Or that." Gavin turned his head and took one last look at the Axis counter. "She's going to call 911 if he comes back."

"I'm holding my breath."

"Yeah," said Gavin in a grim tone. "Let's go."

They turned and retraced their steps out the front doors, squinting against the bright afternoon sunshine. They crossed the hot concrete and got in the Explorer.

"Lunch?" asked Karl. "I know a good place right around the block."

"Might as well," said Gavin.

Karl put the vehicle in gear and slowly dropped the wheels off the sidewalk. Gavin leaned back against the headrest and stared straight ahead as Karl navigated the traffic.

"Damn, I'm tired," said Gavin. "And *parched.*"

"Three o'clock call-outs and the sun will do that to you." Karl turned into a strip mall and found a spot.

"That and I never sleep good when I'm on a case. I dream and dream and dream, and not one of the bastards are good." Gavin yawned, then took a deep breath. "I thought we had him," he said.

"Maybe we do," said Karl.

Gavin followed his gaze to a blue Mazda with a rental car license plate that had pulled into the space behind them. The driver's door swung open, and a Black man got out. He stood facing the Explorer, his arms loose at his sides, waiting.

Gavin and Karl piled out of the Ford, pulling their pistols. "Get your hands up!" snapped the detective.

"Relax," said the man. "I'm not the one you want."

"We'll decide that," said Gavin.

"Hands! I won't tell you again."

The man sighed and rolled his eyes, but he lifted his hands up to his shoulders. "I'm not armed."

"Turn around and put your hands on the car," said Gavin as he slid a step closer.

"Listen, this is—"

"Do as he said!" snapped Karl, his voice harsh and unyielding.

The man's gaze bounced back and forth between them a few times, then he heaved an exaggerated sigh as he turned around and rested his hands on the car.

Karl looked a question at Gavin. When Gavin nodded, the detective holstered his Glock. "Don't you move." He pulled out a set of cuffs and walked across the hot pavement to the man. He frisked the Black man quickly, then reached for his right hand.

"This is unnecessary. I'm here to help you. I purposefully used a card I knew you'd be watching."

"Why?" asked Gavin.

"Your ambush didn't work," said Karl at the same moment.

"No ambush, Karl. And the why is easy," the man said. *My name is Kai Washington.*

Karl froze, then glanced at Gavin. "I heard it," said Gavin. "Cuff him. Let's take him in."

I'm betting my future that you know who I am, sent Kai. *I'm betting Miss Adeline has told you quite a story starring my mother and me. I'm betting she told you I was dead. If you take me in, Agent Gregory, I will be. Cuff me if you must but take me somewhere safe.*

29

Pull into the garage, please.

"I wish you'd stop that," said Karl. "It's creepy as shit."

"Sorry," said Kai. "Old habits die hard."

"You've got your clicker somewhere, or do you want me to crash through the doors?"

"Oops," said Kai. He blinked, and the garage door rumbled up.

"Or do that," said Karl. "Because why use something as mundane as a remote?"

Kai shrugged. "We'll be safe here. I bought this place through a blind trust, and I've never spent any time here."

"Oh, of course. A blind trust. I have one of those, too."

"Detective Santana, I'm sorry I snuck up on you, but there was really no other way. I had to make sure Adeline's Program goons weren't following you."

"That Charger?" asked Gavin.

Kai nodded. "And the Caprice. Did you ask her about them? Bet she played dumb."

"She did. She told us they were probably not following us, but if they were from the Program, they were probably there to help us."

"Yeah, like they helped you at the Miami Beach house."

"What do you mean by that?" asked Karl with an edge to his voice. "And why the fuck did you make me take pot shots at Gavin?"

"You've got it backward, Detective," said Kai. "One of Adeline's pet puppeteers ran you. I'm the one who kicked them out of your head."

"Then why did you run? Why not talk to us there?"

Kai glanced at Gavin in the rearview mirror. "The Program Special Activities team. That place, and everything in it, is blown. I can never go back there, not while Adeline is in power. Using that credit card to draw you out represented an incredible danger, but I did it because you need my help. This morning's fun should have taught you that." The garage door rumbled down as Karl brought the Explorer to a stop. "We'd better go inside before the sun fries us like eggs. I've been living up north—I'm not used to the heat."

Karl grunted and shook his head.

"In for a penny, Karl," said Gavin.

They followed Kai inside, deadbolts popping open without keys, without anyone touching them. "Ah," Kai sighed. "Air conditioning." He looked down at his handcuffed wrists. "Can we dispense with these?"

Karl looked at Gavin and twitched his shoulders. "Sure," Gavin said. "Here…" He stepped forward, pulling his cuff key out of his pocket.

Kai smiled at him, and the cuffs unlocked and hovered in midair until Karl grabbed them and put them away. "Would you like something to drink?"

"I thought you said you never come here."

"That's true, Detective Santana. I pay someone to keep the place up, to keep it stocked in case I had to bolt for cover. Like now."

"Who is killing these women?" asked Gavin. "Why didn't your grandmother want us looking for you? You said she's after you. Why?"

Kai grinned a little. "Well, I'd like a soda." He walked to the refrigerator and opened it. "Oh! Dr. Pepper. That's my favorite."

Karl sighed. "I'll have one. Unless you have orange juice?"

"Sorry, Detective. Nothing that isn't shelf-stable." He quirked an eyebrow at Gavin. "Agent Gregory?"

"Water, then. With ice.

"You've got it. Why don't you two make yourselves comfortable in the family room? I'm betting there are high-end recliners and probably a sectional that's good enough to sleep on."

Karl and Gavin exchanged a glance. Neither one moved.

"Really, Detective Santana, Agent Gregory. You're safe. Why would I save you from the puppeteer this morning, then concoct this elaborate scheme to…what? I can't even make it up."

Karl took a deep breath and huffed it out. "Might as well call me Karl. After all, you've been in my head."

"And it's Gavin."

Kai smiled and turned to the cabinets. He found the glasses on his first try and put three down on the counter. "What did sweet old Miss Adeline tell you?" he asked with a casual air about him. He glanced at Gavin over his shoulder. "Adeline isn't my grandmother, by the way. My mother was her granddaughter."

"How old *is* she?" muttered Karl.

"That's a question that's often asked and never answered. All anyone knows for certain is that she joined Majestic in 1947, and that she'd already had a few babies, though she took no part in raising them." He grinned at them. "She looks good for her age, doesn't she?"

"We've never seen her," said Gavin.

"I haven't seen her since March 15, 2000." He handed Gavin his ice water and passed Karl a soda in a glass. "Come on, gents." He walked past them and into the family room.

The family room was a twenty-by-twenty square, with sliding glass doors covered by plywood on the inside. Three big La-Z-Boy recliners sat in three of the four corners, and a wide sectional took up the other.

Kai plunked into one of the recliners and sat his Dr. Pepper on the tray-table next to it. He waved his hands at the other furniture. "Might as well sit," he said. "This conversation's going to take a while."

Suppressing a sigh, Gavin chose one of the La-Z-Boys but didn't put his feet up. With a twitch of his shoulders, Karl picked the last recliner.

"Tell us why you're not dead," said Karl.

Kai grinned and nodded. "Happy to, but first, tell me the lies Adeline told you."

Gavin took a deep breath and puffed out his cheeks. "It's a long story. Hours and hours of it. She even arranged to give us records from the Program."

"Those were fakes, I'm sure. She usually sticks to one of a few scripts, so I don't need to know the details. Give me the broad brush-strokes."

"Before we get into that, I'd like to conference my wife into this conversation."

Kai spread his hands. "Are you sure you want her drawn into this?"

"Adeline has already pulled her in."

"Is she still in Minnieville?"

Gavin gave him a sharp look. "How do you know that?"

"It blinks in your head like a neon sign, Gavin," said Kai. "Maddie. Minnieville. Maddie, again. On and on."

"She's still at our home, yes," Gavin said quietly.

"Call her then."

After dialing her number, he switched the phone to speaker. When she picked up, he said, "Hello, Maddie. I'm here with Karl…and Kai Washington." Things got very quiet on the Minnieville part of the call. "He says Adeline is after him."

"Is he…"

"Hello, Maddie," said Kai. "No, I'm not a serial killer."

"And…there's…proof to that effect?"

"Not as such," said Gavin, "but there are signs it might be true."

Kai chuckled. "I'm going to like you, Gavin."

"Is…"

"Go on," said Kai. "Ask me anything."

"Is Jamilla better?"

Kai lost his smile. "Unfortunately, not."

"Oh. Uh… I don't know how to broach this."

"Beatrice and her reprogramming?" asked Kai.

"Well, yes. We understood you were given false memories of your mother's demise."

"That's true, but Bea rolled the changes back. But let's leave that for the time being. Gavin, give me the overview of what Adeline told you. I bet she started on June 12, 1998. Right?"

Gavin shook his head. "She started by telling me about a dream she says she shared with me."

Karl arched an eyebrow, and Gavin nodded.

"It was during my last case—"

"The Smith, right?" asked Kai.

"—and it wasn't as mundane as it might have appeared in the press." Gavin told them about the recurring dream he had featuring the alley in Manhattan, about their trip to Hawaii, and how Adeline had looked in on them there.

"That's a new wrinkle," said Kai.

"My husband is a very rational thinker," said Maddie. "He needed something he couldn't talk himself out of believing."

"I see. I should tell you, Adeline lied about sharing that dream with you. It's beyond her gifts. As to the Hawaii thing, Adeline is the best bird dog the Program has ever had. She could have watched over you like she said with ease. What next?"

"We gave her a little test—where are we, stuff like that."

"Also easy for Adeline, if you don't know how to block her," said Kai. "I can teach you that, given time. For now, I'm blocking you and Karl. Did she start with my kidnapping after all that about your case?"

"No," said Gavin. "She told us a story about the assassination attempt of General Edwin Walker in 1963."

"Ah!" said Kai. "Story arc number three, then. After she told you about the Man coming to debrief them in person, she begged off? Said she needed rest or something?"

"Yeah," said Gavin. "The next day she started with Jamilla finding you missing in the Rochester airport."

"Sure," said Kai. "And how she swept in, my personal savior, risking life, limb, and position in Majestic to save me from the cruel fate the evil twins and their lover had in store for me."

"Yes," said Maddie.

"Did she at least admit that she's bird dogged a vast majority of Program inductees?"

"Not in so many words," said Gavin. "She did say she tried to remain apart from the Operations groups."

"Ha!" Kai shook his head, a bitter smile on his face. "And she probably said she took part in the Walker thing, then walked away from the team before the Big Show."

"About that," said Gavin. "I have a hard time believing that isn't fiction."

"It's presented as fact in the covert operations training courses the Program offers. Obviously, I'm too young to know, but it's accepted as a victory by everyone in Majestic."

"A victory?" asked Maddie.

"Yes. JFK wanted to bring the Program out into the public eye. He thought the knowledge contained in the Program's records should be distributed to the wider scientific community and that the practice of kidnapping children should stop."

"And they killed him for it?"

Kai hitched his shoulders. "That's what we are taught. It's a sort of double message: 'This is what we do to people who interfere with Majestic' and 'Cross us at your own risk.' But it did come at a cost. Did she tell you about the CIA taking control for a while? That was the compromise between the Man and Johnson's National Security Command."

"She did." Gavin took a sip of water. "I don't understand why she involved herself in our case. What's she getting out of it?"

"Gavin, she's probably *behind* your case. She's the deadly spider at the center of the web."

"You have proof of that? That her killers are behind the crimes?" asked Gavin.

"No proof. But I know Adeline much better than you do. At best, one of her cadre of psychic killers flipped out, and she wants you to flush him out." Kai shrugged.

"That makes even less sense to me. If the killer is one of her special puppeteers, why not send a fixer to make him sane again?"

"Well, she *does* have an operations team from the Special Activities Group running around Miami. You already know that."

"What on Earth does she need Gavin for?" asked Maddie.

"I can think of at least three possibilities. First, she wants to get me, to force me back into the Program, so she helps your husband find me in the guise of finding the killer. Then, she sends a fixer to work on me. Second, one of her special cadre of killers has lost touch with reality or gone rogue and is killing for fun as I said. I wouldn't put that past any of them." He took a drink.

"And the third?" asked Maddie.

"Has she told you about Fry?"

"As a part of the Walker thing, yes."

"Well, there's a lot more than that. Fry is sort of a golden goose for the Program. He's...*different* from the rest of us. Adeline has had significant interaction with him over the years. She wanted to turn him, to *recruit* him." Kai shrugged.

"I still don't understand why that would prompt her to mimic a serial killer—"

"Like calls to like, Maddie," said Kai. "He's drawn to chaos like a moth to the flame."

"How do you know all this?" asked Karl.

"Adeline found him for the Man in July of 1963. I read the operation reports she filed after she brought him in and got him into the research facility. The *real* ones."

"You said Fry is different. How so?" asked Gavin.

"His abilities…they're more like magic than what I can do."

"Arthur C. Clark said that any significantly advanced technology is indistinguishable from magic," said Maddie.

"Maybe so, but does that matter?"

"It will to my husband."

Gavin grinned and nodded. "Thanks, hon."

"Why did Adeline go after him again? She made it seem like he scared her.

"I'm sure he did. He scares everyone, but the Man wanted him. Adeline did anything the Man asked her to do." Kai shook his head. "He wanted to put Fry under a microscope, to test and prod and experiment on him. Adeline found him in Kentucky. In a small town called Middleton."

Chapter 17
Kentucky Fried

I

Adeline leaned forward between the two bucket seats in the front of the van. "He's behind the Methodist Church. Drinking, I think."

"Methodist Church? Where?"

She squeezed her eyes shut for a moment. "Bruen Street. 220 West Bruen Street."

"Got it," said the driver.

Al turned sideways in his seat. "Will he come quietly?"

"That, I don't know. He's…unpredictable."

"Can't you…" Al shrugged. "You know. Peek at what will happen?"

"No. That happens when it happens. I have no control over my prescience."

"That's too bad."

"Yes," she said, though she wasn't sure she agreed. "Prepare for anything."

"Is he armed?"

"He kept the rifle in April."

"Rifles aren't much good in close quarters."

"Not just the rifle."

"You mean like what he did to Gerry Cooper?"

Adeline nodded. "Or worse. We don't know his limits. We don't know anything about him—but that's why we've come, to change all that."

"Right. If we survive."

The van bounced on its springs as the driver cut the corner into the church's parking lot, rumbling through the grass. "Where?" he barked.

Adeline closed her eyes and sent her consciousness out of the van, to the place where she'd seen Fry last, against the far wall, huddled in a shadow cast by the sanctuary and the full moon above. It was empty.

"He's gone," she said back in the van. "Hold."

She circled the church, trying to look everywhere at once—a feat not impossible for her disembodied consciousness but not easy. She zoomed out into a well-maintained grassy field next to the church, but there was no cover there, nowhere to hide, and the only living things she sensed were rabbits.

She widened her search, zipping around the homes to the west of the church, when she came to the railroad tracks, she stopped and spun around. A farmer's fields stretched away to the west on the other side of the tracks, shielded by a shelter belt of trees. *Where are you, Fry?* she thought.

"Right here, sugar," said a voice in her ear—in her *physical* ear.

As she slammed her consciousness back into her body, she felt his torrid breath feathering her ear, smelled his charnel-house body odor, recoiled from his searing, sultry *presence*. She snapped her eyes open, took in the carnage in the front seats, the dripping blood, the rent flesh, the exposed organs, the slowly melting skin, and cried out, her hand going to her mouth, fear-dredged adrenaline slamming through her like a run-away freight train. She tried to jerk away, tried to put the safety of empty air between them, but his fervid flesh pressed and pressed and pressed against hers—obscene, roiling, earthy, skeevy, vulgar flesh rubbing, shoving, thrusting past her skin, past her muscles, into the depths of her. She screamed, or thought she did, and screamed again, long, wailing verses of terror, chittering choruses of dismay, of horror, of dread.

But that wasn't the worst of it.

His mind, his thoughts—his *being*—pressed past her defenses, invaded her mind like fingers thrust between lips, penetrating her thoughts, her memories, her soul. She felt him inside her, felt herself shriveling from his barbarous touch, from his blazing thoughts and fervent lusts and ardent dreams. She backed away from him, not physically—he held her tight against him—but psychogenically. She ran from him, screaming with silent terror as his maniacal laughter chased her, shrieking as the violence inherent in his core snapped at her heels, howling into the dark night, fleeing helter-skelter while he bayed harsh, cackling laughter behind her, flying away until something stopped her.

Glancing back, she saw the van rocking on its springs, back and forth, back and forth, a boat battling an angry sea, flashes of crimson light piercing the dark velvet night without rhythm, without tempo, without pattern, only random flares of unholy, ghastly vermillion, hateful superheated hellfire. She screamed again, a disembodied ghost.

Then, silence.

The side door of the van slid open without so much as a squeak. Darkness bridled the night once more—the perverse blooming red light dead and gone. Her headlong flight died as well, and she found herself turning to face the van. She didn't want to, but a certain gravity pulled at her, tugged her around.

Fry stepped out of the van, his glowing orange gaze sizzling across her disembodied form, burning her, scalding her, demanding her attention. He reached behind him—back into the van—and pulled her body out behind him, letting it flop bonelessly, her head thudding against the doorframe, her sensible shoes dragging on the gravel, her thin dress flapping in the igneous wind, his feverish breath.

He shoved her body toward her imperiously, commanding her obedience with his molten gaze. She didn't want to but couldn't help but float back toward him, couldn't help but stare into his fiery eyes, couldn't help but inhale the sweet perfume of sulfur, of brimstone.

She slid into her flesh like a well-worn robe, and her senses exploded: his rough palm on the skin of her upper arm, the heat of him making her skin burn, his gaze on her heating her from within, making her lust, making her want him, and she screamed again, shouting her defiance into the night sky.

"What in God's name is going on out here?" a husky voice demanded. "What are you doing to that colored woman? What is that inside your van? Who are you to come into my church and perform your perversity in front of the Lord thy God?"

Fry's lips twitched, both corners of his mouth moving as though worms crawled beneath his skin. His orange gaze lingered on hers for a moment, a mere heartbeat, less, then he turned his baleful gaze away, still holding her with his hand but no longer holding her with his will. He turned in a slow half-circle, muscles under his skin dancing with one another. "Hey there, old hoss," he said.

"Didn't you hear me, boy? I asked you a question, and I'll damn well have an answer!"

"Will you?" Fry cocked his head. He drew a long breath in through his nose, as if tasting the man's scent. "Will you, indeed, Wendell?"

"Do I know you?"

"*Do* you know me, Wendell?"

Her wits returning, Adeline leaned out to gaze past Fry, to see her savior. He was a heavy-set man wearing a dark suit, white shirt, thin black tie. He began to move as Fry dragged her closer, his feet twitching and tapping as though he longed to turn and run but couldn't—held by Fry's gaze, by his wicked, commanding presence.

"Who…" Wendell gulped a breath, high color blossoming on his cheeks.

"Look, Miss Adeline, an owl." Fry let loose a barrage of laughter that made her queasy, made her long for deafness.

Wendell's gaze found hers, his confused and lost, hers lost and chary. "Who is he?" Wendell murmured.

"Behold!" shouted Fry. "*I* am the Lord thy God!" His voice rolled across the empty field, seemed to circle around at the same time, harrowing dissonance, unsufferable discordance.

"Wuh… What?" murmured Wendell.

"You begin to bore me, hoss," said Fry. "You need to work on your conversational skills, ole Wendell, old spark. How do you expect to get with the ladies?" He shook Adeline by her arm, rattling her teeth. "How do you expect to get a piece?"

"Huh… Who?"

"Oh, not that tired shit again!" cried Fry. His body temperature jumped, giving off waves of heat and waves of putrid, butcher shop odors. "I've got me a woman, Wendell! Why are you bothering me? Can't you see I'm *BUSY*?" He shouted the last word, and it was as thunder rolling across the sky.

Wendell shrank away, a dark splotch appearing beneath his feet as urine splattered down his pant leg. He held up one hand to shield his face, peeking at Fry through his spread fingers. "Thu-This is hallowed guhground!" he shrieked in the voice of a thirteen-year-old girl.

Fry threw back his head and laughed, each brutal "ha" feeling like a white-hot ax striking Adeline's brain.

Wendell half-turned, looking up at the steeple of the Methodist church. "Lord, help me," he whined.

Fry's insane laughter stopped in mid-cackle, and he let go of Adeline's arm. He disappeared with a faint pop, then reappeared standing behind Wendell. The minister's eyes went wide, his gaze focused on Adeline, pleading with her for help, for protection.

But she couldn't even protect herself.

Fry's face went slack, and his jaw dropped open. He listed a little to the left. Wendell jerked and twitched like he was having a grand mal seizure, then he calmed. He stood ramrod straight and tugged his clothing into place, smoothing the wrinkles. "That's better," he said. His face wrinkled with disgust. "I hate it when they piss themselves." He shrugged and gave Adeline a sultry wink, then turned and walked toward the church.

Adeline backed slowly toward the van.

Fry's pallid flesh listed a little more to the left, an untethered boat on the morning tide.

The minister reached for the door handle, found them locked, then chuckled. With a twitch of his shoulders, the doors exploded from the wall, crumbling to ash in a burst of bright blue flames.

Adeline turned and ran for the van.

Wendell—or his body, at least—walked inside the sanctuary, disappearing into the gloom.

Fry began to drool, his sightless eyes rolling up in his head.

Adeline ripped the driver's door open, grimacing at the plop of liquified, melted flesh and the splatter of blood as the driver's remains fell to the gravel.

A *whoosh* came from inside the church as though someone had thrown gasoline on a fire, and Wendell began to scream.

Fry twitched.

Wendell ran from the church, swathed in azure flames, flesh charring, eyeballs sizzling.

Adeline threw herself into the bloody driver's seat, grasping at the ignition, finding the keys, jerking them around to start the engine.

The entire Methodist church seemed to hop into the air, and the sound of an explosion rattled through the van. Wendell stopped screaming and looked at her, his eyes gone, his lips burned away, the hair of his head nothing but stringy pieces of ash.

Adeline jerked the gear selector into reverse and hammered the accelerator pedal to the floor, tires spitting gravel at the dead or dying minister and the devil standing dumb behind him.

Wendell fell, slowly, gracelessly, onto his face, stiff as a lead casting, and Fry jerked like a man awakening from a dream. His lava-bright gaze snapped to hers, and he smiled.

She slid the van into a J-turn, tires shrieking on the asphalt of the street, body rocking on its suspension. Adeline tore her gaze away from Fry, jerked the gear selector into drive—all without lifting her right foot. The eight-cylinder engine roared, and the van leaped ahead, Adeline squinting at the darkness, feeling burnt and blinded by the memory of Fry's gaze. Behind her, the church burst into ragged blue flames, the fire growing impossibly fast, a live thing, a starving animal.

She drove to the next intersection, slid the van around the corner without touching the brakes, feeling the van lurch to the side, fearing she'd roll it over but not caring—not daring to care—wanting only an escape from Fry's burning gaze. She darted a glance back at the church as she raced away. Bright blue flames engulfed it, shrouding it in what might as well have been hellfire.

She kept her foot planted, ripping through the tiny downtown area of Middleton, ignoring the stop signs, just driving, just speeding away from Fry, just running for her life, for her sanity.

As she raced past the town limits sign, Adeline felt his breath tickle her ear. "Where we going, sugar?" he asked.

Adeline screamed, and the world fell away.

2

A forest near Rarden, OH
date unknown, midday

Adeline came around as if from a monstrous drunk, her head pounding, her stomach doing cartwheels, the taste of sour ash and dead beetles on her tongue. She rubbed away the crud sticking her eyelids together and opened her eyes, but the sunlight filtering down through the canopy of boughs above her stabbed into her brain, and she narrowed them to the merest of slits. The last thing she remembered was leaving her apartment to meet Al and the van downstairs.

"Welcome back to the world, sugar," said Fry in a hideously intimate tone. "I thought you'd sleep the day away." He chuckled—a sound not unlike grinding gears.

She sat up too quickly and putrid food and bile shot into her mouth. Groaning, she turned her head aside just in time to avoid splattering her dress with watery yellow puke.

"Get it all out, that's what I always say."

She shuddered as memories from Middleton began to surface in her mind: the liquified remains of the driver and Al, the minister berating Fry, the squelch of what remained of the driver against her butt and thighs as she flung herself into the driver's seat, Wendell's eyeless, lipless corpse with stringy ash instead of hair dancing in lapis lazuli flames, Fry jerking like a man awakened from a long sleep, her foot slamming the gas pedal to the floor, the Methodist church jumping with the force of the explosion, her hectic flight out of town in the bloody van, Fry's voice tickling her ear as she crossed the town limits. She shuddered and forced herself to get up, to stagger in a small circle, to gaze into the wilderness surrounding her. She couldn't see the van, and she couldn't see Fry.

"Where are we?" she croaked in a voice that had more in common with the croak of a raven than her normal tone.

"Why, sugar… We're *here*. On this here ridge."

"Yes, but where is here?"

Fry seemed to materialize out of thin air, standing in thick shadows at the edge of the sunlight peeking down through the canopy—thick shadows that had no business existing during the day. "Why, sugar, here is here. It's where… It's where we're *at*. Trees, shadows, sunlight. *Here*." Each word was uttered in the hopelessly confused tone of a dementia patient.

"Are we…" Adeline shook her head. "What is the closest town?"

Fry cocked his head to the side, an orange glow seeming to pulse in his eyes with each beat of his heart. "Why should we care? We ain't there, we're here."

With a sigh, Adeline gave up. "Where is the van?"

"Van?" His head flopped to the other side. "I don't…" A long slow blink accompanied a slight nod.

"Oh, yeah. The *van*." He glanced around as though he might have misplaced it nearby. "Why, I don't have any idea, Miss Addy." He twirled his hand in the air. "I'm not great with things like that."

"Things like vehicles?"

"*Details*, sugar. I'm not good with details."

She pressed her lips together. "Are you good with why you've brought me to this place?"

He squinted up toward the branches of the trees sheltering him from the sun. "I was… I mean, *we* was going somewhere—I don't know where because when I asked you, you fell asleep at the wheel. Woo, doggy, that was a neat trick, keeping the van on the road. I had to get behind the driver's seat and reach around you with—"

"And then you decided to go where?"

He pursed his lips, and one hand came up to rest his first two fingertips on his chin, long fingernails tapping his upper lip. "I was"—he cleared his throat—"*we* was headed out of that little town where y'all found me. We was going east, lickety-split, like our asses was *on fire*, sugar, and then…" He frowned down at his feet. He mumbled something she didn't catch, then looked around again like a ten-year-old lost in the woods. "Well, then we was here."

"You *drove* here?"

His shoulders twitched in a quick shrug, and he shook his head a little. "Must've, yeah? *You* certainly didn't. Oh, sugar, you was *out* like a…" His voice faded, and a frown floated on his lips.

Lifting a shaking hand to her brow, Adeline rubbed her eyes with her thumb and forefinger.

"I know what you need," said Fry.

"Oh yeah? What do I need?" She dropped her hand—it wasn't helping her head anyway.

He leered at her. "A little dog of the hair that bit you."

She felt heat rising in her cheeks, her head thudding with each pounding heartbeat. A spot just above her left collar bone began to burn, and she peeked inside her collar at the black hickey. Then a spot on her right breast, then lower on her belly. "You…" She couldn't finish the thought. She felt a certain soreness down below, an uncleanliness. "I was unconscious the whole time?"

"Yes. Slept through all the fun, you did."

"What does that mean?" she snapped. "What fun?"

"Oh"—again, Fry's hand rose to twirl in an absent minded circle—"you know. The trip. Coming here. Misplacing the *damn van.*"

She turned away, but only to the side so she could still keep an eye on him, and crossed her arms. "And *what else* did I sleep through?"

Fry looked lost again, and he shook his head sadly. "Why are you mad at me, sugar?"

"I was *unconscious* and you…you…" She jerked her head back and forth.

"Oh! You mean…" He cocked his head as though listening to something back in the woods, something only he could hear. A moment later, he nodded and said, "I wouldn't do that, Miss Addy."

"Yes, you draw the line at bursting people apart as they sit in a van, at setting a church on fire and burning the eyes out of the minister." Her hands shook with the urge to hit him, to use her nails on his eyes, to rend his flesh.

Fry chuckled. "Well, *sure*, sugar. I mean, it's what I do. What I was *made* for. Chaos. Besides, that Wendell was a hypocrite. The thoughts he had would make the devil blush."

"But you ain't!" snapped Adeline, hating the backwoods accent, hating that she'd lost control of her speech, that she sounded like the poor sharecropper's daughter that she was. She'd fought that accent long and hard, *and* she'd found a way to educate herself, to rise above her humble beginnings.

"Oh, I'm not He of the Pit. No. I kind of think he's a parable. Or is it an allegory?"

"Those two words are synonyms," she said, forcing herself to enunciate each word, speaking slowly, forcing her anger down, away. She still had a mission to accomplish. She could extract revenge later—*if* he'd raped her.

"Are they?" Fry asked, cocking his head again. "Then I must have meant something else. Fable? Myth? Whatever." He half-turned, gaze zipping toward the dark woods that ran down into the valley below.

"Does it bother you?" she asked in a quiet voice.

"What, sugar? Does what bother me?"

"Your memory. Losing the thread."

He frowned. "It *would* if that ever happened to me."

"But it does. For instance, how did we get here?"

His frown deepened into a scowl. "Not this again."

"Play along, Fry. It's an example, remember?"

"An example?" He shook his head. "What was the question?"

"How did we get here?"

He spun in a slow circle, his gaze zipping up the ridge, then down into the valley, then to the trees that surrounded them. "Must've walked. Am I right? Did we walk here, sugar?"

"You see? That's what I mean. *You don't remember.*"

"Oh, well, it's just I haven't et yet. Hungry." He patted his belly.

"I asked if losing your memory bothered you. You said it would if it was happening."

"Well, sure. Who wouldn't feel the same?"

"My friends can help you."

Again, his gaze flitted into the trees and back. "Your friends?"

Adeline nodded. "Don't worry, my friends are far away. Nevada. But I could take you there. I could get them to help you."

He tilted his head back, slightly turned away, and looked at her from the corner of his eyes. "You ain't trying to trick me, are you, sugar?"

"No tricks," said Adeline.

Fry turned to the other side, his gaze going to the bases of the trees surrounding them. "I know I put the damn thing near a tree," he muttered.

Adeline followed his gaze. "What? The rifle?"

"Rifle?" he asked, his face knotted with confusion. "What rifle? My duffel is what's lost." He bent his head, staring at the ground and walking up the ridge a bit to look, then coming back down.

"You see? My friends could help you, so you don't keep losing the important things."

Without lifting his head, Fry looked at her askance. "Did you take it?" It was almost a snarl, venomous, angry.

"No, but I can help you find it." She walked toward him at a plodding, slow pace. "We'll look together."

"Yeah," he muttered. "We'll look together." He had his head down, so Adeline missed his conniving smile.

3

State Road 73, NW of Rarden, OH
July 20, 1963, 9:53 am

Adeline walked with her head down, her feet aching, her back sore, that spot between her legs that caused her so much trouble over the course of her long life finally gone numb. Fry sauntered by her side, his gaze leaping from house to sign, from sign to ridge, from ridge to her face, from her face to the ribbon of black top. His army duffel hung from his shoulder, forgotten, the barrel of the rifle sticking up from its center. His worn-down combat boots made almost no sound on the gravel shoulder.

Her dress looked a mess, gore splattered from the waist down in the back, an unsightly yellow stain across her right breast that she must have earned by vomiting in her sleep. The thin floral print was torn in places but not in the *important* places. Still, she would have sold her soul for a change of clothes. Fry had offered to dig into his duffel bag, but she'd turned him down. The last thing she wanted was his butcher-shop odor wafting up her nose with every breath.

She sighed and slowed her pace a little, seeking relief for the blister developing on her right heel. With their two-inch square heels, her suede Naturalizer pumps might have been fashionable, but they weren't cut out for long walks. "I don't see why we can't," she said, reviving a discussion from an hour prior.

"Can't what?" murmured Fry, not interrupting his dancing gaze to look her in the eye.

"Hitch. You can't expect to walk from Ohio to Nevada?"

"Why?" he asked, sounding genuinely confused.

"*Because*," said Adeline, "it will take months."

Fry shrugged, and his duffel bag did a little dance. "Time is…" His gaze zipped from a ridge to their right to the ridge on the left, then he stopped walking and spun around to peer behind them.

"What's the matter?" Adeline said with a sigh.

"Someone's coming."

"*Yes.* People are going to drive by us, Fry. This is a state road." She tried, and failed, to keep the exasperation from her voice.

"That's not it."

"That's not what?"

"My name."

"Oh? Tell me, then. What is it?"

"Flagg?" He cocked his head, mouthing the word again. "No, that's…" He shook his head. "That's that other one."

"Other one?"

"Never you mind, sugar. Some things is beyond your ken. And they should be."

"Then what is your name?"

"Frire?" He cocked his head to the other side, the person driving on 73 somewhere behind them forgotten for the moment. "Freir?" He scowled at her as though she'd made him forget his name.

"Those words just mean 'fry' in French and Spanish."

"Forfer? Is that it, sugar?"

"I don't know. I've only ever called you Fry because of the name tag sewn into your fatigues."

Fry tucked his chin and peered down at his chest, lifting the shirt away from his body. "That don't seem right, sugar." He shook his head. "Fufu?"

Adeline grinned. "Are you a little bunny, then?"

He scowled at her. "You making fun, sug?"

"No. It's a nursery sing-along. 'Little Bunny Foo Foo' it's called."

"Sang it." His voice was deep and resonant—a growl a grizzly could be proud of.

"It's just a—"

"*SANG IT, I SAID!*" His shout echoed between the two ridges and went on echoing far longer than it should have.

She looked at him askance, then heaved a sigh. "Little Bunny Foo Foo," she sang, "hoppin' through the forest, scoopin' up the field mice and boppin' 'em on the head."

"That's a silly song, sug, but you've got a pretty voice. You ever think about Nashville?"

"We were talking about your real name."

His brow wrinkled. "Oh. I know we was. Four-four?"

"Think on it. It'll come to you. Meantime, let's try to hitch a ride when they get here."

"Who? When who gets here?"

She drew in a deep breath and puffed out her cheeks. "You said someone was coming."

"Yes," he growled, his gaze going back to where the road curved away toward the south.

"Shall we walk until they catch up?"

Without another word, Fry spun on his heel and started walking away, his long-legged stride making her hustle.

4

U.S. Route 59, north of Cloud Creek, OK
July 27, 1963, 11:08 am

The back of the farm truck smelled of hay and manure, but the hay they sat on kept them clean enough. Fry's gaze kept drifting to the west, drawn there as if the land held memories for him.

"What is it?" she asked, shouting over the blatting engine and the wind of their passage.

"There are...people there."

"Yes," she said with a hint of a smile. "I'd say there are people in every direction from any point of this sprawling nation."

"No. *People*. A Nation. They..." He shook his head, then turned his gaze back toward the west. "They think my skin is as hard as stone. *Nun'Yunu'Wi*, they call me. Dressed in stone. That's what it means."

"Indians?" she wondered. "This part of Oklahoma is full of Cherokee, I think."

He nodded once. "Yes."

"Should we stop?" she asked. "Go and visit them?"

Fry shook his head. "No, they wouldn't know me by sight n'more. There'd be explaining, bawling, begging. That kind of shit."

"Good memories there?"

A faint smile surfaced. "I ate well."

The look in his eye made Adeline shiver, and she looked away.

5

Las Vegas, NV
July 31, 1963, 11:08 pm

Adeline smiled at the orgasm of lights bleeding into the lobby from the Strip outside. Fry stood at the reception counter, his duffel bag at his feet. His clothes were travel-worn, stained, and spread the odor of death and fire and blood wherever he went. Two clerks stood on the other side of the counter, pointedly ignoring him but sparing her plenty of sour looks and icy glares.

Fry cleared his throat for the third time, then rapped his fingers on the countertop. One of the clerks finally glanced his way. "Sir, the worst room in this hotel costs twenty-seven dollars. I'm sure a hotel off the Strip would better suit your needs." He cut his eyes toward Adeline.

Fry bent, opened the drawstring on his duffel and rooted around inside for a moment. When he straightened, he held a worn envelope in his hand. He glared at the clerk long enough to make the man blanch and take an involuntary step back. Then he pushed two dirty fingers into the envelope and pulled out a letter that he'd folded and unfolded millions of times by the look of it. Fry unfolded it once more and lay it on the countertop and tapped it with his index finger. "Fat Sammy says different."

The clerk scanned the letter, then paled even further and glanced at the other clerk. "That could be fake."

Fry's cold grin widened, and his gaze sharpened, a feral wolf eyeing his supper. "We could call him if you think so."

The clerk swallowed hard, and again shot a glance at the other clerk.

Fry's hand came up, then slammed down on the stone counter with a sound like a rifle shot. His grin had departed, and a ferocious snarl had taken its place. He leaned across the table and hooked his finger in the man's shirt, pulling him close. With his other hand, he pointed at the other clerk. "Is he the one I should be talking to?" His voice was an evil hiss—the sound a cobra makes prior to driving its fangs into pristine flesh. "Because if he is, *you are of no use to me.*" He tapped the letter again. "Don't believe the letter? Fine. Call the boss."

"My supervisor is—"

"*I didn't ask for your supervisor*! Call the boss, I said, and I mean, *the boss. Capiche*?"

"Yes, sir. I apologize. I'm happy to help you. Our best suite is open. Would that suit?"

Fry unwound his finger from the man's shirt, leaving a dirty smudge. "That would be fine," he said, his smile reappearing as if by magic, though the gleam in his eye still evoked snapping fangs and howling at the moon.

"Right away, sir." The clerk cut his eyes toward Adeline again. "But your negro friend—"

Fry growled and narrowed his eyes.

"I'm sorry, it's hotel policy," croaked the clerk, raising his hands.

Again, Fry wound his finger into the man's shirt, pulling him closer. He strode down the counter toward the closest phone, pulling the clerk along. He reached across the counter and grabbed the receiver. "*Dial*," he snarled, putting the receiver to his ear.

"I'm… That is…" The clerk's eyes had opened wide, pupils dilated.

Fry leaned across the counter, putting his face an inch from the clerk's, and snapped his teeth—a promise of pain and terror and eternal darkness. "*Dial*," he hissed.

The clerk swallowed hard and spun the rotor seven times. His eyelids fluttered like the wings of a moth, and he huffed air like an idling steam engine. Fry shoved him away.

He stood there leaning one arm on the counter and tapped his foot. "Yeah. Who's this?" he asked into the phone. "Oh, hello, Vincenzo. It's Frank. Yeah, Franky Evil Eye, that's right. I didn't know you were out here." He listened a moment. "Oh, yes, I'm here in Vegas. I'm at your hotel." He turned his gaze on the clerk and stared. "Yeah. This little *stronzo* is giving me a hard time." He cocked his head and grinned at Adeline. "Yes, even *after* I showed him Fat Sammy's letter. He thinks it might be fake. Said so, right out loud. Can you believe it?" He chuckled and nodded. "Just a second." Fry held the phone out to the clerk.

The man shuffled forward and took the phone with a hand that shook badly. "Yes, sir?" he said.

Adeline fancied she could hear the *capo* screaming, even from where she stood. For his part, the clerk blanched more and more until she worried he might pass out, repeating "yessir" every twenty seconds. Finally, he said, "But, sir, he has a nigger with him." He jerked the phone away from his ear as Vincenzo started screaming in earnest—and this time, there was no doubt Adeline could hear the man.

"*I don't care, you little toad! Didn't you read the goddamn letter? Don't you know who Fat Sammy is? I'm not gonna get whacked because you are a fucking asshole! I know Fat Sammy explained who the man is in that damn letter—the man you've kept standing around in the fucking lobby. Here, let me make it simple, give our friend anything—ANYTHING—he wants. You pretend he's Fat Sammy himself, capiche? Now put that evil bastard back on the line before he takes it into his head to start killing people!*"

Fry fixed the clerk with a blood-freezing smile as the man held the receiver out. He took it and held it to his ear. The clerk made himself busy getting the keys to the suite and calling over a bellhop. "Yeah, he seems to have gotten the message," Fry said into the phone. "Thanks, Vin." He listened a moment, his cold dead eyes pinning the clerk where he stood. "I'm not sure it's necessary. How about this: he gives me lip one more time, I'll take him out back to the alley." He nodded and winked at the clerk. "Just tell me if I have to keep him breathing. No? Perfect." He flicked a finger toward Adeline, and the clerk beckoned her. "I'd love that, Vinny, but I'm only going to be here the one night. People to see up north. Right, next time, then." Fry hung up.

As Adeline reached the counter, Fry hooked his thumb at her. "Apologize," he hissed at the clerk.

The clerk swallowed hard. "Very sorry, miss," he croaked, then cut his eyes to Fry. "Okay?"

Fry folded the letter and put it back in the envelope. He wrinkled his face into a grimace. "Tell you what. If I don't come down here in an hour and beat you to fucking death, you'll know it was okay."

The clerk swallowed again. "Miss, please accept my *sincere* apologies. Nothing personal, I swear. I'm not a bigot. My wife even has negro friends who do her sewing. If there's anything I can do to make—"

"It's fine," said Adeline, in her best Ivy-league voice. "But do you know what I could use? New clothes. These have suffered on our journey." She looped her hand around Fry's elbow, and he fixed a gaze as cold as death on the clerk.

"I'll have them here for you in minutes." The clerk paled and glanced at his watch. "I'll have my wife bring you some of hers. You're of a size, and I think they'll do. Would"—he threw a fear-filled glance at Fry—"that do?"

"And, you'll have new things here before we check out." Fry narrowed his eyes. "Expensive, of course. Which you will pay for yourself, old hoss."

"Yessir! Of course!"

Fry snatched the key from the man's grasp and pointed at the bellhop. "Take us to our room, spark."

6

Project Firestarter, Nellis AFB, NV
January 9, 1964, 9:08 pm

Dr. Robert Grayson stood grimacing behind the mirrored glass, watching Fry meditate. He sat with his legs bent in the lotus position, the backs of his hands resting on his knees, the last three fingers of each hand extended, his index finger curled up to touch his thumb. Grayson had nothing against meditation or yoga—it was the levitation that bothered him. Fry's butt hung in mid-air, eighteen inches above his mattress.

That, and the fact that even though he stood behind mirrored glass, Fry's glowing orange eyes seemed to bore into Grayson's own.

"How long this time, Scott?" he asked the young man standing next to him.

Scott Mitchell glanced at the stopwatch he held. "Just coming up on six hours, Dr. Grayson."

Grayson grunted. "And he hasn't spoken? Made no demands?"

"No, nothing like last time."

"No run-ins with anyone on evening shift?"

"No, sir," said Mitchell. "At eleven, he just tucked his legs, arranged his arms, and started floating."

Robert Grayson frowned at Fry. He'd seen him meditate before—numerous times, in fact—though usually after a burst of bad temper and the pyrotechnics that accompanied it. The man—if he was, in fact, a man—had shown no compunction against killing a staff member or another research subject when his hair-trigger temper demanded it. Sometimes with a mere glance, sometimes bloody and insane, other times in a burst of blue flames. Grayson had been present for his last fiery murder—that of a security agent who'd had the misfortune of confusing Fry's angry retort with Fry's off-beat humor. His laughter had turned to screams as the azure flames had engulfed him.

At least it had only lasted a few minutes.

Fry had never shown an ounce of remorse, nor had he ever shown an ounce of restraint.

Grayson glanced at his young research assistant. "Stay away from him, Scott. Let him cool off."

"I..." Scott shrugged. "I'm not sure he's even angry, Dr. Grayson."

"Are you sure he's not?"

Scott glanced at Fry, and the freak-show turned his head as though to return his gaze. "No."

"Then do as I say. He has no compunction against crippling or even killing you, Scott—none at all—nor does he care if the real target of his wrath is off-shift. If you're too close when he needs to vent..."

"Is it true that he's a mafia hitman?"

Grayson sighed. "Well, he admits to killing 'a bunch' of civilians for money. By his own admission, he killed most of them because they angered him, some he killed for money, and some just because he was bored." He rested a hand on Scott's shoulder. "I understand the draw of novelty, Scott. Fry is fascinating—an ability matrix that includes all the things he can do is amazing. But his abilities do not originate in the psionic centers of his mind. His manipulation of objects and human beings is not telekinetic nor is it telecheiristiric in nature. His uncanny mind-reading tricks don't use an erg of psionic power. His use of these powers often seems unconscious in nature—the way we might swat a mosquito."

"And the fire? The blue fire?"

"Despite the name of the project, Fry is our only subject who can create fire from nothing. I don't even have a guess as to how he's doing it." He waved his hand at the mirrored glass. "It's in the same category as his levitation and teleportation."

"I wish I'd been here to see that."

"No. No, you don't, son." Grayson frowned at Fry and imagined he saw the man wink at him. "The only time we've seen him teleport was the night he killed thirteen random people because he ran out of cigarettes and it took us too long to run to the post exchange."

"Oh. That's…"

"Yeah," said Grayson with a sigh. "He's all of that and more. If forced to guess his kind and origin, I'd tell you he was a demon straight out of the depths of Hell."

In Fry's cell, blue flames sparked to life, running up and down his arms without consuming the fatigue jacket the man insisted on wearing. Grayson shuddered and turned away.

"Come on, Scott. Let's give the man some privacy."

"But the data—"

"*Fuck* the data, son. It's no good if we're both dead." He turned toward the observation room's only door, and as he did, Fry's body crashed down onto the mattress, his muscles slackening, his orange eyes flashing as they rolled up in his head.

Grayson began to shake a little and froze in mid-step. His mouth drooped open, and his voice warbled wordlessly up through the registers. Scott glanced at Fry's cell, then turned back to find Grayson bending toward him so that their noses almost touched. "Hello, Scott," said Grayson.

"Dr. Grayson?"

"Fuck no, old hoss. You can call me Fry. We're going to have us some fun, boy."

Chapter 18
D j Vu
All Over Again

I

Kai paused and took a long draught of Dr. Pepper. "The Firestarter security logs recorded the research assistant screaming shortly after that. It was the last entry. Ever. He killed them all that night—researchers, support staff, other research subjects—no one survived inside the facility. We know what happened only because of the automatic surveillance devices."

Gavin frowned at him. "You make him sound like a wizard."

"An evil wizard," murmured Maddie.

"Well, he could be," said Kai. "That's as good an explanation as Grayson's demon from the depths of Hell, theory."

"I don't believe in magic or wizards," said Gavin. "Neither do I believe in demons and Hell."

Kai shrugged. "It's been my experience that Fry doesn't give a shit what you believe he is. Or where he came from, for that matter."

"You've met him?" asked Maddie.

"Oh, yes. He was a frequent guest while I was imprisoned there." He grimaced and turned his gaze down to his lap. "He was a sort of father figure to Javi, Dylan, and Rayson. I suppose Adeline left out his involvement at the Compound."

With a grim expression on his face, Gavin nodded.

"Of course," said Kai. "Tell me what Adeline told you, so I know what to fill in."

Gavin told him an abbreviated version of the story.

When he'd finished, Kai chuckled and shook his head. "She has a thing for Bethany and Beatrice—and to some extent for Chavez. They had the gall to stand up to her, to speak out against her crazy ideas about our 'educational needs.'" He sipped his soda. "Basically, everything she accused the twins of doing, Adeline did herself—and more. She ordered Beatrice to reprogram my mother and me. She ordered the memory alterations, thinking that a feeling of isolation would help her mold me into what she wanted."

"What did she want?" asked Maddie in hushed tones.

"She wanted to turn me into Fry, or as close as the Program could get. I was to be the ultimate assassin. Fry, but loyal to Adeline—and note that I didn't say the Program—but less of a cuckoo. Everything was about her. When I performed well, she basked in the glory as if she'd contributed somehow. When I didn't, she threw Beatrice under the bus." He shook his head. "She was willing to sacrifice my happiness, my sanity, for that goal."

"She said Javier Dela Cruz murdered you—"

Kai leaned back in his La-Z-Boy. "Of course, she did."

"—in order to escape, that he killed the other two boys and Jamilla," said Maddie in a world-weary voice. "But how could she…"

"Adeline d'Clara isn't like *your* great-grandmother, Maddie," said Kai. "She doesn't care about her children—never did. She birthed them, then abandoned them, left them to other families or to grow up on their own. She cares about one thing and one thing only: Adeline d'Clara."

"But—"

"She used what happened at the Compound to oust Beatrice and Sam McIntyre. She set it up to make them look incompetent, then she swooped in and took over as director."

"*She's* Majestic's director?"

"Oh, let me guess…she neglected to mention that?" Kai laughed. "Yes, Adeline d'Clara is the Woman these days."

"She's said all along that she can't use her abilities to find the person responsible for the murders down here."

"Remember those three possibilities I mentioned before?" asked Kai. "I learned how to hide from her bird dogging. She *can't* just reach out with her mind and find me. If it's the second option, she turned Javi, Rayson, and Dylan into her personal…" He rolled his hand in the air.

"Her personal guard," said Maddie.

"Exactly. They do whatever sweet Miss Addy asks, no matter how bloody the task. As a reward for their loyalty, they live like kings. But if one of them is out of control... Well, she *does* have enemies both inside and outside of the Program. They would use this to dethrone her. And if it's the third option, well, she can only find Fry when he allows her to, as well."

"I don't understand the point of all this," said Karl. "I don't get why she needs to have women dropping dead in order to find Fry. I don't understand why she cares about the investigation at all if she's behind it. Why waste her time telling us all those stories? Giving us those records? What's she getting out of this?"

"Maybe she hopes I'll reach out to you to try to set things straight—"

"Looks like she was right on that score," said Gavin.

"—and then she can sweep me up. If it's one of her guardsmen who's lost touch, if she controls the narrative, she thinks can manipulate you into acting in her best interest. And if she wants to set a trap for Fry...well, for any good trap, you need good bait. That's where you come in, Gavin."

"Me? Why would Fry give two shits about me?"

"I don't know, but you can bet Adeline does." Kai raised his glass for another sip. "It sounds like she's playing dumb about Fry altogether, and she knows far more than she let on to you. The fact that she found you in Hawaii is what makes me give that option the highest probability. Her explanation that she dreamed your dream and then decided to follow you..."

"Doesn't gel?" asked Gavin.

"Like I said before, it's beyond her. Maybe if she was a snoop, but she has no telepathic abilities. She sent a snoop to sift your memories for something she could use after she found out about you. I bet she wasn't watching *you* in Hawaii at all."

"Glacadairanam," said Maddie in a voice barely loud enough to hear.

"I don't see how that—"

"Remember? Adeline said she might be able to help you with him later. She said his name was Gaelic or something. And you said he was in your recent dreams with Fry—"

Kai sat up straight and stared at Gavin. "You're dreaming about Fry?"

Gavin shrugged. "Maybe. Or maybe my brain is just putting your great-grandmother's stories and my own experiences into a Cuisinart and delivering them rehashed to my subconscious mind."

"What is this Glacadairanam?"

"Some kind of…" Gavin shrugged. "I have no idea what Glacadairanam is. He said he's a 'wrath child,' that his mother possessed a church girl and seduced a priest."

"And you met this person where?"

"He's not a person at all. More of a ghost-gargoyle type of thing," said Gavin, avoiding Karl's shocked gaze. "He 'rides' people, wears them like a coat. Possesses them. Makes them into violent, brutal serial killers in order to ruin them while he gets his jollies killing. Oh, and we believe he eats their memories."

A half-grin twisted Kai's lips. "You mean to tell me you have direct experience with a thing like that, and you still refuse to believe in Fry? At least Fry is flesh and blood."

Gavin shrugged, trying to keep himself from blushing. "He kidnapped Maddie in an effort to force me to kill for him."

"I thought you said he possesses people."

"He does," said Gavin. "He got bored with it. He said there was no challenge in it anymore. He wanted to force me to kill without possessing me. To make it fun again—make me pick between abandoning my principles and Maddie's life."

"I think I see. It's like when Fry possesses someone. If they survive, they lose their memories of what he made them do. Fry never mentioned eating their memories, though. He never seemed to care about the person he possessed one way or another."

Gavin swallowed hard. "The known victims of Glacadairanam all have long-term memory impairments, but if he grabbed someone for a short period of time, they just ended up with a hole in their memory for the time he was in control."

"I'll bet you Adeline knows more than she let on," said Maddie with an edge to her voice. "The way she dangled helping you fight Glacadairanam sometime in the future. That's *her* carrot and refusing to help is the stick." She snapped her fingers. "*That's* why she acted like she did when you told us about the dreams, Gav."

"I don't—"

"You told her about Fry acting like a mafioso, saying *capiche*, and she gasped. And she did it again when you told us Fry said 'Where we going, sugar?' right in your ear. She knew your dreams were real, were dangerous, but she played it off, said it was just déjà vu."

"I remember that. You called her on it, and she got a little pissy with you."

"That's right. And I asked her point-blank if you were in danger. She said that maybe they were just dreams, but the Glacadairanam dreams in Manhattan were more than that. She knew better."

"Yes," said Gavin.

"That's why she played it off!" said Maddie. "Don't you see? Glacadairanam and Fry are connected somehow."

"That sounds like the Adeline d'Clara I know. Duplicity is not just in her nature; it *is* her nature."

Gavin paled and took a deep breath. "I dreamed again last night. Three more to add to the three I told you and Adeline about," he said in an unsteady voice. "The last one was the latest murder. The fourth and fifth dreams were like the first few—mishmashes of the recurring dream, of things that happened on The Smith case, Fry and Glacadairanam, that damn phrase that spooked Adeline so much—the thing he said in her ear before she passed out in Kentucky—"

"Where we going, sugar?" whispered Maddie.

"—but in the middle of the fifth dream...I noticed the bathroom light wasn't on and ended up in a conversation with Fry. He says I should call him Fry or Furfur or the Nightmare Man. I ask him what he wants from me, and he says nothing. Then he says, 'But my son is another matter.' I ask who his son is, and there's a chirp out on the balcony, like in my Manhattan dreams. Fry holds me in the room, and Glacadairanam puts his hand on my shoulder and says the phrase in my ear."

"Fry's son..." whispered Maddie. "Glacadairanam is Fry's son?"

"That's how I interpret it."

"But it was just a dream," said Karl. "And you said this Glaca-whatsit said his *mother* possessed a church girl and seduced a priest. Fry doesn't sound like any priest I've ever known."

"I hope you're right," said Gavin, "because if you're wrong, I'm fucked."

"Maybe not," said Kai.

"Well, if Fry—"

"Think of it this way: if this Glacadairanam holds you in a special place in his heart, why hasn't he come after you already? Why hasn't he taken you?"

"Adeline said he was busy with other things, other people."

Kai nodded. "But that doesn't really make sense, does it? Leave the one person who beat me—who figured out my weakness and turned it against me—

alone to recover his strength, to plan, to gather allies and weapons. That makes no strategic sense."

"Exactly," said Karl. "Adeline has been lying to us the whole time. Kai's already told us that. Why believe that one thing?"

Gavin shook his head. "I'm not sure I can categorize my confrontation with Glacadairanam as 'beating him.' It was more like a draw. I couldn't hurt him, I just used antipsychotics to stymie him."

"But don't you see, Gavin? A draw is the same as a win in this circumstance."

"And," said Karl, "you need to rethink that draw business. Your wife is safe and sound, you aren't a serial killer, the detective from Saint Mary is free of him, and the little beastie's laying low somewhere, licking his wounds… I'd call that a serious win."

"But he's still out there," said Gavin. "He's still free, he's still alive or whatever the hell he is. He can come back at me at any time, but the reverse isn't true at all. When we fight again, it will be in the time and place of *his* choosing. And he'll be ready for the trick I used to block him."

"And if all that's true, why hasn't he come? Why didn't he take the two of us in Maui? Adeline said he was there," said Maddie.

"I can't answer that," said Gavin. "But if Kai's premise is right, and I'm the bait Adeline is dangling to draw Fry to Miami, it may not matter. The bait usually ends up…" He didn't finish the thought. He didn't need to.

"Then you need to get that case wrapped up, Gavin," said Maddie in a voice that shook. "You need to catch Javier Whatsit and get out of there."

"I don't have powers like Kai's," he said. "And if there are two or three of them—"

"You may not have puppeteering powers, but that means you've had to develop *other talents*," said Kai. "As have I, living my life outside the Program, on the run all the time. "Javier, Rayson, and Dylan haven't. If you take away their psionic power, capturing them becomes trivial."

Gavin scoffed. "How the hell are we supposed to take away their powers?"

"Will Debbie's magic pills help?" asked Maddie.

"What are those?" asked Kai.

"Zoraperidol. It's an antipsychotic," said Gavin. "It kept Glacadairanam out of our heads."

"Antipsychotics? No," said Kai. "At least not against the Three Amigos. Maybe against Fry since it worked against 'his son.'" He made one-handed finger quotes as he said the last.

"Then how do we take away their powers?" asked Karl.

"That's where I come in," said Kai. "After all, I've already beaten the three of them *and* outsmarted Adeline d'Clara. I've developed in ways they can't imagine. You see, the Program is a method of controlling psionics, but it also shields them from the world. It wraps them in a cozy blanket, and it takes away the challenges that help most of us to mature, to grow. It has to, in order to keep the participants dependent on the Program."

"How did you beat them?" asked Maddie.

"They asked me to forgive Javi for all the nonsense he put me through. At first, I didn't want to, but Chavez made it seem like such a…grown-up thing to do. I—"

Gavin's phone rang, and he glanced at the caller ID. "That's Adeline's number."

Kai fell silent, his face grim.

"Do we—"

"*No*," said Maddie. "Block her."

"I don't want to do that—not yet," said Gavin. "We might be able to use her later." He swept his thumb across the screen, sending the call to voice mail. He turned to Kai. "But her call is a reminder. We don't have a lot of time. Tell us how you beat them."

Kai nodded. "It started in the beginning of 2000. Chavez convinced me to mentor Javier Dela Cruz, and for a while, that went well. He seemed over his distrust, his hatred of everyone and everything. But then they started holding him back. At the time, it made no sense, but I later learned it was all part of Adeline's plan to turn me into a lone wolf—and to test my obedience. By mid-March, the mentor thing was coming apart at the seams."

Chapter 19
The Ides of March

I

The Compound, under the Sonoran Desert, AZ
March 15, 2000, 07:17 pm MST

Kai grabbed a dinner tray, then turned to the dining room, looking for Javi. He found him toward the back corner, sitting alone, as usual. Kai put down his tray and slid in next to him. "Hey, Javi."

"Hep, hep, Kai. Did you just come from talking to Chavez?"

Kai nodded his head and forked a bite of whatever it was in the meat section of his tray. It tasted like paste, and he grimaced a little. "What is this crap?"

"Who cares. Protein is protein," Javi said in a rush. "Well? What did the man say?"

Kai dropped his gaze to his tray, his stomach churning. "I'm not going to be testing for charcoal this week. He said I wasn't ready."

"Yeah, that's *bullshit*, though. You are stronger than some charcoals already."

"He also said they are holding off on advancing anyone to green. He said there aren't enough beds in green right now."

Javi's lips went white, and his eyes blazed. "But I'm ready!"

"Chavez said there are too many greens. He said we have to be patient, to pay our dues." Kai stole a quick glance at Javi and frowned at the rage simmering in the other boy's eyes. "He said when they open it up again, you'll be among the first to test for it."

Javi shoved his tray away with shaking hands. "Why?" he demanded.

"I told you what Chavez told me."

"Yeah? What did *you* tell *him*?"

"Javi…" Kai shook his head. "Man, you know me better than that!"

"I *thought* I did, anyway. Then again, I used to think you were a little fucking snitch, didn't I. One of those thoughts has to be wrong."

"Look, this is just a minor setback. No, it's not even that—it's just some bullshit about beds. Don't take it personally, Javi. It's probably a test to see what you'll do." Kai pistoned his shoulders up and down. "Just like saying I'm not ready for charcoal. Let them play their games, man. Don't let them see it's upset you. Just put your head down and work. *Make* them advance you." He glanced at Javi's profile. "That's what I plan on doing."

"*You* didn't get re-blued. *You* aren't way behind a bunch of punks that came in after you. You *are* one of those punks."

Kai grimaced and put his spork down next to his tray. "Javi," he said firmly, "I'm on your side."

"Yeah?" snapped Javi, shoving his tray farther away.

"Yeah. Don't mess this up. Don't give them an excuse to justify keeping you back. Do so good that they look like idiots."

Javi turned a furious glare toward Kai, then stood and almost ran out of the room.

2

The Compound, under the Sonoran Desert, AZ
March 15, 2000, 7:44 pm MST

Fear and fury burbled in Javier's mind. He stalked the halls, fists clenched, chin stuck out belligerently. Questions plagued him: *Have the instructors seen through my little act? Did they sic a better snoop on me?* He didn't think so, or they'd have done more than hold him back on some bullshit like bed counts.

No, he told himself. *If they had any inkling of Miss Addy's plans, they would've locked me down—at the very least. Probably, they'd have sent a better fixer to rewire my brain.*

A gaggle of kids—*younger* kids—dressed in green came around the corner, and Javi glowered at them, his gaze scanning their faces, looking for Kai and not finding him. He stopped and stared at them, and one by one, the students dropped their gazes from his and shut their mouths.

They know! a malignant voice inside him screamed. He narrowed his eyes to mere slits and pinned them with his gaze, one by one. With every new face, his certainty grew. *They know, all right, and they find it funny.* That's *why their laughter died when they saw me!* He marshaled his expression, hiding away his murderous rage. He made his face smile, made his eyes dance with mirth. "Hi," he said.

Only one of the green-suiters answered—a kid he'd seen hanging out with Kai more than once.

Kai must've told him. Kai must've told everyone!

Javi turned at the next intersection, then flattened himself against the wall. He slid back to the corner and peeked around it. The group of kids exchanged glances, then giggled and went on their way.

He betrayed me, Javi thought. *Kai betrayed me twice: once when he convinced Chavez to hold me back, and once when he blabbed about it to everyone. He* hasn't *forgiven me. No, he hasn't forgiven me for anything.*

He hissed through gritted teeth, stoking his anger, feeding on his rage. He turned and walked toward the blue dormitories.

3

The Compound, under the Sonoran Desert, AZ
March 15, 2000, 8:16 pm MST

Every time the study hall door creaked open, Kai looked up, hoping to see Javi. Every time, he was disappointed. Every time he was disappointed, he grew a little sadder.

I failed him, he thought. He knew it was bullshit, but he couldn't control the thought. It circled through his mind, robbing him of his concentration, and every time he returned his attention to the formal logic book Chavez had told him to read, he grew more confused by the strange symbols, the weird arguments. *Why do we have to prove odd numbers aren't even? This is fucking stupid.*

His frustration mounted. His anxiety doubled and doubled again. He didn't want Javi to blow it. He didn't even want to think about what might happen if he did—he'd already been re-blued once. Kai had heard the rumors—every student had—that sometimes students fucked up so bad they were expelled.

The door creaked open again, and again, Kai looked up. Again, it was another kid in a green jumpsuit. Again, Kai thought, *I failed him.*

4

Dylan looked at him, not bothering to hide his mistrust. "Yeah, you *say* that, Javi, but you've said a lot of things."

Javi kept his irritation off his face. "Yeah, I get why you would feel that way, Dylan, but think it through. I had to treat you like shit. *Had to.* I had to convince myself I didn't like you so the snoops wouldn't catch me out. The dark lord said it was the only way."

"Right," said Dylan, folding his arms across his chest. "*Fry* told you to treat us like shit."

"Hey," said Rayson. "It's Javi, man."

Dylan shot him a look that said he was the stupidest boy alive. "And why should we believe you? Why won't you 'have to convince yourself you don't like us' again after you get what you want?"

"Listen, Dylan, this isn't my plan. This is *Miss Addy's* plan, but it's a fucking good one. The dark lord said as much. Said it was *righteous*. Miss Addy says if I help her, she'll put me where I belong—in the Special Activities program—and that means a bump to charcoal, at least. And that means no more of this petty shit." He waved his hands in big circles to take in the dorms. "I always planned on taking you guys with me. I always planned on getting revenge on that little try-hard. Miss Addy said we can do whatever we want to him." He held out his hand, palm up. "Come on, Dylan. You *know* me."

"I thought I did."

"You *did*, *chamaco*. You *do*." He held Dylan's gaze for a few moments, trying to look forthright, then turned to Rayson. "You believe me, right, Rayson?"

"A hundred percent. You did it to get in with them, to find out what we need to know to get ahead in this fucking place. And you found out we needed Miss Addy."

Javi nodded once, then returned his gaze to Dylan. "Hey, I understand how you feel, *cuate*. I wanted to tell you so many times, to signal you somehow, but the damn observers were all over me. They even had a snoop picking away up here"—he tapped his temple—"at all hours, trying to catch me out, to find a reason to drop me out. You can see that, right, *güey*?"

Dylan nodded, slow and purposeful. "I guess so."

"Of course, you can. And you can see why I acted like that."

Dylan shrugged but uncrossed his arms.

"Okay, then," said Javi. "I came back tonight because it's time to *do* something. The others either know all about Miss Addy's plan, in which case, we won't get near that little faggot, but I don't think so. I think I've fooled them—at least up to now. But this"—he put one arm around Dylan's shoulders and the other around Rayson's—"they won't miss. We have to move tonight, right *now*, or they'll go back to all the snooping and constant watching. I can't do it again. Fry said it wouldn't work twice, so I had better not fuck it up." He shrugged. "Then again, if they do know, maybe I'll be lucky, and they'll just boot me from the program, and I'll go live wherever the dark lord does when he's not here." He gave both boys a squeeze. "So, what's it going to be?"

"You know I'm down," said Rayson. "Whatever you want."

"And Miss Addy is on our side? She's behind this?"

Javi nodded. "But you'll have to trust me. Can you do that, Dylan? Fry wants you to."

After looking him in the eye for a few moments, Dylan nodded.

"*Chingon!*" said Javi, thumping him on the shoulder.

5

The Compound, under the Sonoran Desert, AZ
March 15, 2000, 9:15 pm MST

Adeline paused outside the door to the ward where they kept long-term medical cases. Anger simmered somewhere deep inside her—anger at Beatrice for screwing up her reprogramming, anger at Jamilla for being so weak. Useless anger. Barren anger.

She glanced at her watch again, anxiety bubbling within her. The plan *had* to work, or she might lose her mind. *Fry, where are you?*

She stilled her mind and pushed that anger down, down, down, bottling it up with all the other frustrations and angers from her long life. She plastered a smile on her face—the last expression she felt like wearing on her visits to Jamilla. Two months of pointless, boring visits, of reading to the girl, of talking nonsense and pleasantries to her, had passed with no change in her mental state. Oh, sometimes she'd answer with the word "left" or the phrase "down in the middle," but never with anything on topic or relevant.

With a sigh, she turned the knob and stepped inside.

One way or another, this is the last time I'll have to waste my time visiting Jamilla. That thought raised a smile.

6

The Compound, under the Sonoran Desert, AZ
March 15, 2000, 9:33 pm MST

The door creaked open, and Kai looked up, knowing it for foolishness but unable to stop. He dropped his gaze after the briefest of glances, then snapped it back up. Javi stood out in the hall, a sheepish expression on his face, twisting the fingers of his right hand with his left. Their gazes met, and exultant relief buzzed through Kai.

He beckoned Javi to come in, but the boy looked around, his gaze marking the other green-suited figures bent over their studies and shook his head. He beckoned Kai, a pleading expression on his face.

Kai grinned and nodded, then marked his place in the formal logic book and closed it. He slid his chair back and stood. As he turned, he caught Javi looking at him with narrowed eyes, and his stomach sank a little. He didn't want another argument. He wanted Javi to go back to the way he'd been before dinner. He tried to keep his expression neutral, but Javi narrowed his eyes even more, his mouth twisting on one side.

As he approached the door, Javier stepped back and let go of the doorknob. Kai followed him into the hall. "I'm glad you came back," said Kai. "I wanted to apologize. I—"

"*You* wanted to apologize to *me*? Nah, bro. Don't be stupid. You didn't *do* anything. It was me. It was all me." He twirled his fingers next to his ear. "It was all the *old me*."

Kai smiled a little. "You're not mad?"

"Oh, I'm mad, *cuate*, but not at you. It's this place"—he waved his hand in a vague circle—"the games, their bullshit."

"Yeah," said Kai with a relieved sigh. "But it *is* just a game, Javi. We have to play it."

"Do we, *chamaco*?" Then he smiled and cut his hand through the air between them. "Either way, we can't let it get between us."

"Right," said Kai with an answering grin. "One hundred percent right."

Javi glanced at the door behind Kai. "You done studying? There's something I want to show you, but I can't do it here." He pointed upward and mouthed the words, "They're watching."

Kai nodded and smiled. "I can spare a few minutes."

"Just a few?" Javi asked, his tone going a little cold.

"It's only an expression, Javi," said Kai, his smile fading a little.

"Got you, *chulo*." Javi laughed and bumped him on the shoulder with his fist.

"What's this secret thing you want to show me?"

A way to beat them at their own game, Javi sent.

Kai froze for a moment. Javi had never spoken in his mind before—he wasn't even aware the other boy could. *What do you mean?* Kai sent.

Just what I said, bro. Come on, and keep the chatter down. I have no doubt they've got a snoop on me—and probably you, too. These assholes leave nothing to chance. I'm blocking them—for now—but they'll overcome it soon.

Kai's expression clouded. "Okay."

7

Adeline paused, closed the book around her index finger, and took a sip of water. Her voice was starting to go raspy, and her throat was as dry as the desert above. Jamilla just lay there, staring up at the ceiling. *Like a damn cucumber. It's hard to believe she's* my *kin, but her daddy was weak, too.* After a moment, Adeline sighed, opened the book again, and found her place.

She'd read four long novels to Jamilla so far. The medics had suggested it, saying that Jamilla could probably hear her voice even if she didn't respond, and that it would be comforting. Glancing at Jamilla's flaccid cheeks, her half-rolled-up eyes, her rubber, drool-coated lips, Adeline wasn't sure Jamilla still existed to hear her voice. She hoped not. She'd always been needy, Jamilla had. Just like her daddy.

Suppressing a sigh, she said, "Now, where were we?" She glanced up at the woman and crooked an eyebrow, but there was no response—as with every other time she'd tried the same trick. "'Meuhlnir cleared his throat, a painful sound.' Child, I can relate to that, let me tell you. 'We fled the palace as if it were on fire, raising the alarm as we went.'"

Jamilla groaned—a sound so soft, at first Adeline questioned whether she'd heard it at all—then, again, louder.

"Child?" she asked, couching her voice in that caring tone all the suckers believed. She narrowed her eyes and stared at the woman's face.

Jamilla's entire body stiffened, seeming to thrum with frantic energy, and foam bubbled on her lips. Adeline stood and beckoned the medic. "She's seizing!"

Jamilla's arm shot out, grabbing Adeline's forearm in a painful grip. Adeline gasped and dropped the book, her gaze going to Jamilla's face, seeing, for the first time in months, signs of life. Jamilla's eyes focused on her face, and her tongue darted out to rasp across her dry lips.

"It's alright, child," said Adeline in a soothing tone, marshaling her features into a caring, hopeful expression. "You're safe. You've been very ill, and—"

"Sssse'en!" Jamilla's face crumpled, and she tried to lick her lips again. "Se'en!"

"Here, girl, take a little water." With her free hand, Adeline reached for the small cup resting on Jamilla's nightstand. She held the cup to Jamilla's lips and let her take a small amount into her mouth.

Jamilla pulled on her other arm, trying to pull herself upright. Her throat bobbed as she swallowed the water, then her eyes fastened on Adeline's once more. "Wuh-wuh-wuh! On!" She shook her head and moaned. She flung her free hand across her body and pointed at the door.

"Relax, now, child. Everything's fine." An icy fear settled in Adeline's gut. *Can she know? No, not possible.*

Jamilla thrashed her head from side to side. "Echk!"

"Shh, now," said Adeline. "Take some more water, dear."

Jamilla slapped the cup out of her hand, then levered herself sideways.

"Help me!" Adeline cried. "She's trying to get up! You have to sedate her!"

Jamilla's gaze zipped to the medic for half a second, then snapped back to Adeline's face. "Echkt! Ka-ka-eye!"

"I don't understand, child," said Adeline.

"Kai!"

Adeline grimaced, her stomach doing flip-flops. "He's fine, dear. He's here. In the Program. He's doing well." Then it dawned on her: Beatrice's reprogramming had come completely undone. *Figures*, she thought. *Never should have trusted that bimbo to do the job right!*

Jamilla thrashed her head again, shoving Adeline's hands. She flung her legs off the side of the bed and shoved with her arms. "Se'en wuh-on echkt echkt!" Then, her gaze snapped to the medic who'd reached the foot of the bed, holding a syringe. "Nungh! Nangh! Na!"

Adeline glanced at the medic and held up her hand. "Not yet." She turned back to Jamilla. "What are you trying to—" She gasped as a picture of Kai formed in her mind. Kai wearing a green jumpsuit—something Jamilla had never seen—walking next to a boy in a yellow jumpsuit. "What's this?" she murmured. "Kai?"

"Yuh! Yes!" Jamilla shot another terrified glance at the medic. "Guh-GO!" She jerked her eyes toward the door.

Adeline reached out with her special sense, trying to find Kai, but she couldn't. Then a thought occurred to her, and she had to fight to keep the grin off her face. "Get me a wheelchair!" She snapped at the medic. "Be quick if you want to avoid my anger!" She reached down to grab Jamilla under the arms. "Come on, child. You'll have to help me. I can't see him."

Another vision filled her mind: Kai lying broken on polished concrete, a boy in blue and Javier Dela Cruz standing over him, grinning. Adeline ducked her head to hide the flash of triumph in her eyes.

8

The Compound, under the Sonoran Desert, AZ
March 15, 2000, 9:51 pm MST

Javi grinned and dropped a hand on Kai's shoulder. "Thanks for trusting me. After how I acted at dinner, I thought you might—"

"No, it was my fault. I didn't say it right. I just blurted it out like an idiot."

Shrugging, Javi guided him to a door marked with the number 7188. He ignored the keypad set in the wall and knocked with one hand, squeezing Kai's shoulder with the other. "Don't freak out."

"Freak out? What do you mean?"

The door opened a crack, just enough for someone to peek out, then opened wide and Javi shoved him inside, following on his heels. Rayson Fergus grabbed Kai as he stumbled past, wrapping his arms around Kai's middle.

"Hey!" cried Kai. "What is this?"

"Get the door, Dylan," said Javi.

Kai wriggled in Rayson's grasp, craning his head. Shelves full of cleaning supplies and stacked linen took up one entire wall. Two janitor's carts and a utility sink lined the one opposite the shelves. Rayson frog-marched him past all that to the back wall, shoving his face against the cold, seafoam green concrete blocks. Behind them, Dylan closed the door.

"Javi! What are you doing?"

"Surprise," said Javi with a nasty chuckle.

"What? Why are you doing this?"

Javi strode into Kai's line of sight, then turned and put his back to the wall. He fixed a lazy grin on his face. "You're our ticket out of this damn place, *cabrón*. Tonight's fun is the price Miss Addy set for that, but to tell you the truth, *pendejo*, we'd have done it for nothing."

"What are you talking about?" Kai gulped and tried to worm his arms free again. "You can't beat me, Javi. *None* of you can beat me."

"Do you know what's special about this room, Kai?"

Kai froze, and his gaze rolled around the parts of the room he could see, lingering a moment on Dylan's. "Dylan, you shouldn't have left the dorms. You or Rayson." Behind him, Rayson Fergus growled like a mad dog.

Dylan only shook his head and rolled his eyes.

"I asked you a question, Kai," said Javi in a mild tone.

"What? This room?" Kai eyed the janitor carts. "Uh…it's a custodial closet?"

"Very good!" crowed Javi. "You win the prize." He nodded at Rayson, and the big kid pulled Kai away from the wall, his arms still pinned to his sides. Javi straightened from his calculated slouch and punched Kai in the solar plexus.

Kai grunted as his diaphragm spasmed, and his breath whooshed out of him with a grunt. He tried to double-over, but Rayson held him up. The pain was intense, a hot poker in the center of his chest, and his face wrinkled into a grimace of pain.

Javi straightened and treated him to a smile. "You missed the crucial difference between this room and the other ones." He waved his hand toward the door and the hallway beyond. He jerked his chin up and to the side. "No cameras in here, Kai," he said in a quiet, yet emotionally charged voice. "And no observers check it. Miss Addy said so. *Fry* said so."

Kai fought for breath, eyes tearing up, nausea bubbling in his guts. He shifted his gaze from Javi's face to Dylan's, pleading with his eyes, but Dylan only rolled his eyes again. "Adeline…wouldn't…" he wheezed.

Javi smiled and patted his cheek. "Oh, it's already done, *chamaco*. And it was *her* idea. She wanted you to know that."

Kai shook his head, and Javier punched him again, this time in the guts. He tried to curl around his belly, but again, Rayson held him up, this time with a grunt of effort. Self-defense moves played through Kai's mind, but none of that crap for fighting multiple attackers seemed like it had any place in the real world.

Besides, he was a *puppeteer*.

He fastened his gaze on Dylan and batted the boy's mental walls down in a savage thrust of his will. Kai dove deep, cutting Dylan's reasoning off from his motor control areas as he had done with Rayson in the dining room, and Javi in the study room. He drove Dylan forward and snapped his hands into fists.

"Javi, look out!" cried Rayson, twisting Kai away, trying to break his control by breaking his line of sight.

Dylan veered around, then took two lunging steps, crossing the room quickly, and smashed his right fist into Rayson's face, flattening his nose with a spray of blood. Rayson cried out, then let go of Kai, raising both hands to his face.

"No!" shouted Javi.

Kai whirled Dylan around and used him to kick at Javi's knees before bringing Dylan's tight fist looping up toward the roof, then back down to smash into Javi's cheek. The boy grunted and stepped back, bumping against the wall. He made Dylan lunge forward, slinging his fist on a flat arc, aiming for the side of Javi's throat. When the blow struck home, Javi staggered to the left, eyes rolling, mouth agape, and he went over sideways.

Rayson roared and charged at Dylan, leaving Kai to sidle toward the door, his arms wrapped around his belly. He spun Dylan around, using his momentum to whip his foot out, sinking it into Rayson's groin.

Rayson doubled over with a harsh cry, and Kai ran Dylan into him, driving both blue-suited boys into the shelves of cleaning materials. Rayson grabbed at the shelves for support but only managed to dump cleaning supplies to the floor. Kai threw a glance at Javi, then spun and grabbed the doorknob.

Javi fought to his feet, one hand on his neck, and Kai spun Dylan toward Javi, pumping his legs like an Olympic sprinter. Javi snapped his face up and stared at Dylan, grimacing. The blue-suiter staggered and went down to one knee. Kai felt the puppet strings stretch and stretch as Jepson pitched forward on his face.

Javi turned a malicious glare on Kai and slammed into his mind, boring inward, driving Kai's walls back and back and back again. His mental touch felt like boiling acid, his anger and fear and *hatred* scalding Kai.

Rayson rolled away from the mess, glanced at Dylan's slack form, and frowned.

"Do...something..." Javi grunted. His hands had curled into fists, and blood suffused his face, turning it beet red. His respirations came hard and fast as he poured more and more power into Kai's mind.

Kai twisted the doorknob, then jerked the door open half an inch. Rayson slammed into him from behind, driving the door closed, slashing at Kai with berserk haymakers and windmilling blows that he barely felt.

Kai counter-attacked, taking control of Rayson and freezing him in place—anger and pain driving him into trying something he'd never done before: controlling *two* puppets at the same time. He made his will into a gleaming silver battering ram and drove it into the center of Javi's mind. Javier shrieked with pain and rage and frustration, fighting against Kai's onslaught with everything he had. Kai hammered at Javier, a whirlwind of willpower. He imagined crushing the boy under his giant heel like a cockroach. He pictured Javi's head in a vice—a vice that Kai controlled, squeezing and squeezing and squeezing. Javi screamed, and Kai redoubled his attacks, driving the older boy to his knees.

9

Jamilla flung her arm to the left, and Adeline threw her weight against the chair, almost capsizing it, almost falling herself, then sweeping around the corner wide, almost slamming into the wall. Adeline's chest burned, ripping breaths from the air as she ran, pushing Jamilla's wheelchair ahead of her like a much younger woman. Her feet ached with each slapping step, her elbows burned, feeling sick and broken, her grip causing her knuckles to pop and snap each time she shifted to take a corner or tried to find a more comfortable position on the wheelchair's handles, pain washing up her arms in tsunami waves.

"Left!" Jamilla cried at the next intersection, and Adeline threw her weight against the chair once more. "Down the hall in the middle!"

Adeline dredged more power, more speed out of her old legs, panting, eyes watering, throat burning.

"Here! Here!" shouted Jamilla, pointing at an innocent-looking door labeled 7188.

Adeline threw herself at the door, but Jamilla beat her to it, jerking the doorknob, finding it locked, then tapping in a four-digit code on the keypad next to the door. She jerked the door open and froze.

10

The Compound, under the Sonoran Desert, AZ
March 15, 2000, 10:01 pm MST

Kai leaned against the back wall of the janitor's closet, breathing hard, his left hand pressed against his ribs, staring at the boy in front of him. Javi slumped on his knees at Kai's feet, his head bent forward at an extreme angle, his hands loose at his sides. Rayson stood frozen, and Dylan lay on the floor, staring up the ceiling, breathing hard.

"What's going on here?" demanded Adeline from the hall.

Kai didn't lift his gaze from Javi's face. "Is it true?" he asked in a voice that dripped exhaustion, pain, and confusion. For some reason, Adeline had brought a janitor in a wheelchair.

"Is what true, child?" asked Adeline.

"He said this was your idea."

"No, Kai, no," she said in her best let's-be-reasonable tone. "What are these boys doing to you?"

Kai squinted at Javi, then flicked his hostile gaze up to her face. "Yes, it is. I can read it in him"—he pointed at Javier—"and I can feel it in you."

"Child, you're no snoop," she said with a hint of rebuke in her tone.

"Kuh-kuh-kuh," said the janitor. "Kuh-ai!"

Chavez! *I need you*! Kai sent the thoughts with all the power he had left, sidling along the rear wall toward the corner. "*Your* plan!" he sneered.

"Now, child, I don't like your tone. Not one bit!" snapped Adeline.

"Has it *all* been you? Has it been you all along?" Kai's voice was more like the croak of a crow than a boy's voice.

"Boy, I've been fighting for you behind the scenes. I've been—"

Kai laughed, but it sounded almost like he'd given in to the sobs. "How could you?" he asked. "How could you do this to your own family?"

Adeline stared at him for the space of five long breaths, her eyes narrowing to slits toward the end. "It was for your own good," she said, her down-home accent gone, replaced by a cultured, la-dee-dah voice of a New England society maven. "You can't rely on people in this world, boy. Not even people of our own race. No one has your best interests at heart. Everything has a price; everyone expects a payday from you. It's high time you learned that."

"So what now?" he asked. "Do you pay Javi's price and help him to do what he can't on his own?"

Javier snarled something no one understood.

"No," said Adeline. "It's obvious he lacks the wherewithal."

The janitor cried out, not words, just the sounds of frustration and worry, and Adeline wheeled her around and shoved her down the hall. She turned back to Kai. "Javier has failed, and I'm good with that." She flicked her fingers at the three boys. "Go on, then. Take your revenge."

"What?"

"Kill them," said Adeline. "You have the power, exercise it."

Kai scowled at her, shaking his head. "I don't think I want to kill them."

"Well, what do you *think* will happen to them once this fiasco gets out? What do you think the Man will order someone like Chavez to do to them?"

Shaking his head, Kai squeezed his eyes shut. "What's wrong with you? Why are you like this?"

Adeline scoffed. "Like what, child?"

"So hard. So cold. So...*broken* inside."

"Ha! You couldn't take ten steps in my shoes, boy," said Adeline in a cold, hateful voice. "If your childhood had a tenth—no, hundredth—of the tragedy mine had, you would've curled up in a ball in a shed and let the Klansmen hang your daddy, instead of leading your family into a swamp full of gators and cottonmouths! Instead of keeping them *hidden* for weeks! You'd have..." She stopped and closed her mouth with a snick of her teeth. She stepped inside the room and snapped her fingers. "You three! Are you stupid?"

Javi turned his head to the side, drool hanging from his chin in a long, roping strand. "Wha..." he croaked.

"Jamilla—this boy's mama—is out in the hall. Besides Kai, she's the only person whose testimony we don't control." She stamped her foot. "Get out there and make sure she *can't* testify!"

Kai stared up at her, his face a mask of anger and pain. "My mother's dead," he said in a harsh whisper.

"Not yet, boy, but that's the spirit."

He lashed out at her with his mind, rage and sorrow mixed into the attack, but she batted him away easily.

"I'm no blue-suiter, child," she said.

Kai leaped up and darted past Javi and into the hall.

"Get him!" Adeline shouted.

He sprinted to the wheelchair, took it by its handles, and ran.

"Left!" Jamilla cried.

Kai turned the corner, almost falling, almost tipping the chair onto its side, somehow keeping his feet, keeping it upright. He poured on more speed as loud footsteps began behind him.

Jamilla flung her arm out to the left, and Kai careened around the corner again. The hall stretched away into the distance, no exit in sight, nowhere to hide, nothing but endless metal doors, stupid numbers painted above them.

"Muh-muh-middle…" grated Jamilla. "Thuh-then left."

Kai ignored her, his mind racing, creating plans that had no chance of working. His gaze darted to the numbers above the doors—7213 on the left, 7233 on the right—but they meant nothing to him.

"Muh-middle!" shouted Jamilla. "Luh-left!" She dropped her left hand off the armrest and jerked up on the brake for the left wheel.

The chair jerked to the left, spinning ninety degrees, and Kai sprawled beside it, breathing hard. "Don't do that!" he rasped.

She leaned to the right, staring him in the eye. "Muh-middle! Left! Kuh-kai!" Her right fingers shook, pointing at the door in front of her.

Kai rolled to his knees, shaking his head. Shouts and pounding footsteps echoed toward them from the direction they'd come. "There's no time for this!"

Jamilla frowned at him, and again her fingers shook but pointed at the door.

To Kai, it looked like any other door. Its number was 7219. "It's probably *locked*," he hissed as he stood and took the handles of the wheelchair again. He tried to spin her away from the door, to point her down the long hall again, but she hauled upwards on the left brake again. "Don't you understand? They want to *kill* us! *We have to get out here!*"

"Kuh-kuh-kuh." Jamilla shook her head violently. "*Kai*! Guh-go left!"

Kai stepped around the wheelchair, more to shut her up than expecting anything to come of her precious door. He grasped the doorknob and twisted, and the door opened. "You're a genius!" He flung the door wide and wheeled Jamilla into a short, dark hallway that dead-ended into another dark hall running parallel to the hall outside.

He pushed her deeper into the Compound's guts, not knowing where he was taking her, but Jamilla sank back in the chair, heaving a sigh of relief. He took comfort from her contentment.

He slowed their headlong flight to a fast walk, breathing harder than he should've, his entire left side aflame.

11

The Compound, under the Sonoran Desert, AZ
March 15, 2000, 10:12 pm MST

Adeline's fury mounted as she followed her three disciples down the empty hall. The boys ranged ahead, running to the next intersection and peering down connecting hallways. She could tell by their growing panic that Kai and Jamilla weren't visible. "This is stupid," she called. "Boys, come here! Guard me a moment!"

She closed her eyes, going for a calm she didn't remotely feel. She focused on Kai, envisioning him in the special eye lodged in the middle of her mind, then sent her consciousness out.

She saw Javier, Rayson, and Dylan trotting back toward her, then raced away, shooting down the hall at a speed no one could hope to match in the physical realm. She flew until she'd passed the point she figured a boy pushing a wheelchair could have reached, then she branched out, following the grid of hallways that defined the Compound.

She felt a tug, let it pull her, peering into the middle distance down the hall, and saw nothing. She raced down the hall, then the tug *changed*, no longer pulling her forward, it now dragged at her back. She whirled around and raced back, but the tug switched directions again. *What in the hell is going on here?* She stopped moving and turned in a slow circle, but the tug pulled her to a blank wall of concrete blocks.

Adeline drifted through the wall, through a closet stacked floor to ceiling with giant cardboard boxes, through the boxes and through the back wall of the storage room. For a moment, she drifted through a small, tight space that ran vertically, filled with pipes and ducts of all sizes, then broke through the other side into one of the staff observation corridors. The tug led to the left, and she headed in that direction.

"You clever boy," she whispered.

Rough hands grabbed her shoulders, and her concentration broke.

12

Kai's ribs hurt more and more with each step, but he didn't dare stop, not with a bird dog of Adeline's mastery and power behind them. It wouldn't take her long to figure out Jamilla's trick.

Slow down, Kai. Regain your strength while you can.

He jumped at the familiar touch in his mind, the touch that could only be his mother's comforting presence. *Adeline—*

Never mind her. She has other problems to deal with. How are…

How am I alive? I could ask you the same, but given Adeline's involvement, I'm certain she had that blonde bitch reprogram us.

Kai slowed again, and again, the pain in his ribs grew. *She made me think you were dead.*

Same with me.

I thought Adeline…

I don't think we ever knew Adeline, Son. I think she's worn masks her whole life, becoming whoever she thought she needed to be to get ahead.

Kai shook his head, recalling summer vacations in Rochester, the fun times they'd shared in Adeline's little house, juxtaposing those memories with the memories of her commanding Jamilla's death as though she were worth no more than a mere pittance, as though she were a game piece to sacrifice. Anger kindled within him, flaring up like a forest fire.

Shh, little Kai, sent Jamilla. *Look at it like this: Adeline brought us together in the end. And together, we can escape this place.*

Kai looked down at his mother's frail form, the way her smock hung from her bone-thin shoulders and arms, the bulbous knots of her finger joints.

Shh, little Kai, she sent again. *Don't worry about me, I'll be fine. Go left at the next intersection.*

Kai nodded slowly.

13

The Compound, under the Sonoran Desert, AZ
March 15, 2000, 10:16 pm MST

Adeline opened her eyes and stared into Bethany's burning grey eyes. The woman had her by the shoulders and was shaking her briskly. Over her shoulder, Adeline saw that her three ersatz guards stood frozen—obviously under the influence of Hector Chavez who stood next to Beatrice a few steps away. "Unhand me, child," Adeline said in her sweetest tone. "Kai has had some kind of mental breakdown. He tricked these three boys into stepping inside a janitorial closet where he attacked them. I was with Jamilla when I sensed it, and now Kai's kidnapped her. He's taken her inside the staff observation tunnels. I was just about to catch up to him when you interrupted me."

Bethany sneered in her face. "You've gone too far this time," she rasped.

Beatrice nodded. *I've already replayed Javier's memories, d'Clara. You'd better pray we can turn Kai around. He's worth ten of you, bird dog, and that's not just me talking. The Man feels the same way.*

Adeline cracked a smile that was ninth-tenths sneer, then twisted out of Bethany's grasp. "Javier is a mental defective, and one with a history of deceiving fixers. Are you three going to take his word over mine?"

"You're goddamn right!" snapped Chavez. "We're taking over as of right now, Adeline. You'll be lucky if the Man allows you to go on breathing."

Dropping her gaze to the floor to hide it, Adeline smiled.

14

The Compound, under the Sonoran Desert, AZ
March 15, 2000, 10:56 pm MST

Kai's arms, shoulders, and back ached—almost enough to drown out the constant pain in his ribs. He plodded along, pushing Jamilla in front of him. He couldn't quite bring himself to call the woman his mother—not when he could recall her death with such clarity.

It's okay, Kai, Jamilla sent, and along with it came a sense of profound weariness. *I remember your death, as well, after we found out about your daddy.*

Is he... Kai shook his head.

I think that's real.

But it could be an implant. If they can make us think each other is dead, they can do anything.

That's right, so it's best we get as far away from here as we can.

But Adeline can find us anytime she wants.

Jamilla craned her neck to look up at him, a crafty gleam in her eye. *During my confinement in the medical ward, I figured out a way to hide from her.*

Ja— Mom, you can't hide from a bird dog. It's impossible.

Here's how you do it...

15

The Compound, under the Sonoran Desert, AZ
March 15, 2000, 11:36 pm MST

Chavez slammed the door to her quarters in her face, and Adeline stuck out her tongue and blew a raspberry at it. She turned and surveyed her entire kingdom—at least until the Man ordered her death. She went to her little desk and pulled out the chair, then woke up her computer.

She opened her email client and sent a three-word email. Then she opened the security suite and giggled. *They should have revoked my permissions before putting me in here.* They could revoke her access now if they wanted, but with the application running and connected, they couldn't boot her out without restarting the server.

She took off her sweaty dress and pulled on a pair of sweatpants and a sweatshirt. Air blew by her, smelling of brimstone and pain, and Adeline smiled. She felt his impossible heat as he came close, as he leaned in to whisper in her ear.

"Where we going, sugar?" Fry asked.

16

The Compound, under the Sonoran Desert, AZ
March 15, 2000, 11:43 pm MST

Kai opened the door and peeked both up and down the corridor, then he flung the door open and rushed across the hall to test the door across from them. He typed in the code Jamilla had made him memorize, and the door popped open.

With a shark's grin, he ran back and pushed Jamilla into the short hallway that Kai recognized, though he'd only walked through it once on the day Chavez delivered him into the cold hands of the Program. He pulled the door firmly shut behind them, then patted Jamilla's shoulder. "Almost free," he said.

She nodded and flicked her fingers at the other door, and he pushed her through into the parking garage. "Left," she croaked. "Middle of the row on the left."

Kai nodded and pushed her wheelchair down the row to the big 70s era Chrysler sedan. He pushed her chair around and opened the passenger door, his stomach already full of butterflies at the prospect of driving the boat. He set the wheel brakes on her chair, and then she surprised him by pushing herself up to her feet.

She stood a moment, swaying a little. *Go ahead, Kai. Get in, I'll get myself in.*

But—

Kai, she sent. *Do as I bid you.*

He knew what that meant: do what I said or get whupped. Grinning a little, he walked around the front of the car and slid in behind the steering wheel.

A car like this is easy to drive. It's an automatic, so that means you put it in D to go forward and R to go back. Just make sure your foot is on the brake. When you get out on the road, stay close to the right side until you get comfortable. In the traffic lane, you'll see a dark stripe. Drive so that the stripe is coming right at you.

Smiling, Kai sent, *You don't have to tell me all of it at once.*

Jamilla smiled back, but her eyes seemed sad.

"We're almost out, Mom. Don't give up on me now."

She smiled and nodded her head. "Stuh-start it."

Kai nodded, grasped the key that sat in the ignition, and twisted it. The engine roared to life. For at least the millionth time, Kai wondered at the ease of their escape. How his mother had been able to direct him to this car by saying "left" and "down to the middle" time after time. "Get in, Mom."

Let's see you drive that thing a little, she sent.

He pulled the gear lever down to the big D, then let his foot off the brake, and the car leaped forward. *Whoa!* He jammed on the brakes, then turned to his mother, a huge smile on his face. *I didn't expect that.*

She grinned at him and nodded, but the grin didn't last. *Try again. Let's see you drive the car over to the roll-up door.*

He nodded and did as she asked. He glanced back at her in the rearview mirror, and his triumphant grin froze on his lips. Jamilla had turned back toward the door that led inside, so he could only see her in profile, but her cheeks were wet with tears. Panic swatted the grin off his face, and he jammed the gear selector up to the P. He grabbed the door handle and pulled it.

No! Kai, no!

He didn't listen. He swung his legs out of the car as the Program door swung open, light slipping out into the dark parking garage, cutting a swath through the shadows. He stood as Jamilla swayed, then staggered toward the door. "No!" he cried, and Javier, Rayson, and Dylan came through the door. He ran the length of the Chrysler before a lanky man wearing military fatigues and a black hoodie strode out the door.

Fry, he thought.

GO! Jamilla screamed in his mind. *KAI, GO!*

Kai froze as his mother broke into a staggering run, throwing her arms wide. He dithered as she slid to a stop next to a pickup's bed, reaching inside. He stared as she lifted the huge pistol.

She glanced at him, terror for him in her eyes. *Kai, if you love me, go. Go, now! You only have a minute! Remember what I taught you. Remember I always loved you.*

Jamilla flashed a sad smile at him. As she turned her gaze toward Fry, Kai took a few tentative steps toward the driver's seat. As she lifted the pistol, he stepped into the car with his right foot. As the man's eyes began to glow, as orange as a sunset, Jamilla fired, the concussive roar deafening, and the man disappeared. She shifted the gun to point at Dylan and fired again.

Kai slid into the driver's seat, tears splashing down his cheeks. He jerked the gear lever down to D but kept his foot on the brake.

Jamilla shifted the pistol again, this time, aiming at Rayson. She pulled the trigger, and another roar blanketed the garage. Fry appeared behind Jamilla, orange blazing from his eyes, leaning forward as if to whisper in her ear.

Kai hammered his fist on the horn. *Look out*! *Mommy, LOOK OUT*! He grabbed the door handle, but Jamilla's voice shouted in his mind.

NO! *Get out of here, Kai*!

Sobbing, he put his hand back on the steering wheel.

Jamilla turned to look at him one last time, the arm holding the giant pistol drooping toward the ground, and smiled warmly at him. *Don't forget*! she sent, and then Fry was on her, chopping her down to the concrete floor.

Chapter 20
Last Call

I

1 Whitetooth Drive, Miami FL
Friday, 5:28 pm

Kai stopped talking and dropped his gaze to his lap. Across the room, Karl looked down into his Dr. Pepper as though it contained the answer to all of life's questions. In Minnieville, Maddie sobbed quietly.

"I take it you got away?" asked Gavin in a shaking voice. "She sacrificed…" His throat closed on the next word, and he dropped his gaze to his own lap.

"Yes," said Kai. "I put the hammer down and busted right through their goddamn roll-up door. I followed the dirt track until it became a dirt road. I followed that until it became gravel, then asphalt, and eventually, all the way to Phoenix. A few days later, I drove to Albuquerque, spent some months there, then on to San Antonio."

"You lived in the Chrysler?" asked Karl, still staring down at his drink.

"Yes, at first."

"And they never came looking for you?"

Kai shook his head, a watery grin on his face. "Oh, they came, all right. But eventually, I got so that I could do my mother's trick all the time. Subconsciously." He tapped his head and then took a drink.

"Fry never came looking?" asked Gavin in a voice that sounded old and dead.

"No. Fry can't bird dog much. He has to have a hook in you."

"And he didn't have one in you?"

Kai shrugged and wiped a stray tear from his cheek. "If he did, my mother's trick worked against him, as well."

"What was the trick?" Maddie asked.

He chuckled. "My mother's breakdown led her to some dark places—a memory of a bigot shaming her father at the fair being the biggest of them. She told me she must have looped through that night eighty billion times while Adeline visited her and read her stories that she didn't want to hear. There was something about that memory that allowed her to think about things that should have tripped her failsafes. Once she figured that out, she malingered a little—pretended to be sicker than she was—and managed to fool the Program medicos. She found the changes made to her psyche by Beatrice. Once she could—"

"Then that part of Adeline's story really is true?" asked Maddie.

"That Beatrice was the fixer who manipulated her? Yes, that part is true. Beatrice did mine, too. The lie Adeline told about both of those things is that *she* was the one who insisted on the changes. She…" He closed his mouth and shook his head. "Even her story about my so-called rescue was full of half-truths. She followed us because she'd had a premonition that I would take control of Reggie completely on that third day, that I would break him and make him take me away. She couldn't have that; she'd spent three generations selectively breeding her descendants—looking for the right combination of genes to produce a child who might match Fry's natural talents. She had the idea that our relationship would bind me to her, that I would be her personal bogeyman and assassin." He swallowed some Dr. Pepper.

"How did you survive?" asked Maddie. "You were, what? Thirteen?"

"At the time of the escape, I was thirteen, but only for a month. As far as survival goes, you'd be surprised how much easier that is for a man with my gifts."

"What happened to Beatrice, Bethany, and Chavez?" asked Karl.

"Adeline happened to them," said Kai. "Beatrice managed to get away—fixers are even more suited to the life I live. I found her in Minneapolis. She undid her reprogramming. Later, she helped me develop my teletechnitic side."

"You have all of them, then?" asked Gavin.

Kai shook his head. "Not a drop of the telezitonic gift. None of my family had that except Adeline, though Beatrice thinks Jamilla developed the ability while she scrubbed floors."

"All the lefts?"

"Exactly. And she had a touch of augury."

"I don't understand how you got away," said Karl—with a touch of suspicion. "The door code, the car with the key in it, the gun in the pickup."

Kai nodded. "All of that was Adeline's doing."

"Wait…she *wanted* you to escape?"

"No, no. At first, she'd planned on having Javi and his crew escape if they managed to kill me. When she saw my mother awake and aware that night, she adjusted her plans for what would happen if I won the fight. She told her about the code, the car, the pistol. She said I was in danger and that Mom had to get me away. She thought she could use Fry killing us in the middle of an escape attempt to depose the Man—and she was right. Adeline never expected her to make a stand, never expected her to have the strength to turn the pistol on our pursuers."

"Her mistake was judging Jamilla's love for you by her own love—or lack of it—for her own children," said Maddie. "She couldn't fathom laying down her own life for anyone, so she never considered that that's exactly what Jamilla would do to save you."

Kai dropped his gaze to his lap again. "Yes." He drank a swallow of Dr. Pepper. "But her plan still worked. She shifted the blame onto Beatrice, Bethany, and Chavez. My escape, plus my mother's death—which she laid at my feet—while she was supposedly under house arrest, fit right into the plan. Plus, she had testimony from Javi, Dylan, and Rayson to back her up."

"And Fry?"

Kai's lips twisted in a sardonic grin. "Why, he was never there, of course."

"Of course."

"They had a falling out—Fry and Adeline—at some point, and he left her to her own devices. She was running Majestic by then and had her trio of pet assassins, so she thought she didn't need him anymore. I don't know if she understands the depths of their relationship with him."

"Another mistake chalked up to her deficits."

"Yes, Maddie."

"What is Fry?" asked Karl. "I mean, what is he *really*?"

"I don't think anyone knows. When he left Firestarter that night, he took most of the data that they'd accumulated on him. And since the scientists all died that night…"

"Does Adeline know?"

Kai shook his head. "I don't think so, but if anyone did, it would be her."

"Why does she need to set a trap for him? Why can't she just reach out the way she did before? Email or whatever?"

"I don't know," said Kai. "Maybe their blow up is the reason. She's never been one to leave a bridge unburned if she doesn't get her way. Like I said, if Fry doesn't want her to, she can't find him."

"Is he there?" asked Maddie. "In Miami, I mean."

"Again, I don't know."

"What happens if he is? What happens if he's on her side? Can you protect Gavin?"

"Maddie, I don't know. From Javi and other Program operatives, I can. As I did when a puppeteer ran Karl this morning, I can kick them out. Actually, it's lucky that Adeline didn't send someone like Bethany. She could burst aortas or something like that, and there'd be nothing I could do."

"How do we know she hasn't sent someone like that?" asked Gavin. "And how the hell do we stop these goddamn murders?"

"The same way you'd stop any other serial killer," said Kai, his voice calm. "With one small difference. You track them down and arrest them, but before you take them in, you let me have a few moments with them."

"Why?" asked Karl.

Gavin squinted at Kai for a moment. "You'll reprogram them?"

Kai nodded, his gaze steady. "I'll take away their abilities. I'll leave the memories of the murders, but I'll take everything else."

Gavin shook his head once, thinking of Tom Madsen, of Angel Kirk, John Jenkins, and Larry Bateman. "That seems harsh."

"It's how it has to be," said Kai with a shrug. "If they remember what they were, they remain dangerous. I don't want to live with a bullseye on my back anymore."

"What about Adeline?" asked Maddie.

"Without her pets? She'll be vulnerable. Someone will depose her sooner or later. She has no friends, as you might imagine. Anyway, she has to succumb to her age sooner or later."

"What's to stop her from sending in another fixer to undo what you've done?" asked Karl.

"That's why I said 'blank.'"

"I don't understand," said Maddie.

"He means he's going to physically scramble their memories. Destructive retrograde amnesia. How Glacadairanam's victims end up, in other words," said Gavin, his gaze resting on Kai's.

Kai nodded.

"I'm not sure—"

Gavin's phone rang again. "That's her," he said. "I'd better take it this time."

"Be careful," said Maddie.

"I'll link you in but stay quiet so she doesn't catch on."

"Check," said Maddie.

He tapped the accept button, then conferenced the two calls together. "Hello? Adeline?" he said.

"Hello, child," said Adeline. "I'm sorry about this morning… It just got to be too much. The memory of them boys murdering Kai was just too much."

"Sure. We understand."

"Yes, I knew you and your missus would, more's the pity." She cleared her throat—a dainty cough that sounded practiced. "I called you a bit ago."

"You did?"

"I did."

"Oh, it must have been while we were in the 'Glades. No service out there."

"You find Javi or whoever it is, yet? Do you at least have something to go on?"

"We're working on it. That's why we were in the Everglades. He rented a car and trucked out there into the middle of the swamp."

"Why on Earth would he do that?"

"He dumped another body out there," said Karl.

"He did?"

To Gavin, Adeline's surprise seemed genuine. "Yes. Turns out it was the first victim. Well, so far."

Adeline said nothing for a moment. "Lordy. And he rented a car to go back out there? After you had his credit cards? I'd think a serial killer would be smarter than that."

"This one's pretty brazen. He doesn't have much fear of being caught. Which I guess makes sense if he's psychic," said Gavin.

"Well, I just wanted to give my regrets. I won't take up your time, not while you're chasing a killer down."

"About that…" said Karl.

"Yes, Detective?"

"He's not acting right. I was wondering if you had any insight and suggestions about how to catch him? After all, you knew them as children… You know how they think."

"Lordy, child. Why would you think I'd know how a serial killer thinks?"

"It's not the serial killer part we're having trouble with."

"Ah," Adeline said. "Well, remember, I haven't seen whoever is responsible for those deaths since the year 2000."

"Sure, but you know the Program. You know how these suspects were *taught* to think."

"Hmm. I guess I could think on it." She hummed a little. "Have you… Have you run into anyone else who strikes you as suspicious?"

"Outside of the guy who puppeted Karl this morning? No."

"Would a puppeteer use his power to make money? Should we look in the big houses out on the Beach?" asked Karl. "Or would he take just enough, knowing he can always get more."

"My, what a question. I'm not sure I can do it justice."

"Best guess, then," said Gavin.

"Javier might take the second path. Dylan and Rayson would probably be in a big house somewhere fancy."

"Okay," said Gavin. "And Fry?"

"Understand I hardly knew the man, but when I knew him in 1963, he lived in an alley. In filth. Living moment to moment, making his luck when he needed it."

"Got it," said Karl.

"Adeline, do you have any ideas about the acceleration factor?"

"Acceleration? How do you mean?"

"The unsub is killing more often, with fewer days in between. If he follows the same pattern, he'll kill again tonight," said Gavin.

"Lordy!"

"And he'll probably kill near the Langfield Sun. To emphasize how much better he is than me. To show he isn't scared I'll catch him. He might even do it in the same park—it's right across from my hotel."

Adeline gave a horrified chuckle. "Lands, boy. I'm glad I don't have your job. I'll give it some thought, too."

"That would be great," he said.

"Okay, then. I'll let you get back to it. If I don't get the chance, tell your pretty wife I said sorry."

"Will do."

"Good luck. To both of you," Adeline said before she disconnected.

"She's still the same," mused Kai. "That accent!" He chuckled. "She taught herself to speak like a White woman before World War II."

"That was smart, Gavin," said Karl. "Think she'll take the bait?"

"Bait?" asked Kai. "What are you talking about?"

"Gavin gave her a little rope. Let's see if she hangs herself with it." Karl glanced at his watch. "We've got a lot to do before sundown, though. We'd better get on it."

Kai turned a probing stare on Gavin. "All that about when and where?"

Gavin nodded. "It works for two of your three possibilities. But she may not take the bait. Or it's that second one, where the killer is really a whack job."

Kai grinned. "Oh, I bet she's already passing along what you said."

"I hope so," said Gavin, "and I hope MDPD can move fast enough."

"Even if they take the bait, it won't be as easy as all that. In fact, having MDPD there might be a detriment, rather than a boon."

Gavin quirked an eyebrow at Kai.

"These men are experienced puppeteers and operatives. You'll need a way to counter their skills and control them if you do capture them." Kai shot a glance at Karl. "In short, you need me there, and I need to be close to them."

"How close?" asked Karl.

"Twenty feet."

Karl whistled and turned to Gavin. "Cowboy time."

"We've got to go, Maddie," said Gavin.

"Be careful. *All* of you. Gavin, call me the second you can."

2

Gavin stood at the rail of Karl's boat, gazing out on Bayfront Park through a pair of binoculars. Despite the warm night, the full moon, and the late hour, knots of partiers still walked the concrete paths, either taking a scenic route toward their parked cars or just strolling along, not wanting their night to end. He dismissed groups of more than two with a cursory glance, paying detailed attention to the couples—especially the men. So far, no one resembled the composite sketch. Not even a little.

"Do you really think this will work?" asked Karl from the captain's seat.

"I hope so."

"If he kills somewhere else…"

Gavin straightened and let the binoculars hang from the strap around his neck. "At least this gives us a chance."

Karl grunted.

"If we didn't try this, and he dropped a body somewhere else, it would be the same result as we'll get if he ignores the bait—we'll get him through proper investigation, linking the circumstantial evidence to him. But if he takes the bait, if he tries to commit another murder and chooses to do it out there"—he waved his hand over his shoulder at the park—"then he's ours, *and* we catch him in the act. That's better than building a circumstantial case any day of the week."

"*If* it works," said Karl.

"Right. If it doesn't, we're in the same boat as we are right now—no pun intended—and no one has to know."

"Maybe we should have called Bobby."

Gavin shook his head. "I don't think so. He as much as said we should do any cowboy policing first and let him know if it produced results."

"Yeah, I know that."

"I can't think of anything we could do that would be more cowboy than this."

Karl grinned with half his face, then pointed at the park. "Should we get in closer?"

Gavin shook his head. "This is close enough. We don't want to spook him."

3

Bayfront Park, Miami, FL
Saturday, 2:43 am

Karl goosed the boat toward the dock between the Bayfront Park and Bayside Marketplace, then killed the engine and let momentum carry them in with only the natural sound of waves lapping at the shore. A woman's tinkling laugh had reached them across the dark water two minutes earlier, and Gavin had spotted the couple as they walked from the Bayside Marketplace and into the park.

As they stepped off the boat onto the wooden dock, the woman's laugh tinkled out of the copse of trees between them and the amphitheater. Karl and Gavin drew their pistols, then walked to the concrete path at the end of the square dock, moving slowly, careful to make as little sound as possible.

They'd agreed they couldn't make a head-on assault. If nothing else, the unsub would see them coming and pull the same trick he had at Kai's house on Miami Beach—puppet one of them into killing the other. Instead, they cut across the concrete parking lot and climbed the stairs hidden by the artificial hill that covered the maintenance building. At the top of the stairs, they paused, peering toward the cordoned-off area, then ran hunched over down the wide sidewalk until they reached the amphitheater's basin. They looped around that, then stopped in the trees shielding its south side.

They were close—close enough that the unsub would hear any broken stick, any careless step, any noise at all. Gavin hid behind the wide trunk of an old oak tree and peeked out, peering into the shadows beneath the trees.

Nothing moved in the cordoned-off area, and he could see no one standing in the shadows. He turned and raised his eyebrows at Karl, who shook his head.

Then the woman laughed again, but it came from the wrong place. From the south, rather than the site of the previous night's murder. He twisted his head, peering across the open lawn toward the kid's pool area, and the Langfield Sun beyond. Karl came up beside him. "The hotel?" he hissed.

"I did say he'd try to kill near the hotel to emphasize how much better he was than me." He stared at Karl for a moment. "How much better would he be if he killed her *in* the hotel."

"The lobby?"

Gavin wagged his head from side to side. "Cameras. Witnesses. People who might stop him."

"Parking garage then? Pool area?"

Gavin shrugged. "I'm thinking even more personal."

"Your room?" Karl turned and stared at the hotel, even though Gavin's room was on the east side and couldn't be seen from the park.

"Where Kai is."

Karl turned a wide-eyed stare his way, and then they were both sprinting toward the Langfield Sun.

4

They ran up the four flights to the floor of Gavin's room. The stairwell dumped them into the long hotel corridor, with its weird carpet and prints of bad paintings. They moved in silence, except for the harsh breath flowing in and out of them, neither man needing to speak, neither needing instructions from the other to know what to do next. It was a kind of simpatico that developed between partners, but usually partners of a much longer tenure.

Gavin approached the door to his room, then paused and pointed at the sliver of light leaking through the almost-closed door. Karl jerked his chin up and down and swung around Gavin to stand ready on the other side of the door. Their eyes met for a moment, then Karl nodded once more, and Gavin stepped into the middle of the hall and kicked the door with all his strength.

As the door banged open, Karl hunched down and charged in after it, his Glock held out in front of him, finger on the trigger, the block's slack already compressed. Gavin came in behind him, standing tall, his own pistol sweeping the space above Karl's head, providing what cover the tiny hallway allowed.

Karl moved straight forward, hustling past the dark bathroom, while Gavin turned his gaze first on the open closet to their left, then the black maw of the open bathroom door to their right. He stood there, sweating, just as he had in Manhattan on the evening he'd voluntarily gotten into the van driven by Angel Kirk, staring into the dark gloom, just as he had that other night, waiting, his eyelids going *snick-snick-snick*.

He knew he shouldn't give up the initiative, that he should reach in and flick on the bathroom light, that he should do his job and clear the damn room—which would take all of three seconds—but he stood frozen. His nostrils flared as he drew a deep breath through his nose, testing the air for the scents of a fresh murder— blood, human waste, fear. He just stood there, waiting.

What are you waiting for? he asked himself.

A chirp, a terrified voice deep inside him answered. *For Glacadairanam.*

Fear throttled his mind, made him ignore the thousands of training hours, the direct experience he'd had in a thousand real-life situations. His eyes widened in a foolhardy effort to pierce the darkness through force of will.

He'd forgotten all about Karl.

When the cold barrel of Karl's Glock touched his ear, Gavin screamed.

5

Kai had sensed their approach—first, his old "friend" and the puppeteer's would-be victim, and later, after he'd wormed into his hiding place, Gavin and Karl. He extended his senses—something akin to feeling around in a pitch-black room—trying to lay his mind on the unsub. As Karl and Gavin had burst into the room, he'd sensed a burst of emotion from nearby. *The woman's terror*, he thought.

Broadcasting a no-nonsense focus Kai recognized right off, Karl came into the bedroom, moving in silence, the only sound the soft scruff of his shoe leather on the garish carpet—a sound that brought Blue Dorm Seven crashing into Kai's mind, but he shoved those memories aside.

Karl stopped, then turned slowly, and *scriff-scruffed* back the way he'd come—if anything moving with even less noise than before. A moment later, Gavin screamed, and Kai pounced.

6

Langfield Sun, Miami, FL
Saturday, 2:52 am

Gavin screamed, and the icy terror unfroze him. He ducked, sweeping his left arm up and back, pushing Karl's gun hand aside, sweeping his elbow into Karl's ribs, shoving him into the closet, and banging the doors shut. He darted across the narrow hall, reaching for the bathroom's light switch, sure he'd see a bloody crime scene, or worse, that the lights wouldn't illuminate anything other than that alley near Third and 36th in Manhattan.

He knew that last thought for what it was— *bullshit*—and he flicked on the lights, bringing his Glock up to sweep across the small room and shower stall.

It was empty.

7

Kai lashed out, painting a thirty-thousand-amp bolt of purple-white lightning striking the top of the puppeteer's head on the canvas of his mind's eye, driving the bolt through his skin, his skull, into the center of his brain. Once there, Kai sent electrical signals in every direction, down every pathway through the man's gray matter, racing through the white matter's myelin-insulated axons, short-circuiting everything he touched, shouting conflicting signals to the man's muscles, scrambling his neurotransmitters, shutting down his consciousness in a flash of purple-white light. The man convulsed even as he fell face-first onto the rough concrete of the balcony.

Dylan, he thought.

In the front of the room, Karl cried out.

8

Karl regained control as he slammed into the drywall in the back of the closet hard enough to leave a crater the size and shape of his shoulders. He flung his Glock down and shoved the closet doors open, lunging out and away from his pistol.

Gavin stood in the bathroom, standing slumped, his gun hanging at his side.

"Gavin!" Karl cried. "Cuff me!"

"Where's your gun, Karl?" Gavin asked in a voice that shook. "What's—"

"*Never mind that*! Cuff me so that bastard can't run me around and shoot you in the ear!"

A crash rattled the sliding glass door that led to the balcony, and a woman screamed.

"Of course," muttered Gavin. "The balcony. Of course. Nothing happened in the bathroom." He pinched the bridge of his nose as though in the grip of a horrible headache.

"Gavin!" Karl stepped into the bathroom and grabbed him by his shoulders. "What's wrong with you?"

Gavin looked him in the eye for a split second, then his eyes rolled back, and his entire body convulsed in one titanic galvanic burst, every muscle fiber contracting.

9

The peculiar chirp dragged Gavin down, down, down into a deep sleep-like state, a nickel falling down, down, down a darkened, abandoned well. His heart thundered, but he stood there, eyes stretched wide open, staring into the looming, twisting shadows.

"Why are you just standing there like a big idiot, sparky-spark?" Adeline d'Clara asked him in the cultured tones of an Ivy-league society maven. "Get a move on, Gav, or you'll miss your chance to get a piece."

A smile stretched across his lips, followed by the sense of relief that washed through him. "Home! I'm home!" he cried exultantly. "Addy! Addy, I'm here!"

"Well, not really, old hoss," said Maddie, her voice dropping through the registers as she spoke, ending on a low, low note that rattled the black basalt building like an earthquake. "I got tired of waiting on you, spark-old-hoss. Had to take matters into my own hands."

Gavin spun in a circle, his terrified gaze zipping from place to place, looking for his love, his wife, fearing for her, fearing they still sat in that disgusting smelling room in New York City, fearing The Smith's hammer was raining down on him, cracking his skull, splattering Maddie with his brains.

This is *wrong! he thought.* Something's wrong.

"Well, no shit, cowpoke. Glad you could catch up to the rest of us. This is getting dadgum tiresome, all this horsing around. You and me, we need to visit a little."

Behind Gavin—always and forever behind him—a peculiar chirp sounded, but he couldn't move, couldn't run, couldn't fight, couldn't do anything to stop what was coming.

"Where we going, sugar?"

He screamed, his hands flying up to cover his ears, even as he fell down, down, down that black-throated well.

10

Langfield Sun, Miami, FL
Saturday, 2:56 am

Karl hung on to Gavin's arms, settling him to the floor, trying to keep him from smashing his brains out on the tub or smashing the shower's glass enclosure and cutting his own throat. "Gavin!" he cried. "Kai! Kai, if you can hear me, I need help!"

Gavin groaned, and his eyelids fluttered. "Home," he muttered. "I'm home!"

Karl grabbed a stack of fluffy bath towels from the stand next to the tub and cushioned Gavin's head with them. "Just relax, Gavin. Take it easy."

"*NO!*" screamed Gavin, his terrified eyes opening wide, wide, wide, and then his entire body seized as though struck by thirty-thousand-amps of purple-white lightning.

II

A hotel room,
Saturday, 2:57 am

Gavin's eyes bolted open, and he lurched up, fluffy bath towels falling from his shoulders like an avalanche, his breath rasping through his throat as though he'd just run a mile flat out, a woman's scream ringing in his ears. Whose? Sweat ran from his scalp in rivulets, sliding down his forehead and into his eyes, thick and hot, stinging, burning his skin and eyes. He grabbed a towel and swiped it across his forehead, and it came away red. Peering into the grave-dark room, he widened his eyes once, twice, and again, but it didn't help, it didn't stop the hemorrhage, didn't stop the blood raining down from the top of his head, didn't leave him calm like it was supposed to.

A basso voice vibrated the stone beneath his ass. "Dang it, hoss! Quit doing that!"

"Whuh… Who's there?" he asked, his voice not much more than a child's squeak. "What's wrong with me?"

Behind him, something cold and scaly wriggled closer, making a slithering hiss across the white tiles, shoving the towels away and snaking around his waist. Gavin cried out and tried to launch himself up and away, but his hands slipped in the blood puddling around him, and he slammed back down, striking his head on the black glass-like stone floor. He lay there, frozen with pain, staring at the inky darkness that swirled above him, a malevolent thundercloud. He thought he could see a shape there, in the pitch-black cloud of hateful, evil, malignancy, could see it undulating, writhing, twitching.

Then a purple-white spear stabbed down at him from the heart of that blackness, lightning from a bruise-colored Florida thundercloud. At the last second, it bent, traveling parallel to the floor, snaking up to his head, and drilled into his brain. All his muscles spasmed at once, from his toes to his eyelids.

"You think squeezing your eyes shut will protect you, spark?"

The pitch-black swirling above him seemed to breathe in a growling, inexorable rhythm, like some engine of war and death and uncompromising destruction, and he felt compelled to match its cadence.

His gaze danced away from the hateful cloud, streaking toward the bathroom door.

"Wait a minute…" he said. "Why isn't the light on? Turn the light on!"

"Told you so many times, old hoss," said a voice that surrounded him, battering him from all sides, hurricane winds and slashing rain, but mostly from the black, swirling death cloud above him. "I DON'T COTTON TO YOU TELLING ME WHAT TO DO!" The sheer volume of the shout cracked the stone floor beneath him, and Gavin fell away from the darkness, sliding down, down, down, a nickel falling down, down, down into a fire-blackened, abandoned well.

"Wait! Dadgum it, hoss, don't you—"

12

Langfield Sun, Miami, FL
Saturday, 2:58 am

Kai staggered to the doorjamb, blood trickling from one nostril. "What's wrong?"

"He's having seizures!" shouted Karl.

"Leave…me…alone," Gavin gasped, shoving at Karl's hands feebly, pushing the towels away.

"Can't do that, bud," said Karl.

Gavin's eyelids spasmed, revealing eyes so dilated his irises had disappeared.

"Is this another attack from the unsub?" Karl demanded.

Kai shook his head. "He's down. Blanked, like I said."

"Your goddamn friends, then?"

"No."

Karl turned his head, narrowing his eyes at Kai.

"Not me, either," Kai said in a world-weary voice. "It's possible a fixer could cause seizures, but there's no reason to."

"Then… Fry?"

"Fry."

13

A hotel room
Saturday, 2:59 am

FRY FRY FRY FRY FRY FRY FRY FRY FRY FRY FRY FRY FRY FRY FRY FRY FRY FRY FRY FRY FRY FRY FRY FRY FRY FRY FRY FRY FRY FRY FRY FRY FRY FRY FRY—

The word multiplied in the blackness surrounding him, drinking him in, breathing him, choking him. Harsh hands buoyed him up, propelling him through the darkness, moving him with ungentle shoves and slaps, punching him, driving the wind from him, sucking the life from him.

He slammed face-first into the sliding glass door with enough force to create lightning bolt cracks in the glass. He stared out at the swirling abyss, his face frozen, his stomach boiling, his hands aching to open the door, his feet creeping forward, bringing him closer and closer and closer to the cold creature floating on just the other side of the thin glass panes.

Behind him, an unnatural, hateful silence filled the room—a silence perfect-made for a peculiar chirp—and then a heavy, sharp-taloned hand fell on his shoulder. "Where we going, sugar?" chirped a peculiar voice in his ear.

"Nowhere," said Gavin. "No...where..."

"You're supposed to say: 'This is a dream.'"

"Is it? Is it really?"

"No, spark, it ain't. It really ain't."

Rough hands spun him where he stood, pointing his face at the dark bedroom and the shadow-swathed hallway beyond. "See? That goddamn bathroom light is ON, spark. ON!" Cold, dead hands spun him back to face the abyss.

"No, it isn't," said Gavin, but he turned his head to peek over his shoulder, nonetheless.

A nightmare vision stood behind him—orange-eyed, dressed in an old army jacket, a hoody up over his diseased skull. The man grinned at him, and the fires of Hell danced in his gaze. The Nightmare Man turned his own head, back, back, back, back, swiveling his face one hundred eighty degrees away, pivoting until Gavin could see only the back of his hood. Without twisting back to face Gavin, he stepped to the side. "See?"

The hotel room was gone. The black basalt tower was gone. The beach was gone. His bedroom was gone. Beyond the Nightmare Man, only the horrible black maw of the alley existed, and in it, two things gleamed as though lit by the brightest of spotlights.

The first thing was a twisting morass of deep dark colors—blacks and midnight blues and bloody swirls of purple-black seen only in the worst kind of bruises.

The second thing was his bed. The one he and Maddie shared in Minnieville. The one heaped with familiar bedclothes. The one in which Maddie lay, reading her Kindle, her face lit by the simple screen.

The spotlight on the bed pulsed in time with the breathing blackness, and with each bright flicker, it grew a little bigger, illuminating the floor surrounding the bed, revealing the tip of the many pairs of work boots, shoes, bare feet, and silver-clawed talons, exposing the poxed ankles rising above them, showing the bottom hem of rough-spun black robes, lighting the blood-red fascia similar to those worn by the bishops he'd known in his youth, revealing the black maws where faces should have been, exposing the orange-eyed man standing behind Maddie, his hood hiding all but his hateful, malicious gaze. Above the bed, the swirling morass of dead colors, pulsed and pulsed, the caustic, venomous heartbeat of nocuous, diabolic atrocity embodied.

"I could take her, spark," said the orange-eyed Nightmare Man. "Any time I want. Hey! Maybe we could make another one! A brother for Glacadairanam! What do you say, old hoss?"

"Touch her, and I'll fucking end you," Gavin said in a voice both cold and dead. "And your fucking son."

"Which one, sparky-spark? Which son?"

"You mean there are more of them?"

The Nightmare Man smiled, and off in the distance somewhere, a woman screamed and screamed and screamed. His eyes widened, and he shouted, "Now, don't you go and—"

14

Langfield Sun, Miami, FL
Saturday, 3:06 am

Gavin lurched awake, bolted up from his unconscious terror, his heart pounding and pounding and pounding, his breath torn out of him in a rasping pant, a woman's scream ringing in his ears. He glanced around in confusion, thinking he was at home in Minnieville, at home in his bedroom. "Where…"

"Jesus, Gavin," said Karl. "You scared the shit out of me."

He tried not to, but Gavin couldn't resist glancing over his shoulder, not knowing what he expected to see, but there was only a mound of fluffy white hotel towels. "What…" He turned back to face Karl, staring at the man.

"Relax. Just relax." Behind Karl, Kai leaned in the door frame, looking like a truck had run him down.

"What's wrong with you?" Gavin asked.

"It takes a lot out of me, to do what I did."

Gavin shook his head. "I… What did you do?"

"What's wrong with *you*?" asked Kai.

"I don't remember. I don't remember."

"Seizures," said Karl. "You had a bunch of them."

"Maybe," said Kai. "You don't remember anything?"

Gavin's brows drew together in a fierce mask of concentration. "I… It was… I…" He blew out his cheeks and scowled.

"Relax," said Karl. "Just relax."

It was there, right on the tip of Gavin's mind. Something amorphous and huge. Something *important*. "I think…"

Karl put a hand on his shoulder. "We caught him, Gavin."

"Who?"

Karl glanced back at Kai.

"Dylan," said Kai. "It was Dylan Jepson."

"Not…" He shook his head. *Not who?*

"Kai says he's safe now," said Karl with a glance over his shoulder. "He blanked everything about the Program, his abilities, all of it."

Kai nodded. "He has memories of a life—of sorts. He will remember the girls he's killed and how he killed them." After heaving a heavy sigh, he went on, "The bad news is I saw Rayson in his memories. He's here. In Miami, and we'll have to—"

As sudden as a lightning strike, the memory of Maddie in their bed, surrounded by those evil monks or whatever they were, flashed through his mind. "*Fry!*" he cried, patting his pockets in a near frenzy. He ripped his phone out of his jacket pocket and hit the icon for Pete's cell. "Come on, come on," he muttered.

"Gavin, what—"

"Shh!" hissed Gavin.

"Gavin," mumbled Pete, still half asleep. "What's going—"

"Pete! Mobilize a team! Get them to my house!"

"Whoa, Gav. Slow down. I—"

"Pete, *do it*!"

"Okay, okay. One second." He clicked over, leaving Gavin listening to the radio hiss of the open line.

"Gavin, what's wrong?" asked Karl.

His eyes danced up to Karl's, boring into them. "Fry," he whispered.

"Oh, shit," said Kai.

The line clicked, and Pete said, "Okay, Gavin. I called the HRT guys watching your house. Everything is quiet. Secure. You can relax."

"Everyone stop telling me to relax, goddamn it!" he shouted. "Tell them to make entry, Pete! Tell them to get to Maddie!"

"What's all—"

"*Pete, for God's sake!*"

"Hold on." Again, Pete clicked over and in the hissing silence, Karl laid a hand on Gavin's shoulder, his concerned gaze on Gavin's face.

"Okay," said Pete. "They're active. Now, tell me, Gav."

"You remember when I called you from Millvale?"

"Pennsylvania? On The Smith case?"

"Right. I called and asked you to put a protective detail on Maddie."

"Yes," said Pete.

His calm voice infuriated Gavin, but he bit it back, corralled the anger, the fury, the fear. "I asked you to do that because there was a threat leveled against Maddie. I just got another one."

"You're not making sense, Gavin. Who leveled the threats? The Smith?"

"In a way. In a way, Pete, but I don't have time to... Look, I'll explain it all when I get back, but not on the phone. And not in the office. We'll take a hike. I'll explain everything, the stuff I held back on The Smith case, everything that's happened here. I swear, Pete. I swear it, but not now, not right now. Right now, I need Maddie protected. I need her somewhere *safe,* Pete!"

"Safer than her own bed, watched over by two teams of HRT badasses?"

"*Yes*, Pete. Yes."

"Is my house safe enough?"

In the background, Gavin heard Gloria say, "Go get her, Pete! Don't wait for him to ask! *Don't make him ask, just go!*"

The phone rattled and boomed for a moment, then Gloria said, "He's up and moving, Gavin. He's going in person, don't you worry. We'll keep her safe for you. We'll protect her. Here's Pete, he's dressed and armed and running to the car."

"Oh, Gloria," he said in a shaking voice. "Oh, Gloria, thank you. *Thank* you!"

"Of course, Gavin."

"Gavin?" asked Pete.

In the background, Gloria said, "Haul ass, Pete," and an engine roared to life, drowning out the rattling voice of the garage door opener.

"Speaker, Gav," said Pete. "I'm on my way. The HRT guys will text when they have something meaningful to say. What are we looking for?"

"I… Pete, I'm not exactly sure. A group of men, maybe, or maybe one guy. A guy in a black hoodie and an old olive-drab army jacket. Pale. Freaky looking."

"The Smith?" Pete's siren came on, accompanied by the shriek of abused rubber scaring the macadam.

"No. Maybe, in a way, but no."

"Gavin, you're not making much sense here."

"I know, Pete. I know, and I'm sorry. My mind's jumbled."

"He's just had three seizures," said Karl in a loud voice.

"Seizures?" Pete asked.

"Irrelevant," said Gavin. "I need her protected, Pete!"

"I'm on it, Gav, I swear to you. The four HRT guys are there already. The only other thing I can do is deploy a full HRT team to your house—in tactical gear and on alert. Do I need to do that?"

"I… I don't know. Oh, God, Pete, if she's—"

"Don't even say it, Gavin," said Pete. "I'm eight minutes away."

A lifetime! thought Gavin. "Promise me, Pete. Promise me."

"Promise you what?"

"If she's… If she's… Don't say you'll identify her so I don't have to. Don't say, 'I can do the ID, okay. Let me do this for you.' Just tell me. Promise?"

For a moment, the only sound transmitted from Minnieville was the roar of Pete's V8 engine. "Okay, Gavin," said Pete in a worried voice. A chirp sounded on Pete's end.

"Christ, look out, Pete!" Gavin shouted.

The V8's symphony played into the silence, then Pete said, "It's just a text, Gav. You're scaring me here."

"Sorry, sorry. You'll understand once I tell you."

"One of the HRT guys got Maddie out of bed. She says she's fine."

"Oh, thank God, Pete," Gavin said, a sudden enervation robbing him of his strength, and he flopped back into the nest of towels Karl had arranged around him. "But the house isn't safe. I still—"

"I'll take her to our house—as promised. Gloria's already making up the guest room. The security system is on, and she has her twelve gauge out and loaded. Okay?"

Gavin heaved a sigh, the weight of his fear finally sliding off, the stress of his internal vision receding. "Thanks, Pete. I knew I could count on you."

"Always, Gavin, and no matter what."

"I know." He closed his eyes and sighed. "Pete, I know."

Then his eyes rolled up once more, and the phone flew from his hand.

15

Alley near Third and 36th, Manhattan, NY
Saturday, 3:33 am

Gavin stood at the mouth of the alley, his hands shoved in the pockets of his warm-up pants, feet sweating in his running shoes. His breath huffed in and out, in and out, in and out, like a belabored steam engine at maximum throttle. He'd arrived moments ago, arrived in a flat-out run, skidding to a stop and waiting…waiting for…

Waiting for what? *he asked himself.*

Stygian darkness rushed at him, charged him, pounced on him, enveloping him, wrapping him in its cold, dead embrace. "You think it will help, spark? Your men and their guns? Shit, boy, I eat men like that for an afternoon snack."

"No!" Gavin shouted. "No! This is all wrong! Where's the hotel? Where's the goddamn balcony?"

From the dark depths of the alley, a rusty-saw laugh rolled out toward him, circling him, wrapping him up. "Dang, boy! Ain't you got this figured out yet?"

Gavin shook his head, rejecting the voice, rejecting the alley, the darkness.

"I'm so sorry, Gavin-spark. Truly," said Pete Fielding from the alley's grim extremities. "I tried to get there in time, but…"

Horror ripped at the back of Gavin's throat, burning, prickling, tearing his delicate tissues with sharp claws. He dredged the words out, forcing them past the monster tearing his throat apart. "Pete… You promised, Pete! You promised!" He clapped his hands over his ears, shaking his head, denying the words he knew were coming.

"Jesus, Gavin, you don't need to see this. To see her. *I can do the ID, okay?" Somewhere, buried in the black*

darkness of the alley, a clock tick-tick-ticked, mechanical laughter, mechanical mockery, engineered torture, engineered despair. "Okay, Gavin-spark? Let me—"

"NO!" Gavin shrieked. He whirled in a circle and ran, sprinting away from the alley for half a heartbeat, then the world spun, and he was running toward the swirling miasma of cold, dark colors, the swirling tempest of pain, despair, of brutality and lust. "NO-NO-NO!" he screeched. He spun to the left, then back, then to the right, but no matter which way he spun, that goddamn alley was in front of him. No matter what he did, he was trapped in the devil's playground, in a dark hell where fire and brimstone was deemed too cheery, where monsters roamed, free to torture anyone trapped within their reach.

"Hush, old hoss," said a voice as abysmal as the alley itself. "Quit that running, boy, it ain't getting us where we need to git to."

Gavin's leaden feet stopped churning, the dark smoke hissing and slithering around him. His strength drained away, and his breath evaporated in the brutal cold the smoke brought.

"That's better. Just simmer down. Quit that streaking off. I'm here to visit *with you, hoss, but I'm tired of chasing you, tired of dragging your sorry ass back down here. Quit your simpering bellyaching and stand here like a man, sparky. Capiche?" The brutal black burying him breathed, an in-out-in-out as inexorable as death,*

cold breath blowing its killing-house stench in his face. "There, now. That's better."

"What do you want, Fry? Why do you keep—"

"Hush up, boy. I ask the questions in my own goldang-monkey-shittin' domain." He held up a thin, fish-belly white finger, a long, wicked talon at its tip. "Now, don't you go running off before I finish this time."

Gavin opened his mouth, and something icy and hard and venomous slid between his teeth and down his tongue, blocking his throat, gathering in the depths of his chest, denying his scream, denying his questions, snuffing them out, stillborn.

Terror built behind his eyes, a vast inexorable pressure soaring in his body cavities until he thought he'd burst, that his skull would fracture into a million-million pieces, bone-shard shrapnel exploding into the black maw of the alley. His mouth opened and closed, but that algid lump buried in his windpipe let no air snake past, no matter how hard he tried to suck in a fresh, clean breath, no matter how hard he tried to blow the obstruction out, to cough it up.

Then, it came.

At long last, it came, bringing with it a forlorn desperation, a cheerless loveless horror, a doleful resignation.

The Beast came then, rushing out of the black abyss, snarling as it came, singing of wrath and blasphemy and blood and shit and death. The Beast came then, rising up out of the sea of Gavin's despair, ten horns ringing seven heads, ten crowns blinking-blinding-slashing through the dark, the only light, Gavin's only light, gray and gray and gray, shouting its blasphemies, its lies, its threats, its wicked number. The Beast charged at him then, and scarlet death came with it, the harlot straddling its broad back laughing and tossing her golden, blood-tinged hair, her eyes dancing to his, a seductive secret smile slashed across her face, happy at her release from that bottomless pit of despair and wrath and shame and horror.

"Do you see?" roared Fry.

Gavin, who could draw no breath to speak, could no longer bring air into his burning lungs, heard himself chirp then, a strange off-key note from a mistuned bagpipe, a perverse twang from a psychotic cricket, and he could not look away from the whore's abyssal blood-black eyes. The harlot opened her mouth then, and destruction poured forth, the black destruction of his life, his dreams, his love, his hopes. She sang of annihilation, of decimation and desolation then, a harsh lullaby, a grave-side dirge, her voice rising impossibly high, sweeping impossibly low, and for the first time in his life, Gavin knew true fear.

"Do you hear?" roared Furfur, Earl of Hell.

Tears blurred his eyes then, even as his ears rang with the death notes of everything he held dear, yet he could still see the woman on the Beast's back. He watched her as she moved; languid, sensual, carnal, and lush. She swung one leg over the Beast's scarlet shoulder, slid down his scarlet side then, her glimmering dress rucking up past her hips, exposing her sex, her brutal, horrible womb. Her dainty chalk-white feet struck the alley's bricks then, and the death note of the world rang out, its vibrations rattled the walls down around them, cracking concrete foundations, crumbling stone and brick. She approached then, staring him in the eye—an invitation, a dare, a command—and bitter, grievous cold came with her. As she reached for him, his life's warmth seeped away as if in retreat, and his body froze, ice in his veins, in his heart. She touched him then, and visions of savage misery, of murders and torments, of affliction, death, tribulations, poisons, and cruel acts done in the dark, assaulted him, drowned him, held him down in the black deeps, denied him breath or love or humanity.

"Do you feel it?" roared the Nightmare Man, and Gavin whimpered and turned his face away.

Those blood-black, horrible eyes followed him, though, filling his vision until he wanted nothing more than to gouge out his own eyes. Slowly, glacially, the blood-black color drained to gray, then white, then orange. Her alabaster skin roughened then, grew even paler but at the same time ugly and caustic. Her shimmering dress darkened then, became as drab as if color was anathema and banished, turned green and shortened. Her naked legs tanned then, grew pockets, and black boots stretched up from the ground to cover her calves. Her glorious golden hair became black then, *dead, a hood, and she smiled as she finished the translation from harlot to devil.*

The Nightmare Man smiled then, and Gavin's mind reeled. "I think you might be starting to get it, old hoss," he said. "As much as this has been fun"—*he sneered and rolled his eyes, making his true feelings plain—"I'll be glad to move on to other things. Bigger things. Kingdoms without end, without annoyances like you." His voice thickened, hoarsened, dripped scorn. "Lookit, spark. This is the point. You bother me, son. Like a burr under my saddle blanket, if ye ken. Now, I don't cotton to annoyances. Not at all, sparky-spark. Most things, most annoyances, I flat out kill without a second's thought— or a second look—and I'd do that to you, but for my son. You might annoy me, Gavin Gregory, but him, my son, Glacadairanam, you* infuriate, *you fill with* hatred— *more hatred than is his usual, too, which is a feat I'm not sure I can understand or believe. For his sake, I leave you to your life. For his sake, I'll turn my wicked, awful gaze from you, old hoss. I'll leave your woman alone, and I'll leave the new life growing inside her alone, too, though that pains me a mite." He cocked his head and glared at Gavin through narrowed eyelids. "But…" He let it linger there, let the promise of pain and death and destruction hang in the air between them, wriggling like a worm—the perfect stick. He lifted his scaly chin, and his assessing gaze probed Gavin from head to toe. "I could make a place for you, old hoss, in the organization. A priest, of sorts. A missionary. That's within my discretion."*

Magma churned in Gavin's chest, his lungs so long without sweet, cool air, he wondered if its existence was a fantasy, a dream, a lie.

"I'm offering you a chance, spark. A place in proximity to my son, sure. You will see him every day, and that will cause strife, will irritate the both of you, say hallelujah, but for my sake, you will both put your struggles aside. I will make it a safe place." He chuckled. "Well, as safe as any place near me can be for the likes of you."

He smiled then, a sight so grim it almost hurt Gavin, and patted his cheek with one claw-tipped hand. "What do you say, old hoss? You up to joining the family firm?"

Before Gavin could respond, before he could think, the Nightmare Man's pallid expression darkened then, and his eyes grew deadly, acidic, venomous, and wide. He turned his head slightly, gazing into the blackness that surrounded them, and frowned. "No. Don't do that!" he shouted, but at who, Gavin couldn't begin to guess. "Dratnabit! Every goldern time!" His eyes flashed back to Gavin. "You ain't worth all this, spark. This frustration." His gaze crawled away again, focusing on that unseen creature who irritated him so. "I think I'll kill me some women. That'll make me feel better."

The sound of his voice diminished in volume, a rush to its nadir, and when he turned his eyes back on Gavin, they seemed far, far away. "Dadgum, boy. I give up. Think on it and think on what I might do if'n you refuse me."

Gavin could barely hear him, but he understood every word as if Fry whispered them in his ear. Most of all, he understood the threat. He fell away from Fry as if falling backward down a deep, dark well, the creature's body growing tinier with each nanosecond. The icy blockage in his chest disappeared, and Gavin drew in a whooping breath of burning air.

Behind him, a chirp rang out, one that echoed inside his head. A promise of things to come.

Then a cold, pale hand came to rest on his shoulder. He felt a presence behind him, looming from the black nothingness. He felt him lean in close, felt his breath on his ear.

"Where you going, sugar?"

16

An ambulance on Flagler St., Miami, FL
Saturday, 3:53 am

Gavin awoke, gasping for breath, hot tears spilling down his cheeks. For once, he knew where he was in an instant. For once, no fear accompanied his waking, and there were no shadows in the brightly lit ambulance for him to search, to challenge. He blinked, and an EMT leaned into his field of vision. "He's back," he said, and then Karl leaned into his field of vision.

"Thank the Virgin," Karl murmured. "Thank the saints."

"Thank midazolam," said the EMT. "It's responsible for this miracle."

Karl shot the man a disgusted look.

Gavin let his eyes slide closed, exhaustion and sedation ganging up on him. He didn't particularly *want* to sleep, to walk where dreams reigned, but he didn't particularly have much say in the matter.

"I talked to Maddie," said Karl. "She's safe. Hear me, Gavin? She's *safe*. She said she loves you, and she'll be here tomorrow."

"Nnnn!" moaned Gavin, struggling against the weight on his eyelids, the weight on his consciousness.

"Relax, Agent Gregory," said the EMT. "Just relax. We'll be at Jackson Memorial in a few minutes. Rest, now."

Gavin fought to turn his head, fought to communicate to Karl through a look alone, demanding he stop Maddie from coming, but the man only smiled and patted his shoulder. "Your boss is bringing her. She'll be here when you wake up."

17

Gavin awoke, feeling as though he'd been drinking for a week. His mouth felt scuzzy, hot, and tasted of sick, while his face felt slimy, feverish, and sweaty. He heaved a sigh—he hadn't had a single dream. At least, not one he remembered.

"Gavin?" asked Maddie in a soft voice. "Are you awake?"

He opened his mouth, but it felt desiccated and barren, so he settled for a short nod, then closed his eyes against the waves of dizziness.

"Thank the sparkly-vampire gods," whispered Maddie as she came to his side, tears shining unshed in her eyes, and grabbed his hand. "You've been asleep forever."

He looked up into her beautiful brown eyes and twisted his dry lips into a semblance of a smile. He jerked his chin toward the Styrofoam pitcher of water on the bed table.

"Oh!" she said, and a faint blush crept up her cheeks. She poured water into the strangest contraption he'd ever seen. It had the shape like a filter—a clear plastic body, a blue plastic lid from which extended a short, straight tube on one side and a capped vent tube on the other. As Maddie held it out, he wrapped his lips around it and sucked the clear, cold water into his mouth, tasting mana and Maddie's lips and everything else good in the world. "Better?" she asked when he quit sucking the water down.

"Yeah," he said. "You shouldn't have come."

For a moment, hurt played a slow dirge in her eyes, but then she shook her head and forced a smile. "You're worried. Karl said you would be. What a great guy. You lucked out with him." She set down the giant sippy cup and took his hand again. "Now, Gavin, you listen to me," she said in a tone that brooked no argument.

For a moment, Fry's horrible voice rang in his ears, but he banished it with a force of will.

"I know you're worried about me. The dreams. I get it. But, Gavin, I'm here, where I belong, and I'm *staying* until we can walk out of here together." She held up her free hand as though he'd started to argue—he hadn't. "Pete brought me down in the jet, and he insisted on an escort." She nodded to the hall. "Two HRT guys are right out there, and if you give me the slightest bit of trouble, I've already elicited oaths from them that will come in here and kick your ass. Capiche?" She smiled and winked at him, then paled as his face crumpled. "What? What is it, Gav?"

"Don't say that. Don't ever say that," he croaked.

"Say what, honey? It was only a joke—though the promise was real." She flashed a grin, then wiped a tear from his cheek with her thumb.

"Cuh-capiche. Don't say that."

A small frown creased her face for a split second, then she smiled. "Okay. If you don't want me speaking like a mob boss, I guess I can accommodate you. It's only on my mind because of the novel. I'm using it a lot." She rolled her eyes. "Hey…know what's worse than a vampire that sparkles?"

He shrugged and tried for a smile.

"A sparkly vampire mafia hitman."

He closed his eyes and groaned.

"I know, right? But Mr. Story said I had to. Don't worry, though. I've already figured out how I can kill him off before the end."

"Well, that's good."

Her eyes filled with tears, and she leaned down in a rush and hugged him tight. "Don't you ever scare me like this again, Gavin Gregory," she said in his ear.

"I didn't mean to do it this time," he whispered back.

"When you feel up to it, I want you to tell me what happened. Why you freaked out and had the 7th Calvary come get me out of bed."

"Not…not now," he whispered.

"When you feel up to it," she repeated, "and not one second before."

"What happened to me?" he asked as she straightened.

"Seizures," she said. "Karl was there, and he told the doctors about the attack on your room, about taking down The Bogeyman. Based on how hard you've been working, the lack of sleep, and the dehydrated state you're in, the doctors think the combination caused them. They ran some brain stuff while you slept. EEGs or something. He said there are no signs of anything permanent."

He raised his eyebrows.

"Epilepsy. Kai said it might be—" She gulped a breath, and her eyes were once more filled with tears.

"But it wasn't, Mads," he said quietly. "It was the heat and the crazy schedule."

She nodded and wiped her tears. "Anyway. Pete's here. In the hospital, I mean. Karl and Kai left a little while ago—left in a hurry, actually. MDPD searched The Bogeyman's house and found some information on Rayson Fergus. They're going after him."

"I should—"

"Finish that sentence, and I'll have Donny in here in a heartbeat."

"Donny? What happened to Frank?"

"Frank is a figment of your imagination, Gav. Donny is the HRT badass outside."

Gavin smiled, and for the first time in what felt like decades, he felt the urge to laugh. He did so, and Maddie joined him. "I owe Pete an explanation," he said when they'd wound down. "A long one."

Maddie nodded. "Want to start now or rest a bit more?"

"Better to do a thing than live with the fear of it," he said.

"Don't quote Joe Abercrombie to me, Gavin. I'm the one who got you to read those books." She grinned and patted him on the shoulder before going out to find Pete.

Gavin lay in the hospital room, dreading the conversation—not because he didn't believe every bit of it, but because he feared Pete wouldn't. He rehearsed a few ways he might kick off the conversation, not liking a single one of them. When Maddie returned, Pete was with her, looking solemn, but so were Karl and Kai.

Karl smiled at him with genuine warmth. "Glad to see you doing better. You scared me, FBI."

"Hell, I scared me."

Kai gave him a nod and a shy smile.

"Don't keep me in suspense," Gavin said. "Did you get him?"

Karl's smile widened. "Yes. Rayson Fergus is in custody." He glanced at Pete, then said, "Can you believe it? A genuine pair of serial killers."

Gavin turned a solemn gaze on Pete. "How long have we known each other, Pete?" he asked.

"About fifteen years."

"Right. And would you say I'm given to wild fantasy? To flights of fancy? To superstitious nonsense?"

Pete glanced at Maddie, then at Karl. When he returned his gaze to Gavin's he smiled. "What? Is that some kind of joke? You are about as far from those things as a man can get and still be able to breathe."

Gavin nodded. "Right. I'm not gullible, am I?"

"Not at all."

Gavin took Maddie's hand. "Let me tell you who threatened Maddie…and how. I need to start with The Smith case. I need to tell you who—or more appropriately *what*—The Smith is. I need to fill in the blanks, to answer those unanswered questions you let me get away with on Monday."

With a glance at Maddie, Pete nodded. "If you'd rather wait until we can have a private chat—"

"No," said Gavin. "The people in this room know already. And they know about what has happened here in Miami. I want them here because you're going to think I'm crazy, and I want their testimony on my behalf."

Pete squinted a little but nodded.

Gavin told him about the dreams he'd had while tracking The Smith. About the stories Debbie Esteves had told him about the Saint Mary Psycho. About Tom Madsen and the events in Millvale, Pennsylvania.

Pete's brows had furrowed by the time he finished, but he didn't say a word.

"Now, Pete, pretend I'm asking you those questions I started with. Has your answer changed?"

Pete's gaze jumped from Gavin to Maddie, and she nodded. "If it were anyone else, I'd be tempted to call for a psychiatrist, but Maddie's one of the sanest people I know." He grinned a little at that, and the tension in the room eased.

Gavin nodded. "Me, too. Remember Adeline d'Clara?"

"Your mystery psychic?"

"Yes." He glanced at Kai, who nodded. "She really is a psychic, Pete. Not a telepath, but a telezitonic—a bird dog in the parlance of the Majestic Program. Kai, here, is her great-grandson. He's gifted as well."

Pete's slow glance traversed to Karl, then on to Kai, who nodded. He turned back to Gavin. "I don't know—" Pete snapped his mouth shut and turned to stare at Kai, who again nodded. "If you're psychic—"

"I said, 'Gavin is telling the truth. You can trust every word of this.'"

The color drained from Pete's face, and he darted a glance at Maddie. "I…"

Gavin nodded. "Trust me. We all felt the same way. Well, all of us except Kai. The Bogeyman was more than a pair of motivated serial killers. They were telecheiristirics—what the Program calls puppeteers. They have the ability to control a person's body by remote control. Karl can attest to that, and if you need it, Kai can demonstrate. On you."

Pete lost a little more color, then turned to Karl Santana and quirked an eyebrow.

"Absolutely true," said Karl. "I got taken over twice, and both times, I almost shot Gavin. Probably would have, if Kai hadn't intervened—both times."

Pete's gaze tracked to Kai once more, and they stared at one another for a moment. "No, thank you. That's not necessary," said Pete, and Kai grinned and shrugged. Pete sighed and turned back to Gavin. "Okay. If this is true, then your serial killers are about to escape."

"No," said Kai. "The Program has identified five types of psionic ability. Besides the two already mentioned, there are garden variety telepathic and telekinetic skills—we call them snoops and pushers. The fifth, and rarest kind, is teletechnitics—fixers, if you will. We call them that because they can 'fix' your mind—erase or add memories, change your motivations, your beliefs, correct mental illnesses, all of that. Still with me?"

"Sure…I guess," said Pete.

"I have teletechnitic abilities. I used them to fix Dylan Jepson and Rayson Fergus. Neither has psionic abilities any longer, and neither will remember anything about the Program or having the power in the first place. They'll give full confessions, and they'll stay in prison. You have my word."

"Uh…okay." Pete turned to Gavin. "So, this creature in New York—"

"Glacadairanam," said Maddie with a firm nod.

"Right," said Pete. "He's one of these psychics? I mean, really? He has some way of making you believe he's a—"

"No, Pete," said Gavin. "He's what we said he is. A ghost-like creature who can possess people. He wears them like a suit because that's the only way he can interact with the world."

Pete said nothing, just twirled his fingers.

Gavin told him about Fry, about the claims Adeline made about General Walker and JFK, then added the body of his dreams. "Fry is real, too. He says Glacadairanam is his son, though I don't know if it's a lie or not. I—"

"Glacadairanam said his mother possessed a church girl and screwed a priest," said Maddie. "We can't see Fry as a priest, so…"

"Anyway," said Gavin. "Each time I had a seizure, I had another dream. A dream I believe Fry caused, controlled. Except I had some ability to get away—at least at first—though I have no freaking idea what that ability is. It seemed to piss him off, which I like. Anyway, the second to last dream ended with him and a bunch of guys in monk robes standing around Maddie as she lay in bed. Fry said some things…threatened to do some things, and I…" His voice cracked, and Gavin swallowed hard. "That's why I freaked out. It was like the dreams in Manhattan. Where you said those things to me, the things I asked you never to say."

Pete's gaze jumped to Maddie, then switched back to Gavin, and he nodded.

"Those dreams were *true*, Pete. Prophetic. They led up to the evening I confronted Glacadairanam in his warehouse. These dreams about Fry, they're not nightmares. Well, I mean, they are, but they're also *true*. Do you believe that?"

"I believe you believe it, and maybe that's enough for now."

Gavin nodded and shrugged. "Fry…he's out there somewhere. So is Glacadairanam. I don't know how to fight them." He cut his gaze to Kai. "Neither does the Program, for all d'Clara's machinations."

"You can't fight him, anyway. Not until you've fully recovered," said Pete. "Maybe we'll learn more in the meantime."

"You believe us, then?" asked Karl.

Pete looked at him for a long time, then nodded. "Gavin isn't the kind of man to make all this up. Maddie—well, she *is* the type of person to make this up, but it would be in a novel. This man"—he pointed at Kai—"talked to me inside my head, offered to drive me around a little. That provides a bit of credibility." He chuckled. "And I have no reason to doubt you, either, Karl, though we just met."

"Then what do we do?" asked Maddie.

Pete's joviality died on the vine, and he crossed his arms. "I don't know the answer to that, Maddie. I don't know that I ever will. It feels more like a question we should be asking a priest." He sniffed. "For now, we protect ourselves, and Gavin recovers. We don't know where this Fry and his little gargoyle are at the moment, so we can't pursue them anyway. But we can pursue evil in the world. There are a lot of serial killers out there, and we're perfectly suited for those battles. We keep on catching them, while trying to find out more about these supernaturals. Hopefully, by the time we find them, we'll know how to deal with them."

Gavin heaved a sigh of relief. "Thanks, Pete."

"Obviously, this won't be written up back at work."

"I wasn't planning on it," said Gavin with a grin.

"After all, it isn't pertinent, right? But we will have to decide what to do about Kirk Haymond."

With a shrug, Gavin said, "I'm not sure we have to do anything. Jim's sticking to his guns."

"What about the lieutenant down here?" asked Pete, looking at Karl.

"He's good with the results. He won't make waves about anything else. Plus, our unsubs are going to give full confessions." He turned a grin on Kai.

"Good," said Maddie. "Then everything is all settled?"

Pete looked at Gavin and quirked an eyebrow.

"Sure," said Gavin.

"Then my husband needs some rest, gentlemen, though we thank you for coming. We don't want more seizures." As the others turned and began to file toward the door, she said, "And, Pete? I think he might need more time off."

"Take as much as you need, Gavin. That's an order."

"Yessir," said Gavin with a grin.

18

The chirp of his cell phone brought Gavin out of a light sleep, his heart pounding. "I've got to change that damn thing," he muttered.

"No. He's resting," said Maddie. "He had some issues after they… What?"

He could tell by her tone that the caller was Adeline d'Clara, and he was willing to bet that Adeline could pick up on that tone as well. "It's okay, Mads," he said.

She glanced at him and shook her head.

"Put her on speaker."

Maddie rolled her eyes but switched the phone to speaker and lay it on the bed next to his side.

"Hello? Gavin?" Adeline asked in her best down South accent.

"Hello, Adeline," he said.

"I saw on the news that you got him. I'm calling to congratulate you."

"Uh, thanks."

"Is Detective Karl around as well?"

"No," said Maddie. "He's with his own family. That or running the interrogation."

Adeline chuckled. "Oh, I doubt he'll get much from him, what with him being crazy and all."

"Them," said Gavin.

"Eh? What's that, child?"

"Them. As in two of them."

"I'm afraid I don't—"

"Their names should be familiar to you. Dylan Jepson and Rayson Fergus."

Adeline said nothing for a few breaths. When she did speak, her accent wasn't as thick. "That must be a mistake. Those two boys died in—"

"Right. Javier killed them, right? Is he there with you, by the way? Right now, I mean."

"Child, I… I'm not sure I know what you're talking about."

"Yes, you do, Adeline," said Gavin.

"I really don't know what you mean, Agent Gregory."

"I don't believe you, *Miss d'Clara*. Sorry it didn't work out as you'd hoped."

Again, silence stretched between them, and as it stretched, Maddie slipped her hand into his. When Adeline did speak, it was in the even cultured tones of an Ivy-league society maven. "You found my great-grandson, didn't you?"

"I found Fry—at least, sort of. Which was the outcome you preferred?"

"Either. Both."

"Tell Javier he's on his own now. His partners will never be getting out of prison after their full confessions."

"You understand I have the power to have you picked up and interrogated?"

"Sure," he said. "*If* you knew where we are."

A few moments of silence stretched between them. "Ah, neat trick," said Adeline. "You *did* find Kai."

"I'd tell you he said to say hello, but he didn't. His version of events in between 1998 and 2000 were markedly different from your own. I guess his greeting is the fact that you can no longer find us."

"Is he still in Miami? Kai?"

"I don't think I'm going to answer that."

"I'll have the answer by morning," she said with a snide laugh. "All it will take is a snoop."

It was Gavin's turn to laugh. "Go ahead. Send one around. I'm sure we can find room in a cell for them."

"A fixer, then." A furious undercurrent thrummed in Adeline's voice.

"You're not used to being denied your every wish, are you?" asked Maddie. "Sad. And it's sad what you did to your own children. Do you look back and think it was a waste?" She laughed. "No, never mind. I know you don't."

"Anyway, Miss d'Clara, send whoever you like, just don't expect them back."

"Kai's not that strong. He never was."

Gavin shrugged and smiled at Maddie. "I'm sure you're right."

"*Where is Fry?*" Adeline hissed.

"Why don't you look for him?" asked Maddie.

"Because, you stupid bitch, *I can't see him!*"

"There it is again," said Maddie. "That eleven-year-old girl stomping her foot, demanding everything she wants."

"You don't know nothin', tramp!" Her Southern accent was back with a vengeance, but this time, it sounded real. "You White. You never had to put up with bein' treated like an animal, hunted by good ole boys in them pointy hoods, havin' no cross burnin' in your front yard while your brothers and sisters wail and carry on. You never—"

"This is boring," said Gavin. "If any of that *did* happen to you, Adeline, it was decades ago—half a century. These days, *you're* the good old boy in a hood."

"Bull pucky, *child*," she sneered. "There ain't a goddamn thing I can do that will ever equal what White mens like you did to me. Where is Kai?" As she spoke, her voice sounded farther and farther away. "Tell me, or things will get ugly."

"No," said Gavin.

"Then I wash my hands of you. Don't complain when the puppeteers come, when the pushers start poppin' blood vessels."

"Don't threaten me, d'Clara," said Gavin with venom in his voice. "Don't give me a reason to come find *you* and slap steel around your wrists."

She stopped talking then, and a laugh boomed across the line for a moment, but then, as with her speech, it receded, the volume dropping away. After another moment, it faded altogether.

Maddie turned the phone toward her and looked down at the screen. "Disconnected."

"Call her."

"Gav—"

"Do it," he said. "Please."

Maddie shrugged and called the phone number Adeline had given them in her letter. It rang twice, then a man picked it up and said, "Pontillo's Pizza. What can I get you tonight?"

"That can't be right," muttered Maddie. She hit the redial, and it rang four times, then an automated voice said, "We're sorry, the number you have dialed, 604-555-6433 is not in service. If you think you've reached this message in error, please hang up and try your call again." Maddie looked at Gavin and shrugged.

"Easy come, easy go," he said with a smile.

"Did you mean those things? Are we protected from her?"

"Kai assured me we are. He'll be close, whether we know he's around or not."

Maddie nodded, then picked at one of her nails. "There's something I need to tell you, Gav."

"I already know. He or she will be safe, too. I promise, Maddie. Whatever I have to do, you'll both never come to harm."

She looked at him with wide eyes. "Did Kai—"

Gavin shook his head. "No. Fry did."

"Fry…" she said, her face twisting in a moue of concern. "How can we—"

"One day at a time, Mads. Just like everything else."

She smiled then and lay next to him on the edge of his bed. "I love you, Gavin Gregory."

"I love you, too, Francine," he said.

Their laughter lasted a few moments. Their kiss lasted longer.

I hope you've enjoyed *Black Bags* and are dying to read *Devils Dance*, the next book in *The Rational Man* series. You can preorder it here: https://ehv4.us/4devilsdance. To be among the first to know when I've got a new book coming out, please join my Readers' Group by visiting https://ehv4.us/join. Or follow me on BookBub by visiting my profile page there: https://ehv4.us/bbub. Or, if you prefer to stick to Amazon, you may follow my author page: https://ehv4.us/amausa.

If you haven't already read *The Bloodletter Chronicles*, you can view all three books on Amazon (please note that if your local Amazon marketplace supports series pages for Kindle ebooks, all three links point to it rather than individual book pages): https://ehv4.us/4demonking, https://ehv4.us/4thehag, and https://ehv4.us/4ourladychaos. For my complete bibliography, please visit: https://ehv4.us/bib.

Books these days succeed or fail based on the strength of their reviews. I hope you will consider leaving a review—as an independent author, I could use your help. It's easy (I promise). You can leave your review by clicking on this link: https://ehv4.us/2revbb

AUTHOR'S NOTE

It's 3:18 am, Friday, March 26, and I've just finished my rewrite of *Black Bags*. I'm itching to start another story *right now*, but, hey, it *is* three in the morning. I hope you enjoy this novel, as I have, and will stick with me through the rest of this tale—which Mr. Story would like to see continue for a bit and a while.

Supergirl and I have enjoyed watching a show about game wardens and state police officers in the state of my birth—Texas. Those fine men and women inspired some of the dialog in this book, though thinking back, it was mostly the dialog of villains. For that, I apologize. We do love hearing that bit of home (Supergirl spent a few years in Texas before we met) and one day we might find our way back.

I want to speak a bit about the racist assholes portrayed in this book. I want to assure you, my friend, that just as the protagonist in this tale does, I *do* consider them ignorant, racist assholes. You might wonder, then, why I gave them the space to spew their ignorance in these pages. I did it for two reasons. First, many people—*good people*, mind—don't get to just exclude it from their lives. People whom I consider friends—some of the best people I've ever known— must live with this vile, hate-inspired nonsense, and I can't stand it. Full stop. Second, *not* allowing it only allows those mindsets to hide out of sight. We need to drag them into the light, those crazy, hateful ways of thinking, and burn them with fire. That goes for racism, antisemitism, misogynism, so-called able-ism, hell, any old kind of difference-based hatred-ism. I don't cotton to it, spark. Not one bit.

Well, that got a bit serious, but it's a serious issue.

Now, on to more pleasant climes…

This week has been hectic. Mr. Story brought a guy back to life, changed a good guy (woman) into a bad guy (Ivy-league society maven) and brought Pete Fielding in out of the rain. Yes, in the past four days, Mr. Story turned this book on its head. At the same time, he showed me what the series is all about, and what the next step in this wild tale will require, and what the title of it probably is. I actually have a tab in my story bible for the series entitled "HOLY SHIT." That's why I love him so.

This week also saw me finish proofing the audiobook of *Wrath Child*, and I have to tell you how much I love it. I found a terrific actor who *performed* the book, rather than narrated it. His name is Kerr (pronounced like "care") Lordygan, and when he told me he was drawn to the project because he used to sing in an Iron Maiden tribute band, and the song, "Wrath Child" was one of his favorites, I knew I'd met a guy I could work with. Then I listened to an off-the-cuff audition of sorts and knew I'd met the right actor for the job. He's going to perform all the books written this year for the series (and hopefully beyond).

I wish you all the best, friend, until next we palaver together. May your journey be happy and your path smooth. As they say down in Texas, I appreciate y'all and will visit with you soon.

ABOUT THE AUTHOR

Erik Henry Vick is an author of dark speculative fiction who writes despite a disability caused by his Personal Monster™ (also known as an autoimmune disease.) He writes to hang on to the few remaining shreds of his sanity.

He lives in Western New York with his wife, Supergirl; their son; a Rottweiler named after a god of thunder; and two extremely psychotic cats. He fights his Personal Monster™ daily with humor, pain medicine, and funny T-shirts.

Erik has a B.A. in Psychology, an M.S.C.S., and a Ph.D. in Artificial Intelligence. He has worked as a criminal investigator for a state agency, a college professor, a C.T.O. for an international software company, and a video game developer.

He'd love to hear from you on social media:

Blog: https://erikhenryvick.com
Twitter: https://twitter.com/BerserkErik
Facebook: https://fb.me/erikhenryvick
Amazon author pages:
USA: https://ehv4.us/amausa
UK: https://ehv4.us/amauk
Goodreads Author Page: https://ehv4.us/gr
BookBub Author Profile: http://ehv4.us/bbub

Printed in Great Britain
by Amazon